ALERT! ALERT!
DEMONS AT RAINBOW BRIDGE!

"What have we got?" Josef asked Tobrush, who was manipulating about nine different sets of instruments with her back tendrils, while keeping eyestalks fixed on a long scan.

"Something very strange, Captain," the Julki responded. "An intruder from the Mizlaplan side, moving through our territory."

"Warship?"

"Impossible to say at this range, but I'd say not. It is only doing Force Six."

"If they do not deviate from their plot, where are they headed?" he asked.

"They *must* deviate, Captain," Torush responded. "If they do not, then they are heading right off the star maps to where stars only have numbers, and planets are not fully charted."

What the hell?

"Message from Frontier Command in highest-class code, Captain," Desreth reported. "We are directed to maintain pursuit. Their experts believe they know where the ship is headed, although not what is there, or so they say. There have been repeated distress calls on Exchange frequency and in commercial code from a point very close to where the ship is heading. Frontier command states that the distress call is quite peculiar."

"Did they send a copy and triangulated estimate of origin?"

"Yes, sir. The estimate of origin is almost forty light-years off the maps. I'll put the distress call on the ship's intercom."

"All ships . . . any ships . . .this is Research Vessel Wabaugh. Send assistance fast. They're all dead. They're all in there with the demons and they're all dead. Only one left. Can't leave. Approach with extreme caution. Demons at Rainbow Bridge! Coordinates . . ."

"The man is mad," Josef muttered.

Baen Books by Jack L. Chalker

The Changewinds
The Demons at Rainbow Bridge
The Identity Matrix
Downtiming the Nightside

THE DEMONS AT RAINBOW BRIDGE

JACK L. CHALKER

THE DEMONS AT RAINBOW BRIDGE

Copyright © 1989 by Jack L. Chalker

A Baen Book

Baen Publishing Enterprises
P.O. Box 1403
Riverdale, NY 10471

ISBN: 0-671-87887-5

Cover art by Darrell K. Sweet

First Baen printing, August 1998

Distributed by Simon & Schuster
1230 Avenue of the Americas
New York, NY 10020

Printed in the United States of America

For Cliff Simak,
who loved the idea he partly inspired,
but then didn't stick around to see
what I did with it.

AUTHOR'S NOTE

When writing *The Demons at Rainbow Bridge*, I immediately ran into the problem of representing nonverbal communications. In the book we have various characters and creatures, some of whom communicate in whole or in part directly with the mind of another. When added to internalized dialogue, this began to make for a page that was both confusing and typographically unwieldy.

The late George O. Smith, when faced with this problem, decided that the easiest way to resolve this problem was to use a different dialogue delimiter so that the reader would instantly know which communications were spoken aloud and which were mind-to-mind. I have often marveled that others never took up this practice, but it seems practical here and throughout *The Quintara Marathon*. Thus, to alert you, italicized text delimited by single *guillemets* (e.g. <*Watch out on your left!*>) is telepathic or mind-to-mind dialogue throughout this book, joining the traditional "Watch out!" for verbal communications and *better watch out* (no delimiters) for internalized dialogue. It might jar right at the start, but as all sorts of furious dialogue flies in all directions, I think you'll find it remarkably easy.

—Jack L. Chalker

Two Demons In Amber

The ship that roamed the sea of stars descended from heaven toward the blue-green eden below, as always, looking for the snake.

In the colorful terminology of Sector Mapping, the world below and its solar system were in the area labeled in the common language of interstellar commerce as Rainbow Bridge, after the sounds used to translate the X-Y plotting coordinates on a map. The words used for the symbols had no intrinsic meaning, and there was no indication that the union of these accidental words would be prophetic.

For nine days the small, crossbow-shaped scouting ship had lain off the planet, while its carefully laid satellites, like the eggs of a giant bird, had circled and crossed every square millimeter of the planet's surface, photographing and mapping. Other eggs of a different sort had been sent first to the atmosphere to sample and test it and then gently to the ground in selected spots, and even on and under the great seas that, from a height, seemed to engulf and dominate the continental land masses. All of these sent a steady stream of data back to the mother ship, where computers compiled, checked, sorted, double-checked, and evaluated the flood of information received from its children.

The process could, in fact, have been totally automated, but very smart beings had learned over the years that you would never remember to program it for all eventualities, and that ships with their own artificial intelligence and evaluative skills ultimately never seemed to have both a sense of aesthetics and the horse-trader's know-how that could tell the measurably right from the commercially right. The ship *could* do it all on its own, but a second opinion from a different breed was always required.

The breed of living evaluators that accompanied the swift scout ships into those blank spots on the star charts known only by their colorful coordinates might have feathers or scales, fingers or tentacles, might have been hatched from an egg or grown from a pod; it might be male, female, neither, or all of the above, and while it usually breathed oxygen, it might well be more comfortable breathing water or methane or a half dozen other substances. For all that was a single breed, distinguished not by its form or race or birthright but by the fact that those of that breed called *scout* had to be of a singular mental bent.

It was a fact that all scouts were mad; the debate still raged as to whether the demands of the job drove them mad or whether they were mad at the start. In their pasts, most races had seemed to have a very small number of the breed no matter how different they otherwise were; these were the pathfinders, the wilderness explorers, the ones who pushed on alone into blanks on the maps. It had been suspected that some factor—anything from genetic engineering to just too much civilization—would breed them out of existence, and it was true that a few races now dominated the field, but, somehow, whenever someone discovered a new blank on some map, a scout always seemed to be there.

This one happened to be named Cymak, a bipedal creature of the basic Class II shape, with two arms and two legs and a thick torso. He also happened to have lumpy, mottled skin the color of rotted sewage, which was so thick some bullets wouldn't penetrate it, and a triangular-shaped head that seemed to bob about as if it were on a spring rather than a segmented neck. His ancestors, before the age of synthetics, had fed on giant insectlike creatures by punching holes in them while they still lived and sucking out the fluids. He called himself and his physical race *Xymanths*, which, of course, basically translated as "human being," like most of the exotic names that intelligent life forms called themselves. For terms like racial origin and planetary names the interstellar tongue deferred to the local one. Otherwise there would be several hundred "human beings" who considered all but their own kind "nonhuman," and almost all of them would refer to the mother world of their races as "Earth."

The triangular head bobbed and weaved like an unattended jack-in-the-box in the wind, as it looked over the data digests on the screens. So far, the data looked good. So far, in fact, it looked *too* good. Worlds well within the carbon-based life zone that contained a readily balanced oxygen-nitrogen mixture within half a per cent of optimum along with the proper water balance were quite rare. Normally you took what you found and then brought in an Exploiter Team to reengineer the world into something useful, or, even more frequently when these kinds of worlds were found, there was already some form of higher life calling it home.

Not here. There were vast forests and dense jungles all right, and high mountain ranges, and it was perhaps a tad too volcanic for absolute perfection, but so far the surveys had shown no signs of an indigenous race of sentient beings. Oh, you could find the basics there—creatures that took the ecological position of insects, some high-level herbivores and the inevitable carnivores preying on them and pruning their herds, and some rather odd ocean life as well, but nothing to show that anything higher than that had ever evolved here.

Of course, as Cymak knew well, you could never be a hundred per cent sure, even if you stayed a month. Intelligence came in the oddest packages and didn't always fit the conventional molds. More than once he, and almost all the other scouts, had certified a world as "exploitable," only to have Exploiter Teams later discover rather nasty surprises down there. That was what Exploiters got paid for.

Cymak's job was to check the obvious. Structures, signs of environmental alteration, patterns that would show species dominance, that sort of thing. If there was any kind of real intelligence on this world, it wasn't the conventional sort.

"There is an anomaly," the ship's computer reported to him. "I had a number of passes made when it showed up, just to make certain, and sent in the highest resolution photographic gear once it was isolated. It is on the east coast of the smaller continent in the northern hemisphere. It is definitely an artificial structure."

"Just one?" The Xymanth responded.

"Yes. One structure on the entire planet."

That was bad. Worse than a horde of screaming natives, in fact, because one could often do something even with a primitive population—but a single structure probably indicated that somebody else had found the place first.

"Identification?"

"Unknown. That is, the structure is of no known type either in the Exchange or in the Mycohl or Mizlaplan groups. In fact, I did not report it immediately because the readings it gave off indicated malfunctions in my own equipment."

"Put up your best shots on the screens," the scout instructed.

The screens blinked and then showed various passes in full three dimensions. Cymak immediately understood the ship's problem—the artifact was unlike anything he'd ever seen before. In fact, the five views presented to him didn't even look much like each other.

"These are not five separate structures? These are all views of the same single object?"

"One object, same coordinates. You can see why I suspected a defect. I checked for all known types of shielding and found nothing in the registers. As far as I can determine, there was nothing to filter or distort the shots you see. The material and basic dimensions, at least, are consistent."

The first view showed a structure that resembled nothing so much as a great amber-colored crystal of fine quartz perhaps forty meters long, its various facets showing clearly, its far end apparently rounded, its near end coming to a multifaceted taper ending in a point. The second shot showed something the same size and color, but now it seemed concave, as if the top were turned inward. The third shot resembled the first, but the smooth sides of each facet were different, as if the damned thing had somehow *turned*. On the fourth there was no point, but rather a yawning cavity that seemed to reach back half the length of the thing. The fifth was the most disconcerting, with the object seemingly segmented into quarters, with each turned slightly off the other so that the facet walls were broken up and did not match.

"Well, *something* is causing distortion," the Xymanth noted. "Unless that thing is alive and kicking. Composition?"

"Every analysis comes up with indistinct data," the computer told him. "All I can tell you is that it is solid, appears to have some of the properties of glass or glassing plastic, that it is opaque, and that the substance does not appear to exist anywhere else on the planet, either artificially or naturally. There are indications of a low yield energy source there but little else. It is effectively dead to all remote analytical tools. There are no signals emanating from it otherwise, so it is not a beacon, and if it is some sort of downed vessel from an unknown civilization, it is not broadcasting anything we can monitor even as a distress signal, although in any event I would find it inconceivable that such a structure could have flown or even been carried here by any known means of transport or propulsion."

"Life scan?"

"I get no life-form readings that are not consistent with the natural life of the planet. If anyone's home, they either do not match any known type of life or they are very well hidden inside that thing."

"In other words," the scout muttered, "you, the most sophisticated and knowledgeable device any known technology can create and program to answer any question and hazard exacting theories on almost any eventuality with a command of facts and data and a thought speed incomprehensibly better than my own— you are telling me, essentially, that my guess is as good as yours. Right?"

"Probably better than mine," the ship responded. "I do not have nearly your capacity for wild flights of imagination."

"So it's not a spaceship, not a cargo module, not a house built with materials found on the planet, either. So how did it get there?"

"I would not presume to guess. It has been there quite a while, though. It is definitely buried in rock and soil to a fair depth, and there is no sign of construction or melting or other alterations. A good bet is that it has been there a *very* long time, and that the rock and soil have formed around it. It has not, however, been overgrown by the surrounding vegetation or covered by volcanic ash or debris. This indicates that there is some kind of maintenance function within it that still works. Again, if one had to speculate, it would appear most likely that the thing contains a system somewhat analogous to my position in this ship. It is entirely possible that the whole structure is some sort of artificial intelligence in a shell, and indeed that may be all that it is."

"Entirely plausible. You are certain, though, that it is of extraplanetary origin and not merely an unusual feature?"

"Positive. The energy pulses show a clear-cut power source of some kind, and there is some intake and exhaust of gases. Not a sufficient amount to indicate that the whole structure has full atmosphere, but enough to suggest that at least a small part of it has. It would be interesting to get close enough to analyze the gases it expels."

"Then let's get close enough. Roll in a remote unit and let's see just what it's made of and what its reactions might be to an approach. How long will it take?"

"I have already constructed and programmed such a unit, anticipating your actions. However, it is now past dark down there in its area, and I would suggest a daytime foray. Get some food and rest. In the morning we shall test this thing's mettle."

The probe dropped fairly close to the object, in part to see if that would provoke any reaction from it. No scans or other transmissions were detected, and the probe settled to its point just slightly off the ground and proceeded slowly toward the artifact as Cymak and his monitoring computer watched on the screens above.

From ground level, the long, exposed end, which sometimes looked like the rough end of a crystal shard and sometimes like a depression, looked very much the latter, almost a tunnel ringed by sixteen even facets of crystalline substance leading back to a single black point that might or might not have been an entrance of some kind.

The probe did not at first try an approach to that point, but instead rose up and did as much of a survey of the exterior as it could. The initial measurements held up; it was a hair over forty meters in length, seemingly embedded or wedded to the bedrock, the exposed portion a bit under four meters high from ground level. There were no observable or measurable openings, but it did seem to "bleed" gases in the broken, or entry, end, almost as if it were somehow selectively porous. The region of atmospheric bleed or exchange went in a bit over six meters and then stopped abruptly.

"Definitely some sort of atmospheric chamber," the ship told him. "It might be the entire inhabitable life zone within the object, or it might be the only one that requires it. At the far end are two isolated spots giving off heat—not a lot, but definitely indicating a coolant mechanism—and that's it."

"See if you can take a sample and analyze it," Cymak suggested, more fascinated than worried.

The probe settled down on top of the structure, anchored itself on three tight suction feet, then extended a small-core drill and attempted to take a small sample. It didn't happen. All the drill did was whirl around and begin to melt in the frustration of going against something harder than its bit, even though the bit was made of the hardest substance known to the Xymanth.

"Whatever it is, it's not quartz," the computer commented.

"Obviously. Well, it's almost certainly an exercise in futility, but run through all the tests and see if we can come up with anything."

Burning, controlled blasting, laser, and other tests proved equally futile, proving Cymak correct. The computer spent four hours doing everything it could to the object and at the end of that time they knew just as much as they had before they began.

"One thing is certain—if we could figure out its composition and duplicate it, we'd have the perfect enclosure and building material," Cymak said. "Something built with this stuff would be the first construction that really would last down through the ages."

"I am not at all certain it is the material," the ship responded. "I just took another series of measurements and they differ slightly from our earlier ones. Not in gross proportions—we are talking slight changes here—but definitely different. In fact, I have now completed a third pass and it is different still, yet the surface is not moving at all. It is very much as if the object is indeed changing its shape slightly and almost constantly, yet I can not directly measure such a change in progress. It is almost as if the thing were not—quite—totally in our universe. As if our physical laws don't quite apply to it."

The Xymanth was surprised. "You mean—another universe? That it has somehow poked into our universe without quite losing contact with its own?"

"In layman's terms, that is about it. If it were not quite in phase with us, either temporally or in some other dimensional level, that would explain why it seems impervious to all that we have tried to do to it."

"Is that possible?"

"I have never heard of such a thing, but at a guess, faced with reality, I can find no other theory that might explain all its properties. We know very little of the geometry of parallel universes. We exceed the speed of light and travel as far as we do because we know some of the properties and topology of one, but here we may be touching a different one. That theory explains much, if true, although I have never heard of such an intersection actually being discovered. It would certainly explain the properties and characteristics of this object, as well as how it got here. Whoever or whatever built this thing did not fly it here, they simply moved it to a parallel intersection point and shoved it through. To what purpose, however, I cannot speculate."

The Xymanth thought about that for a moment. "I

might hazard a guess. What is our logical next move?"

"Why, to try to gain entry, of course."

"Yes. I am reminded of the *mothryx* traps of my own people. Weblike constructs that one lays upon the ground, partly concealed, with a one-way entrance. The *mothryx* comes along, crawls in the entry, and is trapped there. The trapper then comes along later and the meal is locked inside, fresh and preserved. A random probe from a curious race able to do this on a far larger and more sophisticated scale might serve the same purpose. It is simply here, attracting attention by virtue of its being unlike anything else, waiting for the unwary or the overly curious to crawl inside."

"A fascinating theory. Shall we test it?"

"By all means."

"It might be fruitless no matter what. If the thing is out of sync with our space-time matrix, then transmissions from within it may be impossible."

The Xymanth had thought of that. "If so, it will be most disappointing, but then we will transmit what we have and leave it to the military and the Exploiter Teams to deal with. Proceed."

The probe moved forward again, then down, facing now that forward region that looked like quartz shards from above, but like a gaping mouth from level ground. The ship re-angled a repeater so that signals broadcast horizontally from the probe might be caught and retransmitted upwards, then sent the probe carefully on its way toward the black spot at the center of the shard walls.

"My sophisticated measuring devices are going mad," the ship reported, "but the basics are holding. Atmospheric pressure constant, temperature rising but slightly, visual breaking up on direct but holding well with the repeater. Distance, however, is skewed. According to my readout we have already traversed the length of the object and yet we are just now approaching the entrance."

"It would be a pretty elaborate joke if it took us in and immediately expelled us out the other end," Cymak commented. "A single door."

On the screens that "door" now loomed wide, its edges regular, but the blackness was not a hole into the interior but rather a tough-looking membrane. The probe stopped perhaps centimeters from the surface and extended a small silvery handlike probe to first push against the seal and then to use its three "fingers" to attempt to sample the material. It did not get the chance to do the latter, for at its touch the membrane seemed to rotate counterclockwise and fall back.

"An iris," the ship noted. "At least we are welcomed in."

"Yes," agreed the scout, "but welcomed in to where? Can that be the interior of the thing? It is *huge*."

"As I surmised, the object is not fully within our continuum," the ship commented with some satisfaction. "The constancy of our signal transmission is the only bridge we now have to wherever the probe actually is. I cannot get accurate measurements; the figures shift wildly now, far greater than the exterior measurements, yet I believe my instruments are actually functioning. They were simply never designed to measure something this alien to our experience."

It was a great chamber made of the same quartzlike material as the exterior, but it was irregular, with great columns of crystal rising from floor to ceiling like majestic towers, each illuminated with a cold inner light that was crimson in some, golden in others, and blue and green and colors without names that Cymak could speak. The overall effect was quite beautiful.

The floor was uneven, almost a miniature rolling terrain, the ceiling no more regular than the floor, and the walls seemed to curve this way and that, all catching the light from the columns and blending, twisting, and distorting it into rainbows of color that were not still but slowly writhing back and forth, in and out.

"It is not the light sources that are pulsing or changing," the ship noted. "Rather the walls, floor, ceiling, even the columns are subtly shifting in size and shape as we go through. I believe that to be an illusion produced by our inability to see and measure such conditions accurately. This geometry has been heretofore theoretical in nature. My best guess is that my initial theory was wrong; this thing does not exist outside of our continuum but rather in a multitude of continua simultaneously, ours included. I think it is a tesseract of some sort, although how one would build such a thing and make it real and accessible is beyond any knowledge our world possesses."

"Far more interesting than *how* is *why* someone would build it," Cymak commented, fascinated "And, for that matter, *who*."

"There are inner chambers. I am having problems with transmissions now on a level and scale for which I might not be able to compensate for very long. Still, we will explore so long as we have some sort of control and line to the probe. I fear, though, that if transmission is cut for any time, even a few nanoseconds, we might lose any chance of recall. We will try the nearest central chamber and see what we might see." The probe went forward, the images becoming jerky on the screen, more like a succession of still frames than a moving picture, as it crossed into the new chamber.

"Less illumination here," the ship reported. "I think I . . ."

Conversation stopped. Cymak felt his breathing stop too as the contents of the smaller center chamber suddenly came into sharp focus.

It was a dark room, with but two great pillars in the center. Both were illuminated fully by inner yellow light, but this time they were not at all transparent. Suspended within the columns like insects in amber were—*things*.

Cymak had never been religious. His people had too many gods, like most races, none of whom had done anything particularly for those who invoked them or asked their blessings, but in whose name a lot of wrongs were often committed. Now, however, he was beginning to reevaluate those opinions.

The Empire controlled thousands of worlds upon which hundreds of races had settled, both before and after they had been absorbed into the Empire. The races were of every conceivable shape and form and type; they breathed water and methane and lots of other junk as well, and some were so alien from the rest that they were barely comprehensible to outsiders. And yet, somehow, all had developed at one time in their past theologies and cosmologies, many as different as night and day and even more incomprehensible, but with a curious single commonalty among them that had fascinated and puzzled anthropologists from the start.

The pair in the columns were that commonalty in the flesh.

Each stood perhaps two and a half meters high. Their feet were great cloven hoofs; their legs, slightly bowed, were covered with thick purplish hair to the midriff, while their chests were bare, dark and hard-looking, almost like bone rather than skin. The arms came down from great, broad shoulders and seemed much too long, furred like the legs, but terminating in great clawed hands. The faces were skeletal mask's, grinning horrors with broad, clownish mouths, snoutlike nostrils, and large, dark eyes that seemed almost as black as space, set off by thick purple brows angled down toward the bridge of the nose forming a connected, thick V shape. From their heads grew ugly, misshapen horns.

Their descriptions varied slightly from race to race and even from culture to culture within a race, yet none would have had any more difficulty than Cymak in instantly recognizing them for what they were.

"By the gods of my ancestors," he breathed. "Demons!"

The ship's computer was equally impressed intellectually, but did not carry the burden of having grown up in a sentient culture, acquiring along the way a bit of nerves about monsters and bogeymen.

"They are not quite identical, other than the obvious differences in the horn length and shape and the fact that the one on the left is a bit shorter and thinner," the computer noted clinically. "The briefs they are wearing make it impossible to tell for certain, but there is a possibility that they are a mated pair. Calm down, Cymak—they are definitely embedded in the stuff and certainly not about to come to life."

The Xymanth, however his rational mind insisted that he'd simply happened on a major discovery, could not shake the feeling that he had instead intruded on a temple of the truly supernatural. The strangeness of the object, its less than solid nature, its bizarre shiftings, and now demons.

Almost every race had such demons, and almost without exception they represented all that was truly evil and malevolent in the universe. This pattern also held true among the races of the Mizlaplan, as he well knew, even up to the Mizlaplan themselves, who had set themselves up as gods. Only the Mycohl regarded the ancient and apparently universal demon figure as an agency of good, but the Mycohl had always been perverse.

"This is a discovery of monumental proportions," the ship enthused. "For centuries we have looked for traces of the demon figures as early common visitors to the races of ancient days, but in vain. Now, here at last, is proof that they exist—that demons are a real, unknown, perhaps very advanced race. We shall go down in the history books for this, Cymak!"

"Break it off," the Xymanth said with firmness. "Pull the probe out—*now*."

"But I want to—"

"Do as I say!"

"Very well," the ship responded with a very human sigh. "Get hold of yourself, though. You have traveled farther and seen more and fought more than any two others alive or dead. You can not allow yourself to be undone now by silly superstitions and psychological leftovers from your childhood."

"They are *evil*!" Cymak snapped. "Remember that! Almost universally they are the symbols of pure evil! And that, too, must have a reason, an origin in antiquity that has been passed down to us as a warning!"

"Evil is relative. Besides, the Mycohl consider them good."

"And what sort of society and values do the Mycohl represent? That evil should worship evil is hardly shocking. No, pack it up and get it ready for transmission without delay."

"So you are not so frightened of two apparently dead ancient ones that you will not report it."

"I dare not ignore it. It is unlikely that we could destroy it or cover it up, and if I don't stake this planet, then a Mycohl scout or a Mizlaplanian group will stumble upon it. I just pray that those who come after to study this will not loose a horror upon us all that has been kept bound here for millennia. So, sound a recall and prepare the report. We will do no more work here ourselves."

"Very well. I would not worry so much, though. It is by now mere archaeology, mere objects of study. That pair is long dead and preserved here as in a grave site. If we accept, as is generally agreed, that memories of demons among so many different races so far apart were caused by some ancient visitations, it must have been tens of thousands of years ago. No one except priests, psychics, and psychotics has seen a demon in the flesh since then."

"It is not a grave site," Cymak responded firmly. "Graves are sealed among those who use them. They are not maintained in chambers of an unknown technology still active and responsive to visitors. And ten thousand years ago this was a far different place—certainly geologically, and probably climatologically as well. Our figures show a minor ice age in between. Yet there it sits, still active, still working, with its terrible inhabitants frozen there, not buried in rock or overgrown by vegetation, its door open in full operational condition. That thing is alive, at least as much as you yourself are alive, and perhaps more so. Still alive, still active, still functional, and smart enough to keep from being buried or embedded or undercut or overgrown through the centuries. I fear this is a discovery I will rue until my death."

"Perhaps. It will certainly shake things up, anyway. All is prepared and organized. Do you wish to review it before I transmit?"

"No, I know what a good job you do. Send it, but append this from me. Say, 'I, Cymak, Scout of the Exchange, send you evil from Rainbow Bridge.' Say—say, 'Here be demons.' "

Book One:

Exchange: The Blue Team

Soap Opera For Spacers

Jonah And The Worm

The Erotics had zeroed in on him now, but while he'd watched their dancing with enthusiasm and wondered once again what it must feel like to have a tail like that, he wasn't at all interested in the follow-up.

One of them, maybe senior, nosed out the rest and headed over toward him with all the sass and sexy moves she had. She had all of them. He watched her come, resigned, and drained the last of his drink. No loss there; in a place where everybody was drinking and popping all the wrong stuff, he was limited to fruit juice.

Up close, she was no less erotic but far less human; what seemed almost a stage costume from afar took on a far different cast when you could see that it was no costume but truly her. In the capital of the central world of an empire encompassing hundreds of races spawned by incredibly divergent evolutionary forces, she nonetheless seemed artificial, unreal, like some kind of animated stage prop created by some bizarre artist.

Which, in a way, was just what she was.

She was almost as tall as he was, taller with that thick mane of hair rising from her head and sweeping behind, although he was, to be sure, rather short and thin himself. Her skin was light brown, her face and torso out of some adolescent male's fantasies, the eyes unnaturally large, the lips too thick and sensuous, the face and form perfect, the breasts ridiculously oversized and far too large to be as firm as they were, the nipples ever erect. The brows, however, were thin and angled upwards; the blush and eye shadow were not cosmetic but part of her, and above the outer edge of each eye, about midway between the eye and the hairline, were tiny, perfectly rounded short horns.

She had no navel; about where the navel should have been was a covering of short, incredibly soft darker brown hair that went down to her feet. Her hips were a bit odd-shaped and supported two thick legs that were somehow both equine and sexy, ending not in human feet but in two graceful hooves. From the small of her back trailed a magnificent golden tail of the sort that he'd seen on show horses when he was a kid back on his native world; her hair spilled down her back in the same color and style.

She slid up to him. "Hey, bad boy—want a feelie?"

He looked at her. Only something beyond the painted eyes, deep inside her, revealed her hardness, her many years at this trade, and her sense of entrapment in it.

"Nothing tonight, luv," he responded. "Just here for the scenery and the atmosphere, nothin' more. Maybe some other time."

She'd been around too long to take that as a final brush-off. "Aw, c'mon, big man. You got needs and I can fill 'em."

"*Shove off!*" he said in such a tone that she actually took a step back. Coldly, but less threatening, he added, "You with all your years got no idea of my needs. Go find a paying customer and get happy."

She stared at him. "You a guv or som'thin'?"

He tolerated the question because he knew it was a natural comment. "I ain't no guv, girl, not by a hoop. I want less truckin' with them than you do. I just don't want no tumble tonight."

Her brow furrowed in puzzlement. "Then why in hell'd you come in *here*?"

He felt sudden anger and stood up quickly, almost knocking the stool over. "I don't have to explain nothin' to nobody, least of all a long-tailed piece of ass." He walked briskly by her and out the door and into the street.

He walked about a block in the crowded district before his anger cooled. He'd been out of line there and he knew it, but what the hell could he say or do? She was just doing her job, the only job she could do, the job she'd been *designed* to do in some genetics lab. Hell, why *had* he gone in there, anyway, knowing the scene was inevitable?

Why, indeed, come down here at all? The tourists, the business people, the crews on leave, the conventioneers and politicians—these were the mobs in this gaudy district. He looked around. People, people everywhere, and he was the only damned human in sight.

Maybe that was it. Maybe he'd gone to the only place where he could be certain there would be other human company, no matter what the type and no matter that, down here, those from human stock weren't exactly creations of nature. You could be close, closer than relatives, closer than blood brothers, to a half dozen creatures who were so different from you that you had little in common except the job, and find them the best friends and mates you could ever imagine, but every once in a while you just felt like you had to be with your own kind, no matter who or what they were.

He took the cross-town tube and headed back for the hotel. He felt depressed and mad at himself, and somehow cut off not just from his own kind but from any kind.

That was the problem, really. Not that he was cut off from his own kind by any barriers or occupation but that he was the one who was different. The others in the glit, they were human, and he had less kinship with them than with the Erotic. Maybe that was why he'd gotten so mad at her. That sense of her entrapment; a mind inside there that was maybe curious or smart or ambitious but that couldn't really do much about it. With that body, those urges, the built-in genetic compulsions, she might be bored and hate the whole life but she could literally do or be nothing else.

Somebody else had made that decision for her at her conception, within some computer-controlled bio lab that created endless themes and variations of her to fill an age-old market demand. It wasn't bad enough to have a thousand races to keep track of; there were endless variations of them as well.

He hadn't been like that. He'd been born in the normal manner from material supplied randomly by two parents, even though he never knew who one of them was. Born poor and raised in the filth of an interplanetary backwater, but he'd been smart and he'd had ambition. The Erotic might be smart and have ambitions, too, but she was trapped from birth and she knew it.

He, now, was different. He'd trapped himself. He'd sold his soul for his ambitions, his dreams, and now that he had them they were hollow, for he couldn't enjoy his fruits. When you're poor and without much hope you don't look too hard for the devil's fine print.

Inside his room he relaxed, then removed his clothes. When his back was bared, there was a small furry ball down at the base of the spine, a ball that unrolled slowly and began to gradually inch its way up his back and toward his shoulder. It resembled nothing so much as a large slug, but covered with fine, thick baby-blue and snow-white hair. He sat on the side of the bed, letting it climb all the way up.

<*Poor Jimmy*> said a tiny, whispery, barely audible voice in his head. <*Grysta let you out on the town and she senses your unhappiness. Did you want that girl?*>

He sighed. "No, not *that* girl."

The tiny creature made it to his shoulder, then slowly oozed its way toward his neck. He lay down on the bed, knowing that it couldn't be crushed or hurt in this way. He could have sat and pressed against a steel plate and it wouldn't have hurt Grysta, or dislodged her.

He thought of the creature as "her" even though, strictly speaking, the race was unisexual. Jimmy understood creatures who were bisexual, or trisexual, or whatever, but only second-hand, as he might understand another race by reading about it. That was part of the problem; Grysta seemed to understand him quite well, while he couldn't really understand the tiny creature at all. The biology, yes, but not the culture, not the attitude, not her relationship with him.

He turned on his side and Grysta stretched out, tiny "head" against the nape of his neck, body stretched out rigidly along his spinal column. Microscopic tendrils shot out from her underside, penetrating his skin in a thousand places They were long enough to reach right into his nervous system, yet so fine they could not be seen without aid. There was no pain; there was no real sensation at all, until Grysta had control.

Then his mind seemed to fog, his depression vanishing for now, rationality giving way to waves of pure pleasure washing over and through him. Orgasmic waves traveled to every nerve and cell in his body, an ultimate high that few could ever know or understand. And while it went on, while he writhed in ecstasy, Grysta fed, gorging herself on his blood, yet taking none that would be missed in the morning, and she, too, was undulating in pleasure, and whispering to him, <*Love you. Love you, Jimmy.*>

<*You are depressed.*> Grysta noted. <*Did not I please you during the night?*>

"Yeah, you pleased me," he mumbled, bringing himself erect and managing to get his feet over the side of the bed. "You always please me, Grysta. Like a habitual pleasure drug or a stimulator on the brain's pleasure centers pleases. Nobody can please like you, Grysta." That last was said in a tone of resignation and with a tinge of sarcasm as well. The attitude would be lost on Grysta, he knew.

<*You constantly complain that I have deprived you of your inalienable right to be miserable. This I cannot comprehend, even after all this time. If you really wish to be miserable, I can make you so.*>

"No!" *You're doing a good enough job of that just being here*, he thought sourly to himself. At least he had that one bit of privacy—although the communication was mental in a way, Grysta was not a telepath, and required "interfacing" physically with her host for that. It could be the softest of whispers, but Grysta did require that he really talk to her. It always struck him as ironic that he could have mind-to-mind contact with a hundred different kinds of beings but he had to talk to the one he couldn't get away from. Grysta thought on different wavelengths than most of the universe.

Grysta was always a "her" to him; he even heard the voice in his mind as that of a woman, although she really was asexual. A strong, assertive woman's voice, less like a lover's than that of a boss, or maybe a mother.

<*What is it you want, then?*> Grysta asked him. She always asked him, but she never could understand the answers. How do you explain to a creature, however intelligent, who required a host to see, hear . . . feed . . . that the host resented her presence? No, that wasn't right—he didn't resent her presence, he resented her control. Not that she would hurt him, but neither would she allow him to come to harm, for that would be like setting fire to a room in your house.

"I want a drink," he told her. "I want to get rip-roaring, stinkin'-arse drunk. I want to pop some aphros and go out on my own alone for a night on the town, that's what. I want to pick a fight, go bloody roughhouse, get tossed in the tank with all the other arse-kickin' fools blowin' off steam. I wanna check into an Erotics parlor and indulge all my silly dreams for a bit, that's what. And I wanna do it *alone*."

<You know I can't permit that, Jimmy. Such things are destructive of mind and body, risking at best ill health and at worst injury or death.>

"But that's what I bloody *need*, you furry little slug! Risk. The risk that comes with independence. The risk that's the right of all citizens of the Exchange!"

<We've taken risks on many a hostile world, and come close to disaster.> she noted.

"*We* take the risks! Aye, *we* do, don't *we*. Because we have to work, because we have to be able to afford the basics of life, and because there ain't no other kind of job that would tolerate the two of us, and if we couldn't do that, then your dispensation from the coppers wouldn't hold water and we'd both be discreetly disposed of and you know it. And even now we might be faced with such a thing, being without a ship or crew or commission because your hesitation caused a *Thetian* life. Who's gonna hire us now, you bloody worm? We're Jonahs—bad luck. And there's no shortage of folks in the Guild Halls to fill the available slots. At least most of them can get some kind of menial job dirtside to tide them through from berth to berth, or they can get off this metallic dirtball and find some colonial job. We wouldn't even pass the physical for that. You remember the one time we tried that. I hadn't known until then that burning at the stake wasn't a mere historical curiosity."

<If I had let you save the Thetian, it would have cost our own lives,> she pointed out. <That is known and on the record. Don't worry so much—we'll find something!>

"We better," he responded, sounding like he hadn't

much hope of it. "We're down to our last few hundred, and when that's gone we'll have only ninety days of Guild maintenance."

He got up, pulled on a shirt to conceal Grysta, then opened the door and trooped down the hall to the communal bathroom. Even as he did so, Grysta was manipulating his internal chemistry, providing stimulation, suppressing the usual aches and pains, generally cheering him up a bit so that while his depression wouldn't go away, it would be at least tolerable and he could look himself in the mirror.

He was getting old, he thought, and not even Grysta could stop that, only make it easier to live with. The face that stared back at him in the bathroom mirror was lined and weathered, the curly hair about half-gray, the thick, close-cropped beard streaked with white. He was beginning to look more and more like his late father, and Da always did look like he'd survived a bomb blast but the repairs hadn't totally took.

Here lies Jimmy McCray. His life was a waste of his own time and others', his purpose was to serve as the eyes and ears of a parasite. Here lies Jimmy McCray and Grysta together; even in death he couldn't get rid of her.

It was past midday when he left the Guild hostel and headed to the Hall in his daily exercise in futility, but if he didn't stick his name in religiously, they'd toss him out as a shirker. At least they fed you there.

The City was over a hundred and forty by ninety-five kilometers; a massive complex that spread out as far as the eye could see, and contained within its boundaries well over forty million souls, souls whose only common link was that they were all from someplace else. The whole thing was metal and plastic and other synthetics, and that even went for some of the people and most of their occupations.

The fact was, the whole place could have been run

by computer and maintained by robots, but such things as robots on the level of personal or city or company maintenance were banned. The cabs that floated by as he walked toward the train station were various colors for the various racial groups, so that a *Drukin* wouldn't attempt to fit in a seat or space engineered for a *Klive*, or vice versa, and so that you could be assured that the internal environment was to your liking.

There weren't many blue-and-whites, cabs for *his* kind. His kind of humans were all over the vast, nearly nine hundred-world empire, but they were a very small minority here.

Such cabs would have human drivers, just as the crimson and gold *Kluvian* cab over there had one of the ash-white pyramidal Kluvians driving the thing. Hell, if you let robots do the driving and pick up the garbage and clean the streets and vacuum the hotel rooms, why, the vast assemblage here would be out of jobs and without means or purpose. Though the Empire was truly one that prized individual freedom and the work ethic—including the freedom to starve to death if you didn't have money for food or bleed to death if you couldn't afford treatment—its leaders were fully conscious of the fact that millions or even billions of people of all races who were starving and bleeding in such huge numbers would quickly form a desperate, revolutionary mob.

The train floated in and stopped, and he entered the small blue and white compartment, alone as usual—except for Grysta, of course. There were some other spacers staying in the hostel who were human, but they were younger and more ambitious than he and they'd been at the Guild Hall when the doors opened at the crack of seven. Berths could open up at any time of the twelve-hour day the Hall was open, but the young eager beavers always were paranoid that the perfect position was going to be there at seven on the dot and filled by seven fifteen.

After several stops through a multilayered mass of buildings and overlapping roadways, walkways, tramways—you name it—that always reminded him of being trapped in the basement of a giant's office building, the train broke into the open and there was the Exchange in full view, surrounded by a very pretty if odd-looking park. To him, real parks should be varying shades of green and have trees that didn't look like melted candies or great tentacled monsters of red and blue and yellow, but it was still very pretty and nicely landscaped. In the center of the park, visible from any top floor in the city, rose the smooth, sleek crystalline Exchange Building itself, resembling nothing so much as dozens of monstrous clear quartz crystals bunched together and neatly tapered at the top so they reminded him of organ pipes. Any job that might reach the Guild postings would start there, and the Exchange had far shorter hours.

The train suddenly went into a tunnel underneath the park and the Exchange, and rode for a while in eerie darkness, although, of course, there were lights in his cubicle. Suddenly the vast station burst into view all around him and the train slowed, then stopped. The place, always packed during Exchange hours, looked like somebody's *Alice in Wonderland* nightmare no matter what race you were.

Here, bustling, hurrying, scurrying, slithering, and all sorts of other movements were constantly in view and it seemed like no two creatures, or at least no more than two or three, were alike. They were all *people*, all citizens, but they had exoskeletons and no skeletons, claws and tentacles, two arms, four arms, two to what might have been forty legs, with teeth, mandibles, suckers, you name it. They were every color and shade anyone could imagine and a few that nobody had imagined until they saw them. They came in every shape and size, and perhaps one in five required some kind of aid, from a wheelchair to a breathing apparatus to a full-fledged pressure suit, to get around.

He was watching the parade, getting something of a kick out of it, when he caught sight of a fellow human— a tall, strong-looking but very attractive redhead in a powder-blue jump suit and spacer's boots—having an animated conversation with a *Jurian* and a *Sloge*. Jurians looked to most humans like three-meter land prawns; Sloge looked like giant snails in ringed, curled shells with toothy mouths. They always seemed ready to eat anything that couldn't eat them first.

He wondered what she was doing there, and considered a telepathic scan on the theory that at least one of them would be readable, but before he could more than note the conversation, the train glided off and was soon back in the darkness. It had been a long time since he'd seen a normal human woman, particularly one that looked as good as that, and, with the red hair, possibly Irish.

Probably just as well he didn't try the scan in there, though. The accumulated mass of thought in that tight space would most likely have overwhelmed him and given him a real bang-up headache.

The next stop was the one for the Guild Hall, and he got off and made his way up the moving stairs to something like street level in the crowded and confusing mass of the city.

The Hall itself was a big building with the Guild emblem atop the big double doors that opened for him as he approached them. Inside was the main hall, with its noisy, milling throngs of out-of-work spacers scanning the big computer boards for what openings there were. Some were also color coded if there was some specific race desired, although most were just the usual white printing on blue background for generalized positions. Few companies were race specific unless they had a particular job that required a particular type, or, of course, the ship was one of the few run by life forms that either breathed the wrong stuff or had one of those nasty living environments.

He pulled out his Guild card and went to a terminal, inserted it, then watched the small screen in the unlikely event that he was just what somebody was looking for. Nothing of that kind showed, and he quickly scanned the ships and positions currently listed to see if anything looked really promising. Most of it was the usual stuff, but there was enough that he punched for a printout. The terminal hummed and then disgorged a small folded document and he took it with him to the cafeteria.

The one trouble with eating in the place was that the guy next to you might smell like rotting meat and be noisily ingesting a huge bowl of creepy-crawlies, and with the preparation of dishes based on the racial breakdowns gleaned from the Guild cards, there weren't too many choices for his kind of folks. Soup and a sandwich was fine; he lusted after a beer or at least a cup of coffee, but Grysta disliked stimulants and depressants and made sure that if he took one it made him unpleasantly sick. Sitting down with his tray as far away from other diners as he could, he started eating, then unfolded the printout and studied it in more detail.

There wasn't a whole lot. Black gang stuff, mostly, although that term had lost most of its original meaning. Ship's engineering assistants, general electronics repair and maintenance, shuttlecraft technicians, that sort of thing.

There were only three areas where telepaths really were desired. One was as security officers, since a good one always could tell something was wrong. The second was on First Teams, the first ones in to a newly discovered world, whose job it was to show up and see what tried to kill them. The third was on ships crewed by races that couldn't physically speak to each other without lots of elaborate hardware; the telepath knew no language barrier, although often the thoughts were bizarre and the frames of reference of alien races were nearly impossible to grasp.

But the bulk of spacer jobs was on the big ships, freighters and liners, where Talents were pretty well limited to security, medical, and the officer corps. The jobs most common in the Guild listings—repairmen, monitors, quality control, and the like—weren't for such as he. Talents were not all that common, and weren't well liked or appreciated by many people. Ones like him, from families without known Talents, and clever enough to realize what they had as soon as the Talent grew and concealed it, hadn't had to work all that hard, either, until they were found out. You didn't have to know anything; you just had to read the mind of the smartest kid in the class to get a good grade. He'd been about twelve when the strange dreams and voices he'd heard intermittently over the growing-up years had suddenly coalesced into full strength.

It was rough; you either got control, forced everything else out, learned how to tune in or turn off, and quickly, or the mass of thought would drive you crazy. Many of the unrecognized ones *were* nuts, particularly those who'd been born and raised in cities. He'd been a farm boy on a sparsely populated world, and it had given him the edge he needed.

It was said, however, that sooner or later everybody got caught, although he was never really sure how they knew that. If you didn't get caught, they wouldn't know they hadn't caught you, right? It was kind of like the perfect murder. They all said that there was no such thing, but, if it was perfect, who would know?

But they were good at catching Talents. The Empire's most elite, highly trained special branch was devoted to doing nothing else. They'd finally caught on to him— they never told him how—and then they gave him the treatment. The little finger on his left hand was indelibly dyed with concentric white and black rings that would

never come off and could not be concealed for long—
the damned chemicals burned like hell if cut off from
air and light for any length of time. And, of course,
the most powerful computer-augmented hypnos in the
Empire implanted a bit of ethics in your mind that you
couldn't wash out, either, because you couldn't tell what
was you and what was them. Even the Mycohl did
something like that; nobody trusted Talents, least of
all other Talents.

Like most telepaths, he kept it shut down most of
the time, or, rather, down to a dull whisper that his
consciousness could tune out. Non-telepaths never
understood how terrifying it was to open up wide in
any sort of crowd, to be suddenly flooded with all sorts
of alien thoughts in a monstrous mess, like everybody
speaking at once. That was why so many telepaths didn't
live to adulthood, and why some who lived but never
learned to shut out the world went violently insane.

He stared out at the vast Guild Hall and silently
chuckled to himself. What would most of them think,
he wondered, if they knew that if he bothered
eavesdropping on their thoughts, he would probably
be bored to death?

That afternoon he did put in for a couple of Exploiter
Team positions that advertised for telepaths, and actually
interviewed for one, but as soon as Grysta came up—
and in the close confines of a Team you couldn't exactly
not mention Grysta—the "Thank you very much, we'll
be in touch" flag was raised and that was that.

After dinner there was the usual nothing to do, and
so he wandered back over to the District, as he
sometimes felt compelled to do.

<*I don't understand why you keep coming,*> Grysta
commented, puzzled. <*I don't really care one way or
the other, and I could understand if you were actually
entertained or found companionship or something but
all it seems to do is depress you.*>

"*You* depress me, you little worm," he muttered. And yet, Grysta was right. He couldn't go on a tear like he wanted to do—Grysta would see to that—and there really wasn't much here otherwise. There was in fact only one club on the whole street that catered primarily to humans, and he'd found nothing there the past evening. Still, what the District offered him was quite tangible, quite real. It was *live*. The street was *alive*, teeming with all sorts of creatures with nothing but fun on their minds, in a city that seemed otherwise as curiously inanimate and deathly silent as its masters, the Guardians, that curious, ancient race that really ran the Empire.

And the crazy thing was, not a soul here even knew what the hell they were.

At least you knew that the Mycohl, masters of their own empire, were some kind of communal parasitic organism; they had a biology, a reality, of sorts. And the Mizlaplan, while not very mobile, at least had a known form and known evolutionary path and were very real to the citizens of their own empire. But here, in an empire that didn't even have a name, let alone an emperor, in the only free society of the Big Three empires, nobody at all knew who or even what the bosses were. Their great cities, like this one, were built by others for the comfort and convenience of others. The Guardians themselves had no cities, no monuments, not even an official history—not one they let anybody else know about, anyway.

Some thought them a great computer or assemblage of master machines; some thought they were beings of pure energy, pure mind. Many deep down didn't believe they really existed at all, but were just some construct created by the board of the Exchange as a false front for their own rule. Unlike those citizens of the Mycohl Empire or those of the Mizlaplan, however, the Guardians—whatever they were and if they existed or not—were not thought about much at all by the people of their empire, which seemed to suit everybody just as well.

He looked in on the Club and saw that the stage review, in the round, was in full swing. It was dirty enough, all right, if you were into bestiality. Big, goat-horned satyrs doing obscene and unnatural things with the sexy equine dryads, who were able to twist into amazing positions. It was rough and brutal, to the sounds of overly loud canned music, and it did little for him.

<I don't understand why they go in for the half-human, half-animal thing,> Grysta commented. <But if that's what sells, you'd think they'd have more varieties of animals.>

"They do," he told her. "This particular lot is booked in for a week or two, then they'll have mermaids or centaurs or any one of a thousand varieties of mixes, while this group moves on to one or another of the big cities on the other worlds. This one just happens to have that theme."

<It seems to me that they'd be more of a stimulus if they just used attractive people.> Grysta didn't really understand much about this kind of sexuality, let alone perversions for sale, but she was getting at least an academic concept.

"That's a no-no," he told her, thinking he'd told her this several times before. When Grysta was trying to figure something out and having trouble she often asked the same questions every time the subject came up. "It's called prostitution and it's done, of course, but rarely. Too many really nasty quick-mutation sexually transmitted diseases. Space travel, strange suns, odd atmospheric balances, and varied radiations—the same sort of stuff that caused the birth of Talents—also caused brand new birth defects and mutations, and a nice variety of human diseases, particularly viruses and other tiny buggers. In fact, these Erotics were actually created in an attempt to stamp out such things. It was a crusade for morality on many of the human worlds."

<I understand enough to know that that is not morality on that stage. Ethics, morality—some of it might be silly but it is at least comprehensible. Genetic manipulation to that degree amounts to human slavery.>

"Yes, you'd recognize slavery, no matter how subtle, wouldn't you?" he muttered, mostly to himself. "But they aren't what you think. They're constructs, androids— genetically engineered, yes, but from synthetic materials, not human stock. One of the few legal uses of the advanced science of robotics allowable, created and programmed to do just what you see, and they neither want nor think about anything else. And because they're synthetic, human viruses and diseases can't survive inside them."

He turned away, walking back out into the street. Grysta was silent for a few moments, then commented, *<I can see darker uses for that sort of technology.>*

He nodded, although it was meaningless to the creature. "Fortunately, it takes a bloody fortune plus lots of expertise and research to do that sort of thing, and various components that can be rigidly controlled. The Mycohl, for example, have been trying to find out how it's done for decades and failing. The Mizlaplan, of course, consider the whole thing an abomination."

<And you do not?>

"I think it's probably done what was intended with no harm to anyone. There are still perverts out there, and people either desperate or stupid or defenseless that fall prey to them, but it's way down, perhaps as far down as a society that doesn't engineer its people and dictate their minds can bring it. Every cure has its price."

As Grysta considered that, he relaxed and looked around the streets and alleyways and opened up his mind a bit.

<GOBBLEGOBBLEGOBBLEGOBBLE. . . . !>
Oops! Too wide. Bring it down to a dull roar.
<Gobblegobble . . . went to the wall on that one . . . gobblegobble . . . chanted the Fifth Order Cycles . . . gobblegobble . . . first maze Sudura crimped . . . > What the hell did *that* mean? So many races, so many odd concepts and ways of thinking. It was strange that something like eighty per cent of carbon-based life used bands within a rather narrow range for primary-level thinking. Secondary and deeper thought levels were often way off the mark, beyond all but the most powerful and expert to even touch, with a great variation in the bands even among people of the same race.

But on the primary band, most species did their thinking within ranges that even telepaths of totally alien evolution and biology could intercept. Mostly, of course, he just heard what they were saying aloud to someone, or what was foremost on their minds. You couldn't go on a fishing expedition in somebody else's head—that took machinery and psychophysicians—and there was a lot of mostly banal stuff on the surface. Listening to races that were off his bandwidth and beyond his powers, he still got the sense of someone or something there, like a silent but active channel on a radio. And, every once in a while, he'd feel the odd twinge of a mind instinctively pushing back, of some kind of barrier—not usually hostile, just automatic, like he himself did when another telepath scanned him.

What disturbed him, though, particularly here, was something he couldn't really explain to any non-telepath, not even Grysta. The street, the immediate neighborhood, was to a telepath like a living organism, a kind of mental life that could be felt as something tangible. But on this particular world, even in crowds, there were occasional and jarring dead spots.

Unless he picked them out and scanned them exclusively he couldn't spot them, but they were here.

Black holes of the mind, dead to Talents, dead in other senses as well. Zombies, perhaps, or so he and most others thought, but the one link between the Guardians and this mass that were always there.

They were called cymols. Real people, living people, who were no longer themselves, who had as part of their brains a small controlling computer. They were the losers, mostly, in this society—habitual criminals, murderers, suicidal types, the incurably insane. Their minds, some said their souls, had been replaced, reprogrammed by the Guardians. They could plug in to each other, or to the computer grid, and perhaps to the Guardians themselves.

As far as he was concerned, they were all coppers, and scary types to boot. They looked, talked, and acted just like regular folks, and none but some of the Talents could tell them apart from the crowd.

There'd be a bunch of them down here, of course, checking on the crowds, checking, too, on the people and companies that ran the District, looking for serious criminals and clip artists, making sure that the most wanted didn't vanish into this deliberately created cesspool.

In truth, so long as you weren't arrest bait, this was one area in which the vast majority who had no Talents had the edge. They could conveniently forget that the cymols existed, just as they could ignore the Guardians, and interact with them in ignorance as if they were just ordinary blokes. Talents, though, particularly telepaths and empaths, had to know them for what they were, and it gave them all, including Jimmy McCray, the creeps.

He turned and walked quickly down the street, turning off into a dark alley where the glitter and noise of the District barely reached, cursing himself for having opened up so wide in a place like that without thinking about the obvious presences he would touch there. Odd to think that there were presences that stuck out because of the absence of signal.

<*This isn't the safest of courses to take,*> Grysta noted nervously. They'd been on a lot of worlds that were sheer horrors, but always with a team—backups, protection, and weaponry at their disposal. Jimmy ignored the danger of dark alleys and side streets here, but Grysta felt suddenly very exposed and insecure. <*Don't you think you ought to take one of the main ways out?*>

"Cymols," he muttered, shivering. "You know how they give me the creeps."

<*Dark alleys in bad sections give me the creeps.*>

"Oh, relax. We're not exactly defenseless, and even if we got pounced on, what in heaven's name have we got worth stealing? Besides, I'm still open on the primary band. We'll not be surprised."

It was a telepath's confidence, something a non-telepath could understand but not really accept. Nor, of course, was it fully warranted. Some of the best crooks could fool a telepath, and, while Talents weren't all that common, one telepath who was slightly stronger or more skilled could easily fool a lesser. And, here, on this world, there were plenty of the one race no telepath could scan.

<*AGH! YOU HORSE-ASSED BITCH! I'll teach you—!*>

It was a man's "voice," very loud on the primary band and only slightly less so on the hearing level, so strong and powerful that the speaker had to be very close, but, save for its virulence, Jimmy didn't think of such things as any of his business. He was no voyeur. The sounds of a nasty electronic buzzing and the subsequent screams of real pain in a loud female voice changed that.

Telepathy had uses, but it wasn't very directional unless you fixed on the subject visually, and the layers of the great city, like some monstrous metallic wedding cake, created echoes and false signals. He looked around, tried to pick out the likely source, and saw a very dark, narrow service alleyway to his left. He headed for it, then broke into a trot as the victim's screams and the man's curses both grew stronger and louder. He could see a glint of light pierce the darkness for a moment with each electronic sound.

<Are you crazy? This isn't any of our affair! They're probably trying to lure you in there to take your head off!> Grysta protested, to no avail. She had the power to stop him, of course, but her own strange moral code made it very much a last resort.

Jimmy wasn't sure just what he'd see when he got there, but he wasn't quite prepared for the sight ahead of him.

They were on a loading dock in back of the Club, the human Club, and there were two of them in near total darkness. The only illumination came from a tiny yellow safety light on the back door, and a blue-white electrical light that flashed intermittently from something in the man's hand.

He was a big man, that was for sure, although there wasn't much else you could tell about him in this light, and he had a foot on some dark shape on the dock, holding it down, and as he cursed and screamed threats, the blue-white light flickered once more and became a jagged whip-like pencil of energy, which he brought down on his captive. As the energy whip struck, she screamed again in pain and pleaded nearly unintelligibly for him to stop.

"Hold it, mister!" McCray cried out, his own voice echoing down the narrow street and up the many layers of the city. "You're in civilization here, and that sort of thing just won't do!"

The man at first didn't seem to hear, but then at least the fact that somebody else was there and yelling at him seemed to penetrate his thick, angry skull. He paused, but did not move to free his captive. Instead, he flicked a thumb switch on the electric whip, changing it into an electric torch that suddenly illuminated McCray and nearly blinded him.

"Hey! What . . . ?" The man muttered, a bit confused. "What the hell are *you* doing here, sport?"

"I heard screams," McCray responded calmly. "That's not done on this world, even in this place."

"You mind your own bloody business!" the big man snapped. "If I want to kill this fucking bitch—or maybe not-fucking bitch would be a better term for her worthless hide—I'll bloody well do it. She's bought and paid for and got no rights." The torch swung suddenly off McCray and onto the hapless victim, and McCray took a breath.

It was one of the pretty equine Erotics.

"You ain't no copper I got to explain nothin' to," the man added, "and I can do what I damn well please with my property."

<That's it. You said they were synthetic and all that. Say you're sorry and let's blow this place,> Grysta said urgently.

Jimmy McCray looked at the girl with the hooves and tail, lying there, stark terror on her face, part of her hair singed and bloody welts on her skin. In a legal and technical sense Grysta was right, of course, but no one seeing that terror and that pain could have walked away and not also left his last shred of honor and dignity. His honor and dignity were pretty much all he had left.

"You're right, I'm no copper," he responded to the man in that same even tone, "and I'm no lawyer, either, but where I come from, whipping dogs or horses is still a crime even if you own them. Cruelty to animals, they call it, and *that* is far more than a dog or a horse. In fact, we tend to whip the owners of the mistreated animals so they know what it feels like."

"You arrogant little Mick bastard!" the man spat. "A thousand years of gettin' your asses kicked in and you're all too dumb to ever learn a thing!"

Jimmy stepped closer, almost to the edge of the loading platform. "Maybe I just never had a good enough teacher."

The man glanced at McCray's left hand, always a precaution before you got into these things if you weren't fillet with rage. Mixing it up with a hypno or a telekinetic would be suicide.

"Telepath, eh? You damned mind readers bleed for everybody, don't you? Well, Swami, after the first move, that little talent don't help you one bit in a fight and you know it." The thumb moved the switch back to the whip. "And all I got to do is get *you* to make the first move."

He raised his arm, clearly intending to bring it down once more on the helpless Erotic, and Jimmy moved. With near effortless motion he jumped from the street to the platform, and at the same time the big man varied his wrist motion to bring the whip straight over onto McCray.

The man was a good head taller and maybe forty or fifty kilos heavier than Jimmy, but what Jimmy lacked in bulk he more than made up in speed and agility. Although the big man slashed in a couldn't-miss pattern, McCray bent and ducked and jumped and the lash did in fact miss him. Before the arm motion could be checked, Jimmy crashed into the man's chest, driving him backward into the rear wall of the club. McCray's hand shot out and twisted the whip away from him, sending it flying into the alley.

The big man's knee came up, catching Jimmy, but he was quick enough to anticipate the move and partly deflect it by a backward motion. It still hurt like hell, but it wasn't the debilitating blow the big man intended.

Still, the big man bellowed his rage, now transferred

entirely to Jimmy, and he used his momentary advantage to charge forward. Both he and McCray went down on the platform, but McCray was able to take advantage of the man's forward motion once again and roll backward with him. The result was that the big man fell off the platform, while Jimmy barely stayed on.

Up until now, Grysta had been totally against this whole thing, and still was, but now they were in a fight and that took precedence. Pain suppression on, adrenaline on high . . .

As the big man was picking himself up from the alley, McCray stood and then jumped him. The man went sprawling again, but McCray's acrobaticlike balance served him well, and he remained on his feet and started in with karate kicks that landed painfully on the larger and still-disoriented foe.

The big man was a street brawler type, the same kind of big bully Jimmy McCray knew all too well when he was growing up. The same kind that had driven him, out of pride and a need for self-preservation, to attain the sort of gymnastic skills he now used, and to study the martial arts as the only way a small fellow could best a bigger one like this lug. Such martial arts weren't well-known to the average human of the Exchange; the vast bulk of Oriental humanity had wound up in the Mizlaplan.

Like most big men, this guy could hardly believe he was being struck hard and kicked in the face and beaten bloody while his fists met only empty air. McCray was about to set the man up for what could have been the kill, But in this case would only be the knockout blow, when the man's thoughts checked him:

<Damn it! He's a pro!>

Aloud the man gasped, staggering a bit, "Enough! Enough! There's no more sense in this!"

Being a telepath, Jimmy could tell that the man was sincere. He knew when he was beaten.

The big man managed to make it to the side of the platform and collapse against the side, sinking down and breathing hard. Jimmy, who knew that he would feel tomorrow what Grysta was blocking now, took a few moments to get his own wind back, then walked over to the big man.

The Erotic handler was taking in air in heaves, but now he seemed to have some of his control back, and he sat there and began to laugh.

"So you beat the big man in a back alley brawl," he managed, between gasps for air. "So what did it get you except a few bruises and a little Irish ego?"

The comment took Jimmy McCray by surprise, and he struggled to recover. "I stopped the beating."

"For the moment. Now what do you do?"

McCray frowned, then jumped to the platform. The Erotic girl was still there, curled up a bit, still sobbing from the pain. She looked up at him, but it was an odd mixture of gratitude and fear. "Are you all right?" he asked her gently. "Can you stand? Do you need help? Come, come! You have nothing to fear from me!"

Like all the Erotics, she was on an off-band. He couldn't scan her, just get a kind of soft, empty hiss.

"She feels good she lived long enough to see somebody beat the crap out of me," the big man called from his resting place, a smugness in his voice. "And she also knows I can't let the others hear of this or there'd be discipline problems for the next six weeks, and we close here tomorrow night."

"Kill me," her voice said, almost too soft to hear, and cracking slightly. "Kill me and ship me back."

Jimmy was totally, completely shocked. He turned and walked back to the edge of the platform, where the big man was just getting unsteadily to his feet, still chuckling a bit between grimaces from the sore spots.

"You touch her, let alone kill her, and I'll come back and finish the job I started on you," Jimmy growled.

The big man shrugged. "Got to, sport. I got forty in this company and I'm hypno-bonded. Now, if you'd lost this fight, it'd be different. A nice lesson for her to take back to the forty-odd rest of the company. You give 'em the idea that some little guy interfered with my discipline out of a kind heart and beat me square, and they'll start pushing, taking advantage, screwing up just to get even. Maybe even gang up on me. Time we got through I'd be beat up worse than this and I'd also have to deal out some real nasty discipline, maybe even slow-kill a couple, to get 'em back in line. Better to lose one now and have done with it than go through all that, maybe have to also abort the tour and ship home early, which will cost a lot of money. And you kill me, the whole group gets shipped home under seal by the coppers. They'll all be outcasts when they return, and the cops'll be after you for murder. You see how it is, sport? Your little act of kindness just did nothing but give you a little smug satisfaction and kill your damsel in distress."

As a telepath, Jimmy McCray understood instantly that the bastard was telling the truth. The worst part about it was, the big man wasn't too thrilled at the idea of killing, but considered it just part of the job.

"And what you say isn't murder?"

The big man sighed. "Hey, sport—I don't make the rules. They ain't *people*, remember. They're designed by a computer and grown in a lab someplace. They're like machines. Machine goes bad, you see if you can fix it, and if you can't, you toss it out and get a new one. I was doin' the fixing tonight and you stopped that. Now I got to toss her out."

He looked back at the Erotic, who suddenly seemed so tiny and helpless, her body trembling a bit, her face all too human in spite of the animal-like parts and the artistic design.

He turned back to the big man, who was walking

down to retrieve his whip. "What if she went with me?" he asked the man, the question just forming of its own accord. "You're leaving tomorrow, you said. Off-planet, I gather. She wouldn't see or talk to the others, and your problem would be solved."

The man sighed and shook his head in wonder. "Sweet Jesus, man! I'm supposed to send them all back, so none of 'em are unaccounted for. Besides, what the hell would you *do* with her? They're not all that bright, they're designed for only one thing, really, and they have no citizenship or rights. You rich enough to keep her around as some kind of household accessory?"

That last was just humorous enough to bring a dry chuckle to his throat.

<Holy shit, Jimmy! If you wanted a pet, a cat or something is a lot easier to take care of and a lot cheaper to feed!>

"I can't let him just kill her," he muttered under his breath. "Particularly not if it was really my fault."

<I warned you not to get involved! Damn it, now you've got us in a hell of a fix! With her our cash is cut in half; and we're saddled with somebody who's a dead weight. It brings our starvation closer and only postpones her own fate.>

"Let me have her," Jimmy told the man. "You're a bright lad. You'll figure out a way to explain why she wasn't sent back. I'm sure there are a few lies you can tell to get permission to dispose of her on the spot. It's either that or we'll have to go at it again until you're out for the night, and while I doubt I could hide her forever, I could certainly outlast your ticket out in a day or two in a city of this size."

The man shrugged. "You want her, you take her, sport. Then, when you got to get rid of her, you just call the Club here and they'll tell you where to send the remains. No skin off my nose."

McCray turned back to the Erotic, who had stopped

shaking and was now looking at him as if he were some sort of god.

"Here, here! None of that! He's probably right," Jimmy told her, feeling a bit embarrassed by the look. "Can you walk?" He put out his hand and she took it and got unsteadily to her feet.

"They're fast healers," the man told him. "If they weren't, I wouldn't be using this kind of thing on them. Good luck, sport. You're gonna need it. I almost hate to see you do this. Been years since I got licked in a fight, and I kind'a like you. I can't figure out why the hell you're even doin' this."

"No," sighed Jimmy McCray, "I suspect you probably can't." He turned to the girl. "Can you walk? We'll have to get to a train."

"Yes, master. I can do whatever you wish me to do," she responded softly.

"We'll have none of that!" he snapped. "My ancestors spent too many years as other people's lackeys. I'll not be legitimizing the process! You'll call me Jimmy like most other folks."

She smiled. "Jimmy. That's a nice name."

Besides, he added silently to himself, *I'm hardly in a position to be the muster of anyone, being a vassal myself.*

<Jimmy what the hell have you done to us now?> Grysta wailed.

"Shut up, Grysta," he murmured, and offered the girl his arm.

Cheap Thrills And Bad Dreams

Once the principles of subverting the speed limit of light are discovered, usually by accident and with nobody really believing it, the age of a people's interstellar expansion and colonization begins and starts moving so rapidly that vast changes take place at lightning speed.

On Earth, it had been a team of scientists from several western nations working on a particle physics project having nothing at all to do with space travel who stumbled on it at a government lab in California. By the time they realized what they had, and the government also realized what it had, part of the cat was already out of the bag. By the time it was funded on even a limited basis, nine other nations had stolen the process. In fact, the only reason it was finally fully funded and supported by the nations that discovered it was because at least three other nations had practical ships built first. In fact, Earth came very close to having the nuclear war it had dreaded over who owned what.

Fortunately, by that point, several international blocs' initial probes had established a surprising number of interesting and potentially habitable worlds out there. In full egocentric arrogance, a treaty was finally hammered out dividing the *galaxy,* of all things, into spheres of influence, with all preexisting claims recognized where they were. The fact that once you made the initial horrendous investment to create the machines and materiel that could build the machines

47

and fuels required, interstellar travel proved cheaper per trip than interplanetary travel, also had something to do with it.

Within only a century after the first ships had left Earth, humanity had over a hundred solar systems within its grasp, although, to be sure, most of them were totally worthless and held on to only for pride, speculation, or because they were between two places worth going to. It was an impressive array nonetheless. During that period, the first extraterrestrial life forms were discovered, and whole massive new fields of extraterrestrial study opened up. No other sentient races were discovered in this period, but hope springs eternal, and all sides had no doubt that sooner or later *their* bloc would be the first to meet a truly alien race and convert it to *their* way.

One bloc included the United States, Canada, and most of western Europe except the French, who made an ingenious deal with some of the major Latin American nations and a few of the better-off African nations to form their own Latin bloc. The Japanese, refusing to sign on as junior partners in the West's coalition, formed a full partnership with China that put politics on the back burner and formed another bloc, while the Russians formed an eclectic bloc that included not only their usual worldwide allies and client states but also India, desperate, like China, to find new worlds for an impossibly large population.

All of them competed with each other in the usual historical ways, and all established colonies among the relatively near stars of the spiral arm which Earth was a part of. Certainly there were strains, but there was also a lot of optimism that this was going to go on forever.

It took almost two hundred years of expansion before humanity met its first sentient nonhuman races, and when it did, it had a shock. When a scout for the

Exchange first discovered a Western bloc colonial world, it didn't exactly send greetings.

Instead it claimed the colony as property of the Exchange and gave orders on just what to do next.

The ancient and sophisticated empire that discovered Earth's colonies had been through this many times before. Reports indicated that the discovered world was a mere colony, and relatively new at that, and that there were a *lot* of people colonizing worlds out there.

Almost as soon as word spread through the Exchange of this new race, spies from both the Mycohl and Mizlaplan Empires sent the same details and coordinates to their own masters, who quickly tried to guess the origins of this new race and its obvious pattern of colonial spread. A rush was on once more, but this time three old and wily empires were in a race to gobble up as much of humanity as possible.

Even facing a common threat, humanity only reluctantly joined forces, and when they did, they discovered that their foe was massive, at least a few thousand years more practiced at this sort of thing, and that there wasn't much they could do about it. Later, historians would note that the greatest cost to humanity hadn't been the loss of its autonomy but the crushing of racial ego. In just a bit over two thousand years humans had gone from feeling themselves the center of and model for creation to accepting the role of relatively insignificant subjects of a universe far more vast and complex than they had allowed themselves to imagine.

The bulk of the Western bloc and also most of its affiliated Latin bloc had gone under the Exchange simply because their world had been discovered by an Exchange scout. The Sino-Japanese bloc had fallen mostly to the Mizlaplan, while the Soviet-led bloc went to the Mycohl. The fall was in some cases nasty but quite swift and absolute. The Exchange had over a hundred and forty "member" races; the Mycohl had almost that many, and the Mizlaplan slightly more. They had been at this a very long time.

In the end, some adjustments were made for the sake of practicality among the three conquering powers, but the basic divisions of humanity remained. In the freewheeling Exchange, the Western bloc and Latin bloc remnants settled in quite well into a system that allowed them to remain very much as they were, although a minority and subject people. The Mycohl and the Mizlaplan probably hated each other more than either one hated the Exchange, but both were united in insisting that new subject peoples were to be "culturally unified" with the rest of their empires. The Exchange conquered territory and live bodies; the Mycohl and the Mizlaplan wanted the minds and souls as well.

Within a very few generations, humanity had become more divided than it ever was on Earth, groups having more in common with fellow members of their empires who were spawned by different and bizarre evolutionary paths than with those with whom they were racially linked in the other empires.

Still, reduced to minority status, a small group within a huge empire, all three masses of humanity did recognize that there was only one way back to status and power within the terms of their new cultures. As the primitive, junior members of their empires, they bred like rabbits in a trio of multiracial ancient cultures that by this point bred rather slowly and in tightly controlled fashion. This worked best in closed, somewhat unitary cultures, where numbers meant strength and power and influence. The Mizlaplan had gotten the Chinese and the Mycohl had gotten the Indians, both large population groups, and could claim more positions, more room, and more worlds for themselves quickly.

The Exchange had gotten the Latins, and allowed them to maintain local control over the worlds they had colonized. But access to wealth and power came harder in a society where new worlds were not distributed but sold in the marketplace, and where everything you needed had to be paid for with something somebody else wanted to buy. In the capitalist empire of the Exchange, ironically, humanity had fared the worst, and was still very much a junior partner.

The heart of the Empire was the Exchange itself, the great tubular building in the heart of the capital city deep within the Empire. Inside, virtually anything within the basic limitations of the system could be bought or sold.

One great quartzlike structure contained the commodities brokerage, where resources and futures could be bought and sold. Another was strictly a shares exchange, wherein one could buy, sell, and trade bits and pieces of the millions of companies that ran much of the empire's vast economy. There were other, smaller, more specialized brokerages as well, but the heart of the Exchange and its physical center was the grand Hall of Worlds.

Here, exploration corporations, with vast numbers of scouts always searching the still unexplored reaches of the galaxy, took the findings of their far-flung searchers and placed not companies, not resources, but whole worlds, even whole solar systems, on the block. Buyers ranged from racial groups needing worlds to expand upon, to speculators betting on new finds, to interest groups looking to prove their own ideas of social or political systems by establishing colonies based on their particular values.

The Exchange really didn't care what you did on your own worlds, or how, or why, so long as you obeyed its few basic rules, recognized its extraterrestrial sovereignty, and had no truck with the Mycohl or the Mizlaplan except through the Exchange itself. But from these simple rules came a surprising level of control. The Exchange alone controlled an independent and mostly cymol and robotic interstellar military system; the Exchange alone settled disputes between companies or worlds that could not be settled between the principals. The Exchange alone controlled the interplanetary purse strings through its banks and trading houses. And the Exchange alone controlled the flow of discovery through its control of export patents and enforcements.

It also maintained a public consular corps on every world in the Empire to provide eyes and ears for the unseen Guardians, and a very private and very secret group known as the Special Corps, whose job it was to watch the watchers, find out what wasn't very public, and to find out what the Mycohl and Mizlaplan might be up to.

The humans who had attained some wealth and power within the Empire had done so by voluntarily serving in the consular, military, or Special Corps with distinction. They tended to be the best of their people, but, in a cutthroat society, just what they were best at was the subject of some argument.

Modra Stryke was one of the very few people who tended to look back on a nightmarish descent into hell with wistful nostalgia.

It had been a typical Exploiter Team contract: a new world discovered and purchased on speculation by an agricultural combine who wanted to know if their pig in a poke had reasonable potential as a new source of revenue.

The combine was the kind of employer only a Team like Lankur and Stryke would take—one that would only pay off if they found something there and if the usual nasty surprises and cost estimates weren't outrageous.

Not that the contract didn't call for an ironclad payment no matter what; it was just that these kinds

of jobs came with only enough front money to mount
an expedition, and if you didn't come up with anything
of value, you'd find that the corporation that hired you
had all the substance of a soap bubble and would vanish
just as fast. It was what First Teams always faced, and
why only small private companies like theirs did First
Team work. Strike it rich for an employer a few times
and you'd have enough of a bankroll to establish yourself
as a real company, with lots of ships and crews and
resources, and forget your worries. The trick was to
stay alive, pay the bills, and cover expenses until you
did.

Few did.

Modra Stryke was a tall, attractive redhead with a
strong face and voice and with too strong a romantic
streak at twenty-four to "get into the baby business,"
as she referred to it. Having inherited a little money
from a doting uncle who'd been an Exchange agent
and had parlayed those connections into a small
commodities trading company, she'd rejected the usual
path of getting married and using the family business
as a solid basis. It was too dull, too mundane, and too
dead-ended for somebody like her, particularly at her
age.

Instead she'd sold the business, left her native
Caledon, and come to the capital of the Empire with
dreams of romantic adventure and untold wealth still
buzzing around her head from all the old stories she'd
heard.

She hadn't been in the city three days when the
Widowmaker had limped into port, barely functioning,
its crew half dead and completely dead broke, a last-
gasp First Team that had run out its options. She'd gone
down to see the ship just out of curiosity, and the same
piece of broken-down junk that the spaceport yard had
decided was fit only for scrap looked to her like the
most amazing and romantic thing she'd ever seen.

And there was big, burly Tris Lankur, with full beard and curly black hair and flashing eyes, sparring with the dockmaster and threatening to fight off all comers if they tried to take his ship for back fees. He looked and acted exactly the part of the romantic spacefaring adventurer in all those stories and vidplays, and his crew, a motley batch of nonhuman creations with the same kind of madness in them, had been the perfect supporting cast. Modra had money but needed experience and a way in; they had, by the looks of them, plenty of experience but, between them, the crew of the *Widowmaker* didn't have cab fare. Lankur had taken one look at the tall, shapely redhead, listened to her offer, balked at the idea of taking her along, and finally made the deal.

She remembered it like it was yesterday, but it was actually nearly five years ago.

In that five years, taking First Team assignments, looking for the big one, she'd had the kinds of adventures that, while not at all the glamorous sort of things the glorified fictional versions promised, were certainly exciting, introducing her all too soon to the wonders of Exchange medical science. She'd repaired just about every sort of damage short of death, giving her all the experience she ever wanted or needed, but still she'd had very few jobs that really paid off, and none that paid off so great that they didn't have to do it anymore.

And, finally, it had been down to one last mission, pay off or forget it, on a world poetically named 2KBZ465W. A world that almost literally finished their saga . . .

Beautiful worlds were often like beautiful people— all bloody and nasty-looking when you got under their skins.

Modra Stryke always hated to be first in on a new planet; first in often meant the first to die.

This place was so new they didn't even have a name

for it yet, not officially, although already the forward Exploiter Team had a lot of names for it, none suitable for children.

No matter how good they made the environmental suits, they never had been able to get rid of the smell, she thought glumly. It didn't take many hours inside one, even with all the so-called filtrations and absorptions put into it, before you could smell your own fear-induced sweat and other body odors you never knew you had. The suits hadn't been developed for humans, necessarily, although this one was designed to her unique personal form and requirements. In spite of the fact that the dark-blue suit looked rubbery and skintight and left nothing of the wearer's form to the imagination, it was made of the toughest synthetics ever developed, able to withstand enormous ranges of heat and cold, cushion against most projectiles, even basic flash guns, and keep the wearer comfortable and cozy inside. You could even pee in your pants and some kind of suction would remove the waste, convert it to power, and leave you dry. She could attest to its efficiency there; she'd once been stuck in her suit for three days. It neatly got rid of and used everything—but it couldn't get rid of the smell.

Attached to the suit was a lightweight helmet made out of a more rigid form of the same stuff. You hardly knew you had it on, but it could provide water and something that at least passed for food for several days.

She gave a mental command and instantly the dark, dank swamp she was trudging through changed from a place of darkness and foreboding into a riot of brilliant colors. She looked around but decided that infrared was impractical here, where even the water seemed alive, and switched it off again.

"Tris? Where you at?" she called nervously, hoping her heavy breathing wouldn't betray her fear. Even now, after all this time, she still felt the amateur of the team, and that she was always under examination to see if she would fail.

"Forty meters to your left," Tris Lankur's voice came back to her, sounding far more distant than that. "Closing on I.P. Watch those long vines with the thick tendrils. They appear to have minds of their own and are looking for free samples."

She nodded, although she couldn't see the vines or him. "I've already had to teach a few lessons. This place looks like midnight in Hell."

"I think it has a certain charm, myself," came a third voice, hollow-sounding, guttural, almost like someone using belches to speak. "My ancestral world probably looked no different except in the details."

"Yeah, well, that's why I never accept your invitations to visit your home world," she responded sarcastically.

"And I thought it was because you feared my intentions," the strange voice retorted. Biologically, the pair had about as much in common as they did with these trees.

"Where are you, Durquist? Still in the trees?" she called back.

"About twenty meters up and about fifty to your right," the creature responded. "The ecosystem of this world is fascinating. There is a veritable garden of totally different plants growing off the tops of these giant weeds."

That, in fact, was the trouble. The place looked fairly decent from the air, with a broad, meadowlike matting of light brown moss and lichen providing a surface through which brilliant, bright, and colorful flowers grew. From that vantage point the place was beautiful, which was why somebody had been interested in it.

In truth, it hadn't taken them long to discover that the world's beauty was literally skin-deep, its sun-drenched exterior a thin veneer covering this hell beneath, like an animal's skin covering the ugliness of the body's interior. The carpet soaked up rain like a sponge and slowly released the bulk of it below, causing a steady mist and drizzle that eventually collected on the swampy real surface, watering the huge internal plants that supported the outer layer. The upper-level plants also appeared to have some form of photosynthesis, but what fed the big plants in such quantity that they could grow tall and thick enough to support an entire outer layer hadn't yet been discovered. That was one of their jobs.

The only way to start in on a new world, after you'd poked, probed, measured, and sent robots down to see what was there, was to pick a spot that looked interesting, go down, and see for yourself. There was a final question before heavily investing in a place that had to be answered, and bitter experience had shown that ultimately it could only be answered by one method.

The place has some potential. Now, before we go further, you all go on down there and see what tries to kill you.

It was a hell of a way to make a living, but it paid well, if you lived to enjoy it. Leader parties commanded the best short-term high-risk pay in the business, partly because experience had shown that they were the best— and most cost-effective—way to find out the worst quickly. The crew of the *Widowmaker* didn't like to take this sort of work—nobody did—but coming off two flat-out busts where the purchasers of worlds had gone bankrupt before paying anybody off, they needed a real infusion of cash or there wasn't going to be any ship, any team, or any job. Exploiters who lost their ships by going broke weren't exactly in demand by other teams, either. Everything they had was tied up in their ship and equipment; repossession meant more than ruin, it meant starvation in the harsh domain of the Exchange.

"Only an idiot would think of buying a place like this," Hama Kredner's high-pitched *Derfur* voice chimed in. "An idiot or a *Durquist*, anyway."

"What's your position, Kredner?" Tris Lankur asked, slowing making his way through the muck and trying to figure out a route between the dense black trunks. They didn't dare cut through—not with that canopy up there.

"Twenty meters to I.P. north of you. I should be directly opposite you with the I.P. in the middle."

"I'm hung up for a good route forward," Lankur warned. "Don't go any further in until I reach an equal position. Any visibility?"

"I've got the I.P. beacon registering loud and clear but I can't see a bloody damned thing in this crap. Got fungus hanging all over the place like a curtain. I bet this place stinks to any race known to any civilization."

"Oof!"

"Tris? What happened?" Modra called out, climbing up onto a huge angled trunk. She tried to squeeze through an opening that reason told her was impossibly small, but that the suit's computer said just might be big enough.

"I'm all right," he responded. "Tripped and fell on my face in the mud is all. This stuff is *slimy* as hell. Those damned roach-sized amoeboids or whatever they are that live in this crud are all over my suit and trying to burrow their way through. I may need a moment to burn them off."

"Take it easy," Modra cautioned him, and, by extension, everyone. "No need to rush this."

Tris Lankur was covered with the things, which experience had already shown couldn't be simply washed or brushed off. The only way to get rid of them was to divert power and feed a small charge through the exterior of the suit. It didn't kill them, but they tended to let go and get away fast from the burning sensation.

Modra looked to her left and saw a faint blue glow, her exterior sensors registering a sharp crackling sound. "I see you. Fry them little bastards!"

"'That got 'em!" he announced with a note of triumph. "They're still splashing and making for the bottom to cool off the hotfoot!" He sighed. "You know, they say that in ancient days the real estate business was very peaceful and relaxing."

"Appraising a planet is a bit more complex than appraising a house," the Durquist noted matter-of-factly, missing the irony.

She let it pass. "Durquist—can you make all our beacons?"

"I have you and Tris in view; Hama I cannot see. Must be something in the way."

"I'm here," the Durfur responded. "I'm stopped, but I wonder if that's such a good idea. I'm getting something, feeling something real bad. It's all around me, somehow. Like there's something here, so close I can almost smell it, but I can't put my finger on it."

Modra was an empath, able to sense emotions and sometimes manipulate them. The early surveys of this world had found nothing on any of the known telepathic bands beyond the most primitive animal life, but empaths read a different sort of band, one that covered a broader range than telepathy. Modra had insisted that there were intense pockets of emotion on a primal but very nasty level throughout this swamp. Alien life took many forms, and often did not have much in common with the ones they knew. Even thought, if there was any thought, could take unknown forms, although there tended to be a narrow set of bands for carbon-based life and another equally well-defined set for silicon-based, the only two higher forms of life known. But no telepath could tune into an intelligence as low level as a beehive; an empath, however, could read the hive's agitation and growing rage.

"Uh-oh," the Durquist commented sourly. "Prepare to be defecated upon by rotten fruit."

There was a sudden series of crackling noises high

above, and then several small objects fell, caroming off one branch and another, bouncing off spongy moss, on their way to the bottom. The pretty flowering plants that lived on the carpet above bore fruit, and every once in a while that fruit would get too heavy and break off. They had measured the falling fruit from afar but had not been right under it before.

"Almost got me," the Durquist reported. "It isn't just one that lets loose. When a big one goes, it takes a lot more with it."

"You're telling me!" Hama exclaimed. "They're falling all around me! *I—by the Three Gods of Sumura! The water! The—ackh!*" The last wasn't just on the radio band but was a panicked telepathic burst so strong that all had the sense of confusion, fear, and outright horror in their heads before they even heard the words. Yet no pictures of what was attacking the telepath came through. Hama had lost control.

"Hama!" Lankur cried out. "Stay there! We're coming!"

There was a snapping and crackling on the line, and Hama's voice was broken and strained. *"No! No! Stay back! Get out of the water! The water! It's—"*

"Hama!" screamed Modra Stryke.

Modra looked around and saw the water begin to move near her, as if it somehow had congealed into something alive. Damn it, it *was* alive, no longer frothy but suddenly gelatinous as if something were underneath. She didn't waste any time; she jumped for the nearest large trunk junction and attempted to climb to the branches, three or four meters above the water.

Behind her the water itself seemed to form into a giant waving column, like some sort of tentacle, and reached out for her. It was translucent, pulpy, yet it had definite structure and form, and—my God—it was *huge*!

It rose up as if to grab her, to pull her down and into

the muck, and she instantly switched suit power to external. The tentacle swiped at her boot, there was a crackling of blue energy, and it recoiled. It tried again, and again, seeming to add whatever mass it needed from the water, and each time it got a shock and withdrew. After a number of times it hesitated, as if finally learning, but it continued to circle around her below. Somehow, although it didn't seem possible, the organism knew just where she was.

She took advantage of the pause to climb as high as she could, but at about eight meters up the trunks grew together and twisted, and she could go no higher.

She watched, aware that her helmet lamp was slightly dimmed even now, then drew the pistol attached by its cord to her suit, and when the thing tried again she fired straight at it. A beam of blue-white light went out and caught the top of the tentacle, bathing it in an eerie white-hot glow, and when the glow faded, the top meter of the thing was gone with it.

But there was no blood, no oozing of ichor, just an irregular mass at the end of the tentacle where the disintegration had ceased.

And, slowly, as she watched, the gelatinous mass drew more substance, apparently from the surrounding waters. She could see the tentacle bulge, then the injured top began to swell, and she watched as *it reformed the tentacle she'd just blown off as if nothing had been done to it!*

"Durquist! Tris! Hama! Where the hell are you?" she shouted, forgetting her tough-as-nails act and starting to panic a little.

There was a crackling and popping in the radio, but she heard the Durquist say, "I saw your shot! Hang . . . Coming . . ."

There was a sudden horrible screech and squeal on the intercom that almost blew out her eardrums. She instantly tuned to another frequency, then another, not getting much improvement. The noise was far too loud to bear for more than a moment; she had to will the intercom off.

The sudden blessed silence made her relax for a second, and the thing in the water seemed to sense that and swelled up for another attack. By now there were several other shapes in the water, tentacles growing upward like the first. She barely missed getting grabbed and pulled down, then started sweeping, horizontal motions with the pistol, cutting off rather than disintegrating the tips. There was a lot of splashing as long, curling tendrils dropped into the water, but then her light showed her a sight that froze her blood.

The tendrils seemed to gather themselves up, then swim, snakelike, to the nearest large tentacle and merge with it, followed by the bulging and the slow rise to the top once again.

Son of a bitch! You can't kill these things! she thought to herself. If the little ones could do that, what was to stop the bigger ones from merging, growing into tentacles forty, fifty, even sixty meters high? Those suckers could reach the surface if they had to!

If, that was, they were smart enough to realize it.

She tried the radio again, but there were still the unbearable screeches and she quickly shut it back off. Somebody's suit, probably Hama's, was penetrated; energy was leaking out all over the place and the radio had been open when it happened. She couldn't keep it on, couldn't hope to get through that screech, but now the silence seemed at least equally awful and she suddenly felt very, very alone.

Now she knew why the old-timers wouldn't go out on an appraisal without a telepath.

She looked around in the gloom. The tentacles were holding off for the moment, as if massing for a new attack with more caution—although they couldn't be killed, the gun obviously stung—but she knew it was only a matter of timer. She looked around, trying to figure out if she could somehow move, force the tentacles to chase her from down there.

They didn't appear to be very bright, just single-minded, or they would have had her by now. The falling fruit had stirred them up, maybe even fed them, and they wouldn't go back to rest or whatever state they usually were in until they'd eaten everything in sight that might possibly be edible. They didn't seem to have muscles, but they sure as hell had some strength. If one got her head and the other her feet and pulled and twisted in opposite directions, she'd be cracked like a nut.

Maybe that was what had happened to Hama. Taken by surprise, grabbed by several of these things, which twisted and broke his suit seals before he had known what was happening. The energy discharge would keep them away from his body for a while, which didn't help matters much since they were then free to slither over toward her. It was probable that he wasn't even good to eat.

Another volley, another repeat of the cutting off, the slithering together, the melding, the rising up and rebuilding. Why hadn't they attacked before? Why had they waited? And why hadn't Hama been able to detect them long before this? It didn't make any sense at all.

She wondered again if she should move—and if she could. The Durquist was still high up in the trees and not under immediate attack; the creatures wouldn't know about him. Trouble was, the last message from the Durquist had reported seeing her shots, so that meant staying here or risk losing the only hope of short-term rescue. On the other hand if the Durquist came down here, they'd go after him too. A Durquist had limited mobility in that suit, but couldn't breathe this shit any more than the rest of them could.

And what if it wasn't her shots the Durquist had seen?

What if he'd seen the discharges from Hama's suit or maybe Tris firing?

She checked her energy levels. Fine for now, but this couldn't go on forever. Get away first; later she could find the others.

Maybe.

If the energy pack lasted, and if the suit beacon wasn't drowned out by the interference, they might find her.

There wasn't any clear-cut way out or up from this point, and she didn't dare go down. Damn! Looked like a hundred of them down there now, and more energy used with each swath she cut. Maybe there was a better use for those shots. . . .

She set her pistol to its thinnest cutting beam and fired to her side, carving out a small and jagged, but possibly useful, series of handholds and footholds in the trunks. They proved pretty damned solid, as she'd guessed; they could hardly be mostly water or pulp and hold up that huge canopy.

Maybe, just maybe, they were enough to get across on.

She let the pistol recharge to full, then gave a particularly low cut to the tentacle forest, knowing she had maybe five or six minutes before they reformed. She eyed her steps, and made for the first cut, then the second. She would have to descend a bit in a few more meters to get around, but by then she'd have a near wall of trunks between her and the main body of tentacles. She had no doubt that they could flow around or under or whatever, but that would take more intelligence than they had so far exhibited. If she could fake them out, get over there quickly, they might lose her. It was worth a try, anyway.

She fired another thin cutting beam and almost at the same time made her move, going down, through, and around, then climbing as quickly as possible wherever the possibility presented itself. Finally she stopped and looked down. The sound of her own hard breathing was the only sound around. There didn't seem to be any activity at all; in the murky gloom of the canopy, illuminated only by her helmet optics, she saw only peaceful swamp.

She half expected a giant tentacle to suddenly rise up and grab her, but after a little while she realized that, perhaps, at least for this short time, she'd made it.

Yeah, she'd made it—so hip, hip, hooray! Now she was only stuck here in the middle of nowhere without communications, waiting until something set the things off again.

Think, Modra! Think! She forced herself to be calm, got her breathing regular, took a drink of water, and tried to figure out what to do next. Her beacon was on, so maybe the Durquist could home in on her when things settled down. Now, *that* was a thought. . . . She switched to scan mode and tried to see if there were any other beacons in the area. Yes! For a moment hope soared, but then the small viewer against the helmet began to show more plots, and more—tons and tons of beacons. Damn it! Hama's all-frequency overload was tromping on the beacons as well, creating hundreds of ghost images. So much for that idea.

There was nothing for it but to try and make her way back to the shuttle. She doubted that the tentacles could do much to it, and it was in one of those holes in the canopy that the life below seemed to avoid. But there were fruit-falls all over this damned place. They'd been lucky, or maybe unlucky, to come in this far without one to trigger that—whatever it was. They'd come in overland, in the swamp, too. Doing it via the trees might not even be possible.

What the hell *were* those tentacle things, anyway? It was almost as if the water had come alive, yet the water was water—they'd tested *that* and a lot more.

With a sudden shock she realized that they weren't creatures at all, or at least not creatures in the standard sense of the word. Those bug-sized slimy slugs—they covered the swamp, living just under the surface. Somehow, she realized, they had to be the creatures— that something, maybe a chemical signal, was triggered in the water when the goodies from above hit. But *why* did they form new units? Not to eat fruit, surely. To grab things, maybe larger things—now *there* was a cheery thought!—or, perhaps, simply to move. Maybe they battled each other as colonies for the food, the swamp floor a constant battleground for what was needed to survive.

It didn't matter. Somebody might do something to this world and make it reasonable, but it would be damned expensive to do, and the ecosystem was odd enough anyway that the university types would probably put some kind of hold on it until they could determine the potential for this kind of life form. This one just wasn't going to pan out for them, and that meant deep, deep shit.

Of course, not as deep as the immediate problem, which was getting the hell out of here.

Idly she considered making some kind of armor or shield out of the trees. Clearly they couldn't eat the trees, and if the activation of a colony was chemical, they might not even be aware of her.

No, silly idea. No saws, no woodworking shop handy.

She looked around and saw, not far off, occasional flashes of varicolored energy lighting up the dark swamp like some kind of fancy light show. *There* was the real problem! If she could make it over there, shoot Hama's body, disintegrate it, damn it all, no matter how hard that was to do to a comrade and friend, she'd also get that radio. And with the radio gone, the interference would be gone. Her own radio and locator beacon would then work, and, of course, the I.P. was still sounding off as well.

She had no choice. While it was calm, before more fruit rained from above, she had to silence that noise.

She made her way cautiously toward the glow, which was intermittent but more than enough for the suit scanners to detect. Anything powerful enough to overload all radio frequencies and the beacons as well wasn't going to just vanish.

When she finally made it, it was an ugly sight. The tentacles had ripped the little Durfur almost to shreds, cracking both suit and body in a number of places, then seeping in. The half-eaten corpse was twisted and broken, crawling with those tiny things that could so easily combine to kill.

The sight sickened, enraged, and frightened her. Almost without thinking, she whipped out the pistol, set it to full charge, and began frying the scene. The slug-covered body shivered as the beam hit and enveloped it, and smoke from the burning of remaining hair and flesh as well as frying slugs rose up. She kept at it, steady as a rock, and much of Hama's remains did go up, but not enough, not enough. The suit material was still protecting the interior, including the equipment. Damn it! The pistol didn't have enough power at this range!

As the small warning of power drain began flashing and sounding, she suddenly sensed movement near her and whirled, her finger still on the trigger. At the exact moment the beam came to bear on the intruder, it cut off.

Tris Lankur climbed right next to her and touched helmets with her. The helmets were small, almost form-fitting, the visor shielding the eyes and allowing for mental control of the various screen displays. If all else failed, the helmet contact provided a very weak low-power communication.

"Good thing we bought the pistols with the safeties," he noted, his voice sounding distant and tinny but so very welcome. "Otherwise you'd have fried me, too."

Each suit's code was programmed into the logic of all other suits; that made it impossible to fire on one of your own team, even by accident. The only reason her suit had allowed her to fire at poor Hama's body was because the suit break and monitors showed that the team member was dead.

She practically fell into Tris's arms. "My God! I thought I was the only one left alive!"

"I was having my doubts, too," he admitted, sounding his usual calm and strong self. In all these years, she'd known him to be sarcastic, flip, calm, cool, and collected, but never did he seem frightened or out of his element. He was the bedrock of the company, and of her.

"I was trying to fry that damned power supply," she told him.

"It's under water," he responded. "I had the same idea, but the back of his suit's obviously intact and shielding the pack. How much power do you have left?"

She checked. "Not much. Ten per cent, no more. I've had to use a lot."

"Uh. Okay, I'm reading forty-four per cent, so give me your plug and I'll transfer some. Then we'll both hit him full strength at the same time until we're down to fifteen per cent or that racket stops. Combined, we might have enough power to do it."

She nodded and hooked up, watching her energy gage rise as his fell. When he declined to twenty-seven per cent, he cut it off.

"Okay," he told her, "Don't miss. Count down from five and then go. Remember to cut off at fifteen per cent. If we haven't burned through by then, it's not going to give."

She nodded, took a braced position, aimed, and started only a fraction of a second after he did. In a couple of seconds the two beams converged on the target and stayed on it. Lankur's presence calmed her, and she made this count. At the fifteen per cent mark they both cut off, then quickly checked the radio. It wasn't silent, but there was no longer any screech, just hissing and crackling, through which they could hear each other, although not much better than by the helmet touch method.

"Well, we got it, or most of it," he said with satisfaction. He shifted the scan. "Your locator's on okay, but I don't get the Durquist at all. Damn! Tran might not be able to pick out the beacon through the canopy." He sighed. "Well, he'd better. Nothing to do now but wait."

The exterior sound monitor suddenly filled with a crackling noise of its own, and her blood ran cold.

"Oh, my God! It's going to rain fruit again!"

For seven hours they had been trapped high in those giant trees, with declining power, in a world illuminated only by a failing electronic sensor system, intermittently attacked by tentacles rising from the ooze, the rest of the time in silence much more terrible, waiting for that telltale sound of crackling, falling food.

And through it all, Tris Lankur had told dirty jokes and made rude comments about the world and the situation and kept her alive.

Ultimately, though, they had to start shutting down suit systems to the bare minimum and deciding whether or not to waste precious energy taking out a tentacle if it arose. Pretty soon even the air recycling system would give out, and that would be the end of them.

Tris had even been philosophically fatalistic about that.

"I always thought I'd go this way," he told her. "Sorry to have you here as well, but if I have to go, this is better."

"Better?" She looked around at the stinking hellhole. "Better than what?"

"Better than dying in the poverty I was born into. Better than the mud and filth and real emptiness of dying of starvation. Better, or at least more honorable, than being shot by a copper in a getaway after stealing a couple loaves of bread. Better than bein' just another geek who never even had a chance at this."

The Exchange hadn't been terribly kind to humanity, just letting it go. Her home world was at least pastoral; few there had much in the way of riches or access to major technology, but nobody starved and you could carve out a decent if simple life. Tris's home world had been uglier, had gone horribly wrong without the means or contacts to straighten it out, and nobody had cared. She knew that, academically, but she'd never been on any of those kinds of worlds, never really wanted to see starving children with distended bellies and know that her world could produce enough to feed them but didn't have the cash to transport the food where it was needed.

Sitting there, perched in a tree, all systems failing, her old home, which had seemed so boring and so unromantic, now seemed almost like utopia. She had faced death many times since taking over the *Widowmaker* company, but never like this, never slow, never in such horror. In all that time they'd had many close calls, but this was the first time they'd ever lost a team member, the first time she'd had to look down upon the body of a friend and comrade and imagine herself there as well. Hama, at least, had gone quickly, not like *this*.

And for what had he died? For what were they now going to die?

At that moment, any sense of the romance of this job, the thrill and excitement of it, the very appeal of it, died within her. Even if by some miracle they got out of this one, and somehow found the money to keep going, she wasn't sure now that she could keep going—or even that she wanted to. This one was probably going to get them, but, if not, the next one would, or the next, or the next.

The team, and she along with them, had been crying most of the time about not making the big haul, having rotten luck time after time, but they'd been wrong. They'd been lucky indeed up to now, and now the due bill was at the door. One by one, or all at once, their luck would desert them, they would all wind up just like Hama, just like the vast majority of teams always did. They weren't different, and they had just about used up their dispensations.

The tentacles were just getting stirred up again, with neither she nor Tris having sufficient energy to shoot them anymore, when suddenly there was a vast, explosive sound above them, followed by a horrible whine, and then, all around them, the darkness fell away and a great shaft of sunlight filled the whole forest region. The light, touching the water and the tentacles, seemed to act like acid on the creatures, who dissolved and writhed and sped away from it.

And then the *Widowmaker*'s aging, banged-up shuttlecraft descended, going this way and that to avoid the bigger trees, until it hovered very near them.

"I've got them! They're alive, but just barely, from the looks of it," the Durquist's odd, grumbling, nonhuman voice came to them. The creature, looking somewhat star-shaped in its special suit, emerged from the hatch, jumped to the trees and clung as if born there, then slowly made its way to the two figures. Tris had enough strength left to help the Durquist get Modra in, then allowed himself to be helped inside.

"My apologies for taking so long, although I calculated how much energy reserves you might have had," the creature told them. "We figured that the only place you could be was around Hama's body, since it gave out a signal that'll drive instruments crazy for parsecs, but I couldn't come down and get you until after sunrise. The only way I could deal with those tentacles was to burn them with the sun; otherwise I might just as well have sent you falling into them."

The ride back to the capital was very strange, a mixture

of relief and sadness. Tris alone seemed in a relatively good mood, feeling that he'd cheated death yet another time and that this alone was a victory worth drinking to. Modra had been uncharacteristically silent, keeping mostly to herself, and rejecting alcohol or feelgood pills.

"No report until we get paid—cash," Tris told Trannon Kose, the *Ybrum* who ran the ship and was the theoretical safety backup for the team on the ground. "I don't want them paying off, reading the report, then stopping payment and going bankrupt before we have ours in our account."

"What we'll get will cover expenses and repairs and some dock fees," the spindly, trumpet-nosed Ybrum pilot responded, "but with this kind of report we'll get no more. They'll pay in specie, or they'll learn nothing— I've been stifled enough by this time to know how the game is played. A few intimations that we get ours now or the report gets left in somebody else's hopper does wonders. But unless we get another job, it won't be enough to do more than maintain us."

"How long?"

"A month. Two tops. Depends on what I can sneak out of their offices with."

Tris Lankur sighed. "Okay, we've been down this far before. With that much time I can find something to keep us going."

Modra stared at him grimly. "Another one like this? A First Team job? I don't think I can take another like this."

"Well, unless you have a magic wand for finding us another pot of gold like the one you brought when you signed on," Lankur responded, "we'll have to. Hey—you know the rules. The only reason the possible payoff's so good and the only reason it's a way out for races like ours is because it's damned dangerous. This one was worse than most, I agree, but we made it!"

"All but Hama," she retorted softly.

He sighed again. "Yeah, well, sooner or later everybody dies. When you grow up knee-deep in bodies, some of them your relatives', you celebrate the victories. You don't spend much time mourning your losses, or life wouldn't be worth living at all."

She smiled at him. "Five years ago talk like that sent a shiver of excitement through me. Now—I—I just don't know anymore. I *do* know I need a break. Some time off. Some time to get myself and my head together again."

"I got to admit, when you first joined up none of us thought you would cut it," Tris told her. "You know that. But now you're tough, Modra. Tough, experienced, and gutsy. It's in your blood now, and once it's there, it never lets go."

"Maybe. Maybe you're right. I don't know. I don't know anything anymore," she told him truthfully. *He* still slept soundly; she hadn't had a single period of more than fitful, nightmare-filled sleep. "I think I want to find out, though. When I get back, I'm going to cable my folks and have them advance me a ticket home. Just for a little while. Just to see if I go nuts back there, stir-crazy from boredom or whatever. Maybe to clear my head and find out just what I do want. I do know I need the trip, though. Even if you're right, I'm not going to be any good without it."

He shrugged. "Yeah, okay, if that's what you want— technically, you're still the boss. What if something comes up while you're gone, though?"

"Let me know. If I come back, then we'll both know."

"Fair enough. For me, the last thing I *ever* want to do is go home."

She *had* gone home, even though something inside her pulled at her to stay. At the time it seemed the only thing to do.

But, God! If she could roll back time now and stay back with the ship. . . .

Purgatory Is For Losers

Modra Stryke seemed radiant when she returned to the capital, and she looked fabulous as well. She was made-up, dressed in a fancy outfit that certainly wasn't cheap, and she'd had her flaming red hair redone by somebody who really knew what they were doing. Dressed, made-up, even bedecked with jewelry, she looked so fine that had she not been well-known around the grungier end of the spaceport, she most certainly would have been mugged.

Each of the small, independent teams had an office there; nothing more than a cubicle in a run-down warehouse, but it was an address nonetheless. She waltzed in jauntily, getting compliments from the humans who could recognize her and stares of disbelief from the other races who knew her but didn't understand human vanity at all.

The central "receptionist," was a *Quamahl* with six arms terminating in pincerlike yet soft claws and another at the end of a long, trunklike snout. It was a creature who could not appreciate human appearance at all, and acted as if there was nothing different about her. In point of fact, the Quamahl probably *couldn't* see any difference, considering its own standards were so different and also considering that it had never met a human it didn't find repulsive-looking.

"I see you are back," grumbled the Quamahl.

She smiled and nodded, used to the creature. "Anybody up there?"

74

"Just Lankur right now, probably sound asleep. The Durquist is working on the ship and Trannon Kose is in the city at the Exchange on some kind of business errand."

She nodded. "Tris will do just fine." she walked to the square lift that was the only way so many different shapes could be accommodated and said, "Four." The lift immediately hummed, and rose with her to the fourth-level catwalk.

She walked past various small offices she knew well, noting that most were dark, then got to hers, opened it and walked in.

Tris Lankur was not asleep; in fact, he was on the phone arguing with somebody, but when he looked up and saw her he said, "Look, something's come up. I'll get back to you." He hung up, then settled back and took all of her in. Lankur was one of the few in the complex who *could* appreciate her, and he gave a soft whistle.

"My, oh, my! A few weeks home does wonders," he commented.

She smiled. "I came right over. Besides, I wanted to keep looking like a woman for a little while longer."

"You certainly do that," he agreed, "although you don't look too bad without all that and in a skintight team suit, either. At least nobody would ever mistake you for me." He paused a moment, sensing there was something more on her mind that she was reluctant to broach. "You work out your problems?"

"I—I think so," she responded, her expression suddenly serious, thinking about how to say what she had to say. Finally she sighed and said, "Oh, the hell with it. Tris, I got married."

He was so surprised that he stiffened, and his brow furled, and he grew suddenly a bit cold. Then he chuckled. "Married? Baby, *nobody* gets *married* anymore. Not around here, anyway, and not in our kind of business."

"Yeah, well, I used to think that, too, Tris, and maybe for most people it's still true, but—well, it was like me taking over this company. An impulse, a gamble, but one that felt right for me."

He stared at her. "You're serious!"

She nodded.

That chill stiffness was suddenly back. "Who to? Nobody I know, I feel certain. Couldn't be anybody you knew, either, unless it was some old sweetheart from the home fires."

She sighed, cleared the junk off a stool, and sat down. "Look, this is kind of hard to explain. I'm not even sure I can explain it. It just—*happened*—that's all. After that last job I was just a wreck. Call me a coward or just call it the one that put me over, but that was the case. I had nightmares, I was paranoid, I kept expecting tentacles to rise from anything liquid, even my soup. I needed company, somebody to lean on right then, and I met this guy who was very nice and very understanding and very interesting. I kept it up with him because we both came from villages in the same county back home, and, at first, it was just because he was nice, and then it was also because I discovered he had money, and finally because I enjoyed his company. I think I was somebody exotic to him, too; a First Team owner who was from the same place he was but who had been through the kind of experiences he'd only dreamed about. I think maybe that was part of it—I lost my feel for the romance of this job, but he still had it."

"So you have a nice time, you have a few laughs, maybe even a roll in the hay, and you have a new friend and contact," Lankur responded. "You didn't have to *marry* this guy!"

"I know, I—look, this is hard for me, okay? It just seemed so *right*, somehow, and the longer it went on, the more right it seemed, at least for me. He was, just, well, very kind and very gentle and treated me like I hadn't been treated since before I left home, only with respect, too. Hell, *I* had to seduce him, he was so nice. When I was with him I didn't have the bad dreams, didn't feel so insecure, got some of my empty spots filled up again. And I gave him something, too; like his overlooking all my faults and thinking of me as if I were his romantic fantasy. I'm an empath, remember. I could feel it, and feel his genuineness."

She could feel now, too, and it disturbed her. Around and in Tris Lankur there seemed to be a cold, utterly dark emptiness, a mixture of barely controlled rage mixed with tremendous—*sorrow*. It wasn't what she expected at all. Surprise, yes, but his emotional reaction was more akin to a husband who thought he had the perfect marriage learning that his wife had run off with another man.

"Damn it, Tris! Stop it! We weren't married! We were—are—partners!"

He stared at her with a cold hurt inside him that was physically painful for her to bear. "You could'a married me if you had to be married. Somehow I just never saw you as the type. Hell, we spent five years together and never even screwed for fun."

She felt acutely uncomfortable, her earlier mood completely destroyed by her empathic awareness of his pain. "You said it yourself—people out here, outside home and culture, don't get married. Least of all you. I know I turned you on more than once, and you turned me on, too, but if we'd had sex, it would have changed things and you know it. I would have been demoted to on-board whore and there would have been no sense of equality at all. You're too much in love with this lifestyle to love somebody personally. Sex you got back here, probably better than I could do it."

"And you didn't?"

"I—I wasn't any virgin when I came here, I'll admit that, but I decided when I wanted to get into this business that it would be everything to me, that until lightning struck I wouldn't have any sex life, and I didn't. Not until I was on the way home. It happens when you're an empath. There's no mistaking lust for love. The way you're feeling right now is like I betrayed you or something. We're not lovers, Tris! We never were! Just like you, I was in love with the job, the life, the thrills and challenges, not with anybody personal. Oh, I *do* love you, in the same way I love Tran and even the Durquist and poor Hama, too, but it's not the same kind of love."

Nothing inside him died down or quieted, although he remained on the surface a model of control as always. "So now what? You quit or sell out and go hobnob with the business types and be a good little wife and make tons of babies?"

"No, no! Not exactly, anyway. Yolan—my husband— is a partner in a company with a seat on several exchanges. He's about to switch from commodities over to the full Exchange, the big one. He won't be making the real decisions, of course—I don't think any human has that much status yet—but he can influence the implementation of the investments. In effect, we've become, through my marriage and the agreements we signed, a subsidiary of his company. Automatic business—as much as we want, with a good bankroll to boot. We keep going, just like before. The only difference he insisted on, and the way the last one went he didn't have to insist very much, was that I not be a member of the ground team. Tran's wanted to get off backup for years, ever since I knocked him out of his slot by coming aboard. I know the ship and I've had the experience on the ground now to do backup. That way I'll be the intermediary between the company and the team. To you and the others, it won't seem any different, except that Tran will be going down instead of me. It's perfect, don't you see?"

His hurt was rapidly being superseded by rage, and he finally couldn't keep it in any longer. "Business as usual, huh? Nothing changes, except that we become some damned salaried employees and lose our independence and I have to work with you close as ever knowing—" He paused. "Why did you come back? Why not at least have enough feeling for me to sell out and vanish? I could handle that, sooner or later, but *this*—!"

"Damn it, I was always out of reach before!"

"Of *everybody!* And not out-front unattainable! Damn it, this changes everything! And, sooner or later, Mister Broker's gonna want kids 'cause it's the final fulfillment and you'll be sitting there bloated and pregnant with *another guy's kid* and—fuck it! Fuck you!"

She felt so awful at his reaction that she groped for what to say. "I—I had no idea this would be your reaction! I—I don't know what to do now."

"Undo it! Get a divorce or annulment or whatever it takes. Cancel the deal. Go back to square one again!"

"That's not fair! I've finally found somebody who loves me for me and I finally have a few things right! I'm not going to throw it all away!"

"Not *fair*? *Not fair*? You bet your iron heart it's not fair!" He suddenly got up and swept all the papers, phone, intercom, and most of the contents of the desk onto the floor, then stalked out and slammed the door so hard that had the window been glass, it would have shattered.

She hadn't cried in years, but she had to cry now, and she still wasn't absolutely sure why she felt so guilty, but she stared at that door for a very long time.

She was still there when the Durquist came in.

To everyone, a Durquist was called simply a Durquist. Although they were as individual as most other races, they all seemed to have the same personality to others, and they all looked and sounded pretty much alike except to other Durquists. The Durquist culture somehow got along without names; they tried to explain it to others, but such comments as "Why do we need names when we know who we are and we aren't anyone else?" quickly spun non-Durquist heads and the subject got changed.

Strictly speaking, a Durquist was shaped like a five-pointed star around a central orifice that looked very much like a huge set of jet-black human lips, behind which, mostly invisible to the onlooker, were row after row of sharp, pointed teeth. Brain, stomach, and all the internal organs were somehow clustered inside that hard center. From it emerged the arms—fluid, sucker-clad, able to stretch and twist and bend in almost infinite ways, yet with incredibly powerful muscles. The Durquist's eyes were a stalked pair, one on each side of the mouth; it allowed the creature to assume almost any posture from walking upright on any two arms of its choice and looking weirdly humanoid from a distance or on any combination of four.

The Durquist came in bipedally, the only practical way to get in the door, and the two eyes fixed on Modra. "They said that you came in, and shortly after, Tris left as if he were on his way to blow up the Exchange and anything and anyone else who got in his way," the creature said. "You want to tell me about it?"

She nodded, and proceeded to recount the whole tale, sparing nothing. The Durquist settled back and listened intently, interrupting only a couple of times to clarify a vague point.

When she finished, the creature was silent for a moment, then said, "I do not fully understand your people, you know, for all that we live so closely together, but there are constants among the bulk of races, particularly when more than one sex is involved, and I am curious and observant by nature. It may be that I am totally wrong in the way I interpret these things, but I find it personally astonishing that you would think that he would react any differently than he did."

"I thought he'd be surprised, maybe have a little bruised ego, but nothing like what I got," she responded.

"I would have thought an empath in particular would never be taken that way. I know that an empath supposedly can tell lust from love, but it is possible that being too familiar for too long would blur the interpretation. What you could instantly divine in others you could not in him, because it was slow, steady, day-to-day, and, in essence, you tuned it out."

"He—has great control, too, until today," she told him. "An ability to damp down what rises, to lessen what was there. They say that telepaths can read the surface thoughts but often miss what is way down deep. I think maybe it's that way with me."

"You felt his growing respect and concurrently growing affection, and it was what you wanted to feel from him, so you dug no deeper. The cause of most misery in any history isn't the lack of data, but the misinterpreting and distortion of the data. You have brothers, I believe?"

She nodded. "Yes, two."

"You mistook him for another brother, then. It is—comprehensible, at any rate. The respect you earned caused him to love you, but you, an empath, could not tell one from the other. Being neither empathic nor telepathic himself, he was free to fantasize. Were he an empath, he would save done the opposite of you and mistaken the respect and affection for love. There is a great tragic saga in all this. In fact, I think I saw it on one of the entertainment channels the other day."

"Don't go your usual cynical ways on me right now," she implored him, sincerely trying to figure it out. "I need advice."

"Why? He loves you. You do not love him. It seems a perfect tragic impasse."

"But I do love him—just not in the same way."

"No. You do not love him. you love what he represents—what we all represent. More of that bad entertainment,

You came here with all you had because you were in love with an idea. You found us in a time of need and you fell in love with the team and the lifestyle. What you love in Tris is his near perfect personality for the kind of cast you sought. Adventurous, brave, daring, highly competent, but a rogue. Not quite the sterling, perfect hero of fiction, but with enough of those qualities that you could ignore or tune out the flaws. You laid upon him your romantic vision, and even your empathic ability could not be allowed to soil he image. Yet you are intelligent enough to know that fiction ends before the romance goes bad; that there is no happily ever after with that kind of person. If there was, he would cease to be the person he was and become, in a word, dull. You want Tris to be what your romances imagine him to be. To have settled on him would have been to destroy the very qualities in him that you loved. That is not difficult to understand. Naive; juvenile, perhaps, but understandable even to someone like me."

"You're making me sound like some kind of idiot."

"The ignorance of the immature is common, regardless of age or experience. Tris in his own way is living out a romantic fantasy and is as guilty, if not more so, as you. But it is you who made the choice, not him, because he *is* a permanent adolescent. You needed more. You finally looked death in the face and you didn't like it. You found that you needed solidity, permanence, some kind of security, some guarantee of a contented future no matter how this went, and you needed it just as much, but no more, as you needed the team life and somebody like Tris. In your naiveté, and emotional upset at the admittedly horrible experience you survived, you saw a way to have both. The solidity and fallback that your broker offered, and the adventure and challenge of the team. Even now, you have been sitting here because you do not want to accept the reality that you cannot have both. you must choose—Tris and the rest of us, or the solid and loving if comparatively dull life of a broker's mate, possibly getting a job in his firm."

She felt suddenly angry, as if an orderly and perfect world had just been burned to ashes before her eyes. "And why should I have to choose? I'm the true owner of this company. I hold the majority. If he's not happy with it, he can leave. So can you and Tran. I'll find others, if I have to."

"It is not that simple. I'm getting on in years, and there are younger ones in the Guild Halls right now looking for any position I might fill. I have greater experience than they, but that only makes me more expensive to a prospective hire. The same with Tran. We might eventually find other work, but when you go through this so many times you become insecure. Nobody in this buyer's market is secure unless they are already working, and nobody voluntarily gives up a berth for that same reason. For Tris it is even worse. This is all he has. He's spent his whole life crawling up from the most abysmal beginnings on a world of perpetual poverty and woefully short lives to where he is captain of a team. Not much of a team, and not much of a ship or bank account, but compared to where he started, it is higher than he ever dreamed of getting. To ask him to walk out, to give it all up, when whatever we are he built, is to ask him to commit suicide. He *can't* leave. Even less than the rest of us, he has nowhere else to go. There are only two things that matter to him in this whole universe, and they are this company and you. You have removed yourself from even his fantasies and he could not stand to work with you as usual, when every contact with you will reinforce the hurt. In one moment you removed everything he had, even his dreams."

She sighed. "Shit! I feel like a rotten bastard, but I don't see a way out. Back home, when we went to get married, they of course sent us to some psychs—hypnos,

as usual. The psychs approved the marriage, said it was
the best thing for both of us, but with conditions. They
said I needed this team life, too, but to continue with
it, being away from each other for many weeks at a
time, me with Tris, and him back here maybe wondering
if he did the right thing, the only way they'd sign off is
if we both submitted to a hypno bonding. No matter
what feelings I have on other levels for Tris, I feel no
physical attraction to him at all—or any other man but
one, and that one only wants, desires, or can get it up
for one woman—me. No doubts, no questions, no
insecurities, you see?"

"You can do the same thing to your mind with drugs
and chemicals and not have to bother with all the
paperwork," the Durquist grumbled. "Still, we have what
is classically known as a 'situation' here. I just hope
Tris isn't off to do something rash and stupid. Is your
husband here in the city and well protected?"

Her head snapped up and she stared at the star
creature. "You mean—! Oh, my God! He _might_, too!
But, no, wait a minute. The marriage isn't registered
here yet, so he can't look it up, and I never gave him
Yolan's last name or even a company name, let alone
an address. But I think I should call Yolan, anyway."

"Indeed. Tris, as you well know, can be quite—
resourceful."

She suddenly snapped into action. "Get hold of Tran—
I don't care where he is or what he's doing. I'll call
Yolan and fill him in. Might be an idea to call the
Prefecture and have them on the lookout as well. If
Tris has really gone round the bend, they can help,
and if not, he's bound to wind up in one of their holding
cells sleeping it off."

But when a man like Tris was hurting like he was
and yet was as resourceful as he was, in a city like the
capital, if he wanted to stay invisible he very well could
do so. A day passed, then two, then three. Even Trannon

Kose's underworld contacts couldn't turn up much—or wouldn't. Humans were such a tiny and insignificant group here on the capital world that those who were not a part of the system tended to be very clannish; it would take a human who knew the underworld to find a man who didn't want to be found.

At the end of the fourth day following Tris's disappearance, she began to think, even hope, that the Durquist had been wrong. After five years she hated to part with Tris in this way and with this much hurt, but if he couldn't bear working with her under the new conditions, well, then good luck and Godspeed to him.

But in the middle of the night, in the high-rise comfort of the big apartment she now shared with her husband, the phone awakened her and the robotic switchboard put it through because it was from one of the few who had the right to preempt.

It was Trannon Kose.

"I think you better get down here," the pilot told her. 'District Four, Hospital Nine, Intraspecies Intensive Care."

She was suddenly awake. "Why? What's the matter?"

"I found Tris. Or, rather, the coppers found him. I—I think you better get down here as soon as you can. I've called the Durquist and he's on the way."

"Why? What's the matter?"

"I just think you ought to come down here, Modra. Now. There are decisions to be made." And, with that, he cut the connection.

Yolan offered to take her, but she told him to get back to sleep. He had a long day ahead and this was her business right now, not his.

Running a hospital capable of handling emergencies for such a wide variety of species wasn't easy; most hospitals were in districts mainly populated by only two or three races and set up for them. Transport was swift in any event, and, even for humans, there was at least someplace within minutes of an emergency that could handle a human. Expert care was not as much of a problem, but for quite different reasons.

Trannon Kose was a *Ybrum*, a creature that looked like a set of oval pods connected by spindly, furry, giant pipe cleaners. He looked fragile, but moved with a swiftness and grace that belied his appearance, and the Ybrum were a pretty tough bunch when they had to be.

Modra barged in, spotted Tran and the Durquist, and went right to them. "All right, now what's all this about?"

"Apparently I was quite correct in my basic analysis," the Durquist responded. "Tris was suddenly placed in an untenable position, losing what he most cared for and yet unable to leave as his sanity demanded. We feared that this would take the form of violence, and it did, but not in the way we originally thought."

"He apparently headed straight for the District and went under," Kose put in. "He popped so many feelgoods and so much else that they had to send his blood up for chemical analysis just to find out how much was natural. He stayed like that for the past three and a half days, in a hole provided by an underworld friend for whom we've done some favors now and again. Apparently he overdosed, awoke, and felt the massive depression that coming down from such a chemical high produces, which added to his existing depression. He shot himself in the head, apparently with some sort of archaic projectile weapon he either owned or got from somebody down there."

She took a sharp breath and stiffened as the shock hit her. "He's dead, then?"

"That is the usual condition one finds oneself in after blowing one's brains out," the Durquist responded pragmatically. "The question now is whether or not to let him stay that way."

That shocked her almost as much as the initial news. "Huh? But you just said—"

"That he is dead," the Durquist completed. "In most cases that would be it, but we're in the capital. The technology available here is quite a bit more advanced than they allow us mere citizens, since all the surgeons are cymols capable of plugging themselves in and reading into their own brains, or whatever is inside those heads, the exact medical data and skills they need for any race It appears that we and Tris have blundered into a moral, legal, and ethical conundrum of the Guardians themselves. Ah—here's the physician in charge now. We wanted you here for this, since in a way it's up to us."

The surgeon turned out to be a human, or at least a human in appearance, and a rather young and delicate-looking woman at that, with dark features and very short hair, dressed in a surgical gown. she was walking a bit oddly, and there was something unnerving in her manner as she approached.

To Modra, there was an additional unnerving aspect as well. She was an empath, and while she could damp it down, it was never completely suppressed, and, being tired, she was even less able to do so. Almost everyone in this reception center radiated *something*—fear, concern, joy, sorrow—all those things common to almost all sentient life forms. All but the surgeon and a few of the others in medical garb. She almost had to force herself to ignore that sense she had that most did not, and remember that the doctor was really there. There were no emotions, no feelings, emanating from the doctor at all, any more than from the walls or desks or chairs.

"I apologize if I seem out of sorts," the surgeon told them, "but at the moment I have just finished five procedures on five different life forms and I have the data, from anatomy and physiology down to the molecular level, as well as the psychological data on all of them, inside me. It often creates problems, as all are equal in my mind at the moment and the human one is, shall we say, outnumbered."

"That's all right," Modra responded, able to comprehend the problem if not the kind of brain that could hold that much data. "Now, what's this all about?"

"Your associate committed suicide, but we were able to have a crew there within a few minutes, get him tanked, and perform a data readout before full electrochemical activity ceased in the undamaged areas. The damage was quite extensive but mostly to the forebrain area; the way the human mind stores data is quite complex but is not generally in those areas, which are used primarily for synthesis. We lost much of the newest information but got most of the rest into storage. It's routine in these cases, and helps us understand the various races better and also why and how these things happen."

"Let me get this straight," Modra said, feelingly bit odd, as if this weren't really happening, but some sort of dream. "He's dead, but you have his memories in some kind of storage bank, like computer data?"

"Something like that, yes. It is not terribly common that we can get this much—the damage is usually to areas further back as well and we usually get to the victim too late—but it's not unheard of. We get a few dozen cases a year, mostly from accidents of course, so there are procedures to be followed. Your company insurance was paid up only three days ago after long arrears, but it was paid up before this occurred and there is a determination that the two actions, the premium payment and the suicide, are not related. That is, the patient didn't know about the insurance, and you three did not suspect the patient would kill himself. As an employee, he is therefore fully covered for any procedures we might do."

"Somehow the fact that we're insured is not very important to me right now," Modra said dryly.

"No, it simply calls for a decision on your part, since the patient has no declared next of kin and is, therefore, subject to your company's decisions."

"You mean," Modra asked, mild hope growing within her, "that you can actually restore him to life?"

"In a manner of speaking only. If it were simply a matter of being able to restore him, we would do so, curing at the same time the root cause of his psychosis, of course. The insurance would mandate it, since the death benefit is huge. What *is* possible in these cases is to perform the cymol conversion, then read back in his memories and simulate as much as possible of his old self, just as all of the information for five races is now inside me."

The implications of this were staggering. "You mean— remove his brain, essentially, and replace it with an artificial brain, a computer of some kind capable of running the body and then feed it data to convince it that it was still him?"

The doctor reached up to her own hair and tugged at it gently, removing the natural-looking wig as if it were a hat She was totally bald beneath, without a sign of hair—or surgery—but on one side of the skull was a large rectangular metal plate that seemed to have hundreds upon hundreds of tiny silver dots on it. "It is not quite as bad as all that," she said.

Modra sank slowly into a chair that wasn't really built for the human form. She just had to sit down, though. It was strange—somehow she felt curiously unreal, disconnected, as if this weren't really happening. Still, she was there, and clearly the other two were deferring in some measure to her as owner of the company.

She tried to think about this, but really couldn't. Finally she said, "So it would look like Tris and have Tris's memories but it wouldn't really *be* Tris."

"Yes and no," the doctor responded, replacing her hair and looking more human again. "At the root level, he would be cymol, not human. His personality would be synthesized from his own recorded self-images and from any that you all provide, but it would be synthesized, a layer atop the cymol. He would not be the same, but he would seem—close. The psychochemistry would no longer be there for many things. Emotions would be synthesized, rather than real, and would never be out of control. Certain drives that are brain-driven would no longer exist. Things like sexual urges, rages, even endorphin highs, would be impossible, of course. My body, for example, requires rest but my brain requires no sleep."

"I don't want some inhuman android going around animating his corpse!" she snapped, then realized how that sounded. "It's different with you and the others. I mean, I don't know you. I didn't know you before you became a cymol, and I have no personal attachments or biases."

"I believe," the Durquist interjected, "that the real questions here go beyond that. I find the decision distasteful, but I am forced to be totally pragmatic here. If we say yes, we get back an approximation of Tris Lankur. If we say no, he dies completely."

"Essentially. I must add, at the risk of sounding insensitive, that you would in that case forfeit the death benefit from the insurance, since the cymol route was available and was offered."

"I don't care about the damned money!" Modra snapped. "Damn it, I was the one who caused this! I was the one who killed him! Isn't that bad enough? Isn't that enough for me to have to live with? Do I have to work with a living, breathing reminder of what I've done?"

"Fascinating," the Durquist commented, mostly to himself. "This is a most intriguing wrinkle. One that Tris, wherever his spirit is now, if such a thing exists for humans, must find cynically amusing. By his action, he has precisely reversed your positions, handing you the very situation that you presented to him. Instead of his being forced to live and work on the ship around you, with a constant reminder of what he can never have, it is you who would be in that situation."

"I—I don't think I could do it any more than *he* could!" she told him.

"Then you could quit the team as you suggested he do. Unlike him, you have an alternative livelihood. We already have to hire a replacement for poor Hama; finding an experienced empath would not be much more of a chore. You can leave, or you could work with him."

"I could let him die!"

"A singularly selfish act, although I fear one in character at least as far as the new Modra is concerned. Having a cymol on the team would transform us from a second-rate and never-was broken down company into one that would be almost, if not absolutely, unique. The access to the master data banks alone would be invaluable. The competitive advantage alone would be *enormous*. The potential staggers even me. Not to mention having someone who could carry with them the skills and data for everything from highly technical analysis to patching up a Durquist or a Ybrum. And, although imperfectly, it would go a ways to undoing what you originally caused. For competitive, commercial, economic reasons you *must* approve it. And for selfish reasons, too. A team is no better than its members. If you alone remain, with that dilapidated ship and trash-filled office, your husband's company will hardly send business your way. They'll write you off. A team is called a team because it always works together, knows each other. That is how I was able to find you back on that slime world. How you and Tris could find each other and work together so seamlessly. No husband worth anything would let you go out with a totally new, green crew. No Exchange member corporation would tolerate it."

"And," Trannon Kose put in, "you owe it to him."

She looked up at them in anguish, looking for friends and finding only torturers. "You two really would want *that*?"

Of course not," Tran responded simply. "We want Tris back. But, if we can't have him, then we want the next best thing."

"And there is the pragmatic side," the Durquist added. "We do not do this sort of work because it is a fun game. If I could sacrifice the advantage presented here and have the old Tris back, I would do so, because the integrity of the team comes before all else, and because he was my friend and comrade. We cannot have the old Tris back. He is gone, and I am still here. Hama is gone, but I am still here, too. Unlike poor Hama, however, Tris left us a legacy which can profit those of us still here. I am not inclined to refuse it because *you* might feel just *awful* to get it. I will supplement Tran's sage comment. You owe it to *us*. Or would you rather slink back to your kind husband and fancy apartment, with two more so-called friends and long associates to add to your list of victims?"

She didn't have any reply to that, and just sat there for several minutes, not really able to think. Finally she looked at the surgeon and asked, "Just how much of what we'd get would be Tris? And how much would be illusion?"

The surgeon hardly blinked at that one. "To be truthful, a fair amount of him will survive. The nature and area of the wound, and its precision, well, it almost seems as if going cymol was what he had in mind all along, as incredible as that may seem."

"Not very incredible," commented the Durquist. "It would be just the sort of revenge he'd come up with, and just the type of gamble."

Modra gave the Durquist a killing look, but realized it was true "Honestly, though—how much of the real him would—come back?"

"Memory, habit patterns, that sort of thing. Much of what made him a unique individual. What is damaged beyond repair, and would be replaced in any event, is the control center, as it were. The central processor. But there are no guarantees. There is shock, trauma, and bleeding that needed to be tended to and that took a bit of fine surgery just to get him to this point. As to illusion—as long as no fraud is involved, why worry? I am not saying that he will be the same. He won't. But he'll be close, for all intents and purposes."

"Look, I've had four hours sleep, and right now I'm just wrenched and drained out. Can't I have a little time to think this over? Sort it out in my own mind?" Modra pleaded.

"Maintaining a body under these conditions, as well as the storage, is quite difficult and quite expensive," the surgeon noted. "The insurance company wants an immediate decision for its own cost containments, and, of course, every hour we wait decreases the chance of a successful operation. I'm afraid that no decision is a decision."

"I don't know why you hesitate," the Durquist noted acidly. "What you are being offered is exactly what you wanted, isn't it?"

"*No!*" she snapped, but her anger wasn't really directed at the Durquist. She felt upset, confused, as if everything she'd taken for granted just shattered. This wasn't *fair*, damn it! *She* didn't put a stupid gun to her head, or his. She'd always had a full measure of confidence in her dealings with others because her empathic talent gave her an edge. Now it, too, had betrayed her.

But wasn't the Durquist right? Hadn't she been so self-centered, so blind to anybody's interests or feelings but her own, that, in fact, she had caused all this? From her own viewpoint, from a practical and day-to-day point of view, wasn't this *exactly* what she had wanted?

No! Damn it! She had loved him. Really loved him.

There was never any real doubt in her mind about that. She just didn't want to ruin him, and what she needed would have ruined him for sure.

Well, he couldn't be more ruined than this, could he?

She should have just quit, should have just walked away and given Tris his damned company back and to hell with it. Clean break. She knew that now, understood it, but it was hindsight. It had seemed so *simple*, so *perfect*, only a few days and an eternity ago. Complicated things always seem simple to children, and in this she'd been acting like a child all along.

But, as Tris had said, once it gets in your blood you can't just walk away. It wasn't that easy, particularly when she did love him, too, in a far different way than she loved Yolan. And, suddenly, she could see the Durquist's angry point, and the quiet Tran's as well.

She could have walked away at the start, and none of this would have happened. But to walk away now would add callousness to her insensitivity. It would leave all these terrible events with no meaning at all.

But did this decision involve Tris at all, really? Tris was dead. Gone. It was done, and she couldn't undo that, as much as she wanted to, craved to, undo it. She would replay this over and over for the rest of her life, living with regrets and might-have-beens.

More important right now were Tran and the Durquist. It was more than just self-interest on their part; she understood the unspoken code they were insisting upon. Hama's death had been nobody's fault; although they'd been lucky up to then, that kind of risk came with the job. But the team was a team or it was nothing. To them, Tris's tragedy was the direct result of her actions, and that meant it was due to one member of the team letting down another. This decision boiled down to more than just her feelings and Tris's continued existence in some way. What they were really saying was that her own feelings and interests were against the feelings and interests of the team. If she refused what they wanted, she would be in effect dissolving the team. If she said no, there wasn't a being on a hundred worlds who would trust her to make coffee, let alone make decisions that might mean their lives. If she said no, she would not be a team player; her name would be passed around and her story told so that no spacer would ever even speak to her again. To make a mistake, even one like this, was understandable; to violate the team code was the unforgivable sin.

She hadn't worked five years for that.

She had made a mistake and it had cost. Now they wanted to know how much it had cost, and whether it really *was* just a mistake.

Most spacers never struck it rich; most spacers lived the same kind of hand-to-mouth existence they had, kludging and coveting their rickety ships and equipment to keep going, doing whatever they had to do, always according to their own code and their own ways. she had not deliberately caused this thing; they would accept that. But if she said no, against the team now, she would lose the only things a spacer really had: pride, honor, and a sense of belonging, things that were earned the hard way, and the last things tossed out. No matter what, her thoughts and memories would force her to live with what she'd done. But to quit now, walk out on the team, would be to walk out on the only important thing she'd ever done or earned on her own.

But *damn* Tris for not sticking that gun barrel in his mouth and making so much of a mess of it that this wouldn't have been an option!

"I cannot go against the interests of the team," she told them softly, in a voice without much expression at all. "You have my vote to proceed, Doctor. How long before we would get him back?"

"A matter of a few weeks. It's not as easy as all that.

Only when we begin the process will we have an idea of the length and problems."

"Do what you must, and the best you can for him. Tran, Durquist—we'll need another telepath. That's not going to be easy. Most telepaths are so unnerved by just being in the same room as a cymol that they'll starve first."

The two others visibly relaxed when she had given the go-ahead. Suddenly it was business as usual.

"Not to mention the practical problem that we lost a team member last time out and then had *this* happen on top of it," the Durquist noted. "For a while we will have—what is it you humans call it?—a Jonah reputation. Yes, that's it. This will not be easy. We may have to take what we can get."

"Do what you have to—only, if possible, we want somebody with experience. Somebody who's used to working with an established team. We have a few weeks, and I can cover the bills until then. There's no rush."

"I know. But the only ones that have that kind of experience and would work for us under these conditions are probably Jonahs themselves. It will be difficult." The Durquist paused, its big black lips almost clenched for a moment. Then it said, "Modra—go home and take a pill and get some sleep."

She nodded wearily. "I plan to do just that," she said, and got up to leave. The doctor had already left, since there was no point in remaining at this stage. Drained, Modra Stryke headed for the door.

"Modra," the Durquist called softly.

She stopped, turned, and faced the star creature. "Yes?"

"Welcome back, Modra."

She didn't smile back. Instead, she said, quietly, "We all make our own beds, I guess, and wind up doing what we have to do."

Choosing Corpses

Jimmy McCray was also wondering how the hell he'd gotten into this kind of situation, but his problem stemmed from an act of kindness and compassion. He'd never really believed that there were such things as Jonahs, simply passing off "bad luck" spacers as incompetents, but that was before he had become one himself.

Not only was he unemployed and without prospects, he'd saddled himself with a ward who could offer no service he could use and who was also without citizenship, status, or connections and was totally dependent upon him. The worst thing, however, was that Grysta hadn't shut up about it since it happened.

"Nag, nag, nag. Don't take it out on me," he grumbled to the *Morgh,* who was something of another useless dependent herself. "What was I to do? Walk away and let some innocent be slaughtered?"

<*I have to take it out on you. There's no one else I can take it out on.*>

Well, that was a fact, at least. Still, "At least *you* have somebody to take it out on. I have nobody, but I've all the responsibility, both for a hairy worm on my back and for a half-girl, half-goat, neither of whom can do anything useful or productive."

<*Who are you calling a worm?*>

"If you don't like the situation," he told her, "you can always find yourself another host."

97

<*And get killed by the coppers as soon as they found out. No thanks.*>

"Then shut up and let me think."

The Syn girl had come along meekly with him when they'd left the alley, almost like a small child, and it didn't take him long to realize that for all the sleaze of her past life, a child was pretty much what she was. Worldly only in her own element, she was apparently ignorant of all else. She seemed slow, even a bit stupid, but it wasn't clear yet whether that was part of her programming or simply the result of the course she'd been forced to take.

Her mind was an open book to him, but it gave him no answers. She didn't seem to really *think*, at least not in the way he defined that activity. There was no brooding, no real curiosity, no thinking about the future. He got the impression that she didn't so much act as react, and what little she did think she said aloud. It was as if she had no ego at all; that she existed only in reaction to others. Looking out the train window she had no real thoughts of her own as such; only occasional concepts like "pretty" or "dark" or other impressions, instantly made, instantly forgotten. In a way, she was more alien and unsettling to him than most of the bizarre life forms that made up the Exchange.

She didn't even really have a name, just one of those long numbers she'd memorized that meant nothing to anyone except maybe to her makers and the road company that had owned her. Some of those who got to be star dancers and the like got names, or nicknames, but she was strictly minor league. If the customer wanted a name, she asked him for his favorite one and took it for the evening. Jimmy changed that on the way home the first night.

"Anybody from now on asks you your name, you tell them it's Molly. If they want a full one tell them you're Molly McCray." He'd always liked the name. He'd had the hots for a Molly once, back when he was in school, and it was also the name of one of his grandmothers.

"Okay, master," she'd responded docilely. "For you I be Molly McCray."

"No, for *everyone*. From now on. Understand? And never, *ever*, call me 'master' again. You will call me Jimmy. Everyone calls me Jimmy."

She nodded, although he wasn't sure how much sank into that pretty head. "Okay, Jimmy. I do whatever you say."

It was almost with a shock that he'd realized she meant that literally. Slavery was illegal except on some of the very primitive worlds, and it was morally repugnant to him, but she wasn't a real person with real status or rights; she had the same position in the empire of the Exchange as a robot or computer, even though she was a living, breathing person.

"Do you know how to do anything except dance and lie with men?" he asked her.

She looked at him blankly, as if the question itself was absurd. Worse, the picture patterns that came into her mind in reaction to the question were all of things very much related to just that.

She reached up to scratch her cheek and for the first time he noticed her fingers. Four long-nailed fingers on each hand, but no thumbs. None.

"Do all the Syns lack thumbs?" he asked her, genuinely curious. In all these years he'd never really noticed.

"All the ones I know," she responded matter-of-factly. "I think it a rule or something."

A deliberate design flaw, he thought sourly. To keep them from ever being anything but what they were, and to make sure they were only useful for what they were intended. It sure put limits on what you could do, anyway. Even opening containers, twisting knobs, that sort of thing, would be extremely difficult. Hell, you used thumbs in almost *everything*. There wasn't an intelligent species without opposable thumbs or pincers or prehensile tentacles or the equivalent.

In the days ahead he learned more about her and her kind, and he also learned how very dependent she was. She couldn't brush her own hair, and the knobs on the shower were beyond her. She could manage something like a sandwich, awkwardly, but she dropped a fair number of other things. The fingers she did have didn't seem to have much muscular independence; they closed pretty much as a unit and opened the same way, and the individual movement of each wasn't that great.

About the only positive surprise was that she seemed to be able to metabolize just about anything organic— a cost-saving measure, most likely—and her natural body odor, which he'd feared might be goatlike, seemed sweet and even slightly perfumed.

And, when she was told to figure out a way to do something, such as operate the shower or tidy up, she put herself single-mindedly to the task. She wasn't always successful, but she always tried to do exactly what she was told.

The biggest surprise to him, though, was that she was a broadcast empath.

She was just sitting in the room, staring at him, and suddenly he began to get very, very turned on. Had it not been for Grysta, he would have thought it simply the normal reaction to the situation, but the Morgh seemed to sense something and jolted him just a bit. Then he saw in Molly's mind a single concentration on him, and was able to break it.

"Are you doing that?" he asked her. "Trying to turn me on?"

"Isn't that what you want?" she responded a bit seductively. "Why else do Jimmy want me?"

"To save your life, remember?"

The comment should have triggered a series of thoughts in her, but it didn't; instead, it triggered only vague confusion and a quick thought-burst that took him a moment to make sense of. When he did, he was shocked to realize that she had no real understanding of his actions, because she placed no value on herself beyond her function in life and saw that function as her sole value. She saw no reward in having her life saved, because she placed no value on it; it was somebody else's to save or take. The Boss Master had been hurting her; she had cried out, mostly mentally, against it and McCray had shown up. McCray had fought the Boss Master and won her as the prize.

Until this moment, he hadn't realized just how alien she was.

First things first. He wanted no more surprises.

"Can you read feelings, or just *cause* them in people?" he asked her gently.

"Mostly just make men want me, make things real nice, so it always go just right."

He nodded. He knew of few broadcast empaths who could also receive clearly, just as there were only a few receivers who could do any kind of broadcasting on even a very low level, but you never knew when somebody was designed rather than born. It was likely she could broadcast almost any emotion, and over a fairly broad range and with some power, too, although she probably was unaware of it, being untrained and untested. It explained the effect the beating had on him, too. He'd heard the screams and protests both aurally and telepathically, but reinforcing it was the empathic broadcast. He had literally felt an echo of her fear and misery, and that had made it nearly impossible for him not to do what he did, although, even now, he liked to think that he would have done it anyway.

"Why couldn't you use this power to stop the Boss Master from hitting you?" he asked her, knowing the answer almost as soon as he asked the question.

"Boss Master like hurting us," she responded matter-of-factly.

To a sadist, that kind of broadcast would be confirmation of punishment well-inflicted and maybe a real thrill, too. That, in fact, was just the kind of man they'd hire to manage and shepherd a bunch like the Erotics.

He sighed. "This is going to be very hard for you to understand, but you must understand it. First, you do not do that to me, ever. It won't work, anyway. Second, I did not save you to have my own slave or live-in lover. I saved you because I do not like seeing anyone hurt, and I do not believe in letting anyone be killed. You are here because, having done what I did, I am now responsible for you. That is not what you are used to, but it is what is true."

To his surprise, she *did* understand it, to an extent—and it made her feel miserable. If she wasn't to be his lover and slave, then she had no value or purpose at all.

"Is that all you want to be? Have you never dreamed of being something else, doing something else, finding other things to do?" he asked her, growing exasperated.

She looked at him very seriously and said, truthfully, "No."

"All right, all right! Now, I am going to show you why you can't make me happy—and, believe me, it isn't from a lack on your part." With that, he removed his shirt, then turned his back to her.

She stared at Grysta, flattened out like some black and white woolly caterpillar in the small of his back, and, for the first time, she showed real curiosity. "What—what *is* it?"

"That, my dear, is Grysta. Grysta is from a planet where there are a lot of big but dumb creatures. Grysta's race is parasitic—they can only live if they are in some way attached to somebody else."

<The word is "symbiotic," not "parasitic," you asshole!>

"Depends on how you look at it," he mumbled.

Molly didn't know the word parasitic, but she got the idea from the rest of what he'd said. "You mean it sucks your blood or something? I be told of things like that."

"It's a little more complicated than that, but let's just say that Grysta can only eat through me and in fact can only see and live through me. Don't worry—even if she *could* live off a Syn's body—which is something we don't know and which I actually doubt—considering how much of your system is devoted to keeping you disease-free, she wouldn't move. She's quite happy with me, and the coppers know about her and would kill her if she *did* move to somebody else."

"But you be not happy with her there," Molly responded, surprising him again.

He sighed. "Just like you were the property of the Boss Master, I, in a way, am owned by Grysta."

"It—*think*? It tell you what to do?"

"Yes to both questions, although I don't necessarily do what she wants me to. She argued that I shouldn't save you, for example. Some things, though, I can't help. In her mind, and in her race's way, she is married to her host, and she is jealous. Some of the people you serviced were married, but they didn't bring their wives with them or probably even tell them about you. Grysta must go everywhere with me."

"And she not let you touch me."

This is crazy, he thought to himself. *She's gone from feeling sorry for herself to feeling sorry for me!*

"That's about it. Now you know that I spoke the truth about why I fought for you and why you are here."

Now Molly exhibited at least one other human trait—the common reaction when anybody learned of Grysta. "How it come to get on you?" she asked him. "And where are others of it?"

He chuckled. "Don't worry—you won't go to that

world, ever. Nor will, most likely, anybody else who might be a suitable host. I'm a spacer, or, at least, I *was* a spacer, when I had a ship and mates. We explored new worlds, and Grysta's was one of them. Her race had developed a fair intelligence and mostly lived off the big dumb creatures I talked about. I am a telepath. You know what that is?"

"You read minds. Can you read mine?"

"Sort of, but never mind that for now. I read some very complicated thoughts in the big dumb critters and we saw that they had built a kind of civilization. Not very modern, no machines, but grass houses and some roads and things like that. But the creatures just didn't have the brains to do it. I was one of those sent in to find out who did have the brains, and I found out. The story isn't very exciting, really. I sat in the village and tried to communicate and before I knew it, they'd slapped Grysta on me. At least we found out, I suppose, but by the time I was picked up, Grysta had so figured out my insides and got so comfortable, she'd have died if they took her off, and maybe killed me in the process. She'd have to tidy me up to move on, you see. It looked for a while like I was going to be stuck down there for life, but the rest of the team studied me and Grysta, and figured out that she couldn't lay eggs without another of her kind and she was *very* smart and so came under the Sentience Law—if a race is found that's smart, that can think, it has certain rights. At the time, some people saw real advantages in this combination, although that idea was later given up. While they had it, though, they decided I could leave, with Grysta's promise not to move off me to anyone or anything else or she'd be killed. That was six years ago."

Molly kind of followed the story, showing more of an attention span than he'd given her credit for, and some logical sorting ability as well, but her conclusion was still very Molly.

"Then you not my master. My master is your master."
<That,> remarked Grysta, *<is the absolute strangest line of thought I think I have ever heard.>*
This time, Jimmy McCray gave her no argument.

The solution to his most immediate predicament didn't really leave him overjoyed, but there wasn't any other way that he could see, and it *did*, at least, seem to make everybody but him happy, as usual.

Educating Molly, making her into a more independent sort at least—she could never really be anything but dependent for the basics, due to her physical limitations—proved exasperating. There were flashes of curiosity about things that directly concerned her or him, but not beyond that. Certainly she didn't see any value to learning anything that had no immediate and obvious benefit to her. Occasionally she'd show flashes of real intelligence, but they would be brief, transitory, and as soon as the problem was solved or the question answered, she went back to her normal near-vegetative mental state. It was certain that she had no concept of abstraction or any sort of ambition.

The problem was, neither he nor Grysta had any idea whether her mental limitations were simply because of her previous life or were programmed into her very core by the genetic engineers.

There was, in fact, only one thing she really wanted to do, and it was Grysta who finally suggested to Jimmy that a solution to their problems might be in letting her do it. He resisted for a while. His upbringing and spacer outlook recoiled from the idea, and to go through with it would mean shucking the last sliver of pride he had, but he finally realized that for the immediate future it was really the only thing to do.

He had someone who was quite literally created as a sex object and who wanted to be one, and he had access to the Spacers' Guild Hall and the contacts that went with it. That hadn't gotten him any job, and the fact that he now had Molly made shipping out even less likely in the future, but such contacts could get *her* into a sort of ancient employment.

It was quite typical of the way his life and luck had gone that an act of sheer kindness prompted by the highest moral values, had wound up turning him into a pimp.

The male human spacers took to her readily; for many, it was easy, cheaper than the District, and much more convenient in a location of their own choosing. And, ironically, the only thing he'd had to do to make it legal here was take out a small-business license.

There weren't *many* humans through here, but there were always some, and it wasn't hard to find them and hook the interested ones. More surprising was that business also came from the human resident community. Men who for reasons of marriage or reputation couldn't be seen in the District proved a better market than the spacers did.

He was astonished at how quickly the money came in, and how quickly it grew. It was quite easy to move out of the Guild hotel and into a small but comfortable place in a better part of town, one more convenient and safer for the residents. They weren't going to starve and they weren't going to sink into poverty. Oh, even at her speed they'd never be rich, but they'd never really want for anything, either.

Syns had no legal status and no rights, but neither did he have a true legal claim to her under the law, a nervous Grysta pointed out. When word got around, various unsavory elements might find it expedient to appropriate Molly for their own, or employees of valuable brokerages might move some power levers to get her exclusively. Again, it was Grysta who also came up with an answer.

<No doubt about it, Jimmy. You're going to have to

marry the girl. Do that and you have a legal bond. Then it becomes kidnapping, not property rights.>

"But you can't marry a Syn!" he protested. "They aren't even legally people! It's just not done!"

<Yeah. And that's why I'll bet there isn't a single law or statute covering it. They'll hem and haw and try to figure every way around it, but I bet they can't stop it if you insist, and the marriage would make her a citizen as well, which is more than they'll let me be. You know, this is probably the only world in the Exchange where you could get away with this, too, because they have only the imperial law here and they have to cover so many different races but no native ones. Try it. What have you got to lose?>

And, as usual, Grysta was right. The cymol clerk nearly blew a fuse when he saw the bride and checked the classifications, and, for the first time, Jimmy watched as a cymol removed part of its hair and plugged itself into a master console. There was no way of knowing if the thing was simply scanning at unnatural speeds every statute and legal decision in the Exchange's half million-year history or if it was passing the buck all the way to the Guardians, but after about twenty minutes the hair patch went back on, the connector went back in its socket, and the cymol returned to them. Looking a bit distressed, he said, "The unit is reported as deactivated and destroyed by its owners, so there are no claims. There also appears to be no precedent. The only question is one of consent, since, legally, you are asking to marry a machine. However, subject to legal challenge at a later date, there doesn't seem to be any reason why a citizen who is certified legally sane can't marry a seat cushion."

"What do you mean 'subject to legal challenge'?" Jimmy asked him.

The cymol shrugged. "If someone should lay claim to it in court, you would then be faced with a court case on the validity of the marriage, or, say, if someone with cause sued to dissolve the marriage, well, you would have to defend in court. There is, as I say, no precedent, although I must say there are precedents for things that make this look simple by comparison. But the burden would really be on a challenger, not you. Very well, let me get the records going here. I assume you don't want a ceremony."

<Yes, we do,> Grysta responded.

"No, just the legal part," McCray said.

That amounted to no more than stating the answers to a few basic questions by each of them in front of a recording device and it was done.

Molly had no idea what all this was about, and no real concept of the legalisms; her thoughts seemed to indicate that she saw this as a kind of legal bill of sale, officially making her his property, the way a farmer would transfer a cow or a horse to another owner, and dissolving any claims her old owner had.

Of course, Jimmy also considered it pretty much of a sham; the only fellow ever married who wouldn't be allowed to consummate the marriage, although half the males through here could do it for him.

Of course, if she ever really grew up, was *capable* of growing up, it would also be easy to get an annulment on that basis, which was comforting.

Getting her documents to make her real also provided a bit of amusement, since immediately after name and address you had to enter "racial code," and, quite naturally, there was no racial code for a Syn. There were a hundred and forty-six officially recognized sentient races of the Exchange, a hundred and twenty-nine known sentient races that didn't duplicate the others for the Mycohl, and a hundred and six non-duplicative sentient races for the Mizlaplan, but none of them really fit her. Of course, being an efficient bureaucracy, they *did* have a 'None of the preceding" category, after which one had to go through a lot of stuff defining not only what the applicant *was* but why he/she/it wasn't any of the above. He simply put down the basic truth, which would have the best legal standing, and submitted the whole thing.

The electronic terminal seemed to blink, hesitate a bit, then there was a series of noises and out of the slot came a nice glossy holograph ID card with her new name, official picture, and the basics beyond encoded on it so that it could be read by other electronic devices as needed. The racial code, however, was 999-999, the classical "None of these," which, in a legal sense, put Molly in the same racial category and group as Grysta. That fact, and the thing actually going through and being accepted, made him thankful that Grysta had never gotten this marriage idea herself between species. He fervently hoped that an involuntary mating such as they had wouldn't be so easily recognized. With all the races and worlds and customs, polygamy and polyandry weren't all that uncommon in the Exchange.

Well, if Grysta got the idea, at least he felt he could convince her that it would be against his religion, which it would be, if he still had one.

And, perhaps he did, for he was still alive, and the vestigial remnants of his ancestral religion was probably the only explanation why he hadn't done away with himself.

The problem was, the only thing that kept life at all interesting for him was now forbidden him as well because of his situation. Space was his true love, his erotic passion, the one thing that mattered above all others. Space was not merely his romance, his dream, it was the cruelest mistress of all. Had he not been infected with it, he'd not have one creature on his back and another out whoring for him. Space was a sadistic lover, and he was masochistic enough to want her back.

And that was why, when the Durquist had called for

an appointment—and he knew that Molly held no charms for a Durquist—his heart skipped a beat and he could not contain himself in spite of knowing that anyone remotely interested in him would be repelled by his excess baggage.

The Durquist settled its starry shape against some pillows and looked at him with both stalked eyes. Jimmy tried to read it but got mostly mush. Although the Durquist wasn't a telepath, it had obviously been through a good training program for thought shielding, which was impressive. Unless the star-shaped being let its guard down, this would be strictly voice.

"Let us get some preliminaries out of the way to begin with," the creature began. "We are aware of the Morgh, and your past history. That, in and of itself, should tell you something."

Jimmy nodded. "You need a telepath pretty bad and you can't get one. Why? There must be a hundred experienced telepaths on the rolls, rotting here right now."

"More like three hundred," the Durquist acknowledged. "Some we couldn't consider simply because their physical requirements would require too many expensive modifications to our ship. Others have their own problems, including some who are past their prime and won't admit it, and still others are, frankly, not the sort I'd like at my back in a fight. Most of the rest refused us for other reasons I will get to presently. That left a comparative handful of people such as yourself, and I'm down to you on that short list."

McCray frowned. "They *refused* you? In *this* job market?"

"In a moment. First I would like to know just what happened on your last expedition with the *Zumaqualash*. We have read the official reports and debriefings, and heard a bit second hand from various spacers, but we'd like to know just why you were fired by your own side."

He shrugged. "Not much of a story, really. We were doing a First Team evaluation of a dirt ball out at Cue Veranzas, near the Mycohl frontier region but free space, and it was the usual thing."

The whole area looked like a sea of blue-white sand, and in it and all over it were rocks; horribly twisted, shaped by blowing sand and steady wind into every shape and size and needing little additional imagination to see in them sinister shapes and figures. Yet, as twisted and bizarre as that were, like massive blotches of gray and orange paint formed into globules when dropped in water, they had a certain—regularity—about them, almost as if they were, somehow, planned, shaped, sculpted even, but by a mind too alien to fathom.

Throughout the landscape were the dust devils— hundreds, thousands of them, all whirling about and careening into things and stirring up sand and dust. Yet the instruments and probes had shown the dust devils to be nothing more than that, potentially dangerous but not terribly substantial, and the rocks and sand were composed of known compounds. Anything out there unmeasured and unseen would remain so to the robotic probes and instruments; anything that left tracks had remained out of sight, and any tracks it might have left would have been smoothed over by the bizarre dust devils' madcap dances.

"Nothing particularly weird," Jimmy McCray remembered. "There were certainly no life forms down there that answered to the known carbon- or silicon-based formulas that serve as our definition. Of course, I don't have to tell you that our definition of life needs a lot of work."

"Indeed," the Durquist agreed. "And certainly in your case."

McCray nodded. "It was funny. All our instrumentation, the robotic probes, you name it—all ignored. The atmosphere was rotten enough that we couldn't drop live animals for any kind of meaningful test, so we dropped a few dead ones. The only thing that seemed to happen was that some of the dust devils moved in and over them and buried them in the sand. No big deal, and nothing really suspicious enough to ring any alarms."

"You dismissed the fact that the dust devils had moved in and over them as mere coincidence?"

"Sure. Wouldn't you? I mean, you could watch those little buggers going this way and that with no apparent purpose or consistency and not see any sense at all and, hell, there were so *many* of them, a few were bound to cross over. And they were so insubstantial, really, that the figures said there'd be no real problem breaking out of one if you walked into it or it rolled over you."

"So they were laying for you, as it were."

"I'm not sure. I'm still not sure of anything there. We hit the ground, fanned out, did the usual routine, and it was like ten or maybe fifteen minutes before the ship controller noticed anything really odd. I mean, hell, we're looking at potentially hostile or intelligent actions, right? We were so concerned with avoiding the damned dust devils that it never occurred to anybody, not even the ship's computer, that the dust devils were avoiding *us*.

"Indeed. The pet that made no noise. An old error, but a common one."

Jimmy shrugged. "Well, everything went just fine until Almuda—a Thetian and our geological evaluator—went over to one of those weird rock protrusions and decided to drill a core sample. As soon as he started, they just went *wild*."

"The rocks?"

"The dust devils. They had no natural enemies, or at least no natural enemies left, and no matter how chaotic they were, they never seemed to hurt each other, so it wasn't like we sprung a trap or anything like that, or that they had any hidden weapons or powers—but they sure blew their corks. And, in just doing that, and converging on poor Almuda, they used the only kind of weapon I guess they had—they began picking up massive amounts of sand and then hurling it, in effect sandblasting him. The suit was enough to protect him from that, of course, but it was a *godawful* amount of sand and thrown at great force and it quickly started to bury him."

"Did they turn on the rest of you?"

"No, just him, with more of 'em coming every minute."

"You tried to help him, I assume."

"Well, every time we made a move for him, a bunch turned on us and started spitting sand so hard it knocked us back. When we retreated, they stopped. We tried the pistols, we tried every kind of weapon we had that wouldn't have killed Almuda, and they had no effect. It was like shooting air. The computers got us to back off after that, and they tried a wide beam from the shuttle above the dust devils, trying to superheat the air and maybe dissipate them or something, but whatever they tried didn't work. The heat just made them stronger. It drove us absolutely nuts, hearing Almuda's cries, his pleas for help, and not being able to do anything."

"I see, and with a forty-hour air supply . . ."

"Yeah, you get it. Most of the team couldn't stand it anymore. We pulled back and tried to comfort him, and we hoped that maybe if the dust devils finally buried him completely and couldn't see or hear him anymore that they'd give up, but they kept at it. Night came and they kept at it. Day broke and they kept at it."

"They must have built quite a sand dune."

"It was a monster, covering even all remains of the rocks. They finally did stop, after maybe thirty hours, but they didn't move off or move away, and they kept keeping us away. It was as if they knew, somehow, that he had a limited amount of time. After a while we figured out how. Somehow they could intercept his radio, maybe sense the broadcast energy or something. Everybody else had sort of given up, just on a deathwatch at that point, but I couldn't. I finally figured that if we could get an accurate fix by beacon, then he could kill his power and maybe that would end it and I could get to him. By that time he was near panic and willing to try anything. He cut his power, which gave me about twenty minutes before he'd have to turn it back on or suffocate, and, sure enough, the things lost interest and started to drift away. We all rushed in immediately with whatever we could bring in, and started digging. We quickly found we couldn't use the automatic stuff after a while—the sand was so soft it kept filling in, burying and jamming the controllers, and potentially shifting him as well. So, after we got as much off with the equipment as we could, there wasn't any choice but for us to just go at it like demons with shovels."

"You didn't find him?"

"We didn't get the chance. I didn't have a timer on him, but he turned his damned power back on. It was close—*real* close. A couple more minutes and we'd have had him. I pleaded with the others to help, but somebody yelled that the dust devils were coming back strong and they just backed off and left him there, and me digging alone—more or less. I am never exactly alone. We were so damned *close*! I'm still convinced that even with them starting up again I could have gotten to him, and, if I had, the shuttle could have taken him with the grappler and hoisted him up out of range. I didn't want to quit, even with the devils starting to spit again, not with Almuda so loud in my suit that it was like we was touching helmets at full power. Grysta began yellin' and screamin' at me, but I would hear none of it, and I kept at it, and she finally gave me a series of painful shocks that stopped me dead, then shot my head full of fear and adrenaline. She was in control and I couldn't do anything except drop the shovel and run like hell."

The expression on his face was tense, his eyes wild, his voice filled with the emotion of that time, as if he were doing it all over again. Suddenly, he seemed to snap out of it and sank back into a relaxed posture in his chair.

"Almuda stopped talking to us about an hour after that, and I could only get brief fragments of his thoughts, which turned very dark. He just, well, gave up. I tried to argue with him, even screamed at him, but all he finally said was, 'Farewell, comrades, it has been an interesting life.' Then he shut down all systems, and, about one minute later, there was no doubt as to his location. One whole area of the huge dune just exploded outward. He'd put his energy pack on emergency overload. Killed himself."

In spite of his professed lack of faith, Jimmy McCray crossed himself.

"I do not see what else you could have done," the Durquist commented, trying to sound as sympathetic as possible. "Even if you had gotten to him, the grappler could only have taken one of you up. The creatures would have simply replaced your shipmate with you and there would have been the same problem with a different victim."

"That was Grysta's analysis, but she has a shipmate and crew of one other. Almuda was a good fellow, and he was my friend."

The Durquist was silent for a moment. "Um, yes," it said at last. "But the rest of your team blamed you for this?"

"Yes, curse their miserable souls to the lowest Hell! Not me, really—Grysta. They blamed Grysta. Did a lot of good what-ifs and decided that she'd killed Almuda by making me quit. Never mind the fact that the whole lily-livered lot of them had cut and run far ahead of me. That was the hardest thing to take of all. If I'd cut and run at the same time they had, we'd all have been comrades in cowardice together. Because I had more guts than the lot of them, I alone got blamed for Almuda's death. Grysta and me, anyway."

"I see. If it was Grysta's fault, then it wasn't theirs. Create one, or two in this case, scapegoats and you absolve everyone else of blame and redirect guilt into anger. You were the only human on the team?"

"Yes. I've never actually worked with another human in a team operation, odd as it might sound."

"Not odd. I was just reflecting. The team's reaction seems like such a human thing to do. Never mind. These kinds of situations are rather common for us, I fear. I'm not certain I don't prefer your last world to our last one, where we lost our telepath. One can almost sympathize with your whirlwinds. An entire existence based upon sculpting forms out of rocks, in which the artists outnumber the desecrator by thousands. One wonders if they attacked your poor comrade as a violator of some serious religious law or if it was simply the case of artists murdering what they considered to be the first art critic. No matter, I don't think that this incident says anything bad about you. Indeed, it sounds like you're a better team member than the others. I wonder if—"

At that moment the door slid open and Molly walked into the living room from outside. She spotted the Durquist immediately—the creature was pretty hard to miss—and stopped. Her eyebrows went up. "Sorry. Not know nobody here but Jimmy."

"That is quite all right," the Durquist responded pleasantly. Then, to Jimmy, it said, "We heard on the street how you were making ends meet, but I do not believe I am familiar with her kind. She looks human, in a way, yet animal as well."

Jimmy McCray sighed. "Okay, I guess it's time for my second sob story." And, with that, he told the Durquist all about how he'd rescued Molly and what had developed from it.

"That's why we're probably wasting your time," he concluded after giving the basics of the story. "When I took her I became responsible, and she's just not self-sufficient on her own. The only place she could exist without me would be down at the Club, and the Entertainers' Guild would never permit that. That means, where I go, she goes. She's a broadcast empath, within a limited range, so she has *some* talent other than the obvious, but she's a lot more limited—maybe programmed—than would be useful in the dirt. As much as I'd like to go back to space, I can't just leave her here. I was forced to walk out on one person before and leave 'em to die. I can't do it again."

The Durquist thought it over. "We have an empath—the company owner, in fact—but she's not broadcast. Molly is basically human—the little tail and the hooves wouldn't be much problem to allow for in a suit—and rather small and light. But would she be loose equipment?"

Jimmy understood what the creature meant. "No. I've never seen a less aggressive person in my life, and she'll obey just about any command. About the only thing is, she's totally incapable of harming anything or anybody unless her empathic sense tells her that they want to be hurt."

"Well, the job we have in mind won't even involve a dirtfall, as such," the Durquist told him. "It is not risk-free, but it's not the kind of thing you had last time. About the only problem I can see with her is that she is programmed to provide human sexual favors."

"I see. And no humans on the team."

"On the contrary. The owner is a human female, in fact. And the man . . . well, that's the problem."

Jimmy McCray sat back and stared at the Durquist. "I've been pretty open with you. I think it's time you told me why so many turned you down, you had to come to me."

"Yes, I think so. Settle back and I'll go from the beginning. Bear with me, please, but, even if, at the end, you turn us down, I suspect you could sell the story to the entertainment business."

Jimmy McCray listened to the whole tale, told rather dispassionately in the strange and inhuman tones of the Durquist, and had to agree that it was what his mother would call a real tearjerker all right. Even Molly stopped munching on a *dzir* fruit and seemed raptly attentive after a while, and Grysta made no interruptions at all.

But when the payoff came, the trio had somewhat different reactions.

"A cymol! They made him a *cymol*?" Jimmy McCray was appalled. "You don't know what that does to a telepath, being around a cymol for any time. The playacting is good enough for most folks, but to a telepath it's like working with a corpse! No *wonder* nobody's interested!"

<*Romantic idiot*,> Grysta commented. <*Anybody that screwed up is better off half-machine anyway. I just feel sorry for that poor woman.*>

"Is very sad," Molly commented softly, and Jimmy was startled to see a real tear run down her cheek. "She do one dumb thing and make everybody sad."

"There may be parts in her that are yet undiscovered," the Durquist commented thoughtfully.

"Unfortunately, they're undiscoverable by any known means," McCray responded glumly. He thought it best not to relay Grysta's comment, and the Morgh didn't press for it.

The Durquist summed it up rather well. "Look, this particular job we have lined up is ticklish as hell, but without a telepath it's simply impossible. We're not even the first to try and crack this nut, but the profit potential is enormous, which is why the franchisees haven't sold or relinquished the option. It's quite possible that this job is impossible, but on the remote chance that it's not, nobody dares let others have access. It is also near enough to the Mycohl frontier that abandonment is out of the question. There's already been some evidence that the Mycohl have snuck in and had a crack at it themselves between expeditions. The nature of the thing is such that if they could crack it before us, it wouldn't matter if we had legal claims on it or not. It's never been tried with a cymol directing operations, though, and we think that gives us an advantage. There are very few cymols not directly working for the Exchange."

"But—my God! Day to day with a cymol . . . And you said there'd be no dirt work, so it's entirely cooped up on shipboard." He shivered.

The Durquist moved to the humanoid position, as if it were going to leave. "Consider this, McCray. You can always be a procurer, but the freakish circumstances we both find ourselves in will almost certainly not occur again. If you want space again, you have to take all the terms and conditions and personnel we select. You have stones about your neck and you are sunk neck-deep in water. A dead man is holding out a stick and inviting you to grab it. I am now going to interview the last two potentials on my list. I shall take the first 'yes' I get, no matter what the baggage, because we are desperate. But if we get no affirmatives within the week, then we will cancel the contract. If you decide, call the *Widowmaker* Company at the northern civil spaceport. If we still have an opening, we will take you. I can waste no more time on this."

McCray sighed. "I just *have* to think it over, talk it over. Uh—just out of curiosity, where did the ship's name come from?"

"The name was inherited with the purchase of the ship, I believe," the Durquist replied. "Before my time, really. I believe someone once said it referred to a domestic animal owned by some fictional character. One gets these bizarre names all the time, as you know, considering how much trouble it is to rename anything once it's registered. Good day."

As soon as the Durquist left, Jimmy began pacing, trying to decide in his own mind. To be cooped up in an old clunker of a spaceship with a cymol in command for who knew how long . . . And yet, it was space. It was a team again. It was, as the Durquist pointed out, his last and only chance, not only for his first and only true love, but to perhaps accomplish something, to keep from dry-rotting forever.

<Well? Are you going to take the job or not?>

"You don't have a preference?"

<Well, as the Durquist said, you can always be a procurer. And even I have to admit to being more than a little bored after only a few weeks. This life will kill you, Jimmy. I know that. But this is one I just can't call for you.>

"You don't know what it's like for a telepath to be around a cymol too much."

<No, I only know what it does to your blood pressure and other parts of your anatomy and that's bad enough. That's why I won't make this decision. But, from this non-telepath's standpoint, it seems to me that if the choice is between working with a walking corpse and becoming a walking corpse, I know which one I would choose.>

"Logical as usual," he muttered.

"What is cymol?" Molly asked, curious. She was used to these one-sided muttered conversations by now, but felt no hesitation about listening in.

"A person who's had most of his brain replaced by a computer," he told her. "A machine in a dead man's body."

"A Syn?"

"No, not a Syn. This man was born normally, grew up like other men, had a life, but died young and a suicide, leaving his body intact. So they used it and stuck in a sort of brain of their own."

"He talk like machine?"

"No, in fact if you don't have a Talent, you couldn't tell a cymol from an ordinary person. But you'll be able to tell, and so will I. You know how you can tell the feelings of anybody you're close to?"

She nodded.

"Well, did you ever get that from this chair? Or that piece of fruit you ate? Or the door over there?"

" 'Course not."

"Well, that's what you'll get from him, too."

"Like man we got papers from in office. Or police in clubs."

He nodded. "Yes, they're cymols."

"Only brain get switched?"

"Yeah. So?"

"Was wonderin' about other parts of body."

He chuckled. "They're still there, but they're not important to the fellow anymore except as decoration, looking right. You might say that the flesh is willing but the spirit's not there at all."

That went by her, but she got the idea. "So nobody on this ship for me?"

"That's about it. Could you stand it?"

She shrugged. "Is no big deal. Is just a *job*, you know."

He had to chuckle at that. Every time he thought he had her figured out she threw him a curve. Maybe it would be interesting to see what others would make of her—even a cymol.

<See? You're outvoted, two to one. Take the damned job, Jimmy, and just hold your nose.>

He sighed. "Yes, Mother."

<Besides, you only got to work with the guy. Imagine

that poor woman having to work there, too. This ship'll smell so much like ancient tragedy, you might even figure you haven't got troubles.>

"That," he responded dryly, "is exactly the kind of viewpoint I would expect from you."

Just Off The Hot Plant

Tris Lankur looked and sounded so much the same that it was easy to fool oneself most of the time that nothing really had changed, that the hospital stay had been for some other sort of injury, that he was now back, hale, hearty, and healthy.

Oh, there were little things, things that you noticed only because you'd been so close to the man for so many years, but those you might force yourself to overlook. He no longer smoked or drank to excess, or vanished into the District now and again; he was a bit neater, a bit more fastidious, that kind of thing—little things, easily dismissed or suppressed—if only she hadn't been an empath.

Every living thing large enough to have a central nervous system gave off some sort of emotive radiation, even if it was just the fear and biochemical surge that a bug felt when chased by a boot trying to squash it. Emotional readings of aliens were often confusing or bizarre, and some couldn't be properly interpreted, but, unlike the telepath for whom there were races outside the common telepathic band, there was just about nothing living that was without some empathic radiation. To somebody born with that sense, it was simply a part of things, a part of life, a part of everyone's identity, as much as color and shape and voice and smell. To the empath, a person without this radiation was analogous to someone missing arms or legs or cruelly disfigured;

it might not make a lot of real difference, but you could hardly avoid noticing it no matter how many times you saw them.

On the empathic level, no matter how he looked or sounded or seemed, Tris Lankur had no more presence than the water cooler.

That had hit her as soon as they met him on discharge from the hospital. Her first hesitant words to him were ones she probably had never before needed to speak.

"How—how do you feel?"

He smiled his old smile and shrugged. "Fine. Pretty good for a dead man, anyway. Is there anything wrong? Did they put my head on backwards or something?"

"No, nothing like that," she responded, not smiling at his typically flip humor as she would have in the past. "I'm an empath, remember?"

The reminder actually seemed to surprise him. "Huh. You know, I never thought of that. Until this point, I hadn't ever understood why Talents got the fits around cymols. I'll be damned. Hey—I'm sorry, but there's nothing I can do. I can't broadcast cheer or sadness or whatever. I guess it's just one of those things you're gonna have to learn to live with."

That's not the only thing, she thought sourly. Damn it! It was *worse* than she thought, because he *wasn't* really different. If he moved differently or talked differently or had a major personality shift, it might actually have made it easier, but this was *Tris* here— Tris, with something very important and very dear very obviously missing.

"Do you know what happened to you?" the Durquist asked him.

Tris sobered up and nodded. "Yeah, I know. I don't really *remember*—I have a few gaps here and there all over the place and nothing since we left that canopy world at all—but I know. I think it's best we don't dwell on it much. I never really figured on the empathic business, though. Telepaths are easy to understand, but it just didn't translate over to empaths as well. Think she can handle it?"

"I don't know. We have a job that has been waiting on your discharge, and that will tell the tale."

"Has she been seeing a psych?"

"Yes, but I gather that they want her to go on this one just to convince herself that it's over for her. I think they want her to quit and this is the cold shower, and I think she will. You are, after all, a walking knife directly in her guilt center."

Tris Lankur gave a soft, wry smile to himself and said, softly, "Well, maybe there is a bit of justice in all that."

The Durquist's eyestalks quivered in its equivalent of raised eyebrows, and it wondered for a moment if there was more Tris and less illusion here than they had indicated. Who, after all, but a cymol, and its Guardian programmers, knew just what it was like to be one? Indeed, the nature of the beast made it probable that not even any two cymols were exactly alike.

"You've found a telepath that will work with me?" Tris asked the Durquist.

"Yes, but I have grave reservations about the package I had to buy with him. It wasn't easy, Tris. We are talking the bottom here, not of the proverbial barrel, but the bottom of a black hole. I'll fill you in on the way. Tomorrow the two of you will meet in the briefing and then you can see what I mean, and we will see just how much this fellow wants out."

That night, Tris Lankur did not go to his small apartment. Instead, he remained in the shipyard. Because a cymol still had a human body and part of a human brain, some rest was required, but very little compared to the normal person, and never quite true sleep. If need be, he could rest parts of his body in stages, and go for a very long time without really resting at all.

He had left the hospital with a small suitcase; now, with everyone else gone, he opened it and carefully removed two gray, oblong boxes. One had a handle and was his portable unit; the other he spent several hours installing in his cabin on the *Widowmaker* so that when he was done, it was well-disguised but linked into all ship's systems, including communications and the master computer.

Then he went back to the office, rooted around, found some beer in the small refrigerator and a box of stale cereal, and did what he could. The body was still the body and it required what all bodies required, something he had to be constantly mindful of. This wasn't what his body needed for peak efficiency, and he would have to insure that a proper and exacting balance of such things was aboard or programmed into the food synthesizer on the ship, but it would do for now.

Finishing the "supper," he went to the box with the handle and placed both thumbs in spots only he could sense and which were attuned to him and him alone. A small crack appeared about fifteen centimeters from the top, and he slid it back with his thumbs. Then he disconnected the master cable from the rear of the master terminal on his desk and plugged it into a socket inside the box. Next, he pulled out a long, thin cable with a small, membranous end, then pulled over his big reclining desk chair and sat down. Holding the box cable in his left hand, he reached up with his other hand and removed a thick segment of hair, putting the very real-looking hair patch on the desk. Where the patch had been there was now visible in his skull a small plate composed of myriad silver contacts against a flat copper-colored backing. He fixed the cable to the plate, smoothed out the membrane, settled back, and appeared to fall fast asleep.

❖	❖	❖

Jimmy McCray felt the oddest mixture of emotions of his life sitting there in the common briefing room, and he knew that the redhead, Modra, the empath, was probably getting it double, feeling like he felt and also getting his own drift. He wished he could damp it down, but there was no way even Grysta could help very much here.

Cymol . . . That's a dead man there.

Trannon Kose, the somewhat introverted creature who was the team controller, came out of his shell when it was all business, and began the meeting.

"This is a job like no other," he began. "Three other Exchange teams have had a crack at it and come back empty, and we're pretty sure the Mycohl have snuck in and had more than one go at it themselves. In all other cases, we have had a planet at least well-mapped and checked out by automated equipment under the command of an experienced scout—for all the good that does."

That produced some wry smiles, among those who could smile.

"This one, though, we *can't* go down on. Nobody can, or could, at least that we know of. We can't even say exactly what's in it, although you'll have full spectrographic data that'll say it's more ordinary than it really is. It is an anomaly a kind of object that doesn't fit current knowledge or theory, and it's driving scientists and master computers as crazy as it has the teams who've tried to crack it. It doesn't even have a name. For reasons that will be quickly obvious, the franchisees have accepted the scout's descriptive name and simply called it the Hot Plant."

The room darkened, and suddenly there it was—far away at first, then closer, until it nearly filled the wall.

"That's no planet," Jimmy McCray commented. "That's a *star!*"

And, indeed, that was exactly what it looked like—a common yellow sun.

"That is the impression," Trannon Kose agreed, "but if it is a star, it is not any sort of sun we know. First, although its color is roughly that of the common G-type sun, its mass is infinitely greater, and its size is smaller than the common white dwarf. In fact, the density clearly shows that the damned thing should either collapse into a black hole or blow up, and it certainly should *not* be as relatively cool as it is nor that color. Attempts to penetrate its core or to read the core composition have failed. Either the probes are destroyed or they send back meaningless garbage. We don't know if that is because the core is something totally new or because its other activities scramble any attempts to get meaningful data. You see, it has the annoying habit of occasionally and randomly spewing out all sorts of crap. It threw something at the last team there, which blew all the instrument readings off the scale and took the team along in a wild ride at nearly the speed of light. It was as if it were possible to bunch together gravitons and spew them out in a mini, terribly dense, little planet. They barely escaped with their lives and won't go back."

That caused a stir.

"There really is no safe place to monitor this thing from, but activity is so random and so unpredictable that the odds are at least as good that nothing will come at us as that everything will come at us."

"That comforts me greatly," the Durquist remarked wryly.

Trannon Kose ignored the interruption. "Normally, this would be a matter of sheer science, not involving folks like us, except for the most incredible and inexplicable fact of all.

"It is inhabited."

That caused a real stir. "Hold on, hold on!" McCray called out. "How the bloody hell can you *tell*?"

"That is where you come in, McCray," Tran responded.

"With amplifiers you will have no problem verifying that for yourself, nor Modra either. There is definitely something, a lot of things, alive on that hell, something that *thinks*, and that makes it the key to the whole puzzle. Just suspend your skepticism for a moment and accept what I say."

"That is not easy to do," Tris Lankur said flatly.

"It is things like this that make civilization worth saving," the Durquist noted, and nobody was sure if it was being facetious or not.

"All right, just do it for the sake of argument. Imagine any kind of life that could have evolved down there. Things must change constantly. Their environment, their very composition and makeup, is unlike any kind of life as we know it, and their existence must be so alien it would have little or nothing in common with any of us. They certainly don't see or hear or do anything else in the ways we do, but logic dictates that they probably are unaware that there is even an environment outside of their own. They live *on* the place, not in the outer layers, so there's no probability of awareness. The mass at the core is enormous; they would have no way, short of getting blown by one of those instabilities, to escape from it, and if they did, they would surely die—and do. We've monitored their deaths."

"You mean—telepathically," Jimmy McCray commented.

The oval head bobbed in the equivalent of a nod. "Yes, telepathically and empathically. We think their entire communications level is on the mental bands. It's possible, even probable, that they are some form of bonded energy creature, that they are, in fact, effectively disembodied minds. Don't ask me how that's possible. Some of the top scientists in the field are now under the care of the best psychs in the Exchange after looking into that question, and the number of careers in physics alone that this thing has already ruined are beyond all but the greatest computer's ability to count.

Fortunately, our job isn't figuring that out. What we're expected to do is figure out some way to make contact with these—people—or whatever they are."

"The first step is simple awareness," Jimmy McCray pointed out. "If they get contacted—even if they can't understand any of the framework—so that they are aware of another and alien intelligence, then that's the wedge. I can't see why that's so hard."

"Everybody agrees with you, McCray. The trouble is, they can't handle it. We can read them, but any attempt to contact them—well, so far, at least as far as we can tell, kills them. The prevailing theory is that, being pure energy, when they make telepathic contact they immediately link minds. When they do, they are suddenly faced with an environment so alien, so cold, so totally unlike anything they could even imagine, their brain or whatever passes for it interprets our normal cozy environment as death—and they promptly die."

"That problem is not unheard of," the Durquist noted, "but in all other cases we've been able to get down there in some kind of suits or protective devices and announce ourselves in their element, providing some kind of grounding for them. If the Hot Plant even destroys our instruments and probes—that is out of the question. I can see the problem."

"And the potential reward if it's solved," Modra Stryke put in. "Imagine that kind of environment, that sort of new life form, down there, in that kind of hell. If we could somehow contact them, link up with them in some way, that kind of power and exclusive knowledge of a whole new branch of physics would have a value beyond calculation and would pay off for generations."

"Is this the first job your husband's firm handed us, Modra?" Tris Lankur asked a bit peevishly.

"They bought into the franchise on a minority basis, yes," she responded. "They're running out of seed money, after all, and if they don't have a team in on the problem, they could forfeit the rights. At least it's not a smelly swamp on a dirt ball, and while we've killed a few of them, by accident, they haven't done anything back. If they reacted, they'd have to know we were there, and that would be half the battle."

"What about it, McCray?" Trannon Kose asked the new member. "This will to a large extent depend on you, although with our help, advice, and support. You want a crack at it?"

He shrugged. "I don't see what we have to lose. The worst I can do is kill a few hundred more of the hot little devils."

Jimmy McCray sat back in his chair on the crew bridge of the *Widowmaker* and stared at the screen showing the target. The Hot Plant was aptly named; a small but incredibly fiery little bugger about the size of the average gas giant and blazing away like a miniature sun, the filters showing the whirls and eddies of its gases in constant turmoil.

In a sense, it *was* a sun, but, unlike a true sun, it wasn't master of all it surveyed. Instead, this blazing orb was in orbit, along with an incredible amount of junk, around a terribly small but incredibly dense core that wasn't even visible except with instruments. It could be a neutron star or some other object in the process of compacting down to the point where it became a black hole, except for its irritating habit of intermittently spinning off tiny pieces of itself and flinging them out in all directions. It was that sort of behavior that had destroyed several previous ships and which was why, now, there was an Exploiter Team in place instead of the usual raft of scientists. All the monitoring was being done by robot craft that had, according to Tris, a useful life span of perhaps two or three months before they didn't jump fast enough.

He stared at the inferno on the screen and for the

thousandth time tried, and failed, to imagine any sort of life, no matter how bizarre, existing on it.

The core wobbled like mad from the parental bombardment; it had a starlike temperature and climate, and it was as good a definition of Hell as he'd ever seen.

Widowmaker was as close in as they dared, although the computer pilot was primed and ready and the engines were at minimum power in case anything really nasty came by that might require a quick exit. That, of course, presupposed that the dark little bastard at the center of this cockeyed solar system sent something their instruments were designed to measure, and sent it at a slow enough pace so they could dodge it.

Placement was tricky here. They'd all have preferred to be much farther away, but then, even with the amplifiers, there would be no way he could get a reading on anything on that fireball out there, and the time lag alone would have been irritating. Too close, and even the shields wouldn't keep them from frying, or being spun about in all sorts of force whips from the conflicting close-in bodies.

He still didn't like to be around Tris Lankur, and he trusted the cymol even less, but being around Modra wasn't exactly a clutch of jollies, either. He couldn't remember anybody that miserable or that guilt-ridden who hadn't done away with themselves by now. If being there was uncomfortable for him, it was sheer torture for her; she was eating her bloody insides out, and not deep down, but right on the primary band, where it washed over him if he didn't take constant steps to shut out those thoughts. Trannon Kose was a bit easier to take, although his human conversational style concealed an interior thought pattern and frame of reference that occasionally made McCray dizzy.

Molly spent most of her time relaxing in the cabin, listening to godawful music played by who-knew-what on what could only remotely be described as some kind of sound-making machines, but at least she knew enough to keep out of the way. She had the uncanny ability to simply turn her mind off, something he often envied—and would certainly wish on Modra Stryke.

She hadn't quite gotten the idea of how all this had come about or why, but she had remarked that Modra was "all hollow, real, real sad," and that Kose was "mad at the girl for some reason 'n not hidin' it well," while the Durquist "seem to think all us is a neat show." He wasn't sure what that last meant, not being able to penetrate the Durquist's blocking pattern, but he had the uneasy feeling that Molly meant exactly what she said.

<A ship and crew made for us, huh, Jimmy?> Grysta remarked.

"Huh? How'd you know I was thinking that?"

<We been sort of close, you know. You don't need to be a telepath to figure out some things; you just need brains.>

"Intellect without compassion is just a good computer," he retorted sourly.

<Yeah? And what did compassion get you but saddled with somebody half-horse and half-bimbo? Or buried alive if I hadn't stopped you.>

"Maybe—maybe like the woman Stryke, I'm just trying to justify still being alive."

<You'll live a long time, Jimmy. Deep down you don't have the guts to do what Lankur did and you know it. Your only hope is that somebody or something will do it for you.>

He sighed and looked at the chair. "I guess we better get to work. I'll have to experience this to believe that there could be *anything* remotely alive, let alone sentient, in that mess."

The usual crew chairs were on the crew bridge, of course, but there was one extra, before the big screen, particularly large and padded and comfortable-looking. It had odd straps and small handles for handholds, too, and a small control panel under a false armrest on the right side.

Jimmy sat in it, reclined to a comfortable position, then activated the controls by his right hand. Instantly a nearly invisible energy blister surrounded the chair, uniting him with the ship's communications system and putting most of it under his control while simultaneously shutting out everything else, from the usual ship's noises to the sound of his own breathing to any stray thoughts of others. Isolated, cocoonlike, he could first tune out Grysta, now that there was nothing else to eliminate, and then open his mind via the com link pointed at the sunlike world beyond.

He felt the shock that the first telepaths must have felt when they explored this sector; disbelief, amazement, and a large measure of self-doubt that he was getting what he seemed to be getting.

The blazing inferno slipped away; what remained was impossibly alive, in the way that real worlds populated by real people were alive! Good God! The massive, seething babble that swept over him was incredibly powerful.

A telepathic race, he thought. *Of course. They would have to be.*

But a race of *what*? What kind of demonic things could live in Hell and be comfortable?

With a combination of thought control and instrument manipulation he began to zero in, selectively edit out, localize. It was as if you first saw a world, then narrowed to a continent, then to a region, then to a specific city or town in that region, and finally to a particular point in that city.

Not that they had cities; that seemed clear. This was a kind of life that lent new meaning to the much-misused term *alien*. Even if Trannon Kose looked like a collection of misshapen radishes stuck together by fuzzy pipe cleaners and the Durquist like a fat-bellied starfish with hot lips, they were organic, made up of carbon-based molecules, and while they had evolved differently than his own kind, they had evolved according to the rules. Hundreds of races had come out of primordial slime, most forming carbon-based life, a few silicon-based, but otherwise so much within the rules that they defined "life as we know it and understand it."

Not here. This was life as nobody knew or understood it.

He isolated more, locked, tried to read an individual as much as possible. The resulting stream made his head hurt and his mind dizzy. He'd done this with races so strangely different that he couldn't imagine what the hell they considered a coherent thought, but this was beyond all of them. This wasn't even garbage!

He instantly realized the basic problem here, which was the curse of all codes and code-breakers. Because "life as we know it" had certain common origins, even if it did come out looking and behaving so differently, there were always common traits. Most creatures slept in some fashion, or had some concept of rest. Most ate in some kind of fashion recognizable as such, even if what they ate and how often disgusted the onlooker. There was always some relationship of those most ancient elements: earth, air, fire, water. If nothing else, they were aware of the damned weather.

There was always, eventually, something to grab on to, something to build on.

But what the hell did anybody aboard *Widowmaker* have in common, even to the most microscopic degree, with the denizens of the Hot Plant?

There seemed to be no up, no down, no concept of direction that came across in any holographic sense. Instead of a null band, they appeared to have two telepathic bands he could catch, one of which was almost constantly active and probably served as some substitute for sight; the other was the internal thought patterns he was trying to grab.

They floated, they darted, suspended in an enormous band well below the surface activity, but balanced so that they were unaware of gravity's heavy pull. If they had artifacts, there was nothing to suggest it in the patterns, although he couldn't imagine what sort of artifacts you could have without anything solid, without resources of any sort save the energy in which you lived.

He might even have accepted the idea of some single mass mind evolving in that crap, but clearly this was an enormous mass of individuals; if he'd had anything to hold on to, he could have told them apart.

Another commonalty was sensory input. Sight, sound, smell, taste, touch—that kind of thing. Some of the methods evolution came up with were pretty weird there, too, but any thinking being had sense organs of some kind. Not here. That secondary telepathic band seemed to provide the substitute for input, but the information it relayed was of necessity processed into concepts that had no human equivalents.

Aye, that was the rub. He *was* getting their holographic patterns—he just had never had their frame of reference and was unequipped to even imagine it. The pictures meant something to them, but nothing to him.

He realized he was traveling well-trod ground here, but he already felt the sting of defeat. What in God's name could *he* come up with that the best and brightest brains of the Exchange and all those races and all those computers and all the rest could not?

And yet it was frustrating as hell, for the patterns he was getting were both definite and highly complex; there was no question that they were not merely thoughts but very involved ones. It was impossible to explain, but just "listening" to the patterns and sensing how they were grouped and directed, any telepath knew that whatever was there definitely did *think*, and on a plane well above the common animal or plant. The interaction of these patterns also suggested not merely individuals but some sort of coherent if not comprehensible social organization.

But how the bloody hell did you talk to something that had not one single word or picture in common with you?

He isolated what he thought was a single individual, although he couldn't be certain at this range, tracked it for a bit, then took a deep breath and opened up his mind to it, forming a wide-open telepathic link.

Suddenly he was inside the other mind, in a blazing, confusing whirl, where nothing made sense and everything looked like fractured nightmare images, just swirls of color and weird shapes and lines, and bizarre, insane imagery.

At the same time, the creature was also in his mind, suddenly alone, its secondary band sending back effectively no information, all cold and dark and so terribly alone.

He felt it die; suddenly, like a candle being snuffed out, with only some last thought that had to be a cry of terror or horror, and he snapped back into himself, sweating and trembling.

He'd finally found some commonalty of thought, but it wasn't very useful. The creature, whose whole universe was defined by the twin telepathic bands, had suddenly found that universe no longer defined. Whatever passed for a brain in it instantly interpreted this condition and acted accordingly.

Everything it knew or understood or trusted told it that it was dead, and so it died.

<*You better take a break, Jimmy,*> Grysta cautioned, breaking the silence. <*Your pulse rate alone is near the danger level.*>

A flick of the right hand and the energy blister vanished and the link was turned off, but he just lay there awhile. He'd been warned, but he still found it nearly impossible to believe. It went against everything in his own frame of reference.

"I killed it, Grysta," he muttered, disbelievingly.

<*So? You've killed before.*>

"In self-defense, yes, but—not just by trying to say hello."

<*You sure about that? I mean, you sure they're there at all? I mean* really *sure?*>

He thought about that. Could he, in fact, be getting a reading from somewhere else? Did it only *seem* to come from that inferno? No instruments could really do more than measure the strength of the telepathic band; the only reason for anyone believing that there were living, thinking *things* on that burning world was the strength of the band and the gut feeling of the telepaths who had plumbed it.

Certainly his own interface with the com link had indicated that what he was getting was from the Hot Plant; certainly, too, the prior expeditions here would have checked to see if there were some kind of anomaly that was misdirecting them.

But instruments were, as always, only good at measuring what they were told to measure or what they were designed to measure.

The fact was, his heart said that they were there, but his mind still rebelled, and Grysta's suggestion had fed that intellectual sense of disbelief. He decided that he needed a meeting with the team. Maybe that Metal Head would be useful after all.

Tris Lankur was interested yet not very excited by the idea of some sort of telepathic illusion.

"If not from the Hot Plant, then where?" he asked the others. "McCray, you're the only telepath we have. None of us can really experience what you do with the kind of lifelong training you've had. If you, along with all the ones before you, feel that it's coming from there, and the mind recordings bear out that conviction, who are we to question it? And why do you?"

"It was Grysta who planted the idea in my head," he told them, seeing the slight discomfort that went through the others—all but Lankur, he noted cynically—at being reminded of the extra creature aboard. "But she only voiced what I couldn't place. The *wrongness* of it, somehow. Life there simply defies logic. I—all the telepaths—can only go on experience, you know. The Talent says yes, but I've seen many a magician who could fool everyone here with some sleight of hand, and I've seen ghost solar systems show up on instruments, and caught tightbeam signals that seemed to come from nearby ships or worlds that were somehow whipped and curled across many light-years by freaks of nature. They say what goes in black holes might eventually spurt out somewhere else, but we've never found a white hole, so if that's true, where does the crap go when it weighs more than the universe can support?"

"Are you seriously suggesting that we might be getting a reading from an alternate universe?" the Durquist asked, genuinely fascinated.

"In a way it would make a kind of lopsided sense," Trannon Kose put in. "This is a most unusual, probably unique, solar system. The kind of forces that come into play here are mysterious and beyond our current understanding. If there were any kind of door into such an alternate universe, it would be in a system like this, under conditions like these."

"Indeed, and an alternate universe would not necessarily have anything in common with ours, not even the same natural laws," the Durquist noted. "It would certainly account for the total lack of commonalty between our minds. Why, this raises the stakes considerably if true! Contact across parallel universes—it's never been done! It's never been *dreamt* of!"

"Hold on!" Tris Lankur told him. "Calm down, all of you. The next thing you'll be suggesting is that it's some kind of microscopic civilization on a tiny, dense moon of the Hot Plant."

"Unlikely," responded the Durquist, taking the comment seriously. "Such an object would move or at least wobble even if geostationary. It wouldn't be as predictable. Whatever we're getting at least matches the rotation of the Hot Plant. However, an alternate solar system in which the Hot Plant wasn't hot, or perhaps where such things are normal—that would explain it, since that near-singularity out there would almost certainly pop through to their universe—or perhaps is popping through to ours. Now *that's* a thought."

Jimmy McCray sighed. "Then it's irrelevant. We're arguing angels on the heads of pins here. I was thinking, or rather hoping, that the conditions here were simply acting as a distorter, that we were missing the real origin. But whether or not we're looking into another universe, the problem's the same. How to tell somebody we're here, don't die on us, when we've got absolutely nothing in common except a shared telepathic band. Forget it. I should have realized this was a dead end before I called a meet."

Tris Lankur thought a moment. "No, at least it's gotten us all in on this. You know, I've reviewed all the records over and over, and it seems like nobody before us has tried alternate approaches."

"We've beamed on every type of transmitter we have, to no avail," the Durquist reminded him. "What wasn't tried?"

Lankur looked over at Modra, who was very quiet through all this and seemed to be mostly avoiding looking at him. "Empathic bands, perhaps?"

She looked up and frowned, almost as if she'd been a million light-years away and suddenly got wrenched back. "What?"

"They had empathic scans, to ensure that the telepaths weren't all crazy," the Durquist noted.

"Yes, maybe. But they only used them for wide scan, to establish a second level of proof that living beings were actually there. They never tried active empathy in the same way they tried telepathy."

"What are you all talking about?" Modra asked them.

"I think he wants you to go into the amplifier," Jimmy told her. "At least, even if you zero in on one of them, you won't just murder it."

Suddenly the air around them erupted with impossibly loud alarm bells. Almost instantly all of them were frozen where they stood or sat, surrounded in a protective green energy blister deployed by the ship's computer. There was a tremendous crash, as if something huge had struck the ship, and the lights and most of the power went, abruptly, and eerily, silencing the cacophony of alarms in mid-clang and mid-screech, producing a sudden, expectant silence that was the worst of all.

Then it hit.

They were suddenly falling, tumbling in the total darkness, stomachs turning inside out, each on a bizarre looping and whirling ride in the nothingness.

It was over in a few seconds, but it had seemed like hours. The power was restored in stages, as the ship's computer, obviously a survivor, checked out the systems, ran damage control, and cautiously restored what could be safely restored.

Lankur's protective blister vanished first, and he was immediately all action. "Computer! Damage report!"

"Bad hole in the aft starboard hold," the computer responded through the speakers. "Some damage to redundancy systems but the mains held all right. Everything loose went flying, though. Ship and all hands are safe and secure, but the place is a real mess from bow to stern."

"Screw the mess! What happened?"

The others were all released now as well, and bending and rubbing and stretching to release the sudden tension. Modra Stryke got to a waste hole and threw up. Jimmy McCray wanted to, but there wasn't much in his throat except bile. He suspected, although he wasn't too sure yet, that he'd wet his pants.

<They never had that one in fight recertification simulations!> Grysta commented, sounding about as unsteady as the rest of them looked.

"The singularity threw off what can only be described as a spray of particles along a two hundred and four degree arc, impossible to dodge completely," the computer was reporting. "The largest I measured was about five centimeters in diameter, but they were so dense that they were in effect pure gravitons packed as tight as possible. The speed approached light and they took us along for a while, until their spread weakened their collective pull sufficiently for us to break free. I diverted all power to that purpose. The duration of the uncontested pull was one point two five five seconds during which we moved two hundred ninety-seven point three four six zero kilometers. Breakaway took another six seconds, braking another twelve, during which we moved another three hundred and fourteen kilometers, rounded off."

"Wait a minute!" Jimmy McCray commented as soon as he could talk without spitting bile. "You're telling me that we moved nearly a light-year in one *second*, in normal space, under the normal rules, and that from a standstill, we're now better than two light-years away from where we were?"

"More or less," the computer agreed. "That's why things are a mess all over the ship. We might have some temporal dislocation as well, although it is difficult to determine right now. It will take me a little while to effect basic repairs and calculate a return using more conventional power. After that I shall endeavor to contact universal beacons by subspace tightbeam and determine just what temporal dislocations, if any, it caused. I am also running a stress analysis on every joint and plate in this ship to make certain that damage which is not obvious doesn't cause unpleasantries later. You can be proud of this ship. We are not designed to take beatings like that one. I have run the data we dealt with through the simulation loop a few million times and almost every time it comes back that we are destroyed and you are all dead."

That put a damper on conversation for a minute or so. Finally the computer asked, "*Do* you wish me to get us back to the I.P.?"

"Of course," Lankur responded. "Why wouldn't we?"

"Well, considering the simulations, I should say that if we go back and something like this happens again, there is virtually no chance that this ship could hold together a second time, particularly in its weakened condition."

Lankur nodded, then looked at the others one by one. Finally Jimmy shrugged and said, "We knew the job was dangerous when we took it."

"All right, then." Lankur sighed. "That seems to be the prevailing sentiment. Get us back when you can."

Suddenly Jimmy McCray jumped to his feet. "Molly! I'd better see to her! She's probably terrified out of her wits! I'm getting the oddest thought-streams from her." Odd wasn't the word for it. It was a mixture of the aftermath of sheer terror and . . . something else not so easily defined.

He went out of the wardroom, raced down to the cabin they shared, and poked his head in. She was there, all right, but she didn't look terrified and she actually gave him a smile.

"Are you all right?" he asked her, concerned.

"Oh, yeah. Hey, that be *neat*! Was most fun I had in long time. We gonna do that again?"

For a moment he was speechless. *She thinks this is some sort of bloody amusement ride!* Then he said, slowly, controlling himself as best he could, "I certainly hope not."

<Who said telepaths can't be surprised?> Grysta commented wryly.

Modra Stryke was more human than she'd been at any time since they'd set out on the expedition. Jimmy McCray understood that, for the first time, she was less administrator than active participant, and this gave her some reason to be there and to get her mind off her own dark thoughts.

She wanted this one, wanted it more than she'd wanted success in anything, because, as her thoughts told Jimmy, it would be her last hurrah. There was no question that she was no longer fit for this sort of thing, and she knew it. To have this one end in failure might be more than her fragile sanity could bear.

In a sense, empaths and telepaths were very similar, only reading different things. The brain was highly complex, and it used a number of organic mechanisms to do what it did. The analogue was to a tiny closed-circuit transmitter that brought all the elements of thought to the forebrain for assembly and coherent interpretation, much as a computer would assemble the elements in its memory within its central processing unit and then transmit them to an output device.

The amount of energy involved in the organic system was minuscule, but just as radio telescopes could zero in on, scoop up, isolate, and define noises so faint that they were beyond any concept of normal hearing, so, too, a telepath could pick up, isolate, and intercept those broadcasts on the primary band, the one of primary thought itself. The daydreams, the secondary thoughts, were far too weak and could never be separated from the background, but the main forward-thinking could.

But other information rode on that primary band; sidebands of supplemental data that even the best telepath could not receive but only interpolate, sometimes wrongly, from the strength and context of the thoughts. The emotion behind and beneath the thought, the feelings of the transmitter, were one such sideband, and it was this that the empath could read by somehow also suppressing background and isolating it.

The com link served several purposes. It could receive and amplify those bands, both in transmit and receive, and it was incredibly flexible in its ability to keep suppressing background, even from a fairly great distance, until it could isolate for the user a single organism or individual in a massive mob.

Because of the total isolation of the blister, Modra's comments would be smothered, but Jimmy McCray could penetrate it without disturbing either her or the instrumentation, now set entirely to the empathic band.

<Waves and waves of feelings; massive concentrations . . . a living planet. Impossible to believe, impossible to ignore. Identical sensations to scanning any large, inhabited body . . . No question. Something's down there. . . . A lot of somethings are down there. I wonder what they look like? I wonder if they look like anything at all? Pure energy, perhaps, held together in some kind of plasma beyond our ability to see, hear, or understand, perhaps . . . Fixed-form energy, duplicating without matter the kind of matter-energy synergy that our brains use . . . Pure mind, no body at all . . . But shape. Some kind of shape, since they're distinct. A mind of pure energy in an energy container . . . Living transmitters and receivers as well, seeing and hearing by broadcast waves and returns . . . Returns too confusing. Have to go in, isolate . . .>

"She's going in close," Jimmy told them. "She's getting the same sort of thing I did on wide scan, though. From what she's getting, I can pretty well say everybody was right from the start, anyway. They're there."

<Isolating . . . Odd feelings . . .> She shivered. *<Strange feelings . . . What can they mean? No sense of deception, deceit . . . Whatever they are, they're honest and open with each other . . . If all your interactions are by telepathy, empathy, and who knows what bands we might not be able to tap, it would be . . . No traces of envy, greed, jealousy . . . A race with none of the seven deadly sins. If it wasn't for their awful environment, the place would be more boring than heaven. . . . That's a thought. Maybe I'm being too normal here. Maybe I I'm mentally filtering the wrong things. . . .>*

Jimmy McCray sighed. "What she's getting definitely proves they have nothing in common with us predators. You wonder why a species that never has to lie, cheat, steal, or make war needs intelligence at all."

"Perhaps they have simply outgrown it," suggested Tris Lankur.

"Or more likely outlived and defeated it," responded the Durquist cynically. "I refuse to surrender all my preconceptions."

<Do they love? Do they have intimacies between them? Is there kindness, gentleness, charity, mercy down there? Good God! Could I recognize such things in them if there were, when I couldn't even see such things in my own kind or in myself?>

"She's wandering, brooding," Jimmy warned them. "I wouldn't exactly say she's lost her nerve, but she's lost her self-confidence. I hate to say it, but even though we might be on the right track, I don't think she's up to it mentally and she knows it. She's in a brood loop and it's shutting out the whole bloody planet."

Tris Lankur sighed. "All right, then, bring her out. We'll just have to think of another angle somehow. She's the only empath we've got."

At that moment, Molly stepped onto the crew bridge. She didn't usually come up, particularly when somebody was working, but McCray could see she'd gotten bored and started feeling lonely. "What'cha doin'?" she asked pleasantly.

Suddenly all eyes turned to her, and Jimmy McCray got all their thoughts at once—an easy task since they were all nearly the same thought.

"*Naw*, forget it," he told them. "She's got about the mind of a five-year-old."

"Perhaps that's not as much of a disqualification for this kind of work as it sounds," Lankur responded thoughtfully.

"Indeed," the Durquist put in. "She wouldn't spend half her energy intellectualizing why they're impossible or too alien or whatever, or get hung up with her own problems. It would be wonderfully ironic if what was standing in the way of us and our machines was our knowledge and our intellects."

It was decided that a tiny transmitter through which Jimmy's familiar voice could whisper instructions and encouragement was warranted here, in spite of the theoretical distraction it would represent. Molly was never good at doing more than one thing at a time anyway, and she was eager to find out what the machine with the neat chair did, as long as it didn't hurt and somebody told her what to do.

It was a simple matter for Trannon Kose to hook up a small remote to the controls; it not only simplified the job of teaching her how to work the thing, it gave Jimmy some added control and a sure hand at the stick.

"What I do now, Jimmy?"

"Don't talk, just think your questions," he told her. "The—wrapping—makes it useless to speak out loud, but I can always hear you. All you have to do right now is relax and let the pictures come into your mind. yes— that's good. Now . . . what do you see in your head?"

<*Sun. Same one as on big picture screen. Look real hot.*>

"It is. Now, you know how you know the way men are feeling by just looking at them? Just relax and do the same for that sun."

Puzzlement. Confusion.

<It's not going to work,> Grysta grumbled. *<Even Molly can't believe that people could live on such a place.>*

"Shut up, Grysta," he hissed, even though she echoed his thoughts. No matter what, it was too early to give up; they had to at least try.

"Just find out what the sun feels, Molly," he coaxed soothingly.

She shrugged, her mind indicating she thought he was putting her on, but she had nothing better to do. *<If you say so, Jimmy. I try.>*

Instant shock; more puzzlement, total confusion. *<There is people on there! How that be, Jimmy? Why they not burn up?>*

"We don't know," he answered honestly. "That's why we're here. Let me get you in closer. You might even be able to tell different people when I'm done. Nobody in particular, but somebody. Let's see."

<Funny, crazy feelings,> she reported, more fascinated than scared her confusion now completely dismissed because fact had replaced doubt in her mind. *<Not make much sense, Jimmy. They not like us.>*

"No, they're not. That's why it's so hard to talk to them. Take a look at any of them you can feel. See if you can make any sense out of what they're feeling."

She tried; she really tried. *<I be sorry, Jimmy. They not make sense.>*

He sighed and switched off the mike. "No good. She's there and in, but they're as alien to her as to us. Aside from adding a touch of childlike wonder, it's the same dead end."

"Well, it was worth a try." Tris Lankur sighed.

<I wonder why a bunch of 'em's so sad?>

Jimmy's head snapped up and he almost forgot to trigger the mike back on. "What? What did you ask?"

<*Whole bunch be sad is all. Other ones come, try to make feel better. They not do good job of it, though. Maybe I help. Send nice love. Oh, my! I guess I screw up!*>

Jimmy was suddenly so excited he nearly forgot himself. "No! No! You're doing fine!" To the others, he said, "She found some of them feeling sad, maybe grief. Hard to say. I can't pick it up myself, even via her mind, just her responses and reactions. She did her instinctive thing of shooting down some sympathy vibes—and they got it!"

<*Oh, my!*> Molly repeated. <*Everybody get so confused, so excited! I think I do bad thing!*>

"No, no, you're doing just fine!" he assured her.

<*Whole big crowd come. More'n more. They look all over. Most send up. I not know what they send. What I do, Jimmy?*>

"Send more good feelings to them. As widely as possible. As strong and as much as you can."

The Durquist suddenly stirred. "I greatly fear we have just started a new religion with ourselves as the gods. Imagine what would happen if you were at a memorial service for some deceased kin and suddenly everybody got a hundred times amplified blast of love and kisses from beyond."

"I'll take it!" Lankur responded. "We don't have to start discussing philosophy and politics with them. our job was to establish a means of contact, and that we did. Broadcast empathy! So obvious everybody missed it completely! And so would we—if we hadn't happened to have poor, sweet, childlike Molly along. McCray—take the backup chair. Get in on the same beam with her. I realize I'm asking you to pat your head and rub your stomach at the same time, but what if we could get some kind of thought picture from on High while they're still looking? Don't link minds. Just send a simple thought, a simple greeting, a feeling of hello, as she continues to send empathically. Short burst. Don't try for a response—we know what happens when we try that. Let Molly feel the response!"

Jimmy was in the other chair as quickly as he could get there, and just before the blister activated he told Molly, "I'm not going to talk for a few minutes. You just keep sending to them. I'm going to try and send a hello to the same folks while we have their attention."

<*Okay, Jimmy. I guess that would be nice. I not like what they send back now. Kind 'a like this be people I own or somethin'.*>

"Just relax. Activating."

He was in quickly, but had to depend on Grysta's control of his biochemistry to calm down enough to do it. This would be tricky. A simple image, a simple greeting. Open hands? Godlike father figure? No, that wouldn't do. They didn't have bodies like he did, let alone hands. Some kind of burst, maybe just pulses. Yes, that was it. Ah—he had them. He couldn't follow anything telepathically, but he could tell they were pretty damned worked up about something. Here goes . . .

<*. . . pulse . . . pulse . . . pulsepulse. Pulsepulse . . . pulsepulse . . . pulsepulsepulsepulse.*> Repeat Pattern. Twice . . . three times.

Blister off, power off.

"Molly, what are you getting?"

<*Dumb stuff. They keep winkin' on and off to me! Don't maker no senses*>

"Hot damn! We did it!" McCray shouted to them, clapping his hands in a kind of nervous self-applause. "Code—simple arithmetic. But they got it! *They got it!*"

"Grid coordinates are registered," the Durquist reported. "I suspect that will be a holy and well-visited spot from this point on. We can cut her loose."

"I almost hate to," Jimmy responded. "It's sort of like getting a call from God and suddenly being put on hold."

"Better than killing them," Tris Lankur responded. "They can wait. We've done what we were commissioned to do. Our job now is to get the hell out of here in one piece and report to our employers on the means and methods. It'll be up to others, scientists, permanent development teams—you name it—to turn this into a conversation, which it might well take years to do."

Molly's blister winked out and the chair powered down. She didn't get up, but looked over at them "Thanks. I—it not feel *right* what they feel to me."

Jimmy McCray went over and kissed her, an act that both surprised and pleased the Syn. "Oh, Molly, you came through for us! We all love you, Molly!"

She smiled and seemed genuinely pleased. "I did good?"

"You did *wonderful!*"

Grysta was practical, as ever. <*You tell them she gets a full team share for this, Jimmy.*>

"Aye, and a team rating too!" he responded, laughing. "Sweet *Jesus* it's been a long time since something worked out!"

Interlude: Collect Call From Hell

The Durquist found her in her cabin, just lying there, staring up at the ceiling. She glanced over at the creature when it filled her open hatch door, but said nothing.

"You do not look particularly happy at this juncture," the Durquist noted. "Everyone else is celebrating the end of the jinx. Is it because the childish little Syn did what you couldn't?"

Modra Stryke sighed and shook her head. "No, it's nothing like that. I *am* happy we managed it, partly because everybody needed it so badly and partly because—well, it's good to leave on something positive. It *was* a fluke, though. I really wish we'd done it through something we planned and not something we lucked into."

"You display ignorance of achievement," the Durquist responded. "Almost everyone who ever accomplished something very difficult and very major did so at least in part due to flukes and luck. Those alone get you what you wish in only a very few cases, but all the hard work and suffering and strain in the universe isn't enough to hit it big without those breaks. It is part of the way things are. We took the risk and this time the break came our way. It's about time, really, although, many people *never* get the break. We lose a telepath and have to take what we can get, then wind up with one who's got a Syn who's little more than a programmed organic robot with the built-in power to make rakish men spend money to copulate with her, and that little talent turns out to be the key to breaking something that all us smart folks and even smarter machines couldn't break. And in our first real triumph, for which we'll take full credit even if it *was* a fluke, you decide to quit on us."

"I have to," she responded hollowly. "I shouldn't have come on this one. I should have gone in for full therapy and put it all behind me instead of going through this—torture. I guess it all boils down to the fact that I may be as dumb as I thought, but I'm definitely not as tough as I always thought I was."

"Oh, you're tough, all right," the Durquist responded. "Anyone else would have quit this business long ago. And anyone else with the load you put on yourself would have blown themselves away or put in for cymol or something equally drastic. You're just blaming yourself for not being a machine, Modra. But you're not a machine, and even machines make mistakes, sometimes big ones. Look at poor McCray before you sink forever."

She sighed. "I know, I know. I guess I'm probably better off than he is, for all that. I think I *would* die rather than allow myself to become almost property, and that thing on his back just about owns him body and soul. It must be a miserable experience, particularly with that sex bomb around. But it's no good to point out how miserable other people are. I *know* most people live in more misery and squalor and hopelessness than I'll ever understand. It doesn't help, though. At least *his* wasn't self-inflicted; it was an on-the-job injury, really. And what happened, happened only to him. He didn't screw anybody else. That's what the real problem is, you see. I don't have any computerized brain and simulated personality. I don't have any creature on my back telling me what I can and can't do. I'm fine, even well-fixed. I'm not like McCray—I'm more like, well, that parasite of his."

"I still think your quitting is a waste," the star-shaped

creature told her, "although it's certainly better than having a Modra like *this*. We can not undo our mistakes, usually; we can only learn from them. But—do what you must. As for Tris—I wonder sometimes, after viewing him on this trip. To be sure, he is a cymol, and, to be sure, much of what we see was read back into his head, but—I still wonder. When does illusion become reality?"

She frowned. "Huh? What?"

"There was a *phrenax*—pardon, in your culture the closest word would be cousin, which isn't exactly it but is close enough—Hmmm . . . This is difficult. Let me discard reality and put it in what I believe are human terms. The crime the—cousin—was accused of was the Durquist equivalent of incestuous rape. Nothing could be proven, so the head of the clan secretly arranged for one of the rare Durquist hypnos to visit on a pretext. Evidence gained in that manner is, of course, not admissible most anywhere, but the hypno was pretty well able to confirm the act by hypnoing not the accused but one of her victims."

She sat up. "Huh? A *her* raped little *hims*? Now *that's* a switch!"

"Not if you're a Durquist. At any rate, by drawing on clan loyalties and also the promise of great rewards, the clan head convinced the hypno to violate the law and do a job on the accused—cousin—that couldn't be traced. The clan drugged the cousin, then she was put in a room alone with the hypno, and the hypno proceeded to imprint on the cousin that when she awoke she would discover that she was now in the body of one of her victims. The child had already been spirited away, and by common consent the clan treated the cousin as if she were this young male. The cousin felt as if she were the recipient of some supernatural revenge. Within a few months of living the illusion, she molted, and emerged a male—a virtually unheard-of thing, although it is, of course, biologically possible."

"Of course," she responded, hoping she didn't sound sarcastic.

"Yes, but the point was, an illusion had been created out of revenge, but the illusion ultimately became the reality. Descent, inheritance, and much more comes through the female line in my people. Later on, by chance, the cousin discovered what had actually happened, but it didn't matter. She was now a he and would remain so."

"That *is* fascinating," she told him, "but I assume this story also has a point for me somewhere?"

"Perhaps. We hold the brain sacred and we don't even know what the Guardians are, let alone understand the technology that lets them create a cymol. We *do*, however, hold the brain as special. If we lose a limb, we can grow another—or, in your case, have one grown by medical procedure. If our organs are damaged, they can be replaced with synthetic ones that work just as well. Our brains are merely sophisticated organic computers, after all. It's the data, the experience, that makes them unique. A lot of genetic chemistry goes into helping shape who we become, but by our age we're pretty well fixed. They got the data and memories out of Tris. They got a sense of his behavior patterns from us. They then read all that into this cymol brain, which contains what was the real Tris. To be sure, there are problems—various chemical stimuli, some emotional interactions—but, basically, Tris is there. All that he was is there. Is that illusion? Or is that really Tris? And becoming more and more the old Tris as time passes."

She thought about it. "I see what you mean. I don't know. But if you're trying to cheer me up, forget it. You forget that I'm an empath, Durquist. No matter how much of the old Tris is there, even if he's *all* there and secretly reveling in the fact that he got even with me, he's still cold and not there to me. It's like a hole where he should be; more like he was a holographic projection. If I could *feel* him, as I feel you and McCray and Tran and even that little bastard on McCray's back, then it would be something I could live with, guilt aside. But I can't. I'm quitting, and that's that."

"Very well. There's nothing more to say, then."

"Uh—one question."

"Yes?"

"I never really thought to ask this, but—which sex are *you*?"

"Why—male, of course. I should think that would be obvious. If I were female, why would I be out in the galaxy, surrounded by aliens, cut off from my own kind, trying to become totally independent?"

She'd been around other species enough not to be surprised at the comment. After all, the Durquist's motivations weren't all that far from her own.

"Uh—pardon me for asking, and if I am out of line just tell me where to go but—you weren't by any chance one of the victims of that cousin, were you?"

"Certainly not!"

The Durquist left her and continued on down to the wardroom, leaving her there, a bit shocked but at least thinking of something other than herself.

The Durquist had forgotten, as usual, that she was an empath. Most people never thought twice about empaths unless they were trying to lie or cheat or con you. He had been telling the truth in his response to her question, but something else had come through, both in his telling of the story and in his response to her query. There were only two possible explanations for the feelings emanating from him and one was now eliminated. It explained much that had been a mystery about the Durquist, and told her, too, that the star-shaped creature also carried a fairly heavy load of guilt.

So much, in fact, that since he hadn't been one of

the victims, the only other possible explanation was that he had been the victimizer.

They all were there in the wardroom, a bit of apprehension in all of them, since meetings of this kind *after* a commission were rare and generally only called in emergencies. Most thoughts ran to the possibility that the damage suffered in the whiplash effect was more serious than originally believed, but there didn't seem to be quite the sense of urgency that something like that would entail.

Tris Lankur didn't keep them waiting long.

"A little more than an hour ago, we picked up a subspace tightbeam all-call on the emergency bands," he told them. "It's a very strange message, but—well, I'll let you hear it first. Computer—play back message."

"All ships . . . any ships . . . Exchange registry . . . This is Research Vessel Wabaugh. *Coordinates based on special map frontier zone one one four eight two stroke five. Coordinates are Rainbow Bridge. Send assistance fast. They're all dead. They're all in there with the demons and they're all dead. Only one left. Can't leave. Approach with extreme caution! Power adequate for maintenance only. Any Exchange registry. Approach with caution. Demons at Rainbow Bridge! Coordinates . . ."*

"That's enough," Lankur told the computer. "It just keeps repeating."

"It sounds like somebody's gone stark staring bonkers," Jimmy McCray noted. "Either that or it's some kind of trap. That's pretty far out in the frontier. Almost No Man's Land."

Tris Lankur nodded. "We looked it up, though, and it's a valid claim and it is ours. I've reported it, but it'll take hours, maybe days, before my report gets through and others are dispatched. I have no idea if we're the closest Exchange ship or not, but we've gone over the coordinates, and because we're approaching a charted wormhole, it appears that we could divert and reach there in less than three days."

"It's no scales off our appendages," the Durquist commented. "I'd say forget it. Somebody else better-armed and in better shape will get it."

That seemed to be the general sentiment, but Lankur was prepared for that.

"The way this beam's bouncing around I can only figure that it's gone out in all directions. That area of the frontier is pretty dicey. A sliver of Mycohlian claims lies just to the right on the charts and the Mizlaplan has a sliver just beyond that. It's even money that the message would just as easily be picked up by either or both, and being in, as McCray put it, No Man's Land, a lot of nasty stuff could be pulled before any of our people could get there. Just knock off this one sending the distress signal, if that's what it is, and a claim easily changes hands."

"All the more reason for us to forget we heard it," remarked Trannon Kose.

Lankur sighed. "I wish I could, but I can't. As you all know, I'm not a hundred per cent master of my own destiny anymore. If this were a private claim, I could still ignore it, but the *Wabaugh* is not merely an Exchange registry vessel, it's owned and operated by the Exchange itself. I'm obligated to override any of my own interests if the interests of the Empire are involved. I have little choice."

"Then why call the meeting?" Trannon Kose asked him.

"Because it doesn't necessarily involve you beyond the diversion. We can lay well off, and I can use the shuttle to go in and investigate on my own. It just means an extra few days, and if overwhelming unfriendlies show up, you can scram and leave me there." He paused a moment, then added, "Of course, if you're willing to fully participate, there's definitely the possibility of salvage, maybe even a takeover claim here. I'd like to have us work as a team, but I can't force you. The point is, if I go in alone, I'll be going in as an agent of the Guardians, not the team; anything of value that I find will become the property of the state. But if the team participates as part of the normal response to a distress signal, then the team will have a claim on anything that turns up."

"Unless we get stiffed, we're going to get a potload of money as our fee on the Hot Plant," Jimmy McCray pointed out. "The only thing more dangerous than a First Team operation is a rescue mission. If we'd failed at the Hot Plant, or if this was another team in trouble, I'd be more inclined to do whatever was needed than going after a government research vessel when I'm due a big pay."

"You'll get paid, McCray," Modra said flatly. "It's a point, Tris."

"All right, then, I go alone. But while the Hot Plant fees will free us from First Team work and allow us to spruce up *Widowmaker* and maybe have a good time someplace, that's all it'll do. We'll still be a subsidiary operation—employees." He looked straight at Modra on that one. "I should think we might like to be our own bosses at the next level."

"The point is well taken," the Durquist admitted. "Although, having experienced the first really good luck this team has ever had, I feel unease at testing it too far."

"There's security in being a subsidiary," Modra pointed out. "Besides, the likelihood of anything being there that's really worth much is pretty slim."

"Perhaps," said Trannon Kose thoughtfully. "But I am not a great believer in luck, good or bad, and I have to wonder why they kept this one for themselves instead of putting it up for Exchange auction. And with Tris's position we'll be able to call on the whole navy if need be to back us up."

Jimmy McCray shrugged. "We have to go there anyway. Why not?"

"I do what Jimmy say," Molly piped up.

Lankur looked them over. "Durquist?"

"Oh, why not? We may be having a streak."

"I say no," Modra said firmly.

"I make it three, maybe four, to one," Lankur responded. "This team is going in as a team. Modra, if you want to skip it, just give us a release that you have no claim on what we find and stay aboard."

She sighed. "No, I'm in. I just was wondering what the hell you said to a demon."

Book Two:

Mizlaplan: The Gold Team

The Game Of Martyr
And Murder

The Grand Game

Even after all this time, it was still unsettling to step
from a spaceship into a horse-drawn carriage.

The cabbie, a middle-aged cherub with muttonchop
whiskers and a cherry-red, bulbous nose that stood out
all the more because of his tiny, deep-set eyes, viewed
his potential fare with some distaste. This fellow was
simply not the sort that ever strayed from the spaceports,
and certainly not on this world. If he was going
somewhere on business, he sure didn't dress to impress,
either.

The passenger was of medium height but seemed
larger; a fellow with a commanding presence, although
not of the sort that also commanded respect. He was
a muscular sort, thin but not looking it; dark, orange-
brown skin and Mongol-like features, but with what
appeared to be a three-day growth of full beard of the
density not associated with Mongol types. That feature
alone made him look grungy and not quite right, but
added to it was shoulder-length jet-black hair that badly
needed combing, loose-fitting cotton shirt and pants
that appeared to be what he not only wore daily but
also what he slept in, and neglected fingernails as long
as claws. Nor, of course, did his incongruous and
unnerving steely blue eyes indicate a purity of ethnic
back-ground, although spacing tended to be a family
enterprise and minor mutations weren't all that
uncommon. He even smelled a bit—well, foul—and

fungus, grasses, and the rest, but he was not readily
available even in the low places where smoking was

163

the cabbie wondered if he should take this fellow and risk having to fumigate the cab.

The strange man stopped at the cab door, looked up, and said, "Sainte Gree, cabbie."

The cabbie's bushy eyebrows rose in surprise. "But that is a Holy Retreat!"

"I know. Take the long, scenic route, too, if there is one. I've been cooped up inside a can for a very long time and I need to breathe clean air and see green land and blue sky and horizons without walls."

With that, the spacer got in and settled back in his seat and the cabbie sighed, resigned, and flicked the reins to start off.

It was an open coach, although most cabs were covered; when you waited at or near the spaceport in fair weather like today or the most foul weather, you did so with open coaches for just the reason the grungy passenger had given. You had to love space to keep at that sort of job over the years, but there was something in the human psyche that craved clean air and openness, and when they got the chance they wouldn't take a covered or cloistered ride for anything if they could help it. Every cabbie had tales of spacers sitting in the open, getting soaked through and seeming to enjoy every miserable moment of it.

Still, few of them ever looked as grimy as this fellow; they always dressed up when they made a planetfall. And he couldn't remember any of them ever being interested in visiting a Holy Retreat no matter what they looked like.

The spacer relaxed and sank into the cushioned seat, stretched his legs, then reached inside his tunic and pulled out a battered old case from which he took a long, fat cigar. It was another example of the man's totally antisocial appearance; almost no one smoked, both for health reasons and because tobacco was not readily available even in the few places where smoking was permitted. Spacers, however, did develop some bizarre and even disgusting habits, taking advantage of the dispensations awarded for the kind of life they led.

About half an hour from the spaceport most things modern had been left behind. The road was well-built and maintained, but it was hard-packed dirt, with covered bridges over the rivers and streams. The lush green forest was all around, but now and again there were breaks where he could see rolling hills and neat farms, often with grazing livestock. Out here, nothing was motorized, nothing was powered except by wind, water, or muscle, and nothing at all was prefabricated except the society itself.

He had come from such a society himself. The world was different, the land and climate, vegetation and animals, were different, yet it shared a certain simple sameness with all the other worlds of the Mizlaplan.

One People, One Faith, One Way was easier said than done, particularly the latter, when there was so much distance between and so many differences among the people of the Holy Empire and their worlds, but it was far more consistent than not. One needed only to make allowances for local differences.

The credo was, in fact, comforting to those who lived under it; a unity of culture that included the exact same set of beliefs, language, and attitudes no matter how far from home you strayed.

This world was Terran, like himself; however, other worlds he went to within the Empire were the homes of people with scales, people with tentacles, people who looked like lizards, people who looked like rocks, and people who looked like nothing else had ever looked. To the Mizlaplan, the evolutionary origin of one's species and its biology was irrelevant. Many diverse races, yet One People. That was pretty impressive.

"How far is it to the retreat?" he called to the driver after a while.

"Fairly far, sir. Another thirty or forty minutes at least."

He felt no guilt at taking the cabbie so far out of town; it was the man's function to do this, just as his function was to be the captain of the *Faith of Gorusu*, a position he had inherited at least partly on merit and after years of hard work and service. He had been selected for his career after the Examinations at age twelve, and had been sent off to the Space Academy on his thirteenth birthday. After ten years of intensive study and indoctrination in a rigid, monastic setting, with few trips home to visit relatives and no other breaks, he'd been commissioned and assigned as junior on a freight scow going from nowhere to noplace in particular. He hadn't gone home at all after that; his trips home had become less and less frequent with each year away, anyway. That world was a primitive one of nomadic herdsmen in a cold, harsh climate; his world was now computers and high technology, and he and his people no longer had much of anything in common except their genes.

Over the years, too, his competence and abilities had allowed him far too much latitude; they called ones like him bilge rats, from some ancient scourge no longer understood in its historical context. He had become jaded, lax in his personal appearance and habits, a real slob. He knew it was mostly rebellion at all those years of straight-laced conformity, but he didn't care. He'd been to a thousand worlds, seen much of what there was to see. He'd even been over to the heathen—the Mycohl Empire and the Exchange. The former was always a chilling experience; the latter totally unnerving with its accent on the accumulation of wealth, its freewheeling no-morals societies and its totally materialistic and chaotic bent. About the only thing the Mycohlians and the Mizlaplan had in common, culturally, was the inability to conceive of anybody actually living in the domain of the Exchange—rootless, foundationless, with nothing and no one but yourself to rely on even in the midst of a city or town.

All three empires, of course, had other things in common. He could remember well the first time he'd seen Terrans not unlike himself who were not of the Mizlaplan, and how people of the same genetic stock could be more alien to one another than those of other racial stock and other worlds.

Terrans were not, of course, the only races to overlap, but they seemed the largest such group. Spacefaring races who'd broken free of their own worlds and spread out and established rather large realms and thought themselves the lords of creation until, of course, they'd run into the Mizlaplan, or the Mycohl, or the Exchange. Space geometry and bad luck had put his own ancestors in the path of all three, with the result that the last thing one could ever trust was form and race.

He'd been somewhat irritated when the orders for this mission had come in. When a captain took on cargo it was an obligation, and having to dump it off enroute and beg other ships to take it was something he hated doing, but you didn't ignore these kinds of orders.

Discovering that most of the Arm was in retreat out here hadn't been helpful, either, considering that the mission sounded urgent. When the Holy Ones were in their retreats, they were cut off from all things modern, which meant a buggy ride in the country and person-to-person contact. This one smelled particularly unpleasant, too. He much preferred the standard missions, where they were checking out a newly discovered world and evaluating its potential and finding its hidden dangers, or perhaps a fragmentary colony, never absorbed into one of the three great empires, that had to be brought into the Mizlaplan fold before it fell into the hands of the heathen and was corrupted.

The cabbie finally couldn't resist some conversation. "You work with the Holy Ones?" the driver asked, trying to imagine a fellow who looked like that amongst saints.

"I do, when they need me," he replied. "As to why they picked a character like me, I couldn't say, if that's your thinking. They say I give 'em perspective. They spend most of their times in the spiritual world or among the goodfolk, like yourself. I'm a jarring, ever-present reminder to them of what people might become if they don't do their jobs right."

The cabbie half turned, then thought better of it, although he really wanted to get some indication of whether or not his passenger was joking.

They came around a bend and suddenly the Holy Retreat was spread out below them in a shallow, wide valley. The captain had never seen a Holy Retreat before, and he was impressed by the manicured lawns, wooded areas, and impressive facilities. It appeared they would come in by a large athletic field and track that looked as good as any he'd seen; off to one side was a large outdoor swimming pool, along with a number of smaller pools, which, from the rising wisps of steam, suggested hot springs beneath. The place itself was laid out with a large but rustic-looking temple in the center, with dorms and support buildings constructed of wood in a similar style. Had it not been a religious place, he wouldn't have minded spending a week or so there.

There weren't a lot of people around, but those who were seemed to be having fun. It was comforting to see that the saints also had fun now and again, at least to the limit of their own restrictions.

"Is there an angel in residence?" he asked the cabbie.

"Oh, yes, sir," came the response with obvious pride. "I, myself, pray to the Venerated One who is here, dwelling within the main altar of that very temple there."

The captain looked, a bit awed himself at that news, even though there was nothing more to see. He was a cynical, worldly man, a professional sinner and he knew it, but he was nonetheless a true believer. All save the saints lived in sin and would die in sin, and there was no way out of that except the mercy and forgiveness of the gods through their chosen vessels of perfection, the angelic Lords of the Mizlaplan.

For him, any more progress toward salvation would have to wait until the next life at least, since the very thing that was extremely unusual about him and made him the choice of the Arm of Faith, for its work prevented him from ever attaining sainthood in this life. Perhaps that was why he had turned out the way he did. Everybody had at least a crack at instant cleansing and perfection; everybody except the very few who were like him. In older times the people had declared those like him accursed, agents of evil, and had killed them, but the later interdiction by the Venerated Ones had saved him and others from that fate, although he'd had to work triple all his life to prove his devotion and faith.

There really was no choice for a logical man. Those races and people of the Exchange paid lip service to a million different gods and deities, almost all clearly invented by cultures in their own images to fit their own needs. Many, if not most, of the people had no real religious beliefs at all.

The Mycohl, on the other hand, worshiped the forces of evil and darkness and served them, for they were a constant, and although it was difficult to see what that had profited them and certainly it wasn't any sort of life he'd ever want for himself, at least it was consistent. People there followed the dark way because they were born into it and raised in it. Those of the Mizlaplan had no doubts or questions, no chaos and no rituals to dark gods who ignored them and did little or nothing in return except give them a lifetime of fear. Quite probably most of them, deep down, had no more commitment or true belief in their deities than did the Exchange, but at least there was no confusion.

Here, though, within the Mizlaplan, no logical person could doubt the truth of his own beliefs and system. Not when true angels lived amongst the faithful and dispensed justice and mercy and were accessible to high and low alike on a day-to-day basis through the saints.

The coach traveled down to the campus, then followed a road alongside the running track, and both he and the cabbie, ordinary mortals, looked over at the saints. The common folk, like the two of them, wore plain baggy clothing that covered them completely; the women wore long, mostly plain dresses as well and little in the way of adornment, to keep down the temptations of the flesh and promote equality rather than envy no matter what their position. The saints, however, presented quite a different picture, having been cleansed of sin and also made incapable of committing future sins.

Not all the sanctified looked as good as these specimens, but these were the cream of the crop, perfect people; the men all strong and virile and handsome—models of male physical perfection; the women equally strong but stunningly, naturally beautiful, the image of female physical perfection to match the perfection of their souls. Their clothing tended to be close-fitting, often revealing, for they had nothing at all to hide nor were they ever capable of succumbing to temptation.

The cabbie looked with a sigh at a particularly gorgeous, buxom beauty who wore nothing but a skintight pullover and short shorts for running around the track: "I must admit I hate to come up here," he told the captain. "Sights like that awaken in me the most sinful thoughts, and sights like those rippling male muscles there arouse envy within me, and in spite of myself, I keep thinking, 'what a waste.'"

The captain smiled. He knew exactly what the fellow was talking about but it was in his sinful nature to twist knives occasionally, just for the evil pleasure in it.

"Are you suggesting that they are wasted? That becoming a saint and attaining perfection of mind and body is somehow wrong or sinful? They are examples for us to try and emulate, my good man. Their physical perfection is a gift from the gods for this purpose. Are you suggesting that the ways of the gods are somehow wrong?"

"No, no, good sir!" the cabbie responded, suddenly defensive. "The gods placed our souls in these corrupt bodies, and it was that which was talking. Not being perfect, I cannot always control what it speaks to me."

The captain laughed. "Calm down and be at peace, fellow! I often feel the same way myself. I was just having a bit of fun, that's all. Try being cooped up for long periods in a spaceship with one or more women who look like everything your animal ego ever fantasized in its most sinful moments, and know that they are unattainable. Early on I feared I might go mad, and even now it is by compromise in my mind that I survive it. Tell me—are you married?"

"Yes, sir. Thirty years next spring."

"Well, do you love her, then?"

"Of course I do!"

"Any children?"

"Six, sir. Two boys and four girls—mostly grown now but the sort that make you proud."

"Why, then, perhaps you should stop feeling quite so much guilt at what you cannot have and dwell on what you do, which is in its own way as wonderful as what the saints have. Reason tempers the commission of sin."

They pulled up in front of a low, wooden, lodge-type structure and the captain got out and thanked the driver and then climbed the stairs. No money changed hands and no transaction was recorded anywhere; such things did not exist in the domain of the Mizlaplan. Each person worked at what the theocratic bureaucracy determined they were best qualified to do, and each person had equal drawing rights on the labor of others. In a domain, even one that was spread over countless light-years, where Church and State were one and all people were in close association with others and with the Church itself, there was no slacking, just as there could be no fundamental disagreements.

That, in fact, was what people like him were good for. Removed from the omnipresent communal and social system and its constantly judgmental people, he felt less pressure and more his own man. Such individualism was a sin in Mizlaplan society, and a grave one, but it could be tolerated with a smudged conscience if the individual was useful and in the service of the System.

This was basically a Terran retreat: it wasn't that other races were not welcome and treated as equals, but just that each one had different physical requirements and different needs, from food to waste disposal, from how they might exercise to how they might comfortably rest. Morok the Holy Ladue, for example, who was Arm commander, was a *Stargin*, a birdlike and hollow-boned creature who was quite fragile under some conditions and who in any case would prefer a retreat on a world where flight was possible. He would pick up Morok along the way, where the commander was taking leadership courses at Grinshin Starbase. The Klees, being *Leburs* and not any more holy than he, were the other two parts of his permanent ship's crew and remained behind at the spaceport.

There were, however, a few other races represented here; those who could share in and use the facilities as well as Terrans.

There was always something unsettling about being around the saints, particularly ones you didn't know. Behind the main desk, for example, sat a big, bronzed fellow with rippling muscles and perfect hair who, like the others around here, looked just too good to be true. Few of the billions of people of the Mizlaplan knew of or comprehended genetic engineering; to the captain, it was a given, and in places like this it gave him a secret, guilty pleasure to discover that even these examples of perfection had to work hard to keep looking that way.

The captain stopped in front of the man, bowed slightly, noting that the little finger of the receptionist's left hand was metallic green in color, with a red band at the knuckle—a levitator, of no particular concern to others—then said, "Captain Gun Roh Chin, of the *Faith of Gorusu*, Holy One. I am commanded to interrupt the retreats of Savin the Holy Peshwa, Krisha the Holy Mendoro, and Manya the Holy Szin. An Arm of Mizlaplan is commanded to assemble immediately."

The man looked the captain over with the same sort of distaste and urge to run for the disinfectant that the cabbie had shown. It was simply not done to show up like this, and it was almost never done that one of the common folk, rather than one of The Holy, would arrive to summon a saint. Still, there was no questioning this arrival. A command of the gods was a command, and no ordinary person would dare come here unless ordered to do so by the gods themselves.

The big man jotted down the names on a pad. "Very well. Take a seat over there, Captain, and wait. I will have to look up where your people might be and then dispatch runners to find them."

"As you command, Holy Sir. However, with your permission, I should prefer to wait outside rather than in here. When one spends most of his life confined within metal walls, he is eager for whatever open space and fresh air he can get."

"Certainly. Go ahead. Just do not wander far, since I will summon them here." Unspoken was his evident relief in not having to contend with this filthy character in his squeaky clean entry room.

Chin went out and sat for a few minutes on the wooden steps, just taking in the peaceful view. He pulled out another cigar, bit off the end, then lit it with a battered lighter, which had once been engraved handsomely but now was so faded and bent and worn that little intelligible remained. Smoking was not, strictly speaking, a sin, but it was frowned on by polite—which meant all—Mizlaplanian society, as well as being a known health hazard. As such, it was the perfect statement to make without getting hauled off before a church behavioral committee.

The captain knew that it probably was not just his looks and manner that had disturbed the manager. Most likely the manager was a telepath, able to read at least the first-level thoughts of anyone else except another telepath—and a telepath could always tell another by the unique feeling of blocking. To such a one, to *any* telepath, Gun Roh Chin would be horribly disturbing, simply because the telepath would have one sense removed. Chin would be standing there, could be seen, heard, felt, touched, but to a telepath, he would be psychically dead. Chin was not a telepath and could not block one; he was an island, official category Cipher. Therein lay his value to the system, for Ciphers were the rarest of the mental mutations known.

There were quite a number of people with various paranormal powers; it had come from the old days, from the spacefaring units who had spent year after year in ships, subject to unknown forces and radiations, rotated slightly into alternate universes to bypass the rigid speed of light.

Long-term radiation had produced many changes, some positive, some not, and some merely cosmetic. Those with similar changes had tended to inbreed and create, in effect, sub-races. The physical, however, was not the major attribute that caused so much attention, but the mental. Selective breeding here, too, had created sub-races that were physiologically the same as others but who had some kind of mental power or ability not found among normal folk.

Savin was a *Mesok*, a huge humanoid creature, with a hard, rubbery reptilian skin, nasty yellow eyes like some giant cat's, with big, bony hands whose fingers and toes ended in suckers at their tips, and big, bony, dish-like ears that seemed glued to the top of his angular head. He was a fearsome-looking one, all green and black, with enormous teeth that showed even with his mouth closed. The very sight of him was as intimidating as a vision of Hell.

Savin was also an empath; it was nearly impossible to deceive him, for he could sense and read your emotions and could transmit to a degree. He could calm a panic, whip up a mob, or make you feel very happy with yourself. He could also sense any falsehoods or guilt. Empaths made the best preachers, theologians, and psychologists, and were essential to an Arm.

Krisha was all too Terran, a dark-skinned black-eyed beauty who was also a telepath; how good a telepath, only she knew. The average telepath, and the only "official" telepaths, could read only surface thoughts and broadcast their own thoughts over limited distances. The best ones had a vast range of reading the minute energy from the thoughts of creatures beyond their own race, and often even the primitive thoughts of creatures not yet discovered but about to pounce on you on some alien world. No telepath, however, was supposed to be able to reach beyond the primary, or surface, thought waves, down to those inner things everyone thought and preferred to keep hidden. "Supposed" was the operative word, though; Chin had seen Krisha and other telepaths in actual physical contact with subjects appear to bore down to their very souls.

Security officers were always telepaths.

Manya was a *Gnoll*, a race that was quite alien but

looked Terran, at least to non-Terran races. Gnolls were short, squat, barrel-chested gnomes with snakelike forked tongues, huge pointed ears that stuck up on both sides of their heads, and with tough gray skin like an elephant's hide. But they and Terrans could eat the same foods, tended to share a liking for sweets, had similar biological systems, and weren't as far apart in an evolutionary sense as they seemed on the surface. Of course, while Manya wasn't any beauty queen to a Terran, she was most likely the epitome of female Gnoll physical perfection.

Morok, the Stargin who was the Arm commander, was the most feared of all creatures, a hypno, who could scan the broad band of countless alien wavelengths and, looking straight at you, could command your very will. Morok could convince you that up was down and red was black and that you were the Queen of the Fairies. Only a Cipher like Gun Roh Chin, or another hypno, could resist that unseen power, and if it was another hypno, it was then a matter of power and will. Hypnos were priests by definition and absolute commandment; any among the Mizlaplan who were not were satanic and to be summarily put to death—if you could.

Chin sat smoking his cigar and watching the passing parade with some amusement. The priests and priestesses, mostly Terrans, were the epitome of genetic engineering— perfect men, perfect women, beautiful people beyond all the fantasies of the ordinary-born like himself, and all had one or another of the Talents. He disconcerted Talents, and it always amused him.

That fellow there, for instance, stopping, giving him a mildly puzzled glance, then going on lest he call attention to his disadvantage and discomfort. You didn't have to see that the little finger of his left hand was tattooed with alternate black and white rings to know he was a telepath. Telepaths weren't all that directional, so they still depended first on the usual senses before directing their Talent at an individual. The priest had seen Chin, and probably unconsciously directed a query or stab at him, and come up a blank. Not blocked, as with another telepath—one of them could still feel another. To the fellow, born and raised a telepath, Chin had been the ultimate contradiction; a man clearly alive and clearly seen, yet from the telepathic viewpoint simply not there. Chin knew that before the day was out the poor man would go through every possible test of his telepathic powers and then go nuts trying to figure it all out.

That priestess, there—very nice, superlative looks even for one of the Holy Ones. She turned in, and although she could clearly see him, she almost walked over him. Only the odor of the cigar and a last-minute "Whoa, there!" from the captain kept her from taking a spill. She started, staring at him, obviously unnerved, and seemed about to say something, but then thought better of it and walked around him into the main building.

An empath, certainly. Little finger copper with small white banding. Empaths were always highly directional. Many people are pretty much unnoticed by others, and, with an empath, it was inconceivable that even if her mind was a million light-years away, her Talent wouldn't immediately tell her that someone was there. Nothing could block an empath, not even another empath. Therefore, to her, Chin simply had not existed. Perhaps she would be a bit more observant and not as lazy in the future. Certainly she would also go a bit nuts trying to figure it all out.

He had often wondered what it was like to have such powers, and particularly to grow up with them, take them for granted. Sure, they said a telepath could only read your surface thoughts, but it might be fun to be a bit of a Peeping Tom, even if it was a sin. He wasn't a priest; he had no "Holy" in his name. He was born a sinner and would die one, weighed on the Cosmic Scales to see which way his next incarnation would go.

And certainly being an empath would be quite handy when trying to pick up women; the rejection rate would be way, way down, and he'd know sincerity when he saw it, or project a bit of his own lust into the other. Carnal, sinful thoughts, just perfect for a religious retreat. It brought out the worst in him every time.

Being a hypno in the Mizlaplan wouldn't be so hot. The temptation was too great; that was why they were required by law to be sinless priests. Being a hypno was the subject of too many of his fantasies; if he were one, he'd surely reincarnate no more. He would burn in hellfire for eternity. With a price that high, leave the glazed eyes to Morok.

But of them all, his Talent, the rarest of the rare, one that they'd never successfully figured out how to breed, was the one he loved most. Ciphers, or nulls, were the only really secure people in the universe and the only ones who always slept soundly no matter how sinful their thoughts or deeds. His thoughts could not be read, his emotional state could be neither absorbed by another nor altered by design, and, most of all, a hypno would get his lights put out after trying anything with him. True, it wasn't perfect—drugs could make him spill everything, and a levitator more than once had taught him not to fool around with them, but, for the most part, they could have only his body, never his mind and feelings, and that felt pretty good.

And because his Talent was internal, affecting no one but himself, he had no mandatory identifier; his little fingers were unadorned and thus he could move amongst all the common classes of people easily, as one of them, while moving just as confidently amongst the Talents. Very few could do that, and it gave him a perspective and a freedom none of the others had.

And it drove all these people with their perfect bodies

and sinless minds, so accustomed to and dependent on their own extraordinary powers, absolutely stark, staring nuts.

The door opened behind him and he turned to see who it might be, then rose from his perch on the steps and bowed slightly at the sight of Krisha the Holy Mendoro.

Like the rest, she was beautiful. Tall, dark, with sparkling eyes and sensuous lips, with lush black hair cut short and a body men would kill for even though it was forbidden to them. She was fairly young, looking no more than in her mid or late twenties, although she was probably older than that, and her voice was firm and clearly used to confident command.

"You've been teasing the poor Shepherds again, haven't you, Captain?" she asked accusingly.

He shrugged and gave her a sheepish smile. "I was just enjoying the air and sky and a good cigar, Holy Mother, minding my own business. What reactions others might have *is* not my fault, surely."

Her eyebrows rose and you didn't have to be an empath to feel her skepticism at his reply, but she turned quickly to business. "What brings you here?"

"The Arm is commanded to assemble with all deliberate speed," he responded crisply. "Naturally I can't say more, even here, but once aboard I'll brief you. We'll pick up Morok on the way. I assume he'll already have more of the gory details than I have now. From what they gave me, though, it sounds like a nasty one."

She nodded. "Aren't they all? After being here a while and talking with the other priests and priestesses and hearing them excitedly describing adventures we would consider dull and routine, I often have wondered if when the Holy of Holies set the threads of our destinies in this incarnation, it was stipulated that we would get the worst of the worst."

Chin shook his head slowly from side to side. "No, it

isn't hat sort of destiny. We get the worst because we're good. Perhaps the best. All that will do for us in the end is send us to the next incarnation far earlier than most of the others here, but, until then, we are the best."

"Perhaps," she responded automatically. Pride was a sin and she could not sin, but was it pride or truth that he spoke? They always did seem to get the nastiest, most impossible assignments, and so far they had always performed.

He understood her problem with the prideful aspect of his statement and respected it, but he wasn't a holy anything and he felt tremendous pride in himself and the team and in their accomplishments. He also was dead honest with himself. He loved his work.

"Savin and Manya are coming?" he asked her.

She nodded. "They will meet us here as soon as they can get cleaned up and prepared. How did you get here?"

"Taxi from the spaceport. I assume we can get a ride back somehow when we're ready, although this isn't exactly on the regular taxi routes. If not, I can use the ship's communicator and have one of the Klees send a taxi out."

"No, that will not be necessary. I will go back to the desk and arrange for a cart. Someone will come and pick it up later."

He watched as she turned and did just that, and gave a sigh. It wasn't easy being around such a combination of beauty and brains on a no-touch basis, with the knowledge that you hadn't a prayer of ever scoring and that even attempting it would be a sin of the gravest sort. Still, it was sometimes handy if you could pick your confessor and did so judiciously. Somebody who'd tell you to cure your lusts by going out and getting laid. Now *that* was a penance he always religiously obeyed.

Savin the Holy Peshwa appeared, looking as monstrously

handsome as usual, teeth gleaming, pupils just tiny slits now in the bright sunlight. Like Krisha, though, Savin should never be underestimated. He was brilliant, if a bit cold, and a meticulous planner who usually thought of all the angles. The Arm's whip, he was its chief soldier and exceptionally good at it. They all were exceptionally good at what they did.

Behind him came a short, squat humanoid; a gnomelike creature with huge yellow eyes with catlike pupils that changed with the light, and a broad slit for a mouth, inside which, Chin knew, was a very large and very long reptilian forked tongue. The hairless body was elephantine gray, the hide tough enough to stop all but the most powerful arrow or spear, the huge ears rising up from the rounded face like giant leaves, but twitching and turning here and there. This was Manya the Holy Szin.

Manya wasn't all that strong and didn't move all that fast, but she had another rather uncommon Talent that had served her and the Arm quite well over time. She was what they called in the old speech a *chameleon*. If she wished, she could cloud the minds of all around her so that she would be, in effect, invisible—except, of course, to Gun Roh Chin, as well as machines, electronic cameras, and automatic sensors. It was one of the few traits that was not due to the mutations of early spacers; it had developed in a fair percentage of her race as a protective mechanism. So far, only the Gnolls were known to have this ability, and, also so far, there hadn't been another race, no matter how alien or on what brain wavelengths they operated, that it didn't work on. The Gnolls were a Mizlaplanian plus not shared by the other empires; they existed only within the Mizlaplan. This alone had saved them several times in encounters with those of the Mycohl and the Exchange. Many an opponent had failed to account for Manya, and paid the price of that lapse.

Krisha emerged to join the trio, and together they waited for a cart to be brought up. Aside from the usual polite amenities, there wasn't a lot of talk between them. They all knew each other all too well by this time as it was. None of the Holies really wanted to know what Chin had been doing since the last Call, and Chin knew he'd be bored to tears if he asked them the same question. Nor could he tell them anything he knew of the mission, as little as that was, until they were safely aboard and away from this world. This was an espionage matter, and one never knew if an enemy was about in such cases. If nothing was said here that might have the remotest chance of being overheard and reported, then there was no chance of alerting or spooking their prey.

Fairly quickly they heard a dull whine, and from around the back of the main building came a small electric cart with Spartan metal benches in back and an equally uncomfortable sculpted plastic driver's seat. The young priest who brought it bowed to them and then walked away without a word. Questions would have been improper and unseemly—and there would be no answers anyway, since it was none of his business.

The trio of Holies got in the back. There was no question who would drive; Chin ranked lowest of this group on any totem pole except in matters of ship command once aboard, and he didn't mind. Truth to tell, he preferred driving to being a passenger in a vehicle driven by somebody who was so confident of reward in the hereafter.

It took less time to get back by electric cart than it had to arrive by horse cart, even at the magnificent average speed of twenty kilometers per hour, and Chin went straight to the staff entrance. As they got out, a young woman came up and asked, "Will you be using the car again, Captain?"

"No," he responded. "It's all yours."

She got in and drove off, not back to the retreat but simply to a parking area. Somebody would be along to get it sooner or later, or somebody else would show up wanting to go out there. That was the way of things in the Mizlaplan. There was a shuttle waiting for them; he'd seen to that detail before going up to the retreat. As Spartan as the cart, but utilitarian, and fully automated. They got in, took seats, strapped themselves in, and the shuttle hissed, ran its self-tests, then lifted off as soon as clearance from the harbor-master's control computers was received. In forty minutes it was in orbit; ten minutes later it had maneuvered into position to dock with the *Faith of Gorusu*. The airlock interconnects hissed once again, the shuttle gave a gentle shudder, and then they all unstrapped and made for the hatch. Now the protocol was reversed; it was unthinkable to precede a captain aboard his own ship.

Mazarun Klee awaited them. She was a tall, slender Lebur, sleek, supple, with smooth gray skin. Leburs were totally hairless with huge, round black eyes in a thin, almost triangular head, with tiny black mouths and flat, flaring nostrils. Their huge hands each had three fingers and an opposing thumb, and they had equally huge flat feet. Somehow, these features combined to produce an exotic kind of beauty, and they were attractive even to humans.

"Cast off the shuttle and prepare to get under way as soon as harbor clearance gives the word," Chin said crisply. He ignored the Holies he'd gone to so much trouble to retrieve; he had work to do now and they didn't. Besides, they knew their way around the ship by now very well. So well, in fact, they'd required no luggage of any kind.

"Already in progress, Captain," Mazarun Klee responded, using a tiny radio that converted her strong telepathic speech to something audible that a null like himself could hear. The words had a sound to him like that of a beautiful, somewhat sexy human soprano, but that might have been the radio engineers' choice. The Lebur were one-way telepathic with all but their own kind; they could broadcast to a specific person or group, but could not receive any but their own kind's thoughts in return. Klee, of course, had ears, although no more than tiny holes on either side of her flat skull, and could hear and understand him—but the smaller Lebur males were totally deaf and dumb in the conventional sense, able to communicate, even hear, only telepathically among their own kind. Anthropologists said that the Lebur males never fully developed physically and really served only one purpose—even on their home worlds, they were dependent on the females for most things. Fortunately for the males, a Lebur female had to mate or die, and always mated for life.

Indeed, it was Kumazon Klee, Mazarun's husband, who was up on the bridge handling the routine. They might be small and weak, but there was nothing wrong with Lebur males' intelligence and Ku could read the screens and punch in the approval codes as easily as anyone else.

It was because Leburs quite literally had to mate that there were none in the priesthood, but because of their high culture, intelligence, and their strong sense of honor they were as common as humans in ship's crews and prized for their loyalty throughout the Mizlaplan.

"Grinshin Starbase in sixty-two standard hours, Captain," Mazarun told him. "Our sealed orders will be carried with Morok."

He nodded. "Very well." He always wondered about that sexy mental "voice" of hers. Was it actually hers, or was it only in his mind? It was like wondering whether different people actually saw color exactly the same. How could you know unless you could use another's eyes and brain? "Do we have a transfer point for the cargo?"

"No, sir. We'll have to carry what couldn't be unloaded here. It's nothing vital."

"And nothing useful," he muttered. "All right, let's get on with this. I want to see the charts and I want the inventory of the storage modules for the Arm. I do wish we had a medic aboard for this one, though. At least Manya has some lab training."

Mazarun's strange head turned toward him in surprise. "You think we will need one?"

"I think we're going to be treading into a Mycohlian quagmire. I can feel it. The fuel warrants show we've got a long trip, and the added inventories and specific questions I was asked indicate something really nasty."

"We've taken on the Mycohl before."

Chin nodded. "And never come away totally unbloodied. Although I'm quite fond of my body and my position in life, I'm willing to risk it time and again in the surety that at least my soul is safe. Criminals, madmen, revolutionaries, and new alien worlds don't as much bother me as excite me. You know that. But with the Mycohl, even the purest amongst us can lose his or her very soul. Don't forget that, Mazarun. Our previous encounters have been mostly straight up—them against us—for some new speck of dirt somewhere, and that's been bad enough. But I've just got a bad feeling about this one, that's all. Maybe I'm developing into a Predictor."

Actually, his hunches were based not on any paranormal powers but on long experience. The additional inventories, the kinds of weapons, testing and lab equipment, the nature of the reference tapes, the additional security systems on everything having to do with the ship and records, even the amount of fuel allocated—all painted a picture clear enough that he didn't have to have any special power to figure out what was what.

Facing a powerful galactic empire, where good was evil and evil good, where up was down and wrong was right, was bad enough. But when such a civilization was run by demonic spirits who could be literally anybody, not clearly defined in form as were the angels of the Mizlaplan, well, being pure in heart just didn't cut it at all. And although he was a believing man, as they well knew, he was hardly pure of heart, now or ever.

It took three days for him to reach the starbase and pick up the last of the Arm. Morok the Holy Ladue came aboard with his usual brusque manner, barely nodding to the captain and the Arm. Birdlike and hollow-boned, with long, clawed hands at the end of great rubbery gray-black wings that, folded, appeared like some kind of demonic cloak, his bullet-shaped head appearing to be all mouth and sharp teeth so that you missed the tiny but penetrating red eyes, the Stargin was at once fierce-looking and frail on his long spindly legs, one of which bore the metallic blue and gold bands that marked him as a hypno.

Nor was Morok ever particularly happy to be back aboard ship, or in most places other than in regions of low or zero gravity. Stargin were not one of the more common races, and Chin's occupation had never taken him to one of their few worlds, but he knew that on those worlds the Stargin used their wings to fly and enjoyed such freedom, it was a living hell for Morok to spend most of his time under conditions more comfortable to bipedal creatures. He was earning his place in a high Heaven by more than his mere position as High Priest and Arm Commander. He never complained, but his discomfort could be sublimated only so far, and the situation always made him a bit nasty.

Morok stopped, reached into a case he carried with him, pulled out a module with the most holy of seals and handed it to the captain. "Cast off quickly, Gunny. All speed," the Stargin said in that raspy, artificial voice of his that was the only way one of his race could form the sounds of common speech. "As soon as we make the jump to null-space I will want a conference of the Arm in the wardroom."

Chin took the module and bowed slightly. "As you command, Holy One," he responded, and turned and made his way swiftly back to the bridge.

Kumazon Klee had already disengaged from the starbase anchorage and was now taking the ship out and away, awaiting course and speed. The mute Lebur saw Chin come on the bridge through the bank of monitors in front of him, turned, and waited expectantly.

The captain wasted no time beyond a cursory check of the status screens to assure himself that all was correct—a habit, since the ship's computers really did the flying and Klee's job as helmsman was mostly to ensure that all was well and monitor ship's functions for possible mechanical problems. Then the module was inserted, seal intact, in the special input port to the right side of the bridge command chair. The port broke the seal, made the connection with the module, and then it was the module's turn to make certain that the ship was the correct one, the input port was the correct one, and through contact with the ship's computers to verify that only the personnel aboard were actually there and that all was well. If anything was amiss, Chin had one chance to answer satisfactorily any anomalies; if he couldn't, or it was definitely the wrong place, or things couldn't be fixed, then the module would dissolve and short out the ship's computer as well.

All, however, checked out, and the module then began dumping its instructions into the main computer of the *Faith of Gorusu*. Chin and Klee both stared at the main status monitor, waiting themselves to find out where they were going.

The ship began to move of its own accord, gaining speed and setting its course as it went. With all the programs now fed and verified, the screen signaled for

Chin to remove the module, which he did. The seal was burned away, but the module was still good for a single backup just in case they had problems on the way.

He reached over and quickly typed in the questions he wanted answered. The Mizlaplan could easily have built computers that talked, but in the interest of equality and out of deference to those races for whom hearing was a problem, they accepted manual input and projected screen data as an alternative. When Kumazon was on the bridge, as now, he always used that system.

On the screen the basics appeared almost instantly.

Destination: Medara, second from the star called only VX-2664-A. Colonization Project. Classification: frontier. Colonies: 1, prototypical. Inhabitants: 55, of whom the majority were Terran. Mission: prevent destabilization of colony by Mycohlian interlopers.

It was pretty far out. His chart had actually put it outside the Mizlaplan, in a sort of No Man's Land. In fact, the nearest habitable worlds were Mycohlian, as Chin had suspected. They never chose this team unless the job was particularly dirty.

The captain punched up what was known of the Mycohlian worlds. One Terran, which was bad, all things considered, one *Thion*, and one *Corithian*. He liked neither Thions nor Corithians particularly. Neither of them was represented within the Mizlaplan races and each of them was in its own way unpleasant, but at least now they would all know that the intruders would probably be Terran. The other two would stick out rather obviously in the small colony.

The three known empires—although neither the Mizlaplan nor the Exchange liked to think of themselves in those terms—covered more than a quarter of the galaxy at this point and contained, among them, over four hundred sentient, advanced races. Only a relative handful of races had any sort of spaceflight before being discovered and incorporated into one or another of the political giants, and fewer still had discovered the means to cheat light speed and become interstellar civilizations. And, of the latter group, only five existed in truly vast numbers, either because of the age of their interstellar civilization or because, like Terrans, they bred faster than a cold virus.

With almost three-quarters of an entire galaxy left to explore, each empire had different priorities. New civilizations and races were the primary aim of the Mizlaplan; they brought the Truth and Way of Mizlaplan to those ignorant of it, while protecting them from the venal and satanic ways of the other two empires. The Mycohl wanted to extend their power and control as far as they could, to impose their own harsh and brutal system on all they could seize, maybe just because such expansion fueled their empire and justified its kind of rule. The Exchange primarily sought new products and new ideas and new customers, although there was an underlying feeling that they had to protect anyone new from the other two systems.

And, of course, any world that was habitable by any race of the three had to be held, or it would be defaulted to the others. This was a matter of principle that extended even to worlds that were pretty well worthless, uninhabited pieces of rock. Chin thought of it as a kind of intergalactic game of *Go*, the ancient game of his own Terran people, where you had to take all the empty spaces and cut off your enemy. Expansion could never stop, lest your enemies capture all the space around your own vast empire and block it from expanding farther. If that ever happened to any one of the empires, while the other two kept expanding and growing, the cut-off empire would become depleted, lose its purpose, and begin to wither, eventually to be digested by the two victors.

And that was why a bunch of Mizlaplan were out on

a worthless chunk of rock trying to establish a colony. The Mycohl had been turning at that point in the frontier, beginning to threaten a flanking movement, cutting off an area of expansion. Medara was essential to the Mizlaplan not for what it was but for where it was.

And, as he looked at the star maps, that fact worried Gun Roh Chin the most. It was a very long way to the next inhabited Mizlaplan world, although there was nothing in between to speak of. Possession was most of the law in this grand game, too. Until the Mizlaplan scouts could discover another world in line beyond Medara in that direction, Medara had to be not merely claimed but held, possessed, inhabited. If they failed to establish a permanent colony there, someone else could claim it like an abandoned ship. Of course, treaties forbade the other empires from in any way influencing the success of a colonization effort, but everyone understood that this only meant not getting caught at it. An agreement between two empires could always force a decision on the third, so the Council of Empires could invoke penalties on one member if it got caught doing something forbidden by the treaties. On that one point, and in the self-interest of all three, alliance was possible.

The trick, then, particularly in a case like this, with one lone colony so close to enemy territory being defended by the inhabitancy of a mere fifty-five souls, was not to get caught. The Mycohl were good at that.

And the sacred duty of the Arm was to catch them red-handed and present them on a silver tray to the Council.

Gun Roh Chin sat back in his command chair a moment and sighed. As nervous as he always was going into one of these situations, and knowing the odds and the fearsomeness of the enemy, he still couldn't help it.

He loved this job.

Unwelcome Guest

Morok The Holy Ladue got right down to business.

They were all there in the wardroom: the fearsome-looking Savin, the beautiful Krisha, the wizened Manya, and Captain Chin. Mazarun Klee was also there, though not as a member of the Arm. In an emergency, she and her husband might be the only hope of getting out a message or summoning help, and so they had to know what the rest were supposed to do.

Morok opened with the traditional prayer, "May the Gods of Mizlaplan and their Holy Angels watch over and guide their servants in this great task," then got immediately down to business.

"You have all read over the basics on this Medara and I do not have to tell you the geopolitical situation, I trust. Geographically, this insignificant dirt ball is essential to the continuance of our Holy Mission and the thwarting of satanic moves against us. It is always such places that acquire this importance, simply because of their lack of intrinsic value. Were this an inhabited world, we would be justified in bringing in whatever force we needed, but under the stupid games of the diplomats we cannot do so without it being interpreted as an accusation of impropriety and thus an insult to the Mycohl, which they could exploit. So, we are left to play the usual games with inadequate forces and personnel, and the stakes are very high. The forces of evil will stop at nothing on this one; we must be worthy indeed to prevail."

"Has an intrusion been deduced or merely suspected?" Krisha asked the leader.

"A Holy Inquisition has been mandated by conditions, although we've been watching and expecting something, naturally, almost from the start. Of the fifty-five people in the developmental colony, the only priest, Wu the Holy Li Tai, was found dead a week ago. It took this long for the report to get to us, and for us to be dispatched with all speed—alas. We shall probably learn nothing of importance about his death by the time we get there."

"He was murdered?" Savin asked, jotting down some note to himself on a pad.

"Probably, although it is reported as a natural death. It would be, of course. He was found slumped over his desk in his office. The official cause of death according to the colony medical officer is a burst blood vessel in the brain—a stroke, in other words. However, as you all know, that is one of the easiest causes of death to fake convincingly, and the forensic facilities in a colony of this size are limited, even if the medical officer had been an experienced coroner and not the usual internist they send to places like this. Manya, you won't have a lot of work at this point, but do your best."

The science officer nodded her massive head. "We can safely assume foul play, in any event. The first thing anyone would do would be to remove the saint. The Holy was, I presume, a telepath?"

Morok nodded. "Yes Not the only one in the colony, but, of course, the only incorruptible one. They also took advantage of the requirement that saints be cremated three days after death, knowing we could not possibly get there in time to see the body."

"I find the idea that he was murdered somewhat questionable as a starting assumption," Gun Roh Chin put in. "It seems to me that killing the only Holy One, knowing it will invoke an Inquisition, is the *last* thing you would do. You trade one local priest for many, all of whom, unlike the victim, are trained and empowered investigators. And if we find any evidence at all, we will be justified in bringing up whatever force and personnel we need. The possibility that this is in fact a natural death cannot be excluded."

"We exclude nothing, Captain," Morok responded curtly, "but if we go on the assumption that Wu *was* murdered, then your point is even better taken. It implies that the Mycohl no longer care if we come in— or, worse yet, that we are being lured in, either to be used in some nefarious way or possibly to certify that there is no foul play, or to make a rash accusation without sufficient evidence to take to the Council. Either of the latter two possibilities would be as good as giving them Medara by default. We cannot stay forever; a clean bill of health would give them free rein there for quite some time. An accusation we cannot make stick would wind up in the Council awarding Medara to Mycohl as our penalty for bringing a false charge. We did not intend to bring such a charge, but the damage is now done."

"What kind of damage?" Manya asked in her low, raspy voice.

"Our diplomats jumped to the same conclusions we have, but, alas, they blundered in bringing it up, ever so discreetly, with the Mycohl themselves. It was hoped," Morok said sourly, "that this might scare them off."

"And instead they went public," Savin guessed.

Morok's birdlike head bobbed in his gesture of affirmation. "Either they saw the blunder and capitalized on it, or they counted on it and we fell right into their trap. They denied any improprieties, naturally, and made a great deal of indignant fuss almost at once. They went immediately and loudly public in the chambers, challenging us to prove our allegations or to withdraw them, giving us no choice but to make a formal protest."

"Uh-oh," Krisha said, shaking her head in disgust. "Then he better had have been murdered, and we better prove it."

"Indeed," Morok responded. "And that, Captain, is why we begin and end with foul play. Thanks to our own diplomatic stupidity, they have been able to invoke the Munchang Treaty, putting us in an impossible position. They have gone on record actually *urging* an investigation to clear their good name and they have further demanded that, as the Treaty allows, an outside observer be appointed to ensure our fairness!"

They were all suddenly upset except the captain, who kept his silence and merely watched, and Krisha, who seemed thoughtful.

"That is intolerable!" Savin cried angrily. "To have an *alien*, a *heathen*, looking over our shoulder, making decisions for reasons of its own—No! Who knows what motives such a one might have? They would be as much an enemy as the one we seek!"

"Sacrilege," Manya rasped. "This is an Arm of the Gods! We act not just on our own but as the extensions of the Lords of Creation! What if this—*creature*, this—*heathen*—ahead reverse our finding? It is giving Hell an absolute veto over the gods! Such a thing is irreconcilable with our own holy infallibility!"

Morok's birdlike head listened impassively to the arguments and pleas, and waited for the din to die down. Finally, unfazed, he said, "The arguments are correct and well taken, but they have already been argued before a Grand Council of the Mizlaplan itself. Theologically, it was rightly determined that, as an Arm, we act with supernatural aid. Are the heathen not also subject to the ultimate will of the gods? If not, why do we try and convert them? Are they not of the same seed as the majority of the Mizlaplan, ignorant of the truth and as such given to allow Hell equal weight, yet hardly damned. If we do the work of the gods, then the gods must also be trusted to have influence over the observer. That was how the treaty was enabled and how our ancestors could agree to it in the first place, and, overall, it has worked out well."

"But a *heathen*!" Manya was livid.

"It is not as bad as all that," Morok soothed. "In several hundred such cases, when the Exchange has had no stake in the outcome, they have virtually always come down on our side. They are not a pleasant people nor from a pleasant culture, but something in their souls impels them towards the side of the gods when it is us versus the satanists. They resist us, perhaps even fear us, but they truly dislike the Mycohl. It might even be argued that the Observer works in our favor. We only have to prove interference; by virtue of their protestations of innocence and ignorance of this affair, the Mycohl do not even get to testify."

"Unless," the captain noted, "the fellow really dropped dead of natural causes."

He drew icy stares but otherwise silence.

Krisha alone among the clerics had not argued. Now she said, "There is no use in arguing, nor in raising false fears. We have to accept the Observer; to do otherwise would be to hand the world to the Mycohl by default. It seems clear to me that we have a nearly impossible task as it is and will need supernatural aid. From what I hear, I am convinced that this was in fact a plot; that they perceived a weakness in our legation and exploited it. Commit one murder sure to bring suspicion and a reaction, as the captain said. Then draw our people into making an accusation, forcing us to prove murder by their agencies, under conditions where that is next to impossible, or to surrender the planet without a shot. It is diabolically clever; exactly what I would expect from them."

"Do we know who the Observer will be?" Savin asked uncomfortably.

"I have his name and dossier," Morok responded, as the others continued to seethe but kept silent They had no choice but to accept; the decision had been made by Divine Council. The gods themselves had accepted, and so, as far as they were concerned, had decreed the Observer, and above all else the gods must be obeyed. "It's probably phony, of course. The Observers are supposed to be disinterested judges, usually political officers or diplomats, but *we* never send an amateur when we are requested to send an Observer, and we assume the same of them. We can expect this Observer to actually be someone from the espionage or military branch, who will be most interested in our methods and attempt to build information for his own side from our investigation. Captain, you have been an Observer, have you not?"

All eyes turned to Gun Roh Chin, who sighed and nodded. "Yes, Holy One. Twice. Needless to say, neither of the others will accept a cleric from us, since how could any of you rule in favor of Mycohl?"

That seemed to shock them. "Could you do so, Captain?" Krisha asked, finding it inconceivable.

"I can and I have, in one of the two cases," Chin responded, seeing the expressions and enjoying them. "My oath and my honor required it no matter what my personal revulsion A particularly clever Exchange corporation, which coveted a new and rather unpleasant world for certain unique products possible there, spent a great deal of time and money creating the appearance of an indigenous and invisible alien life form that slowly and methodically wiped out a Mycohl hive—that's what they call their political-tribal groups. It was a brilliant and insidious plan, particularly ugly in operation, whose motive was sheer greed, the ultimate curse of the Exchange and its culture. My presence and status allowed the Mycohlian operatives at the Exchange to gather the evidence, and on the world itself I was then able to observe a clever trap laid with knowledge that presented me with sufficient evidence to certify the Mycohlian accusations. It was most unpleasant, but an education."

"To cause the death of satanists is no evil, no matter what the motive," Manya rasped. "To find for the Mycohl is to serve evil!"

The captain was unruffled. "Neither my Holy Lords nor the Exchange saw it that way, nor do I," he responded calmly. "I was taught that personal honor and oaths before the gods are inviolate, the highest standards. To have lied or condoned mass murder knowingly would have violated both of those and made me no better than the Mycohl. Such are the tests the gods give us, or so I was instructed. To have found against evil, no matter what my personal feelings, would have made me indistinguishable from the satanists. Such rulings are difficult, knots that defy tidy untying. That is why judges are so often necessary, and why they are so well respected and live such stressful lives."

"The captain is quite correct," Morok told them. "It is why he is so valuable, and why such as he are members of the Arms even though not of the clergy. We must never lose sight of the fact that the souls of the Mycohl are the souls of the damned, continually reborn into evil, beyond any hope of redemption, but always attempting to gain more converts to their sort. It took great courage for the captain to go in there at all, to be totally surrounded by a demonic society, and not to fall into their masters' moral trap. Captain, it will be your task, as one who has been in that position, to keep the Observer straight and to the task, to facilitate his job, while also making certain he learns nothing but what he is sent to observe."

Chin nodded. "I understand perfectly. This is not done every day, you know. Requests for Observers are extremely rare. It is likely that I can quote chapter and verse of the treaty language better than this fellow can. Besides, it is far easier to work with Exchange people than the Mycohl. The folk of the Exchange are merely lost or directionless souls; they are not necessarily damned." He sighed. "So when do we pick this fellow up?"

"The arc of the routing to Medara takes us at one brief point to the closest intersection with an Exchange region," Morok told him. "At that point we will effect the Observer's transfer to this vessel, then proceed directly to Medara with no other stops or delays."

Chin nodded. "I know the point. That would be in, oh, three and a half days, give or take a few hours. Holy Manya, I know your distaste, but you must give him a thorough and complete examination before we reach our destination. Just as the Mycohl will accept no clergy from us, so we accept no cymols from the Exchange. I should not like a cymol loose on this ship, let alone on a colony of ours, and it is quite a temptation each time for them to try and slip one in on us."

Manya's great head turned toward him, and she said, "I'll have no soulless monsters in our holy presence. No matter what tricks they try, I am better. I personally hope they *do* try something like that. Then we can with full right and justification atomize the creature and not be burdened with this Observer nonsense."

"Be cautious, yes, but correct," Morok warned her, and the others as well. "Remember that unless we can catch the Mycohl in the act and force a confession, the future of this world will depend on us convincing the Observer. If we begin by making an enemy of the Observer, making him dislike and distrust us, then we help the Mycohl and make our task even less likely to succeed. Indeed, if we lose this because of *our* mistakes, we may forfeit divine intervention and aid. I don't say you have to love him, but treat him with the respect due his position."

Krisha looked around the table. "If we are to assume that the death was murder, that the Mycohl are doing something to make the colony fail, then we must also assume that they factored in the Observer."

"It would strengthen their claims of innocence if the colony failed," Chin noted. "A clean bill of health from an independent Observer, perhaps a finding that it was strictly a local crime, would give them a free hand to force our public humiliation. Even if we failed, there are scores of legalistic and diplomatic dances possible, but if the Observer comes down with a definite finding of no intervention, we are out in the cold in a very big hurry."

Morok's head bobbed in agreement. "Exactly."

"Have you considered that one of our own might truly have gone mad and done this deed, and that the Mycohl are just capitalizing on it?" Savin asked them.

"Unlikely," Morok replied. "The prize is too tempting for them not to make a takeover attempt, as we might well have done in reversed circumstances. This was already taken into consideration before we raised the point with the Mycohl."

Krisha frowned. "What I cannot understand," she said, "is why this was not anticipated. We must be growing lazy and lax in our duties. Our best counterintelligence people should have been there from the start, and our best military scientists."

"They were," Morok assured her. "At this point we are called in only because it is a priest who died in mysterious circumstances, not because of local request or need. In fact, I expect some resentment among on-site personnel, since we will, by our very presence, be usurping their function and presenting them with a new layer of higher-ups to answer to."

"If any resent the Arm, they are blasphemous," Manya snorted. "They should rejoice that the gods have sent us."

"Manya, if the common folk of the Mizlaplan were perfect and free from temptation and sin, there would be no need for such as we," Morok noted, "nor would there be need for more incarnations. The Assumption would be at hand. You are very good at what you do, Manya; none better in my humble opinion, but you have blind spots as a minister of the True Word. We are dealing with fallible, corruptible people, people who have not the armor to withstand sin but who want to do the right thing. They need us, but their sinful natures and godly wills are always in conflict. We are at war, not with the other great powers, but against the one great Power that is not flesh and blood, and against which ordinary folk, no matter how brilliant or well-educated or noble, are powerless without our aid. We must all be mindful to deal in what is, not what we would like it to be."

Gun Roh Chin listened to their wrangling and had sinful thoughts, since he felt very happy to be himself and not one of the Holies. That in itself was somewhat blasphemous, because their incarnation was the second-highest possible within the physical universe, and a level his own soul would have to attain at some point, to achieve eventual heavenly perfection. To be incapable of sinning was not the same as having a sinless soul. Only the Holy Angels, the physical angels of the Mizlaplan, were totally free of sin. He was resigned to the fact that he was probably as high as he was going to get right now, and since the Assumption could not come about until all who were capable of attaining perfection had done so, he was inevitably damned somewhere down the pike. It gave him a certain fatalism, but it made life easier to live.

Normally, each member of the Arm remained alone in his or her own cabin except for meals and discussions, praying and studying the materials for the mission, but they were all curious enough to emerge and gather near the main airlock when the ship slowed and stood by to pick up the passenger that no one wanted.

The Observer came in a Mizlaplan naval vessel, which docked and immediately prepared for transfer. The airlock seals were made, there was much hissing and a bit of groaning that would make many people nervous but which the captain understood was normal, then the airlock signal switched to "EQUALIZED—OPEN" and Gun Roh Chin pressed the release on his side and the lock swung back.

First in was a middle-aged naval officer, a *Zrubek*—tall, bipedal, with a mottled, leathery brown skin and flaring nostrils, a face that always reminded the captain of a camel's, looking even more out of place in the traditional light green of the shipboard navy. He bowed slightly in respect to the captain of the freighter, then said, "One passenger for you, Captain."

"Thank you, Commander. We have been expecting him."

The officer's round yellow eyes widened a bit. "I think you might be in for a bit of a surprise, then, Captain." He stood aside, and down the locking tube came the Exchange Observer.

Chin saw immediately what the officer meant. *A woman!* he thought, startled. *And so young!*

"I knew it!" Manya muttered, as the others also stared at the newcomer. "They are mocking us!"

The captain was strongly built but he wasn't a tall man, barely a hundred and sixty-seven centimeters; the Observer was almost a head shorter and slightly built—at least ten, twelve centimeters shorter and probably thirty kilograms lighter than he. She had short reddish-blond hair and big blue eyes, an exotic combination to him, and the palest skin he could ever remember seeing. Although this was paired with a body only a genetically bred saint should have, her face and small size made her seem a mere child, almost too young to be allowed out alone, never mind sent out on a job like this. And, if she were *his* daughter, looking as she did, Gun Roh Chin knew he wouldn't let her walk down the street alone.

She smiled a sweet smile and said, "How do you do, Captain. I'm Kelly Morgan." She extended a hand and he wasn't sure whether to shake it in Exchange fashion or kiss it. He settled for shaking, which seemed right. Regardless of cultural differences or prejudices, he and the rest would have to think of Morgan at all times first as Observer, a species of one, and neuter for official purposes.

It's going to be hard to do that, though, the captain thought wistfully.

"You look startled," she noted, a bit impolitic.

"We, uh, simply did not expect a woman," he responded, deciding that this was *his* ship, *his* mission, and *his* nation and that he was not going to mince words with her.

"I know. The name throws everybody off. The story of my adult life. Does it bother you?"

How do you answer that one without being insulting? "In a sense it does," he responded carefully but honestly. "In the Mizlaplan it is not the custom for young women to travel alone, let alone be on a mission such as this."

"I understand I'm breaking a few social rules, but, like you, I was asked to do this by people I'd have a hard time turning down, particularly for the sake of my future advancement. And it gives me a chance to get to know a bit more about your people and culture." There was a noise behind her and she turned. "Those are my bags. I assume they can be sent to my cabin?"

He nodded dumbly, and Mazarun Klee's sleek gray shape came forward, picked up the two cases and went off with them.

Morgan looked at the Lebur and then over at Krisha and Manya. "At least I am not the only female aboard."

Chin shook his head. "No, but Mazarun is here with her husband and the others are clergy. Come, let me introduce you."

They went down the line as if at a diplomatic reception. Morgan noted the frostiness, and had expected it, so she settled for the customary *pro forma* bow instead of handshaking. Chin couldn't help noting how cool and controlled the woman was. Even he would have some problems shaking hands with Gavin, for example, whose fingertip suckers secreted a smelly resinlike substance which was hard to get rid of, and with the way that Manya was radiating hostility, anyone shaking the Gnoll's hand might come back missing his own hand.

The formalities out of the way, Morgan turned back to him and said, "I assume you want to check me out, make sure I have no hidden implants or whatever. We'd best get that all over with right now, if you like. It'll make the rest of the trip a bit more relaxed for all of us."

The fact that she brought it up, and so soon, meant that they'd find nothing, or she was confident that they would not—but, of course, that too could be a clever ploy, to disarm them or give her time to do something.

"This is Manya the Holy Szin," Chin told her. "She is our science officer and is medically trained. Manya, she is correct. We should do what we must right off."

Making no effort to conceal her ill will, Manya almost snorted. "Very well," said the Gnoll, "come with me."

They went off, and as soon as they were out of earshot, Chin snapped the intercom off his belt and transmitted orders. "Examine and analyze the luggage and all its contents. Don't neglect to examine the cases themselves as well. I want a readout and computer evaluation on everything down to the subatomic level." He slipped the communicator back on his belt and stared at the silent high priests and priestess.

"This will not do at all," Savin commented after a moment. "Manya is correct. They are tweaking our collective faces by violating our ways so clearly."

"I'm not so sure about that," Krisha responded. "I tried to scan her and got nothing at all, although she has no standardized attribute markings. Savin?"

"Nothing," responded the empath.

"A null, like our captain, here," Morok put in. "Nulls are extremely rare but perfect for this sort of work, which is why Captain Chin has twice had missions similar to hers with us. The fact that she seems so young, almost a child, is possibly deception as well. It would be very difficult to take her seriously or think of her as one of consequence. If in fact she is older than she seems, and more experienced, she could use erroneous assumptions to her advantage. The best agents are those whom no one would look twice at or take seriously. I do not think we can underestimate our Miss Morgan or the people who selected her for this. Besides," he added, "we are stuck with her."

Krisha, ever the security officer, nodded. "Captain, the fact that you are Terran, as is she, and a male unburdened with sainthood, makes you the logical candidate to find out what lies behind those startling eyes, and perhaps makes you her most likely target for intelligence as well. Do not be taken in by her so easily. She will undoubtedly attempt to get quite close to you. Let her, but do not let down your guard."

"Indeed? Why do you think she will do anything but merely stand around and ask questions?" he responded, not exactly averse to the thought of her getting close to him, but remembering how he himself had functioned in the role of Observer.

"It is what I would do in her situation," Krisha replied knowingly, "if I were her and if I had no other restrictions, and if I came from a culture as morally decayed as hers, I would not hesitate to use whatever means available for my purposes. Situations like this do not happen by chance, Captain, and the Exchange has excellent intelligence."

Kelly Morgan was poked and probed and scanned and monitored to within an inch of her life, but it wasn't anything she hadn't expected nor undergone in preparation for her assignment. They had also prepared her to an extent for the obvious suspicion and hostility those of the Mizlaplan might have toward an outsider, but it was kind of tough facing Manya the Holy Szin right off, one on one, without anyone else there to act as a buffer.

Although she'd been well briefed, to the point of being told that this particular Arm would most likely be the one sent, she had an initial impression that the others were what anyone would expect: highly competent people doing their jobs. Most of what she knew was about the Captain, on whom there were voluminous files from when he'd worked as an Observer, but the rest were still just descriptions in a briefing book.

That briefing might have been all wrong, or they might all be wild-eyed religious nuts, but clearly Manya was an absolute fanatic, examining banal pleasantries for insults and seeming *very* rough and nasty. It would not do to turn her back on this Manya, she decided. It wasn't completely unknown for Observers of all stripes to have tragic accidents in the course of their duties, particularly if it became clear that a finding wasn't going to go the right way. Supposedly none of these clerics could sin, but sin was in the mind, not an absolute, and was culture-driven and then filtered through layer upon layer of rationalization. These people believed that the Mycohl were truly demons, and if they couldn't make a case, the Mycohl stood to embarrass the hell out of them.

"How old are you?" Manya snapped at her.

"Twenty-four," she responded.

"And you are not yet married?"

"No."

"Nor a virgin, either," Manya muttered. "They send us harlots to judge us."

"I am neither harlot nor judge," she responded, controlling her temper She was in *their* domain, after all. "My people consider women equally as responsible as men. We might marry for love, or not at all, with the same choices men have."

"It is not a question of choices!" the priestess snapped. "It strikes to the very essence of what it means to be sentient."

"I know you do not want me here, but I am here, and I think I am sentient, and I will be fair. Why can't you just leave it at that?"

"Because your people are barbarians!" Manya shot back angrily. "Without rules, there is no civilization. Without a consistent system of behavior, without a clear-cut definition of sin, morality becomes a mere argument over the best way to train animals. Without awareness of sin, there is anarchy and decay and the descent to satanism. And if you are under demonic influences, you can not possibly be fair. You cannot be neutral to evil! That in itself is evil!"

"I am not neutral to evil," she assured the Gnoll. "Show it to me and I will testify on your behalf."

"How can you be other than neutral to evil, when you have no definition of the term? No two people of the Exchange would define it the same way. Even your dictionaries argue about it. No, Miss Morgan. If you are neutral, then you are the enemy of all for which I stand."

"Then that's the way it must be," she responded, not having any other way to respond She had been quite proud of her command of the Mizlaplanian master language, the Holy Tongue they all spoke no matter how ill-suited it was to some of the races, but now she was beginning to discover that it didn't really allow for the kind of sarcastic retorts she was capable of in her own tongue and six other languages.

"That's it," Manya snapped at last, her mottled face showing contempt and her eyes glaring. "Your body is cleaner than your damned soul, although that's not saying much. Lawfully clean, anyway."

"My soul is my own, Reverend Mother," she responded correctly if coolly—there was little chance of her ever winning over Manya, that was obvious—"but it is not my soul that is at issue here, nor my body. I shall try and keep out of the way and be as unobtrusive as possible. This is your problem, not mine. I am not your problem, and will not be, unless you choose to make it so."

A Gnoll's grin was a rather frightening and intimidating sight, particularly when you knew there was no humor behind it.

"I have no problem with you," the priestess told her. "If you are true to your stated goal, it wouldn't matter how badly we treated you nor what we did. In the end, you would still have to testify for us."

That one she was ready for. They'd told her in the preparation classes that something like that comment always arose early on.

"No, Reverend Mother, you should check with your archbishop on that one." She drew herself up to her full hundred and fifty-two centimeters. "See me? I am a very small person, but I have one trillion heads and one trillion swords! In our part of the galaxy any race who would do me harm would harm their own citizens, and the individuals who did so, regardless of the outcome, would be subject to judgment by the other two parties. You may not like the Exchange or its powers, but you and your people respect it because it is equal to your own in that power. I am one small person and I am not Mizlaplanian, but here, now, and for the duration of this assignment, *I am everybody else!*"

She stood there a moment in silence, and Manya said nothing in reply, her face as Gnollishly impassive as ever.

Kelly Morgan took a deep breath and said, in a calmer, softer voice that was nonetheless at least as icy a tone as Manya was capable of using, "Now, if we are through with all this, I should like to be taken to my quarters and allowed to freshen up."

Manya pressed an intercom button and Mazarun Klee appeared as if she'd been waiting outside for just such a summons.

"Take the Observer to her quarters and show her the layout," Manya instructed.

Klee's head nodded, and she beckoned and led Morgan out. The door to the lab and infirmary closed with a hiss that seemed almost a comment on the dialogue just past.

Another door slid open opposite Manya, and Krisha stepped through. "Well? What do you think?" she asked the Gnoll, wanting a first impression.

Manya shook her massive head slowly from side to side. "It is hard to say. She is what she says she is—physiologically, at least. They sent no monsters or hybrid surprises. And yet, somehow, I have a feeling that we are being had. It goes beyond my innate distrust of all heathen, although that is a part of it. It is the heathen brains who chose her for this job that I sense lurking in the air somewhere, leering and laughing at us. She is certainly mistaken if she believes that I underestimate her accursed empire of exploiters and thieves."

"Perhaps your problem is that you *overestimate* them," Krisha suggested.

"No, no. I provoked her here. Deliberately so, while she was still inside the monitor strips. I went so far as to threaten her."

"I heard."

"Her blood pressure started racing, her heart pounded,

and she was about as scared and as angry as it is possible to be without harming herself—all as to be expected. But she did not break down, did not fold up or backtrack. Instead she answered with calm, deliberate reason and counter-threat, so adroitly that had I not been monitoring her with the Terran norms programmed in, I would have thought her made of steel. I do not overestimate; I merely think that the evidence indicates that those who selected her for this might well know just what they are doing. No girl that young has that much poise and self-control unless she is exceptional. I would like very much to know more about her background."

The security officer shrugged. "Perhaps our fearless captain can get it out of her, although if she's as good as you think, it will be only what will do her no harm and us no good. We are only a bit over three days to Medara. We must not forget that the girl is not our true problem; the Medara situation is. If we lose Medara by our failure to support the lodged protest, then what difference does the girl make?"

"We must pray for guidance," Manya responded. "And enlightenment," she added gravely.

"I must apologize, Captain, for looking so poorly, but it has been a long trip under less than ideal conditions," Kelly Morgan said as she entered the small mess area behind the bridge.

The captain stood and bowed slightly. "You look quite—acceptable, I assure you. Please have a seat."

She glided in smoothly, and Kumazon Klee began the service with a silence that startled her. He caught her slight jump at the Lebur's moves and smiled slightly, hoping that the smile would not be seen as offense.

"The Leburs are an efficient and graceful race," he commented. "They mate for life, and each sex has attributes the other needs but lacks, so it's as much a symbiotic relationship as a romantic one. We like to

say that we need one another or we can't do without
the other, and such things—but, with them, it is really
true. Kumazon, here, is both deaf and physiologically
dumb, and can communicate telepathically only with
his mate, Mazarun. Yet his mind is brilliant, on a level
we cannot comprehend, and he can handle things of
minute size and often perform dozens of tasks almost
at once, keeping all progress in his head by some kind
of inborn sense. More than anyone, he runs this ship—
I merely preside, as it were, by virtue of having graduated
from the Academy."

She looked at the food. It was somewhat strange, as
she had expected, but nothing her briefing programs
hadn't covered. In fact, if those programs were to be
believed, this was to be quite a culinary treat. Most
Exchange ships, except for the great liners, used
synthesized meals created out of waste materials. They
were nutritious, they did what food was supposed to
do, but they tended to all taste like—well, nothing much.
While the military and other institutional ships of the
Mizlaplan ate no better, the freighters had a reputation
for good food freshly prepared. They had the room for
it, and with the lonely life of a freighter crew it was
one of the few pleasures they had.

"We are eating alone?" she asked, curious. "Not with
the others?"

He sighed. "I doubt if any of them will eat much on
this trip. The tendency is for much prayer and fasting
before a Holy Mission. In any event, food as rich as
this would probably cause them all to come down with
bellyaches. The priesthood is a rather austere life, with
one foot already in the next world. I myself confess to
being one of the damned. The more I see of them,
the more I appreciate the agony of their lives and the
less I crave such a thing myself. I fear that I am too
content with my lot in life; I shall never progress."

She smiled a bit at that and tried the food. It *was*

good, and she was experienced enough not to ask what was actually in it. Do that enough in alien environments, and you wound up on a fast as bad as those Holy Ones. And this was an alien environment, even if the man across from her was descended from the same human race as she.

"I find your candor a bit odd," she said after eating a bit." It seems to me that anyone who thinks as you do wouldn't be the sort of man they'd trust for this sort of mission."

He shrugged. "I make no secret of my attitudes, and they know it. Manya, and I think Savin, are somewhat scandalized, and I fear quite a lot of prayer time is wasted on me. Morok only appreciates my honesty and says it shores up his confidence in my trustworthiness, and Krisha is too worldly in her background not to understand. The gods have used sinners, even the worst of them, for their purposes since time immemorial. There's not a religion in the history of any people where that is not so. My own ancestors were always pragmatic; they prayed to their gods for rain and got drought, and they prayed for a good harvest and got plagues of locusts, and still they prayed. Morok believes that the gods made me this way because I serve them best as I am; I prefer to believe him."

She gave him a polite chuckle, which he seemed to appreciate. She was beginning to like Gun Roh Chin, who seemed a rock of sanity in this empire of saints.

"You said Krisha was of a worldly background," she noted, trying to get as much of a handle on these people as she could. "I thought the priests were essentially bred, not made. I think I read that they were perfect vessels prepared for the souls of the saints to enter."

"To an extent that's true," he acknowledged, "and most were bred to it. Not everyone who grows up in those perfect bodies winds up a saint, however, no matter how hard they try. It is said that some improper souls get in, or the supply of souls rising to that level is not as great as the capacity to breed physical perfection, allowing some good but not-yet-ready souls to enter. Those are weeded out and then blended into the general population. Others, like Krisha, aren't bred at all but arise among the ordinary folk, and for one reason or another are determined to be saints. Krisha was that way. Born in the normal way to parents she knew, no known manipulation of genes or whatever, raised as ordinary folk are raised, normal childhood and schooling, that sort of thing."

"And one day the local priest, or whatever, saw that she was acting like a saint and took her out of there?"

Chin sighed. "No, actually, quite the opposite. She was a rebel; she rejected most of our society and its standards. She refused the marriage that her parents and the Church had arranged for her, and when it looked as if she'd be forced into it, she ran away. That is what is known as an ecclesiastical crime. They found her, of course, and she was given a choice of recanting her rebelliousness and accepting her lot or facing ecclesiastical judgment. She refused the former and so got the latter. Her family was not without power and influence, and she has real power as a telepath. In such cases, it's not unheard for the ecclesiastical court to find that the accused is a misplaced saint— which they did—ruling that her rebelliousness was caused by this, and she was therefore to be cleansed of her sins and taken before the Lord Mizlaplan. That action alone commands either sainthood or death. She did not die, so here she is."

Like the two master races of the other empires, the Mizlaplan were an ancient race, one of the oldest known. Although no outsider ever saw them, they were far more tangible than the Exchange's own Guardians, where even the highest officials of the Exchange had no idea, or at least claimed they had no idea, just who or what or where the bosses were. The Mizlaplan were small, chunky creatures, dark granite-gray in color, barely a meter high on average, and almost all of that was a great, vaguely humanoid head. They had enormous eyes, broad noses with undulating flaps, and enormous thick-lipped mouths with tiny, almost hairlike tendrils inside and around the lips. More substantial tendrils grew, Medusa-like, on their heads. They had only vestigial arms and legs and were essentially helpless, except for the racial trait that had made them the masters.

There were a number of Hypnos around—Morok, in fact, was one—but while some had great power, it was transitory and faded over time, and was not equally applicable to all races. To come face to face with a Mizlaplanian, however, was to come face to face with a race of Hypnos, a race so powerful that no known other race save the Mycohl could resist their will, from the highest to the lowest, and before which even the most powerful non-Mizlaplanian hypno had no chance. No matter what you knew intellectually, no matter what your background or intentions, when you faced one, you were face to face with a true god—one you could but worship and obey without question or hesitation, not just then and there, but for life. Everyone who came before them was their absolute slave and would obey any command, do anything at all, even kill or be killed, in their service.

Nobody really knew whether or not the Guardians were immune to the Mizlaplanian power, since nobody in the other empires knew any more about that third race than did its subjects. Fortunately, for the Guardians, close physical presence was necessary; you couldn't broadcast the Mizlaplanian power more than a few meters, and if the ancient race still reproduced at all, it was very slowly and their empire was very large.

Those few who did not succumb to the will of the

Mizlaplanian, either died in agony from the experience or were reduced to gibbering, unthinking animals. Even the Mycohl, the one known race that could not be controlled by them, would die in their presence. But a Mycohlian, in a face-down, had been known to take the Mizlaplanian with it when it died. It wasn't hard to see why the Mizlaplan considered the Mycohl the empire of evil, of all that was hellish and unholy.

Morgan could imagine the scene of poor Krisha, who merely wanted an independent life and to make her own decisions, hauled forcibly before the Lord Mizlaplan, her will drained out of her, her spirit redirected to serving, defending, and perpetuating the system she'd rejected. Given the religious instruction that defined sin in her culture and then forbidden to succumb to such sin.

Chin read her thoughts. "They really cannot sin, you know," he remarked casually. "They have sinful thoughts, of course, since they're still people and still in the real universe. They have the same temptations as we—more, I think, than someone like me, who is out in space most of the time—but, unlike us, they cannot succumb, not even slightly."

"I beg your pardon if I offend, but, honestly, I think I would go mad," she told him.

He shrugged. "There's no offense there. I often thought the same thing, but, of course, it's impossible for them to go mad. You see, for you, for me, religion is a cultural thing, an institution, but, deep down, we have some doubts, probe some holes, really wonder about some of it. They can't. They don't academically or ritually or merely emotionally believe it's a hundred per cent true, they *know* it, know with a certainty we can never feel. All the questions, all the doubts, down to the core of their souls, have been removed."

She stared at him. "Do *you* have doubts?"

He grinned. "Madame, part of the benefit of our system is that I received a truly excellent and well-rounded education. In addition, I have a passionate interest in my own people's ancient history and culture, the oldest of any human history known. And, in addition to that, I know just as much of the history and exobiology of the galaxy as you do, I'd say. The most intellectual people I know are freighter captains,, for we have very little else to do out here. There is a small ship's shrine aboard but temples are light-years apart, and the *last* thing spacers want to do is make planetfall on a Holy Day. Many of my colleagues do much penance for that; if they have the sort of thoughts I do, and they must, then every time they make planetfall they betray those thoughts The only way to avoid unpleasantness, shall we say, is to think the correct thoughts. I am quite blessed, or cursed, compared to them; since, you see, as a null, my thoughts remain—my own."

She nodded. "I think I see." Indeed, the presence of a null, and particularly one as sophisticated and worldly as the captain, was an unexpected and quite happy turn of events for her. The number of people with any freedom, even of thought, in this totally conformist culture could probably be numbered in the hundreds; certainly no more than a few thousand. To find one, and one of the even rarer human ones, in this situation, was almost too good to be true.

Now *that* brought up an ugly thought. As a null herself, she could not verify that Chin was who or what he said he was. The mere fact that they would have such a man as their captain in Holy Inquisitions was suspect in and of itself. She was well aware of how easily personalities could be tailored to fit needs. The captain was obviously trying to befriend her as part of his job, and it would be a mistake to underestimate these people simply because they had such a repressive and servile society. They had, after all, managed to impose that society and system on well over a hundred races, some of whom had quite literally nothing in common, and hold it together, and link it all with relatively sophisticated technology, even co-opting features from the religions they superseded and evolving the system as they went. Gun Roh Chin could, in fact, be almost anyone, even a priest himself.

It was true that the clergy could not sin, but "sin" was a relative term in any language. It would hardly be a sin to deceive a nonbeliever, an infidel, from a society that looked to these people like a snake pit. Some ancient religions found no sin in human sacrifice; indeed, many found holiness in torturing and killing nonbelievers. This was a culture whose people were fully capable of suicidally detonating a bomb that would destroy a building, a city, even a world, if their Church told them that it was the will of their gods to do so and that they would attain a higher incarnation by the very act.

Gun Roh Chin sipped some hot tea and settled back comfortably in his old, worn, wardroom chair. Krisha sat across from him, looking a bit wan and weary even at this juncture, but still, without Kelly Morgan's coiffured hair and makeup and jewelry, the priestess was a damned attractive woman.

"You've had several days with her now," the security chief noted. "I want your overall opinions."

The captain put down his tea and gave a slight shrug. "She has certainly come on strong to me, and, I admit, I did little to discourage her. Alas, it is for the same motive: She is trying to gain an ally and friend, and I am trying to win her absolute confidence."

"Modesty, Captain? Or are you truly convinced that she does not find you irresistible?"

He chuckled, but dodged a direct answer. "The question is irrelevant. She has a job to do apart from any personal feelings or desires. She is quite bright; possibly even brighter than anyone here. For one so apparently young, she has an incredible fund of knowledge about almost anything one might bring up, and a consummate skill in betraying only what she wishes to betray while gaining much from me even if I am trying to betray nothing at all. Still . . ."

"Yes?"

"I just have this *sense*, somehow, that, deep down, she's very nervous about something. Not us, not this ship, not the journey, but *something*."

"Now you are no longer a null but a psychic?"

He laughed. "I shall read no tea leaves, I promise. It's the job, more than anything. I must deal with every level of society at one time or another, punctuated by long periods of isolation, which gives me a certain distance and perspective. You learn to read people. No matter what her appearance, she's a pro. She knows that I am her 'handler,' as it were, but she's hiding far more than what one expects such an Observer to hide. You can almost smell it. And it grows, day by day, as we approach our goal."

"What do you think it is, then, other than the usual nerves?"

"I can only wager on the general nature of it. The intelligence service of the Exchange is exceptionally good, unencumbered as it is by the slightest trace of ethics or morality, or by a depth of predictability such as our own people and also those of the Mycohl might have. She is so well-briefed, she is probably overbriefed. I believe she knows far more about where we are going and what we will find than we do."

"But Medara has been quarantined since the murder was discovered. No one new has gone there since . . . oh! I see! That's really the point, isn't it?"

Gun Roh Chin nodded solemnly. "Indeed. Consider our own not untalented Secret Service. A colonial claim is made by a rival out on a frontier that is crucial in our galactic game of *Go*. We and the Exchange may be rivals, even potential enemies, but that is irrelevant.

No matter how much we distrust or suspect or even detest one another, we have a common third-party enemy. I have studied the star maps. Medara is at a critical juncture, at the outermost extension in that region claimed by ourselves and the Mycohl. The Exchange itself has several tentative claims just a few lightyears away, with the Mycohl in between them and us. I have no way of knowing how valuable those claims are, but let us say, for the sake of argument, that one or more of the Exchange's new-found treasures out there is of great potential value. The Mycohl might be tempted to cheat, to bring up forces and eradicate them, *if*, that is, there was no one else out there to monitor such a movement—such as the Mizlaplan on Medara. What would *you* do?"

Krisha thought abut it. "Try and eliminate us first, of course. If we lost Medara, it would push us well back, turn our efforts well away." She suddenly saw where he was going. "Oh! I see—I would make very certain that one of our people was on Medara, reporting on just about everything, making certain that anything learned there was transmitted back to our people. You think the Exchange has an agent on Medara."

He nodded. "It's what I would do. And if I were being sent there as Observer, while the law and the treaties forbid it, I would certainly be informed of this fact, perhaps even the agent's identity. It would be more than a little embarrassing if the Holy Inquisition were to uncover their man in the course of trying to find the Mycohl. An ethical conundrum, but we'd have no choice."

"If you are right," she said, thinking hard, "then I want the identity of that agent. I do *not* want him taken, but I want to know who he is. If we could find the codes and transmission methods he uses without alerting the Exchange . . . it would be *most* helpful. Not to mention making certain that the Exchange receives exactly what we wish them to receive." She sighed. "We shall be busy with the main investigation. You take their man—and if you need help, we'll try and give it."

He nodded. "I was already thinking along those lines. I believe she trusts me, to an extent. I intend to use that first."

"Still," Krisha responded, "be careful. Ask yourself this question: In such a situation, would they send a sacrificial lamb? Or would they send one of their best?"

"I am trying not to underestimate her. I simply hope that she underestimates *me*."

Krisha sighed and shook her head slowly. "This is all speculation, you know, based entirely on your perception of some sense of nervousness while looking into her big brown eyes."

"Jealous?"

"Yes," she retorted, not returning his joking tone. "Not in the romantic sense, of course. Oh! I think this is the worst of it. Being unable to lie is at times a great curse."

He understood, as much as anyone not in her position could, what she meant by that. To be incapable of committing a sin was not the same thing as being without sin. Krisha was still young, still attractive, and, unlike her companions in the Holy Orders, she was not a willing member. They had either been bred for it and raised in it with no thoughts of anything else, or they had come to it on their own and been judged proper for the role. They, too, must have their temptations, their burdens, their regrets, but in all cases their situation was different. None of them, as far as he knew, had been ordained against his or her will.

Krisha was not an example of Mizlaplanian devotion but rather of its justice. She was an example to the others who might be tempted to break free of the system, to harbor less than perfect thoughts. One who had rejected the system and its values, whose punishment was to eternally not only obey all of those rules as no ordinary human could but also to serve them, work to preserve them, and to maintain them. Her primary duty for the Inquisition was not these infrequent full-scale investigations, but rather to travel around, talking to young girls and attempting to identify any doubters or potential rebels—and deal with them as appropriate.

For a personable figure and powerful telepath, this wasn't very difficult; those she herself could not turn back to the proper way, she could refer to powerful priestly hypnos like Morok who, with the local priesthood, could turn almost any doubter into a true believer, with Talents and conditioning.

But, usually, there would be no need for such drastic steps. She was the best walking example for recalcitrants, for she could tell them of her own rebellion and her punishment. They had made her incapable of committing sin, yes, and incapable of not serving in whatever capacity she was commanded to serve, but they had deliberately not altered the person inside.

By this stage, most people had snapped, become fanatics like Manya, totally suppressing or rejecting their old selves. That was what was *supposed* to happen, eventually. Not to break would be to live in eternal torment; forced to behave as you had no wish to behave, forced to betray what you felt was right, forced to obey what you wanted to reject, yet forbidden hypnotics and other means to ease the pain.

The captain feared the inevitability of Hell one day; Krisha the Holy Mendoro was already in it.

"You envy her, then, because she is what you wanted to be."

She nodded grimly. "Yes, that is so. I have confessed it already to Morok, who commanded me to pray many hours that I may expunge such feelings. I do so, but it does not help. The problem is, it would be a terrible thing to wish her misfortune if she were one of us, but she is of the enemy. It is doctrine that the enemy has its pleasures now, for a short while, but suffers horribly for eternity after death, while for us it is the reverse. I do believe this, but I have never been able to accept its unfairness."

"I've been to her realm," Chin reminded the security officer. "While a few live wondrous lives, most are in misery and will never climb out, and those who are on the top, those few, are there at the expense of the others. I began, I admit, with some slight envy for the comforts there, but I was soon overwhelmed by the inequities. It is an ugly place, but those at the top cannot even see or comprehend the Ugliness that supports it. There is a price to be paid for everything, and there is no perfection in this life. There the individual supersedes the needs of society, of the masses. It is a culture of greed. The Mycohl have a structured hierarchy, a hybrid of theirs and ours in some respects, yet one in which masses of people are rated and graded like meat or eggs and whose share is based on that subjective grading system, with the top so removed and debased that there are no morals, no ethics, no system at all but power. Our Holy Ones do not abuse; there is no starving here, nor human sacrifices, nor are innocents brought to slavery, debauchery, even ugly death, to feed the egos of those above. There are always inequities, but, of the three, we are the only one with a sense of values, of obligations to others, a true definition of *sin*. I am one of the few who could live elsewhere. I have seen the others, and I am still here."

She considered that. "Perhaps, then," she responded thoughtfully, "your experience is what is necessary for true peace. We have values, true, and a social system that works, and a sense of sin, but we never see it in the context that you have been blessed to see it. Perhaps if I had seen what you had seen, my soul could be at peace."

"Interesting thought," he agreed, taking out a cigar and studying it for a moment. "Perhaps you can't really appreciate sin until you've come face to face with the real thing."

A Very Ancient Game

Medara may have been in the hands of the saints, but it was certainly no paradise.

The entire forward base, or "establishment colony," as it was called in the jargon of interstellar treaties and conventions, consisted of a set of dull, blocky buildings with rounded roofs connected by a series of enclosed but not heated tubelike walkways. The whole complex was sprawled over only a few acres, the only signs of any habitation on the planet; dull, gunmetal gray pieces of ugliness dropped into a dry, forbidding landscape of dull yellows and off-whites and rounded mountains showing the effects of rugged weathering.

The most noticeable hardship was the wind; it blew constantly and hard, and seemed like some invisible giant's rage, shaking and rattling the whole place. The atmosphere was dense, but lacking in sufficient oxygen for most races, and outdoors almost everyone had to use small respirators. The camp was theoretically sealed and pressurized, with every entry and exit a safety airlock, but the designers had never reckoned with that wind, and there were often breaks in the seals, which allowed some of the precious air to escape. Everyone wore his respirator like a necklace at all times, knowing that sooner or later he would need it. One of the seals had, in fact, blown on the night of Wu's death, and there were still signs of a quick fix in that connector.

At the far end, nearest the dormitory-like sleeping

quarters but far from the labs and research stations, an end module contained the small chapel and sacristy where Wu the Holy Li Tai had been found slumped over his desk, dead.

The tall and eerie-looking Savin tapped his claws on his chitinous exoskeleton in a nervous habit while studying the layout, then shook his massive head.

"It's impossible," he muttered, as much to himself as to Krisha, beside him. "All fifty-four live right next to the scene and have open access. No one would notice if you went in there, even if the place was crowded. We assume the motive; all of them had opportunity. If Manya cannot find the means, or if the means are pedestrian, then it is hopeless to decide which of them did it."

Krisha nodded grimly. "The hard way, then. I have deliberately kept myself shut down and apart, and have met few of them, but it will not take long before they all know more about us than we do about ourselves. That is the nature of places like this. We need to begin interviewing immediately, before they can properly prepare for us. We will use the sacristy. You will interview, and I will sit behind the screen and monitor. Take the Talents here last; it will be better if they are kept guessing as to our own strength and abilities."

Savin made a noise that sounded like a distant, echoing roar but which was, for him, a moan. "Fifty-four! A half-dozen Talents and forty-eight without. This will be a long process."

"Then we had best get to it," she suggested, having no appetite for it either, but, like him, no choice.

On the opposite side of the complex, Manya sat in the tiny two-bed hospital and punched up the controls. The long-dead and cremated cleric appeared in a holographic image, so detailed it almost seemed as if the body were there, although "lifelike" was not the word to describe it.

Grudgingly, Manya noted that colony personnel had followed procedure to the letter; that, at least, was something. As soon as the body had been discovered, all were excluded until the on-site three-person security team carefully photographed and mapped out the death scene in the sacristy. Then the body had been removed to the hospital and run through the full scan, creating a detailed picture inside and out of the dead man down to the molecular level. Now, days later, Manya could slowly but surely strip away layer after layer of the victim, getting more detail than she could have from the body itself, zeroing in and isolating any factor that drew her attention.

The blood and other body fluids showed no significant abnormalities, but she hadn't expected that they would. The contents of the stomach showed no traces of poisons or any substance more lethal than the remains of a very spicy stew. There were no signs of sudden shock, such as electrocution or being struck by a ray, nor any other obvious signs of death. The heart, lungs, and other internal organs appeared in fairly good shape. The worst thing she could find in the initial scans was a significant flabbiness showing that Wu did little or no exercise, and a tendency toward obesity that really wasn't all that unusual in a castrated human male.

She expected nothing different. In fact, the less she found, the more convinced she became that indeed Wu the Holy Li Tai had been murdered. It was an ancient mistake of otherwise very competent and clever murderers. If you wanted a death to appear to stem from natural causes, you should provide some obvious natural cause. The fact that there was absolutely nothing here, not even signs of depression or serious psychochemical disease, to show why a man of this age and condition should suddenly keel over dead was in itself suspicious.

Still, she wished she had the body for comparisons.

Any computer records could be altered, although not without detection by anyone short of a computer genius. Morok, who *was* something of a genius in that area, was working that angle in a room nearby.

With the rest all so busy, Gun Roh Chin and Kelly Morgan were left with very little to do. Since Morgan's role was that of Observer only, someone could have come up to her and said, "Hi! I'm the Mycohlian murderer trying to knock off everybody here" and she couldn't have done anything, not even betray him, without violating her own oath of neutrality. It was up to the Inquisition to prove their case; she could only verify or validate their own work.

Gun Roh Chin's job was to watch her. That was not exactly an odious task even when they weren't doing anything, but, so far, watching her had yielded no results. She seemed no more or less interested in anyone at the camp than he did, and, indeed, if his suspicions about the Exchange agent were correct, she would probably do nothing unless forced to do so by circumstances.

For a while, they toured the station, and personnel on duty were polite but a bit frosty toward her. That was to be expected, of course. If things went wrong, she might well be the one whose testimony before the treaty court would force them out in favor of their most hated enemy.

"Not much amusement, I'm afraid," the captain noted sourly.

She nodded. "The boredom of this kind of job must be oppressive. Are they all volunteers?"

"Mostly," he told her. "You don't send people to live under these conditions in such a desolate and remote wasteland by ordering them to do so and expect to get any work out of them. I think one would really have to like this sort of thing to keep from going mad here."

The winds outside howled and shook the walls and she shivered, although no cold air came through. He had to admit he was feeling pretty much the same way himself, and also very hemmed in. His ship was far larger than this whole complex, and there, even with the Inquisition aboard, he could have all the privacy he wanted.

"What do they do for relaxation?" she asked him. "For fun, I mean. To break up this boredom?"

"You think our faith more austere and rigid than it is. There are many sects, and some have much in the way of singing, even dancing. There is also a good library, and classes are offered on everything from self-improvement to maintenance and repair."

"Sounds really thrilling," she noted tartly.

He shrugged. "The Mizlaplan live their faith and find great joy and comfort in it. It's not merely one of your one-day-a-week, say the right words and pay a small penance type religions. It's more a lifestyle. They are sacrificing for the greater good, and there is much satisfaction in that."

"Yeah, well, maybe. Let's go check in on the others. It would be interesting to see if they have come up with anything."

"I would doubt it, so early on." But, still, he had to admit he longed for some familiar faces and a bit of information himself.

"Even with all the computer aids, it will take me, probably, three days to do a thorough forensic autopsy," Manya told them, a trace of irritability in her voice, not so much from Morgan's presence but from being interrupted.

"But are you leaning towards anything now?" Chin asked, trying to at least keep Manya from going after the Observer.

"Hard to say. He was certainly not sick, not poisoned, not shocked either by internal or external means. Except for the fact that he ceased to breathe and his heart stopped beating, he should be alive now. The most likely hypothesis, having ruled out virtually all natural causes that we know, is the very old method of air injection."

"Eh?"

"Come in, possibly while he slept, with a power syringe set to *load*. Inject major air bubbles into the bloodstream, and when they get to the heart, they cause spasms and death. Because it is just air, there is nothing at all to show in an autopsy. There are air bubbles naturally in blood that no longer circulates and in a body shutting down."

"But I thought that such a method would leave some kind of mark at the point of injection," Kelly Morgan pointed out. "Even a high-speed air syringe would bruise or rupture some pores with that much air being forced in."

Manya's massive head shot up and she looked Morgan straight in the eyes. "Know a lot about murders, don't you? Yes, you're right. Short of having him in some kind of unconscious stupor—and there are no drugs, traces of noxious gases, or the like in his blood to show that he was in any way unconscious, nor any marks of violence to his person sufficient to render him unconscious—you would have to make it a straight, pressed-down, hard, injection on bare skin. That also means that there are only so many places for it to be done, considering that he was dressed in full robes and appeared not to have been moved. He awoke briefly, cried out once in surprise and confusion, then collapsed."

That took even Chin by surprise. "How in the name of all that is holy can you tell that?"

A gnarled finger pointed upwards and they followed it. "Because there are cameras and audio monitors everywhere, you idiot. Everywhere except the sacristy. The viewer on one of the key lab monitors burned out about a week before the Holy was killed and they discovered that they were out of spares for that size.

Alas, not at all uncommon, particularly this long after the last major resupply vessel. It was Wu himself who volunteered the sacristy unit, one of the few of the same size. As a result, we had no backup recording of the deed, but Morok has been able to raise the slight sounds from the audio monitor in the chapel."

Morgan seemed slightly uncomfortable. "Do you *always* monitor every square millimeter? It seems . . . excessive."

"Of course not!" the Gnoll snapped. "But in this position, with such security considerations and the Empire of Evil barely two days away, it is routine. Unless the computer flags something suspicious or there is an incident, privacy, such as it is here, is preserved. Priests of races not otherwise represented here check out the recordings in due course and if there is nothing of interest they are then erased."

Morgan thought about that one. "I see . . . But if this *was* murder, it surely depended a lot on everything going just right, didn't it? I mean, even assuming the murderer broke the lab monitor, he would still have to depend on the priest volunteering his instead of using one from another part of the station. It sounds so complex that it seems as if it would take a miracle for nothing to go wrong with such plans."

"Do not underestimate the forces of Hell!" Manya spat. "Now—let me get back to my work, of finding the injection point!"

"I think we'll check with Morok," Chin suggested none too subtly, and when Morgan nodded they left.

The impressive, winged Stargin wasn't ready to commit himself to anything yet, nor to share his theories with the Observer at this stage. However, he did venture a few opinions.

"I believe that the forensic scan was tampered with," he told them. "It is a good job—no, a *brilliant* job— but I have managed to uncover ghost traces of an overwritten file, which I believe was the original scan. The change in file size is minute; had they added something—perhaps an extra hair or two—to bring the file up to or slightly over the original it would never be discoverable, although adding something that wasn't there might have wound up betraying them to a skillful eye. I might have made the same decision in their place."

Chin wasn't entirely convinced. "We are making this killer out to be a diabolical genius of incredible scale. He knows security, he knows forensics, he knows medicine well enough to almost undetectably alter a full body scan of this magnitude. *And* he is brilliant enough to have gotten here and remained here in close quarters for over a year without detection, while also fooling *existing* heightened security after the death and still tampering with the evidence with remarkable ease. I begin to believe that the only way you could deal with such a creature is exorcism, for it is certainly not flesh and blood."

Morok's bright, reflective eyes darted around the room. "Perhaps," he answered, "but these are all pieces in a puzzle. If we can discover why Wu, and *only* Wu, was killed, the rest might fall into place."

They began walking to the other end of the complex, toward the chapel. Outside, the howling of the wind was sometimes almost unbearable. At one of the quieter junctures, Kelly Morgan commented, "I'm willing at this point to concede that it's a questionable death, but the rest is just too fantastic. If the Mycohl were really this good, we'd all be members of Mycohlian hives by now."

Chin was tempted to agree with her. If the autopsy had been tampered with, there would be no way to absolutely prove from the scan that Wu had been murdered. If the tampering was so good that there was only a suspicion of tampering, not absolute proof, it would be a dead end. What they had might be grounds for Morgan to testify that foul play was a distinct possibility and that charges against the Mycohl were warranted by motive. Which *might* keep Medara in the Mizlaplan, with an admonishment, but it still wouldn't explain things. The Mycohl would have to know that this would be a likely result. Why, then, go to this trouble? And how?

It all seemed to come down to Krisha and Savin and the literal inquisition.

Each of the station colonists was questioned separately, with a small number waiting outside in the chapel. About half the colonists seemed to be human, mostly quite young, all married and accompanied by their wives, to preserve harmony. There weren't any children here, not yet, but several of the young women were visibly pregnant, as might be expected in a place with so little else to do at night.

There were a few Gnoll couples; Kelly Morgan noted that the male and female Gnolls looked almost alike, except for the males' wiry, quill-like whiskers and a single tuft of hair that sprouted from their grayish skulls. None seemed any more hospitable or scowled any less than Manya. Either they were born permanently angry at the universe or a scowl meant something totally different to a Gnoll.

The rest were a mixed bag of Mizlaplanian races, but all seemed to be what Morgan thought of as humanoid— head, torso, arms, legs, that sort of thing. Within that rather broad definition, these included some *Magos* with bright orange exoskeletons and eyestalks that terminated in round, glowing orbs; tiny, triangular-faced *Zailundurs* with tails, who waddled on slight, almost nonexistent legs supported by feet bigger than their bodies; and sleek, pea-green *Ausliks* with pin-sized heads and mouths in their bellies.

Chin studied Morgan carefully as she surveyed the group, but if there was any hint of recognition on either

her part or one of the others, it was a hint he missed. He was pretty well convinced, anyway, that the Exchange agent, if he existed, would be human. With half the complement here human, and with that race one of only two represented here that also had a segment in the Exchange, it was logical. It would be the easiest group in which to conceal a convincing ringer, that was for sure. In fact, it was a fair bet that the Mycohlian was also human, unless, of course, it was truly one of that empire's master race. That was the trouble with the Mycohl; being a collective parasite with enormous adaptive range, they could be almost anybody or anything, if they were willing to take the risk.

Observing one woman whose pregnancy was well along, Morgan whispered, "I wouldn't like to bear and raise a child here, if only for the child's sake."

"Nor I," he agreed. "I am not certain I would even like to be a hermit in this place. Still, children have an amazing ability to adapt. After all, these are not merely a developmental team, but colonists, and to have a colony, one must intend to live there."

"How many Talents are among the group?" she asked him.

"Six or seven, I believe, not counting the late Holy Wu. Only four humans, though. Yes, I see what you mean. There are tricks that may be used to fool telepaths, although I wouldn't bet on such tricks with someone like Krisha, but it is said that an empath can always tell a true Mycohlian. If none are truly hosts for that insidious parasite, then the odds are good that we are dealing with a Talent. Still, in the hands of a good, powerful hypno, aided by conditioning machines, an agent can be buried so completely that even he won't know he's an agent until or unless something triggers the knowledge. If he's gone underground until the Inquisition is over, he will be next to impossible to ferret out."

"What will they do if they can't solve it? *They* must stay until they come to some resolution; you and I will leave in three weeks with whatever report I can manage."

"I don't know," he admitted. "I *do* know that they will use whatever measures are required, and that they are as aware of their deadline, as far as the Treaty appeal goes, as we are. I also know that they are, under law, working as direct agents of the gods, and, as such, there are no limits to their methods or approaches. Their power is essentially absolute, since they are not permitted to fail. They've never had quite this sort of problem nor this capable an enemy before."

"I know I sense some fear in these people here."

He nodded. "Don't let the Inquisition's education or civility fool you into thinking that they are just another batch of detectives. They can be quite ruthless and quite rough. Remember that anyone who is innocent and who is killed by the Inquisition in error is automatically elevated to a higher incarnation and celebrated as a martyr."

At the end of a week, the Inquisition's frustration was showing, both individually and collectively. Clear as well was the onset of near-exhaustion, bearable if it bore results, intolerable if it did not.

"Inquisitional interrogation may be the only way," Krisha concluded, the reluctance and sadness in her statement self-evident to the others.

"Merely using my hypnotic Talent is not enough," Morok responded. "Anyone this good is certain to have anticipated it and had a great deal of computer and therapeutic help. The only way to break through such conditioning to the true personality would be by similar means, but, of necessity, by a hit-or-miss brute force approach Under these conditions, and with this equipment, it is quite likely that we would needlessly destroy many innocent minds, and none would be left unscarred. I would be prepared to do this with a small band of suspects, but to destroy the minds of an entire colony, one in which there are so many well along with child, would be not only reprehensible but also counterproductive. We would simply be doing what the Mycohl wanted—eliminating this colony as a viable unit."

"What about swapping them all out?" Savin suggested. "I am certain from our interrogations that there are no true Mycohlians here. I have had some experience with them before, as you recall. The only one capable of hiding it from me would be Quamong, a very capable broadcast empath himself, but as we know, the true Mycohl never develop Talents themselves and can never use them when in a host. It takes more than having the ability; it takes being born and raised with it, living with it day in and day out, in all sorts of circumstances."

"Swapping them out?" Manya repeated. "You mean bringing out the whole mob of them, placing them in some sort of isolation, while bringing another colony in? If we had months, perhaps, but even then, how do we know that we wouldn't wind up with more enemies than before? It may even be what they want us to do. No. There *must* be another way!"

Krisha turned to the one member who seemed rather well-rested and relaxed. "What about you, Captain? Any thoughts? Or any progress on your own investigation?"

"Yes, and where *is* that girl now?" Manya put in.

Gun Roh Chin sighed. "Many thoughts, no conclusions. Miss Morgan is currently with the wives, apparently trading sewing and design ideas or some such thing with them. To be specific, I believe she is attempting to learn Allusian rug weaving. The women are quite naturally curious about her, and she is someone different to break the monotony here. She has been quite proper and circumspect among the men here and never gone anywhere alone or unescorted. She has also been under constant security-monitor surveillance, and I don't think she's made a real misstep. She is of the opinion that she will return in two more weeks, with an inconclusive report that our own diplomats will be able to use to at least keep this world away from the Mycohl, although not without some very unpleasant embarrassment, such as a public apology by our people to the Mycohl."

"*Apologize to Hell? The* Mizlaplan *apologize to those monsters? Unthinkable!*" Manya almost shouted.

"The captain is correct," agreed Morok. "Either we will be forced to publicly apologize to them with much humiliation, or we will have to hand them Medara. *If*, that is, we can not deliver up a Mycohlian agent."

"Both of those alternatives are unthinkable!" Manya persisted. "If we so ill serve the gods that we can not find the guilty one, then we must come up with him nonetheless!"

Krisha's eyebrows rose. "You mean manufacture one?"

"It is ethical, in this situation," Morok responded. "But not at the expense of one of our own. A volunteer would be required, a willing martyr, and the pool of people here who are not married couples is very small."

"Unless Captain Chin can find his Exchange spy," Krisha noted. "That would be an ideal candidate, even though I would be sad to lose him. If not . . . Savin and I have interviewed everyone. I know of no likely martyrs among them. Besides, we would also have to convince Miss Morgan beyond the shadow of a doubt. Otherwise the martyr shall have no purpose, we would then sin, and we would all surely die. I should not mind myself, but I personally would be unwilling to surrender your lives and your immortal souls to the caprices of that woman."

There was silence for a long period. Finally, Morok spoke. "There is one other way, both proper and ethical in all respects, and which creates no martyrs. It would take higher approval by far than I can give, and fast action to make it in time, but it is, I think, the only course if we agree that this agent is too good for us. I hate to do it, but the alternatives are too bitter to bear, and the burden will not be upon me for it. Keep working. We want the guilty party if we can get him. We want all the agents if they are here. To the end, my solution can be postponed, even canceled. Even though I feel it fruitless, we will start hypno examinations tomorrow. Nothing that we can reasonably do will we not do."

"What do you have in mind?" Krisha asked him.

"If you consider our options, and you remember the definition of a colony, it is logical, and something no agents or their handlers would ever anticipate."

Krisha gasped. "You don't mean—!"

"Not a word outside this room. That includes you, Captain. Miss Morgan is not to know of this."

"I am not quite certain what I am not to betray," he admitted to them, "but it sounds severe. I cannot question your actions, but I also can't help but feel that we are giving up too easily, that we are overlooking the obvious."

"Indeed?" Morok was interested. "Any examples?"

"It's right there—I can almost *touch* it. But I do not have it yet." He sighed. "What about the straight line for now? Who suggested to Wu that he swap his monitor?"

"Nothing really there," Krisha told him. "It was a typical meeting. When the problem was discovered, Chu, the technician in charge, was asked who else had operating monitors of that size. He listed several, including Wu's, and it was then that Wu volunteered. Nothing out of the ordinary."

"What about computer access, then? It must have taken a long time to edit that scan with such skill."

"Again, a dead end," Morok told him. "No one had access for that long a time, and it would have to have been done at one full and lengthy session. The master computer is under security control, of course, but its modules, including the medical one, are not secured. You cannot expect medical personnel to have to go through a hierarchy in an emergency. These are tied into the science modules. You could tap in with the proper equipment at a million points, even from outside, where there are no monitors at all. Even from the religious modules in the still-dark sacristy. There are too many possibilities."

Chin made a fist of his right hand and struck his left palm. "There is *something*! I know it!"

"Well, you have about ten days to find that 'something,' " Morok responded. "After that, things will automatically begin to happen."

Gun Roh Chin sat in the lotus position on a mat on the floor of his tiny living quarters. If anyone had come in, they would have thought him in some sort of mystical trance.

Much of the day, he'd been in the colony security office going over recording after recording, and those who had watched him and gotten curious came away even more confused.

Over the past several days he'd watched hours upon hours of older recordings of the then-still-living Wu the Holy Li Tai going about his day-to-day routine, a most boring exercise.

Then there were the recordings of Kelly Morgan in the women's quarters, in which she could be seen befriending and interacting with the other women there. And the summaries of all those interrogations, all the work and suspected cover-ups Morok had revealed with his particular electronic skills.

Krisha would have accused him of having too much imagination, of building monstrous conspiracies where none existed and seeing childish bogeymen when, in truth, there was nothing under the bed.

Now he stirred, reached over, and pulled several printouts of star maps in front of him. He stared once again at them.

There was the Medaran system, at nearly the edge of the frontier regions, keeping a vast section of interstellar space within Mizlaplanian control. There, close by, was the border of Mycohlian space, also none too thick with real settlements in this region. And then, barely two days across the Mycohl, there was a near crazy-quilt of claims almost intertwining the Mycohlian and Exchange regions.

Clearly someone in the Mycohlian hierarchy had blown it badly in the planning stages. Using Medara, the Mizlaplan had curved inward toward them, forcing them out in a slender thread through the whole frontier region, while the Exchange seemed to be filling in areas on the other side so fast and furiously and with no seeming regard for expense or practicality that the Mycohlians were getting badly squeezed. It was a geographic curse of being the middle.

In his mind, the star chart seemed to vanish, leaving instead a vast grid filled with tiny marker stones of black and white and gold. A three-way version of his ancestors' most beloved game, which had survived so long because it was so simple to learn, so horribly difficult to master, and so—useful.

Go had a very simple set of objectives. Each player placed a stone, one at a time, on the grid. If one player's stones completely surrounded and filled in the area around an opponent's stones, the latter's stones were captured and replaced with stones of the victor's color. When all the board was filled, it was almost always clear who controlled the most territory.

It didn't take a military genius to see that the Mycohl had probably executed a number of people just for losing Medara, but their position wasn't hopeless. Depending on the presence of planets in the region beyond, they could do a no-holds-barred mass exploration and claim, and get through that bottleneck even now. There were still enough open spaces on the grid beyond to avoid being cut off.

It was the tendency of the Mizlaplan to think of the Mycohl as some great beast, cunning but animalistic, and so to underestimate them. No system, no matter how repugnant held on to over a hundred alien races, maintained order and stability to a high degree within their realm, and grew and expanded outwards, by being brutish and animalistic. That approach might achieve great gains in the short run but would collapse over the long haul, particularly since such a regime would not have a war to keep the people unified and directed.

Clearly they had blown it in this location, but it was only one region in space that went on in all directions. Still, this was an important area, with a particularly high planet ratio, and not one that they would wish to abandon. The tendency would be to a brute force approach—take Medara on this side and two or three of the newer Exchange colonies on the other—and open up the lanes again, as it were. That, however, would mean a two-front shooting war against opponents of nearly equal military strength. Combined, the Mizlaplan and the Exchange could chop the Mycohl to pieces, just as the Mycohl could do to either of the others, with some alliances.

When you looked at their position on a map, you got an idea of just why the Mycohl were as nasty and militaristic and paranoid as they were.

It was an equally common error for the Mizlaplan to think of the Exchange more as heathen than as an enemy as formidable as the Mycohl. If the Mizlaplan could surmount those feelings, they could easily join forces with the Exchange and remove the common threat.

Why kill Mu, when it was the one act sure to bring in an Inquisition?

"She knows more about Medara than we do. . . ."

"You mean manufacture *one?"*

"Why send this mere slip of a girl . . . ?"

"To be specific, I believe she is trying to learn Allusian rug weaving. . . ."

Gun Roh Chin suddenly came alive, got up, stretched, and then strode confidently down to Security.

"Any reply yet to my inquiries to Naval Command?" he asked the officer on duty.

"Just came in, not an hour ago, sir," the officer responded crisply, thumbing through a stack of documents. "They asked a lot of questions about the inquiry and didn't particularly like having to answer at all, I can tell you that. Had it not been official business of the Inquisition, I think I would have received a response that could not be stated in front of polite company. Ah! Here it is!"

Chin took the small sheaf of papers, all marked "CODED—EYES ONLY—DESTROY BY INCINERATION," thumbed through them impatiently, then found what he was looking for. He betrayed no surprise as he read it; it was exactly what he suspected.

"There is no need to keep these, watchman," he told the security man. "Follow the disposal instructions. I have what I need."

But that wasn't quite true. He had the basics, yes. He was pretty sure now that he knew why Wu was killed, who the Exchange agent, or agents, were—at least reduced to a manageable number of suspects—and he knew pretty well what was going on here. Proving it, however, was something else again.

In a way, parts of the solution strained credulity, which would make it difficult to convince even one as wise as Morok of its truth. In another way, it merely saddened him.

Now, how in the name of the Twenty-Seven Hells was he going to confirm it? And, even if he did, what could, or should, he do about it?

And, worst thought of all, should he, could he, bring himself to do anything at all?

The Holies were performing a service in the chapel, which made things noisy but also allowed Kelly Morgan to enter without being noticed and make her way through the back of the room into the adjoining sacristy.

Gun Roh Chin was there, alone, perched on the side of Wu's desk, studying an ornately carved board on which there were little white and black disks. He looked up when she entered, and nodded to her.

"The only safe room in this whole place," he commented, betraying no emotion. "And with that racket next door, which will go on for at least another hour, fully secure. All the sacred things are in there; there's no reason why anyone would come in here now."

"Your note seemed a bit—conspiratorial," she responded, frowning. "I am here entirely out of curiosity, Captain."

Chin gestured to the board. "Wu's ancestors were from the same general region of Earth as mine," he said, seemingly relaxed. "Countries, they called them back then, and even our race was divided into races, for they knew no other. We Chinese contributed much to human culture. Writing, the imperial governmental forms, even gunpowder, although I'm not certain that the last is something to advertise. We also created the most ancient of strategic games—*Go*, the game on which chess is based, and my people's real passion. That's what this is—a *Go* board. Wu was apparently quite good at it—there is an inscription on a plate here that says this set was given him for winning a most prestigious championship, perhaps the top one in this day and age. Do you know the game?"

She walked over and looked at the board, not knowing where this was all leading. "No," she replied. "I have heard of the game, but I don't know anything about it."

He gave a slight smile. "Oh, I think you do. you might not know that the game you play is *Go*, but you know it quite well. Tell me—was the identity of the Mycohlian decided upon from the start, or will you simply choose someone at random?"

Her head snapped up. "What?"

"I am not as blind-sided as my compatriots. I am ever mindful that there are *three* sides to this galactic game of *Go*, not two. I do confess to being less than a Grand Master myself; I see the strategy all right, even several moves ahead, but I cannot see the ultimate objective. What imaginable gain could the Exchange achieve by murdering a Mizlaplanian cleric and blaming the murder on the Mycohl?"

She froze a bit, but recovered nicely. "I have no idea what you are talking about. I think you have quite an imagination, Captain. Obviously those long, lonely voyages have bred a streak of romantic fantasy. If you were in the Exchange, you would probably be quite successful plotting mystery thrillers."

He ignored the put-down. "Was it, perhaps, just an accident? Wu, perhaps unable to sleep for some reason, wandering out and blundering into something, seeing something he wasn't supposed to see? I note that on the night of his death one of the seals broke in a connecting chamber, and the wind came howling through and everything came crashing down. The ultimate diversion, perhaps? Those seals seem to be holding up quite well now. Shall we have someone who knows that end of the business closely examine some of those breaches to see if they were indeed the natural occurrences they seemed to be at the time? It wouldn't take much. Someone standing there, a tiny bit of malleable explosive in one of the flex joints, then wait until the wind hits full force to blow it. Who would look for that tiny trace of explosive? Who would doubt that the elements of this inhospitable pile of rock did not do it? In a place like this, all the alarms would go off, everyone would come running, and there would be mass confusion followed by organized damage control and repair. Ample time then to send a coded message to a relay beacon."

"He died at his desk, in his sleep, without a mark on him," she pointed out. "Maybe working on the repairs got to him or something. Your theory doesn't hold water, Captain."

"Indeed? There are a hundred, perhaps a thousand, ways to render someone unconscious that would be easily concealed in a scan autopsy. When there were so many ways to make his death look natural, or accidental, I had to keep asking myself why it was made deliberately mysterious. Then it came to me—obvious, really. The scan had been tampered with. Manya has spent an eternity looking for where the injection mark was erased, and it probably was. With that kind of evidence, almost any coroner would suddenly close in on that idea, the method of death, and perhaps miss the fact that the *degree* of alteration of the scan was the real issue. Death and cause of death would be all that concerned a coroner, or an Inquisitor who was also one. The fact that some tiny nerve damage, perhaps in the neck, which those most skilled in the martial arts can control, causing temporary paralysis, would be as easy to erase as the puncture. The mysterious hides the obvious."

"So? Even if true, it only confirms what I'm already ready to certify—death by unnatural causes."

He nodded. "Indeed. My! They are singing loudly in there! I hope I don't have to start shouting."

He paused a moment, then continued. "Another nicely timed explosion. Seals busted, airlocks closing, much noise and pandemonium. The priest is back here, and starts to answer the call with the others, but someone is waiting for him. A quick, careful, almost surgical set of moves and out he goes. Back in here, into that chair, slumped over his desk. No problems—no monitor. The injection, and he's dead."

"Hold it! You said yourself there were bells ringing and all sorts of other stuff going on. But the chapel audio monitor picked up his cry—much later, when they'd done their damage control and come back and settled down for the night."

"Not a big problem, and one that was useful in shifting the estimated time of death and establishing a wrong set of facts. The entrance to the living quarters is right out there. The killer gives a cry when it is dead quiet, just sufficient to register. If one presses close to the wall on the way out, the chapel's visual monitor can't see you. It has a blind spot, which might well have been known, but, after all, who would be sneaking into the sacristy? Security wanted the picture of the people at the service, not the hundred per cent coverage they required in the sensitive areas. The killer leaves, then goes to bed. The next morning, Wu is discovered. They photograph the room and document the scene, then remove the body to the hospital. They run his body through the scan, then prepare it for ritual cremation. Later, the scan is expertly retouched. There are several days more before we arrive; plenty of time to work that out. It's not difficult to gain access. The scan is stored in the computer used by the science labs. Anyone with the proper security code could call it up, work on it, then read it back in, and I credit any competent spy with being able to gain local codes."

"You really should write this up," she told him. "I could get you some nice money for this one."

"Ah, but that's not the best part. No, no. Wu's been disposed of, the evidence tampered with, but now there will be the Inquisition and a no-holds-barred investigation—with an Observer, yet. The killer cannot be extricated without a finger pointing directly to him, and there might be—other considerations. But the Inquisition is certain to be sniffing for Mycohl blood, and there's none here. Well, perhaps there *is* a Mycohl spy somewhere, but that poor devil, if he exists, is as confused as we were. Now we've had a couple of weeks to find what we were supposed to find and conclude what we were supposed to conclude, but we still don't have a murderer. Sometime in the next few days, however, between now and when you and I are due to leave, I predict we will have the first wind-wall failure since we've been here. This time it will be fatal. The body, when removed, will have on it some of the explosive which will easily be checked out to be of Mycohlian manufacture. An intensive search of the victim's workplace, or whatever, will turn up more of the same. You will then certify that the Mycohl indeed did it, everyone will be happy, case closed, and we all leave. The Mycohl will be confused and furious, but under the Treaty and with all the circumstantial evidence they will be helpless. And the Exchange will have a free hand to keep doing here whatever it is they are doing. How's that for an ending?"

"A good one," she approved, "but without a shred of evidence. If your Mycohl fatality doesn't turn up, it evaporates into the hot air it is."

"Oh, I don't know about that." He sighed, reached into a pocket, and brought out a small box. Opening it, he removed a series of thin, tubular strands and held them up.

Kelly Morgan clearly knew just what she was looking at, which confirmed much of his theory right then and there. "Where did you get those?"

He gave that smug, satisfied smile of his and put them back in the box. "From the hollowed out area in the Allusian loom, of course. I assumed that Mycohlian *mystok* would be rather difficult to get around here, compared to the local stuff used before. That was your job. Somehow your diplomats provoked our weakest link into publicly accusing the Mycohl. It wouldn't be that hard to do—I think I could do it myself without half-thinking. That caused the Mycohl to react, since they were probably pretty sure it wasn't them, and they demanded an apology or an Observer. It would be the easiest way to resupply and brief the trapped Exchange agent here. And they sent you, a woman, to a male-dominated culture. Why? To twit us? No, because this place isn't that easy for a foreigner to act freely in. But male dominance is one of our weakest links, isn't it? All the time we talked about enemy agents, even Manya and Krisha, it was always using the word 'he.' No one pays a great deal of attention to women in such matters here, because, other than the priestesses, they have no power or access to power except through their husbands. Why, no one would take the idea of a female spy here seriously. Particularly if that woman were married and, perhaps, even with child. Nor think twice that a bored female Observer might spend most of her time with our women." He looked straight at her. *"Even less that she was learning rug weaving techniques."*

Kelly Morgan said nothing, but it was clear that her mind was racing.

"A rug weaver, in fact, whose husband is a superb computer technician," he added, then paused again before remarking, "I don't know what's louder—the singing or the chanting. I wouldn't mind so much if they were the least bit harmonious."

Finally, Morgan sighed. "You've already reported this, I suppose?"

"You're still here, aren't you?" he responded.

That was a major point. "Are you going to report it?"

"I have very little choice but to turn in your people. Not to do so would cause worse problems and perhaps cause all of the other people here to suffer needlessly."

"Damn it, man! They've got a kind of built-in

mechanism that will cause their deaths before any sort of coercion can force them to betray any secrets. With these nice little explosive worms, they could just as easily be the Mycohl. Officially, anyway. And that would leave me clear to make my guilty finding without anyone else having to die for it."

"You would so easily throw them to the wolves? Even the child she carries? That's rather cold, wouldn't you say? And catching the vaunted Exchange Secret Service in the act like this would be most—useful."

"Useful to who? You? You'd get nothing out of this! Nothing except a gold star in the celestial book or something. What do you have to look forward to, anyway? A gold watch and a room in the Old Captains' Home after years of shifting crates of this and that from Nowhere to Noplace and back again? There's a way to do this so nobody's harmed. We've actually *helped* you here! There *are* a pair of Mycohl agents here. Our people actually *stopped* them from doing anything. They had a canister, a vicious disease they were going to hook into the pressurization system. Your ineffectual security system would have been helpless. The computer records would show no sign of tampering, nor would there be any such signs left by the time they got through. A distress signal would be sent, and, since the Mycohl are actually closer by than most Mizlaplanian ships, they would naturally answer the call. A Corithian ship from the Corithian hive. The Corithians are more machine than living race. They'd be ready and able to show that Medara was toxic to all carbon-based life, and then they'd claim it under the salvage laws. We stopped them! Everyone here is *alive* because of our people!"

The news of the Mycohlian plot sent a chill through him, all the more because he believed it. It was just the sort of thing they thought might be tried. Still, it had gone too far now.

"Everyone is alive except Wu the Holy Li Tai," he responded flatly.

"They were replacing the tank. Disposing of the toxin outside in the main vaporizer and putting a tank with nothing but oxygen back. By bad luck, even though it was late, Wu saw them with the tank. He didn't think anything of it at the time, but when the Mycohlians pulled anything else off, he'd remember them and the tank. Wu was with another guy but he was easily dealt with, like the others."

"One's a hypno . . ." he muttered. "Of course. And the other is most likely a strong telepath. Heavy-duty for this sort of thing. But hypnos aren't effective with the clergy, and the telepath not only knew that the incident was up front in Wu's mind but that Wu would bring it up again with his companion, and blow all sorts of whistles when he discovered his companion didn't remember a thing about it. Or, more interestingly, remembered entirely different people."

"Look at your damned *Go* board!" she snapped. "There are *two* colors there! Two! Black and white. We not only want the Mycohl squeezed in this sector on general principles, but also there have been a lot of big things—I don't know exactly what, but *big*—going on near them on the other side in our space. We wanted this colony firmly established and protected not only for the usual reasons but also because it would shift major Mycohlian forces, interests, and efforts elsewhere. We knew they'd make a major move and we felt pretty confident that they would succeed. They've had a small support group of Corithians secreted here almost since your colony was built, and you never even spotted or detected or even suspected them. We saved your asses for *mutual* interests. The Mycohl scheduled to die this week are really Mycohl. The finding then will be true, and they won't dare move on Medara again. And you would throw this out?"

He looked at her with a bemused expression. "First, it's throw the agents to the wolves but let me go, then it's a subtle bribery offer, and now it's mutual protection and self-interest. If I hold out long enough, I expect seduction or offers of marriage."

"Neither would be as much of a sacrifice as you seem to think," she replied. "You are quite an exceptional man, Gun Roh Chin."

He rolled his eyes. "Spare me! I am not too certain how much faith I have, but sex in the sacristy is something even my cynical brain finds uncomfortable. I assume that if all else fails, I will be an unfortunate additional victim of the Mycohl?"

"I—I would hope it would never come to that. I meant what I said, Captain. To kill you would be very hard indeed." She paused a moment, then shifted gears again.

"Look," she said, "you're not like the others. You're not locked in either to this mind-set or this theology. You said yourself that there is no such thing as perfection, at least not in *this* life. In the end, this is just a sad situation that can only be made worse by your interfering. Let it go, Captain. We're both humans; our people came from the same place. We have more in common with each other than either of us does with the people we work for. It's only an accident of history that you are standing there and I am standing here. Just—let it go."

He slid off the desk and stared at her, grim-faced. "That is all it is to you people, isn't it? A game of *Go*. But the stones are *people*, not stones, and you can't see that. 'Go ahead, Captain. Commit treason. Let dead bodies lie. It's only a game and the victims are merely black and white stones on a board.' But it is not that simple. Nothing is that simple. Had there been no Three Empires, had the human race spread out, we would at some point come to this same position, me for the Sino-Japanese Bloc, you for the Western

Alliance. Nothing changed, really. *These* are my people; no matter what their shape or background, no matter what they eat or how they eat or what they smell like. I am the captain of a spaceship, and I believe that to be the noblest, grandest position of any secular job. The Mizlaplan gave me that opportunity. No one starves here. No one wants. No one is regarded better or worse, either for their shape or whether they have mandibles or tentacles or hands, whether they are yellow or white or green or purple. It has its faults, yes, but compared to what? *This* is my country, Kelly. *These* are my people. In the end, it comes down to that."

"So what can you accomplish for all that?"

"Retaining the one thing that separates all of us from all of you. Retaining my honor. That may be an alien concept to you, but to me it is everything. It is the *only* thing of true value. Up there, only a few hours away now, is another ship, probably braking at this very moment to come into orbit. Aboard it, in a special area, is a Lord High Commissioner for the Mizlaplan. Morok decided that the puzzle was beyond being solved and put to his superiors the only solution he could think of, and they accepted it. He proposed to ordain the whole colony, to turn this into a clerical outpost and retreat. Everyone would be turned, including the agents, the murderers, whatever. Their loyalties altered, they would have no choice but to come forward."

She paled, visibly shaken by that. "My God!"

"I have become very close to Krisha over the years. Her life is a tragedy. I will not have fifty-six more Krishas on my conscience to snare four guilty parties." He turned and picked up one of the little stones from the *Go* board. "Not stones! *People!* I cannot forget that. I cannot allow it morally, just to win a damned game. *You* could—I know it. That is the true unbridgeable difference between us that makes us not the same, but aliens."

She swallowed hard. "So, now what? This changes everything, of course."

"Of course. Now I will tell you what you will do. You will give me the names of the two Mycohl agents. Together, under the authority of the Inquisition, those four, your pair and their pair, will go up to meet the new ship. Evidence will then be taken, and given, willingly, without coercion. No one else will die, unless the Mycohl people fight it to the death or kill themselves on the way. Care will be taken that they will not know who they will be meeting until they actually do, to minimize that risk. You, then, will take the evidence back. The Corithian outpost, the attempt on the whole colony, will be sufficient as Mycohlian motive, opportunity, and method. Your treaty violations will not emerge publicly, but your people will know, and know that *we* know. That might be useful for more—cooperation—in the future."

She was beaten and she knew it. Finally she said, "I don't see where I have much choice in this." she sighed. "You know, we thought we'd be dealing with some hidebound, insular clerics. Competent but myopic. And we'd have gotten away with it, too, if we hadn't by sheer rotten luck gotten the one honorable, independent thinker left in the Mizlaplan."

He was not above a bit of ego. "One of the few, anyway. A society like ours needs a few like me to keep it working. Or, perhaps there *are* unseen forces manipulating fate."

She made one last, hesitating try. "I could still kill you, you know. Even though I'm very small and a woman, I know the ways."

"I know you do. I never underestimated you, Kelly. That is why, before we came in here, I re-switched the lab monitor and the sacristy monitor. Not so much for self-protection as much as to ensure that I never wavered from my resolve."

She actually smiled at him. "You would have made a

hell of an agent, Gun Roh Chin. One *hell* of an agent. I really do wish that you were on our side."

He knew Krisha was in the security room and made straight for it. When he entered, she looked up at him and shook her head slowly from side to side, as if in wonder.

"How'd I do, coach?" he asked her.

"I would kiss you if I could, Gun Roh Chin. She's right about one thing, though. If we had met before . . ."

"You would have been a young girl climbing the walls of boredom in a big, dumb, lonely freighter carrying whatevers from Nowhere to Noplace, to coin a phrase."

"Oh, I don't know. Loneliness and emptiness take many forms, and if you have the right company, a little isolation might not be a bad thing." She sighed. "I am still consumed enough with bad thoughts to wish we could do more to her than send her back with her tail between her legs, though."

He shook his head sadly. "No, Krisha. That's the saddest part of this. In the end, she wasn't thinking about those people or death or salvation or honor or anything else. She was thinking about how much negative impact this will have on her career, and the damage this will do by giving us so much information about their operations and how these agents managed to avoid detection. To her, there is only one human being and that is Kelly Morgan, player. Perhaps two, with me as the opponent. She has just lost a game, that's all, but all the losses are merely stones. They will never be mere stones to you."

She sat back and sighed. "No."

"She's everything you romanticized and fantasized yourself as being," he told her. "But, right now, she, not you, is the loneliest, emptiest person I have ever met."

By the next day, Gun Roh Chin was infected with a major attack of smug satisfaction and having a very difficult time demonstrating humility, but he sort of managed. He would rather have been a legend, though, than have to continue to fend off congratulations and thanks from the remaining colonists.

Morok and Savin had been in orbit with the Mizlaplan ship, carrying one of the Mizlaplanian demi-gods himself, for much of the time, and it was unexpected that they would return as early as they did, although Chin was actually itching to get underway and put this mission and his laurels behind him. A few months of cargo hauling with only the Klees for company would be just right, he decided.

Morok had handled the transfer of the two pairs of agents quite deftly, convincing them that some tests had to be run with equipment brought in by the new ship and taking colonists up in small groups, putting them through some nonsense, then bringing them back down in staggered batches so that the agents still to go could not notice the absence of those who had gone before.

"Quite smooth, if I do say so myself," Morok commented. "We had them enter through one door, but when we got to the agents, they were directed to another door. That door led directly to an audience with His Holiness, of course. The hypnos put up a slight fight, but it was a trifle to one of His Holiness's ultimate power. All were converted and ordained successfully; there were no deaths, although we now have, I believe, the only priestess ever who is also pregnant. The child, being the progeny of two ordained clerics, will of course be raised within the Holy Church. The four will be returning with His Holiness aboard His ship, be debriefed on the way, and be enrolled in religious studies to bring them to full utility. Miss Morgan will also return with them rather than with us."

"That is something of a relief," Chin responded. "I should think her company would have made our return voyage most—unpleasant."

"That is certainly true," Morok admitted, "but, I fear, the decision was more practical than out of regard for our feelings. We are not yet disbanded as an Arm."

Startled, everyone turned to the leader of the Arm, all eyes and ears on him. This was neither expected nor normal procedure.

"But—what else is there to do here?" Krisha asked him.

"Nothing—here. A new priest who came with His Holiness will take over those duties. I believe we should all say our farewells and return to the *Faith of Gorusu.* What we are charged to do next is best discussed there."

It felt good to Captain Chin to be back aboard once more. It seemed somehow normal, even comfortable. *Correct.*

Morok wasted no time, nor did they want him to.

"Captain, how far from here is the Exchange frontier? In days of travel, not light-years."

"I will have to consult the computers and charts," he responded, "but certainly no more than six days by a safe route that would skirt the Mycohl regions Three, if we exercise the right of innocent passage. That, of course, is to the legal borders."

"Innocent passage!" Manya snorted. "We should ask nothing of Hell, particularly not its permission to carry out holy work."

Chin frowned. "You wish me to go flat out, without filing proper requests, for the frontier region claimed by the Exchange? We could be forced over or blown out of space if we weren't careful. Why?"

"Do you think you can manage it without us being forced over or blown up?" Morok pressed.

"I—I can try. It depends on what is in the area. The frontier is by treaty lightly defended, as you know, and pretty open. We are quite small, and space is vast. If we could add half a day, plot a course that kept us well away from any Mycohl systems and off their usual routes, it's probable that we could get through, at least going in. The Mycohl neck in there is rather narrow, so even if they did detect a single ship, it would be unlikely they could send someone out that could catch us before we were through. Defenses are designed to detect fleets, not single ships. But, once in Exchange territory we would be wide open, and they will be no friendlier than the Mycohl to one coming in without permission—no more than we would be under reverse circumstances."

Morok nodded. "Nonetheless, it must be done." He punched a code into the computer link, then turned back to them.

"What you are about to hear was intercepted by intelligence monitors on His Holiness's ship less than a day ago. It was reported to the nearest star base, and with their help, a triangulation was made. It was sent in the clear by a ship whose transmission has an Exchange header, and, indeed, it comes from the other side of the neck, and not very far on the other side, either. Listen. Computer—play recording."

"*All ships . . . any ships . . . Exchange registry . . . This is Research Vessel* Wabaugh. *Coordinates based on special map frontier zone one one four eight two stroke*

*five. Coordinates are Rainbow Bridge. Send assistance
fast. They're all dead. They're all in there with the
demons and they're all dead. Only one left. Can't leave.
Approach with extreme caution! Power adequate for
maintenance only. Any Exchange registry. Approach
with caution. Demons at Rainbow Bridge!*

Coordinates . . ."

"That's enough," said Morok, and the message cut
out. "It merely begins repeating, but with less coherency.
The message has been, of course, computer translated,
but I must say the emotion and inflection was true to
the original."

"Do we have any way to zero in on those coordinates?"
Savin asked. "They do not sound like any system we
use."

"Ordinarily, yes," Chin responded, "since those are
commercial, not military, coordinates and would be the
ones on just about every commercial ship in the
Exchange. That's why the speaker used them instead
of the military ones, although he didn't sound right
enough in the head to have thought of that. We, of
course, have sets of those for all areas of known space,
but that's the problem. This is near the edge of known
space. That sort of coordinate is not on any map I have;
I can tell you that without even researching. It must
be pretty new."

"Our locators can give you a plot from here to there
without charts," Morok told him. "We have a very good
idea where it is, and it is right on the edge of the
universe, after which all things known drop off into a
great blank sea on anyone's map."

The captain shrugged. "I still don't see why it concerns
us, or how it justifies the risk you are asking us to take.
I'll do it, of course, but it sounds to me like a distress
call from the last survivor of a Mycohl attack on some
distant Exchange outpost."

"Do not our treaties demand that our ships respond

to distress calls no matter what the jurisdiction, if we are closest?" Savin asked him.

"Well, yes, but I don't think that would excuse our cutting across Mycohl territory. And even if we get there, we might face a small Mycohl battle group. This is a freighter, not a warship. We are virtually unarmed and certainly slow and defenseless against any Mycohlian attack craft."

"I fear the translation might have given a false impression after all," Morok said. "Captain, you know the Exchange trading language?"

"I did long ago. It's faded from disuse, but I suppose I could make it out."

"Then listen again, this time to the original. Computer—play original intercept, unenhanced."

The message came through again, weaker, fading in and out, broken here and there, but clear enough to be understood. Chin noted that Morok was right; the computer translator had really caught the emotion exactly. It sounded the same, really, and for a moment he couldn't understand what was bothering Morok. Then it hit him.

"He said *demons*. Not Mycohl, not any nickname or euphemism for Mycohl. It must be a code word or new slang for something. He couldn't have meant actual *demons*."

A Mizlaplan under attack might well use his own word for demon to mean Mycohl; the two were almost the same word, for obvious reasons. But in the Spartan, crisp trading language of the Exchange, it had only one meaning and that was demons of the supernatural sort.

"Did he sound like he was using code words?" Morok asked them all. "Did he in fact sound like he would have *remembered* any code words? In his tongue, if he had been attacked by Mycohl he would have said 'Mycohl,' or perhaps one of a half-dozen nicknames or epithets for them. The word in his tongue is unambiguous. Neither His holiness nor our military intelligence believes it means anything other than what it says."

It was time for Chin's cynical streak to kick in and spoil his current good reputation. "Are you trying to tell me that our people believe that this message is from the last survivor of an attack by real, live demons? *Demons?*"

"Why not?" Manya snapped. "If the Mycohl are frustrated here, they might well be so consumed with evil and those people who failed here might well have incurred the wrath of their terrible masters."

"But—*demons?* Real, live demons . . ."

"This is not a voluntary association," Morok reminded the captain. "This is an Arm of the Holy Inquisition and we happen to be here, closest to it. We are not asked to find out the meaning of this message; we are *commanded* to do so."

Gun Roh Chin sighed. "Yes, I see. Very well. I will go immediately to the bridge and make preparations to get underway. I assume the coordinates have already been fed into my ship's computer?"

"Yes. The course is up to you, but we are commanded to ignore risk and go with all deliberate speed. Naval Intelligence shows no concentrations of Exchange ships anywhere in the region. It is possible that we alone have intercepted the message at this stage. It is also possible, of course, that if it is not Mycohl doings we find, they will have gotten the message as well."

Gun Roh chin imagined coming into orbit around an alien star and facing a Mycohl ship armed to the teeth, and perhaps an Exchange naval patrol vessel at least as dangerous. *Well,* he thought to himself, resigned, *if they're there, I can at last have the satisfaction of shooting Manya at them.*

It wasn't difficult to plot the course, although it was at a hell of an angle. Frontier was *right!* According to the best and most recent maps he had, there was nothing at all there.

Even less difficult was ignoring his orders and programming as safe and sane a route through the Mycohl neck as he could manage. It would add perhaps twelve or thirteen hours, which wouldn't be noticed by Morok or the others, but it would almost ensure that they would at least survive.

Getting back was going to be much nastier. He had no desire to lose his life right now, much less spend the rest of it in alien captivity, but, if it had to happen, he hoped it wouldn't be for such an idiotic reason as chasing after demons.

In a little while, Krisha came up to the bridge. She usually didn't do that, preferring to sit in the wardroom, but she was most welcome.

"Am I intruding?" she asked him.

"You *never* intrude," he responded, meaning it. "Sit down."

"Are we underway?"

He nodded. "Arrival at this mysterious blank on the maps, where we sail off the edge, is about eighty-four standard hours flat out. If they aren't already where we are going, I would say that the Mycohlian patrol ship would be about six hours behind us."

"We all do as we are commanded to do," she sighed.

"Do *you* think there are demons where we're going?"

"I—probably not. But I have been in the presence of the Hosts of the Gods, so I do not reject the idea that demons exist. Only that it seems rather—unlikely— on the basis of that one message. I believe we will find something unpleasant, but that might well be a man driven mad by some terrible but totally explainable tragedy. People who sound like that man do often see demons where only madness lies."

"I know, I know. But our dear Miss Morgan said that the Exchange had something going over there, something they wanted very much to keep the Mycohl away from. Something big, she said. Big, and recent, I would say, if that distress call was really from a research vessel. She didn't know what it was, only that it was. Need to know and all that. What you don't know you cannot tell to Mizlaplanians who catch you with your hand in their candy."

She laughed softly at that. "You have such a way with words. I wonder if your thoughts are the same? You have no idea what it's like for a telepath to come up against someone it's impossible to read."

"My thoughts are such that no telepath who is also a beautiful priestess should be exposed to them," he said playfully. "Actually, I was just sitting here thinking about our Miss Morgan and her journey home on that ship."

"Don't tell me you miss her!"

He smiled. "No, it's not that. I was just thinking that somebody like that, going home in disgrace and possibly ruined, would be thinking of some way in which to mitigate her fate and restore her credibility. It's a ship and crew entirely of priests, His Holiness's personal guard and staff. She's not going to be able to twist their heads or fire up their lusts or get into any security area. Putting myself in her place right now, I think I'd direct my efforts to bringing home some completely new piece of information—unique information. His Holiness requires no locks or bars or security apparatus. No one has ever gazed upon a living one of his kind save those who have been ordained. She is a null, as I am a null. She may wonder—as, I admit, I have wondered—if she perhaps would be immune to the radiance that pervades and influences all others in the Holy Presence. She might feel it worth the risk and just 'accidentally' pick the wrong door."

Krisha looked up at him in surprise. "Captain—I have gazed upon a Holy One and been bathed in his presence. It is on a level different from any paranormal activity, and, as a telepath, I know first- or second-hand just what all the Talents are like. It's nothing like that. It doesn't come over your mind like the influence of a hypno; it permeates to the core of your very soul. You know, instantly, through every atom of your being, that you are in the presence of someone who can only be described as supernatural, so far above you that the gulf between people and the lowliest one-celled creature is as nothing compared to the gulf between you and He. If she should walk in there as you say, she will emerge like me."

"Now isn't that a thought?" he responded, grinning. "It gives a man a reason to survive this thing and get back home, doesn't it? Just to see and speak with Kelly the Holy Morgan, I'd fight ten demons with my bare hands!"

She couldn't help it; she broke up at the thought of it. "For that," she said, "I'll fight ten more demons at your back—and we'd win, too!"

...and, as a telepath, I know that, on some hand, that what all the Talans are like. It's nothing like theirs. It doesn't come over your mind like the suddenness of a liquid attentiveness in the core of your very soul. You know instantly, through every atom of your being, that you are in the presence of someone who can only be described as supernatural, so far above you that the gulf between people and the father we called on ours was nothing compared to the gulf between you and Ra. If we Should stick to there as you suppose will emerge like me."

"Aren't they though?" he responded, grinning.

"He gave a little a reason to survive this thing and get back home. It's just to return and speak with Kelly the Holy Morgan bel fight ten demons with my bare hands."

She nodded, her chin some broke up at the thought of it. "For that," she said, "I'll fight ten more demons at your back—and we'd win, too!"

Book Three:

Mycohl: The Red Team

A Matter Of Death And Life

Masquerade Party

It was the tradition of the Lords of Qaamil that, once a year, each Lord in turn should throw a massive festival in celebration of the eternal continuity of the Realm and its hives in which all the cells of the hive should participate and to which all the other Lords of Qaamil and their Hive Masters and retinue should be invited.

Over the years, this festival had evolved from mere celebration into a sort of contest in which each Lord was expected to outdo the efforts of the previous year's host and thus make the rival Lords look like pikers. It was an increasingly difficult objective, since it did not seem that such things could grow any larger or grander than they now were and because throwing such a bash brought hives to the brink of bankruptcy.

This effect filtered down to the Barons of each cell, who were expected to come up with suitable entertainment for their own races that would impress those also of their race who would attend from the other hives. Some of the races had strange ideas of what constituted a good time, and a few had trouble with the concept. What, for example, did one do to give a good time to Corithians who had no concept of emotions, who ate by absorbing rock, and who reproduced by converting rock into the raw materials of Corithian life and so literally constructed their young?

The answer, at least in that case, was that one did nothing, since doing nothing was more agreeable to the Corithians than any alternative. Most races, however, were far more difficult to satisfy.

The one who was impossible to satisfy was the Lord who would have to throw the next year's festival, since he would be faced with trying to figure out how to outdo the last. It was, therefore, taken as a given that the future Lord Host would do everything in his power to spoil everybody's party.

Humans were a very small part of the Mycohl Empire, the only one of the Three Empires to call itself such and run it in classical style, although without an emperor at its head. Under the law of Equitable Redistribution governing the absorption of new races into the Empire, the billions who had fallen under Mycohl control had been distributed among the various hives throughout the Realm so that no hive had a preponderance of one race and all racial subgroups, or cells, theoretically had an equal chance of attaining primacy. At least at the local level there was enough self-rule to ensure that no race would be one hundred per cent at the bottom of the heap.

The basis and heart of Mycohlian society was the *Qiimish,* or Holy Books, whose distilled essence was drilled into every citizen, from the lowest to the highest, almost from birth:

"The objective of all higher forms of life is the attainment of freedom. . . . Freedom is power. . . . The gods give power to those who can seize it and hold it. . . . All gains in civilization stem from struggles for dominance; a society at peace stagnates and loses its claims to power. . . . The eternal fate of the soul is based upon the hierarchical position it achieves in life. . . ."

The other empires called the Mycohlian civilization one of violence, degradation, and brutality; an interracial collection of gangsters using a religion based on social evolution to justify its own ugliness and excess. The Mycohl preferred to think of their civilization as dynamic, in which the cream always rose to the top and where plot and coup furthered progress. After all, did not the greatest ideas come from violent revolutions on all the worlds? Did not the great technological leaps come mostly from war?

And this was, for all its excesses, a civil war without bitterness; a civilization in ferment, yet watched over and controlled, even contained, by its master race, the Mycohl itself. Being parasites, they could walk among the lower forms and, undetected by the masses, watch and learn and enjoy, even participating at will, intervening only when no other course was open to them. It kept the hives honest, as it were, and everyone on their toes, for while the Mycohl had no Talents as such, they also were immune to them, being able to play whatever sweet mind's song a telepath wanted to hear or an empath to feel, all the time using their great ancestral gift of total disguise, and making even the Lords of Qaamil sleep less than soundly at night.

The setting for the main celebration would look all wrong to one who knew human history; a strange mix of high-tech wonders and medieval primitivism, with a great, gleaming castle lit by a rainbow of fairyland lights overlooking a vast plain of grass and mud illuminated by torches, where barbaric-looking creatures of many races wore rags or crude furs and seemed of another, distant, almost mythic age.

The human woman who walked barefoot through the mud-churned area where drols of two dozen races or more toiled marking off the areas and setting up tents and tables and other things, might not have looked very different from her primitive ancestors of a million or more years past. She might have been beautiful, even a temptress, had she had a gentler past, but her body bore the marks that age one quickly. The tattered brown fur loincloth that was all she wore left the scars on her back easy to see, although they were certainly old; other, smaller scars over other parts of her dark and weathered skin seemed almost a road map of her past, while the small, gunmetal-gray anklet on her left leg and the matching bracelets on her wrists, with their tell-tale metallic eyelets, told as much as that hard face and those ancient brown eyes of a past of toil and degradation.

An observer would have been less surprised if he could have known that she wore a thin prosthesis that expertly hid the small red diamond branded on her forehead above the nose, which would in other circumstances have clearly marked her as an empath.

She had been beautiful once; before all that happened to her, before the deep scar as from a saber had been etched in her left cheek and down into the lip. Oddly, she did not resent that most disfiguring of her scars; it had liberated her as much as her initial beauty had condemned her to house slavery among the highborn of her cell. She had hated the one who disfigured her—another woman, in fact, out of jealousy—but strangling that woman, watching the life drain out of the bitch, had settled that fire. It had been the first time she'd had both the opportunity and the nerve to pay someone back, and the thrill of it had been indescribable.

A huge man, a human of tremendous height and weight and with muscles like a blacksmith's and hair like an ape's, put down the table he was carrying and called to her. He was sweaty, filthy, and probably had so many pests living on him that he qualified as his own private cell keeper.

"Hey! Hugirl!" he shouted. "Hugirl come shake gum tit'n puss fer workin' hard pushman!"

"Pushman got bigger tits than *dis* hugirl—go bendsuck pushman self!" she snapped without breaking her slow steady stride.

"Hey! Hugirl got fuzzhead? No like realmen?"

She stopped and turned slightly toward him. "Hugirl

loves realmen. Pushman find realmen, den call 'er!"

That, of course, enraged the big man, and he tossed aside the table and made for her. She whirled and faced him full on, and although he was gigantic compared to her, he stopped, sensing danger. There was something in her manner, in her stance, in the quickness of her reactions and in the momentary flexing of her muscles that brought him up short. He made an odd symbol in the air, and shouted, "Pushman don't haul wit' no witchbitch!"

And, with that, it was over. She instantly relaxed, turned, and continued to walk toward the castle grounds, while the big man went back to his table muttering, "Pushman got fuzzhead 'self. Ain't no hugirl walk byself 'less she witchbitch!"

She wasn't really angry at the man, nor disappointed she didn't have a crack at him, either. He was just typical of his kind, and he was also a *big* sucker who might have torn a limb off or something before she could have killed him. She could have taken him, if she thought he was really going to come all the way after her, but being an empath had advantages in that kind of confrontation, even over telepathy. Men like that rarely thought through their actions first. A bit of broadcast empathy, calming his rage to where he *could* think and back off, was far more prudent and safe. This wasn't the time or place for killing anyway; it was supposed to be a celebration.

There were not many humans here at all. Over there, were a whole raft of Thions, looking much like giant, wingless horse flies about the size of a human, constructing a grandiose nest out of Thion silk; across from them, tiny *Dhorths*, like blue, duckbilled bipedal lizards, sawed and shaped and carved for their own kind. And so it was across the whole field until she reached the castle grounds. A great black shape suddenly rose before her, blocking her path. It was big; bigger even than the huge man who had called to her, but, while humanoid in appearance, it was made of a black synthetic that would take an incredible amount of punishment and it had only a slit in its otherwise blank face, through which three dull green lights emanated from a triangle of holes.

"Who are you and why are you on the grounds?" asked the guardian robot in a deliberately mandated electronic-sounding voice.

"The Hive Master has commanded my presence," she responded crisply. "Kalia 4KX26, Pusabi Cell."

"Checking . . . Check approved. You are late. Enter through the blue door to your right up this side path and await security check."

She nodded and walked past the guardian, taking the route indicated. There were several doors at the end, all of different colors and bearing different shapes, leading to separate security areas for each species.

Each door had both a hand plate and an eye viewer resembling half a set of binoculars. She looked into the viewer of the door she'd been directed to and put her right hand on the plate. Varicolored lights played for just an instant on her eyes, leaving only a brief afterimage, and she felt a slight burning on her palm. Then the door started buzzing. She pushed on it and entered a small sitting room that looked more like a doctor's waiting room than a security-check area.

If she looked out of place on the grounds, she looked even more so in this air-conditioned and cushioned environment. She decided not to sit; if she was indeed late, through no fault of her own, then they damned well should be out here in a hurry.

The far door opened, and she was somewhat surprised to see another human. It was a man—squarejawed, hairy, and muscular—with thick black hair and a crudely trimmed full beard. He wore a threadbare loincloth and little else, and, although they were clearly from different ancestral human stock, they made a fairly good pair of primitives. He was a tall man, and seemed a bit surprised to find that she was almost as tall as he was, but he recovered quickly even as she tensed in automatic defense. Something inside her, gut instinct born of experience, told her that this man, too, wore a skin patch that hid his Talent brand, and that underneath it would be not the red of an empath or the green of the telepath or even the white of the telekinetic, but rather the blue diamond of that most feared Talent, and justly so, the hypno.

"You have to relax and not fight me," he told her in a deep, rich bass with just a trace of an exotic accent.

Even so, she instinctively tried to avoid his gaze while still seeming to look at him, and she brought up her empathic defenses as well. It was no use; the fellow was good and he was *strong*; one lock of eyes was enough. She couldn't not look at those eyes, and she felt her Talent waning, her defenses collapse. All thought drained from her.

"You will relax and answer my questions without hesitation, and you will clearly remember everything we do or say," he told her soothingly, then proceeded to run through the stock security and loyalty drill. A very well-trained, very well-prepared enemy could fool even a hypno in this situation, but someone who was not willingly so prepared would crack. This was a final check; they already knew exactly who she was from the eye, palm, and perspiration tests, and they'd read her genetic code and compared it to file. The only thing those checks could not verify was whether or not someone had been intercepted on the way by an outside agency and reprogrammed for latent or negative action. *That* he could tell, and he was satisfied in a short while that she was clean.

He gave her back herself. It was an odd sensation, like someone had held you underwater and suddenly you broke free to the surface. She knew it well, but she hated It and would always hate it.

"I am Josef 3BX47, of the Vronsky Cell," he told her, trilling the *r* in Vronsky. There were only three human cells in Lord Skuazos' hive, and as each had their own planet and retained some of their old culture beneath the new, they didn't meet very often. "Please come this way. The others are waiting."

She followed him down a hall and into a larger, conference-type room that clearly wasn't built for humans. Humans, however, had a handy way of being able to sit almost anywhere.

Three others were already in the room, none of them human. One was a *Julki*; a squat, rectangular-shaped creature much like a two-meter slug, with long, curved antennae and four, long, independent eyestalks. The nostrils were a series of tiny brown blips below, and the mouth opened somewhat like a spiral, giving the creatures, to humans, a permanent expression of shock and surprise. Along its broad back appeared to be a thick carpet of long brown hairs; in actuality, they were long, tiny tendrils almost like tentacles, which were capable of most delicate work. Julkis were most useful for a different natural ability, however; give one just a few of your cells, a lick of your skin from its tiny tongue perhaps, and it could synthesize and secrete a whole series of nasty poisons that would protect it from you and make it toxic to whoever and whatever it was around.

The second creature was a Thion. Up close, the resemblance to the common house fly that somehow, like the cockroach and a number of other unwelcome guests, had managed eventually to make it to the stars where humans colonized, was no less pronounced. It had the ability to eat almost anything organic and carbon-based, raw and not necessarily well preserved, either. Few other races would invite a Thion to dinner, although all were tempted to send them the garbage.

The third creature was a Corithian. It just was there, a meter and a half lump of dull silver, rounded, looking like nothing so much as an oval sculpture of a beetle not quite finished. Atop its back, almost centered, were two black egg-shaped bulges that were clearly what it used for eyes.

"This is Tobrush," Josef said, gesturing to the Julki, "and this is Robakuk," now nodding to the Thion. "Our Corithian comrade is Desreth. This is Kalia, and now the company is complete."

"The Hive Master has been notified and is on his way," said an eerie, expressionless voice that sounded less like a living thing than the guardian robot, although it had no electronic component. Kalia never liked or trusted Corithians, and she'd had little experience with them. She couldn't help but wonder where the voice was coming from in that blob.

She looked around at the others. "Does anyone know why we were all summoned here?" she asked. "And why so surreptitiously?"

"I assume it is something to do with security for the celebration," hissed the Julki, forming the words rather clearly by forcing air out of that mouth in odd ways. It, too, sounded very alien, but at least it sounded *alive*. "If you have not been here before, then none of us has, which makes us totally unknown locally."

She nodded. It made about as much sense as anything. She looked over at Josef. "Two humans—one Pusabi and one Vronsky, but no Tripolitan. Since there are few humans here, I assume they believe the Tripolitans will cause some trouble."

The Tripolitans were the third and last, but hardly least, human cell in the hive.

"The Lord Qabar of the Makuut Hive hosts next year's celebration, I believe," the Thion noted, in a high, squeaky voice. "Is not Makuut of your kind? And is not Tripolitania closest to his realm?"

"Ah! I pay little attention to such things, since I am not normally invited to such affairs," she responded a bit ungraciously. Still, it all made sense. Qabar was the only human Lord of a hive in the entire Empire, which made him a brilliant and ruthless man indeed. She knew of him; all humans did everywhere in the Empire. There was at once a sense of pride and an example that humans could not only aspire to, but actually reach, the highest possible position, and equally, a sense of relief that no matter how nasty and ruthless your own leaders might be, they weren't as bad as living under somebody like Qabar.

At that moment, the Hive Master entered, ending all discussion. Both she and Josef dropped to one knee and bowed their heads in respect; the Thion lowered itself in an equivalent gesture so its head was almost on the floor, and the Julki essentially straightened up in his own version of the same. The Corithian remained an impassive lump, as usual.

The Hive Master, like his Lord, was a *Yasbrin*, and they were as mean and formidable-looking a race as the galaxy had yet bred, standing two and a half meters tall on wide, furry feet; eyes the size of teacups, bulging from a thick, mottled, black and yellow face with a short snout that was festooned with so many carnivorous fangs, they spilled out even with the mouth closed.

"Stand and be at ease," the Hive Master told them in a deep, guttural voice that fit the fearsome visage. He settled himself into a chair made for his race at one end of the room. "I overheard the speculation and it is essentially correct. The celebration will be grand and opulent; ships are coming in here at all hours, disgorging specific luxuries for the nobility of all the races that will be represented here. It is a financial strain, we will admit, but we have planned and budgeted for it and we will make it. Lord Qabar, next year's host, is not as good a long-range planner, nor does he pay proper attention to details. He puts things off, and that means he faces ruin next year. That has left him with few options: praying for a miracle, and those are pretty scarce, or making a successful conquest so that the losers pay—and given the relative strengths in the region, there's little likelihood of success there—or, finally, screwing up our party so that no matter what he can manage next year, he looks good compared to us. Of the three, which would *you* choose?"

"Point taken, my Lord," Josef responded. "May I also assume that you believe his plans for such an operation include the Tripolitans?"

"You may. Qabar's own mother was a Tripolitan; the two cells are of different hives but of common ancestry generally, and there is much trading of breeding stock. The Tripolitan Baron Fasil is ambitious and the sort who is not averse to embarrassing us to improve his own position here. We assume competency, or none of them would have risen to their current positions and held them this long. Thus, we also assume they know the humans on our permanent security staff. Their own advance party arrives late tonight, but much of the preliminary work has been or is being done by drols from the Vronsky and Pusabi who, because they are closer at hand, are doing more of the work. Josef, Kalia, both of you were among a pool of people our computers initially suggested; you both come highly recommended by your superiors, and you both have risen from the drol underclass and are comfortable there."

Kalia thought to herself that she would never be *comfortable* as a drol but she could certainly endure it.

"That was why you had us come in in disguise with the work battalions," Josef commented. "But they still will be expecting someone."

"They will, but they won't know who or from where, which puts them at somewhat the same disadvantage as we have."

"Then what are these others?" Kalia asked him. "Backup?"

"And more. Tobrush is a *very* strong telepath, and, as a supervisor of work brigades, will be able to do some random scanning and also perhaps give either of you a little warning if something blows. She will also be testing and checking Qabar's own Julkis to make certain that they do not contribute certain toxins to the festivities. Robakuk is a telekinetic who has proven very capable over the years, and with the large number of Thions present, will be able to not only cover your back but also rally any members of the hive if bodies are necessary. Desreth is an excellent analyst and observer who has other useful abilities as well, and, frankly, we don't believe they will be expecting us to use a Corithian spy. However, since only our own Corithians will be on hand, the rest not terribly interested in this sort of thing and here only because of protocol, all of them will be ours and at your disposal."

"The irrationality of these festivals is beyond our comprehension, and interest," Desreth noted. "However, the fact that they are held and that they represent a threat to the hive we understand. Corithians under Qabar do not have the trust and involvement our hive gives us here. We would not be concerned if he were to be badly embarrassed, bankrupted, or overthrown."

That was certainly clear enough. Although the Corithians were a race that was not only physiologically but psychologically different from just about any others known, and really didn't fit in very well with the rest, they were a pragmatic race. They did crave knowledge of the universe and they did need to expand. The Mycohl had the spaceships and the guns and the sheer numbers. The Corithians had proven invaluable and solidly loyal to the hives that had given them true equal status and access, and many, if not most, of the Lords who had them in their hives were willing to trust what they couldn't understand or directly control. Lord Skuazos had involved them wherever they wished to involve themselves and had used them well, and they had more than repaid him for it.

"Josef will aid those of you who require it in Talent defense. I know that you all have some experience with it, but we must expect that whoever Qabar uses will be very good." the Hive Master warned them. "Be better. Remember that we have only eight more days until we open the celebration. Whatever Qabar does will be done before the celebration officially gets underway and all the Lords are present. To do otherwise, to disrupt the actual ceremonies themselves, would be to incur the wrath of all the Lords for spoiling their fun and would make him the target of everyone. The attempt will be to embarrass *us* instead. It is your function to see that this does not happen."

The meaning of that last was clear to all of them, although said in a businesslike tone. One advanced in the Empire on successes; at this level, the rewards and promotions might well be lavish. Death was not the worst punishment for failure, either. Not on this high level.

The Mycohlian value system was simple and easily understood: Life was a testing ground and you got one shot at it. It was not how high you were born in life, nor how high you rose, but where you wound up at the end that determined your status in the afterlife. Failure meant demotion, then the worst treatment, and then death at that level. For that reason, those above the underclasses tended to commit suicide rather than face demotion; at least you maintained your status that way. Such values were a given from the cradle, for all hives, cells, and races. It wasn't certain if it was true of the Corithians, who had no belief in an afterlife or much else, but in their own culture it was an absolute that first you determined why you failed and sent a report, then you died as a defective. It amounted to the same thing, anyway; Mycohl priests explained it simply by agreeing with the Corithians that the strange metallic race had no souls anyway.

The Hive Master having left, they rose and relaxed again, although Kalia stiffened when Josef turned first to her. He saw it and said, "I realize loyalty is to family, then cell, then hive, but in this case we are all working for the hive. We must trust one another."

"I trust no slaver's eye, nor the brain behind it," she responded crisply "no matter what the family, cell, or hive."

"I have neither the time nor will to prove myself to you," he replied. "You went under far too quickly out there for someone attempting to fight it off. You'll be no help to us if they use a hypno, and they most certainly will. I intend merely to give you some automatic defenses. They won't save you from a strong hypno in physical contact, but they will make you aware of and able to fight off anything less—and give out a mental warning if anyone gets hold of you so that Citizen Tobrush, tuned into all of us, will immediately know. The conditioning will not last; I shall have to renew it from day to day. This technique, however, is not widely known—most others are inferior—and it has saved many people."

Before she could do more than frame a reply, he grabbed her and she felt herself caught in that mental undertow once more, powerless to resist. Much of what he did was not verbal, and bewildered even the others, including the telepath who could follow it. From the manner in which Josef was proceeding, Tobrush got the distinct impression that the hypno himself had no idea what he was doing or how it worked; he only knew that it *did* work.

Again there was that sense of breaking clear of the surface and she was out from under again. Josef wasted no time, going next to the Thion, Robakuk, and repeating the procedure on the creature. She tried to follow what he was saying, knowing it had to be pretty much what was done to her or that someone like Tobrush would know it and say so, but it was mostly nonsense phrases. Finally, he treated Tobrush in much the same manner; Desreth was immune to all the mental Talents; only telekinetics, whose effect was physical, were any real worry to a Corithian.

Corithians, of course, did not really worry; they merely calculated all risk factors.

"Be prepared to go out and assume your roles," Josef told them. "Since the Hive Master coordinates all assignments, we shall all be not only where we can cover one another but also in the areas most likely to be targets. Remember that if you stop someone from sabotage we would prefer them alive but it's not essential. If, however, they manage to actually pull something off, we will need a living perpetrator to prove maliciousness. Our lives and fortunes depend on all of us thinking through our actions rather than merely acting on impulse and destroying what we need."

It was a valid warning, but it made the job a lot tougher.

He turned to Kalia. "What about you? Can you maintain an underclass persona and stoop to drol work?"

"I have never had the power to order others to do my share," she responded acidly. "See that you maintain your own cover, slaver."

"I have no idea how you came to be as you are or anything else, only that the hive computer and the Hive Master's staff says you are good. If you are, then leave your hurts and bitterness and anger here. We can afford no individualists in this. We stand or fall as a team, and we live or die by each other's deeds."

"So long as we watch each other's backs rather than stare into each other's eyes," she came back with a slight sneer, then turned and walked back the way she'd come, toward the drol camp on the field outside.

"We all carry armor against the bitterness and hurts

and angers of our past," Robakuk noted philosophically. "And I doubt that we can just leave them conveniently to the side. Still, she carries more armor than most."

"It does seem that the permanent sneer carved in that once pretty face more accurately reflects what is inside right now," Josef agreed. "But I bet she is a hell of a fighter. Still . . . I, too, started my life in irons. Being a young and inexperienced hypno in a colony of older and more experienced hypnos isn't much different than not being one in this situation. Cutting off those irons became my obsession, and when I did, my spirit soared. Most people I've ever met feel that way. She, on the other hand, may be the only citizen I have ever met that kept hers on."

"She keeps the visions hidden," Tobrush, the telepath, told them. "Perhaps if I were of her kind, I would be able to piece together the images that come into her mind, but I can make only limited sense out of it. Whatever scars we bear, I just get the sense that she drew the worst of the lot. The fact that she is still here and at this level says much for her if that be the case. The only standard I have for her appearance is the one in your own mind, of course, since, to be honest, you humans are among the more hideously repugnant and at the same time incredibly silly looking creatures I know. I gather from your mind, though, that the facial scar is a major disfigurement. As much as the irons, that adds to her enigma, since at her level she could have quite easily gotten it repaired to invisibility."

"Yes, that's true," Josef admitted. "Yet she wears it like a soldier's medal." He sighed. "Well, let us join her and get to work. At least there is no one of her race who would think from her appearance that she was anything but a drol. As for me, I often dream of leading a great army against overwhelming odds, but I will do as I am ordered and guard the Lord's pudding."

❖   ❖   ❖

Although she was an empath, Kalia wasn't completely unprotected from other Talents. One of the things you had to learn first in order to survive above the drol level was how to fool them, how to get around them, and how, sometimes, to use their own arrogance against them. Telepaths were the hardest to fool, but because she had mastered the technique, through much sweat and meditation and practice, she had become very valuable. Not many ever did master the technique, but those who did so and had the will to use it could walk in places no one else dared and do so undetected.

It was easiest to do when among the drols, the lowest laboring class of the Mycohl, who were treated little better than domestic animals by the upper classes. Fewer than five per cent of any population had Talents, and among the drols it was far less than that and usually very weak when it showed at all. Although possessed of a native cleverness, they were appallingly ignorant and even their few customs and traditions were simplistic. The universe to them was a place of magic governed by great wizards, witches, sorcerers, and demons, and it was unlikely that most of this bunch here even knew they were on a planet different than their own. To know that, one first had to know what a planet was.

In an empire that had developed interstellar spacecraft, planet-destroying weaponry, and robots—and could even regrow severed limbs or project three-dimensional images to different stars—the mere existence of the drols seemed odd to outsiders and proof of Mycohl depravity. To the Mycohl, it was part of the natural order. A bottom caste *had* to exist to make sense of the religion and its view of the universe; rough, often brutal treatment of inferiors was a given throughout the hierarchy. To the Mycohl, such layers were necessary to make sense of the universe.

To be sure, the kind of robots and machinery that

had built the great castle, for example, or the ships that brought these drols here from their cell worlds, could easily do in a day what was taking almost a week for these people to do poorly, and by hand. Such was true of just about all work that drols did everywhere. But if one must have drols, then they had to have work. To do things in any other way would be, to Mycohl thinking, immoral.

The key was social mobility. True, most of these drols would die drols, and most would live lives that were brutal, hard, and short, without the benefits of science or other knowledge. Only a few, a very few—the smartest and the Talents—would have the guts to take the chance and rise above it, or get the kind of break that would accomplish the same thing. But as long as it was possible, and as long as every drol knew somebody who knew somebody who knew somebody who had risen up and out, there was always the hope that they or their kids or grandkids would be among the elect.

Kalia had been born a drol and spent her first twelve years a drol. She still found their childlike ignorance and appreciation of the most basic pleasures to be refreshingly honest and appealing, and she could meld with them very easily and be accepted by them as one of their own. Their basic language, which had only a mild level of consistency, was also a wonderful shield against telepathy Shifting to their speech patterns and graceless moves, thinking those basic thoughts in that way, she was able to shift down her more sophisticated self. Just as Josef's hypno blocks wouldn't stop a strong hypno who had you face to face at close quarters, neither would her exercises fool a strong telepath who was trying to pick your mind specifically—but first a telepath would have to pick her out of the crowd, and for that, this mental regimen was almost foolproof.

A supervisor spotted her and immediately ordered her into roustabout work, raising large tents and setting them against the weather. Years of lifting weights and other exercises reinforced by various toning drugs had made her hard as steel and as strong as many men, and she fell right into the routine. If there were any ringers here from Qabar's crowd, they would be pretty damned tired when they had the opportunity to do any mischief.

Josef posed as one of the drol supervisors; although large and strong himself, his lack of the calluses, bruises, and scars that a drol his age and build would have acquired made it impossible for him to fit in on the basic level. Supervisors were occasionally very low-level, low-strength Talents; more often, they were simply bigger, stronger, and nastier than the supervisor they'd worked under, and had finally risen up and killed the bastard and replaced him. Mostly he strode around with the three-tailed whip, cracking it, barking orders, and occasionally using the whip, although sparingly, on someone he thought really needed it. Some supervisors used the whip for power binges and really enjoyed it, but those were few. The smart ones remembered that supervisors were still drols, still had to sleep and eat with the people they bossed, and that too much of that and you'd wind up a dead supervisor very quickly.

Mostly he was studying faces and actions, as convinced as the Hive Master that the only human Lord in the Mycohl Empire would use his own kind to do his dirty work. If so, they would be good—as good as Kalia, at least, who he watched with a sense of admiration. She made no false moves at all, blending in perfectly, even to the curses and other interactions with her co-workers, and watching her lift and steady a log so large and heavy he doubted if *he* could lift it, made him respect her in other ways as well. He could see now why she had been chosen, and he was grateful that she was, at least nominally, on *his* side.

From the corner of his eye he caught something

moving and turned to see what it was. A Julki, from across the way, just standing there and looking mostly at its own people. The trouble was, all Julkis looked pretty much alike to him except that the males had flashy-colored tendrils, while the females, like Tobrush, were mostly that mud-ugly grayish brown.

<*That you, Tobrush? If it is, and you need to talk, wiggle some back tendrils and I'll ease over.*>

Some back tendrils wiggled and at least a small bunched clump made a gesture that was obscene only to humans. He stifled a chuckle and slowly wandered over, as if seeing what a Julki was doing this close to the human camp.

"I have some general thought impressions from your area that are suspicious," the Julki told him. "The girl is good. Maybe too good. I have no idea where she is in that mob. The others, they are good, too, but occasional terms flash by that do not match the gutter speech of the rest."

"You're sure it's not just the girl and me?"

"No. You are both from the majority of the two groups here. This is definitely a third."

"Where?"

"I cannot tell, but the general area is from near the Cell Baron's pavilion. I only noticed when they began collecting there, coming from the area of the dignitaries' tent."

"I'll see what I can."

"Have caution," Tobrush warned. "I received at least one slight indicator of a telepathic scan."

"I'll watch it," he assured the telepath. "Just make sure *you* watch *me.*"

He wandered off back toward the construction and after a while made his way to Kalia.

" 'Ey! Pusabi bitch!" he snarled at her, but with some slight good humor. "Pusabi pushmen got make der hugirls do manwork?"

"Pusabigirl haul asses much Vronsky stringmen, still do hauljob!" she snapped back.

"Pavilion," he whispered so softly he almost just mouthed it. "Telepath, others." Loudly and without pause, he added, "So? Cookplace need woodcarry. Haul ass!" And he gave a little crack of the whip that just brushed her.

She looked at him with a haughty expression, then spat near his feet, turned her back to him, and stalked off toward the large flat area in back of and just to the right of the Cell Baron's most completed pavilion.

The act went over big with the nearby Pusabi men, some of whom started chuckling and making snide remarks concerning which of the two, the Vronsky supervisor or the Pusabi girl, really had balls. He snarled at them and cracked the whip in mock anger and then stalked off, but while it set the men back to work, it didn't stop the sniggering.

Kalia's dossier had said she was expert at telepathic masking, and Tobrush had pretty much confirmed that. He wasn't quite so good at it, but the Qabar telepath had already slipped, letting himself be noticed. When a telepath hit another telepath's shield, he knew it, and was probably still cursing himself out for the slip. If so, he'd keep his Talent damped down until he really needed it, and that was just fine with Josef.

The drol night crew was about ready to relieve the day crew, so he started to make his way toward the pavilion himself. He was hungry enough to eat that slop they fed them by now, anyway, and he wanted a look at the area. The real question was: What the hell did you do to screw up this party for so many different races and cells beyond repair?

Let's see, what was over in the pavilion area? The pavilion itself, of course, but what would be gained by bombing or burning it? Even if your timing was perfect so that it couldn't be repaired or replaced before the big shots got there, it would only inconvenience one group. There was the altar, but they wouldn't touch that. Even if they were believers in nothing, there was still no gain in doing that.

The kitchen area? A possibility. Poison or foul the food. But that was still too limited to make any sense. Again, screwing up one or two cells or just the humans wouldn't achieve for Qabar what he really needed, which was a total fiasco affecting the vast majority of the eighty or so races represented here.

I'm just not thinking dirty enough, he told himself, irritated that nothing was coming to him. *What would I do if the circumstances were reversed.*

The only thing he could think of was a sudden, major blast of cold air and torrential rain or hail, but that would mean sabotaging Lord Skuazos' weather-control center, a really high-tech operation best handled by local security.

No, it was something *here,* something centered right around this area, something that was totally escaping his notice and which, once he'd found it, he'd hate himself for not discovering sooner. He just hoped he'd hit on what it was in time to avert a disaster.

It would have to be something here especially for the festival; something that wasn't normally a part of the complex and thus wouldn't be under the normal scrutiny of the Hive Master's own security forces. But what? From here, what could cause a massive disruption affecting the whole valley and ruining everything?

He went over to the huge fire pit and got his plate of slop. It smelled almost as bad as it looked, and was worse than he remembered it. He passed up the cheap ale; they put something in it that made you sleep like a log so you'd be fresh in the morning. Instead, he got a mug of water. It was warm and had a slightly metallic taste, but it made the slop digestible, more or less.

As he sat and tried to get his meal down, he kept

looking over the incoming mob and wondering which of them was part of a plot to screw this all up, and what had they found that would louse up not only humans but Julkis and Thions and seventy-odd more races who had so little in common that, as foul as this slop was, it was gourmet cooking compared to what those others liked to eat.

Well, if Kalia was smart enough to take the water instead of the ale, maybe *she* could figure it out.

That, he realized, was part of the problem. Cell pride, male pride, personal pride. Deep down, he knew he was almost afraid that she *would* figure it out first.

He sat there, seeing just how many would take that water instead of the ale. Those would at least narrow down the likely suspects. These guys couldn't have brought much equipment with them, if any, and they'd have to have cover stories so they'd be part of some known clan, maybe using a hypno to convince somebody she was really their old Cousin Zim. Whatever they were doing had to be with available material and supplies and almost certainly would have to be done at night.

Well, he'd remain awake for a while and see what he could see, but he couldn't stay awake for the next seven days and keep up the act. Night was the Thions' element—and the Corithians', if they wanted it to be.

The drols were beginning to group into small clans where they could settle in for the night; tired as they were, there were a lot of mating noises going on all over right now, and a few drols wandering around who hadn't yet found anybody they felt like lying with for the night.

" 'Ey! Vronsky Shortlord! What be tune? Vronskyboy turnon from dem bones of Pusabigirl?"

He looked up and saw a woman he'd had in his group when they'd flown in here. She had big bones, big breasts, and a body like a stone hauler's and she looked a lot like his mother probably looked at age fifteen or so. He barely remembered his mother and was never sure which one of the clan women she was anyway, but they all looked sort of the same.

"Yea, bitch try suckup in haulass boat. Want stingtail, Vronskygirl?"

She turned her rear end to him suggestively. "Oooo! Dat be love, Shortlord?"

He gave her a playful swipe with the whip, without pain or force, and she laughed it off.

He didn't see Kalia. Almost everyone had settled in and presumably she had, too. *What the hell*, he thought. *If I don't take supervisor's privilege I'm going to stand out anyway*.

"C'mon, bitch! Show ol' Vronskyboy how best ones do it!"

The sunlight and the noise of the group getting ready to feed woke him up. The big woman was still there, sleeping almost pressed into him, still snoring lightly.

It wasn't unusual for supervisors to get propositioned for the obvious reasons; she'd probably stick near him from now on for that very reason. On the other hand, she *was* kind of cute and as good, maybe better, than she advertised, and she added to his cover. She also had a good wit and a talent for wisecracks, which helped offset her somewhat unexpected masochistic streak.

During the next few days there was little progress, but the effect of the drol life was taking its toll on him. Immersed in it for the first time since he'd been a small boy, he found himself beginning to think in the drol patois and, as a result, found himself thinking and acting more like them than like someone undercover. The ease with which the veneer of civilized freemen society had stripped itself away depressed him even as it continued. He was aching, forever tired, getting calluses and sores all over, and to no profit.

The temptation to use his hypno powers was also

enormous, and he began to think that maybe Kalia had been more correct than he wanted to admit about hypnos not knowing what it was to be on the bottom. In that sense, the experience was a real education for him.

He had also, almost inevitably, picked up a retinue of sorts. The girl had stuck with him, of course, and she had clan sisters who used that as an opening, and even though he knew in the back of his mind that it was his position among the drols that was causing all the attention and not his native charm and good looks, it still fed his ego. Hypnos tended to more or less arrange what they wanted, almost as a matter-of-fact; to receive such attention without intervention was something new to him.

The drols weren't much of a source of information, though. Was there anyone strange or different that they noticed? Well, all Pusabi were strange and different to them. Other than that, no, and they were basically working the pavilion area, helping to install pipes and fitting chairs and the like, following very clearly drawn diagrams. Occasionally a master plumber or carpenter, freemen from the castle and almost never human, would come by to check the work or correct this or that, always explaining the job or problem to the supervisors in clear, patient terms.

He had the suspicion that it was those types who posed a threat; they alone went from cell pavilion to cell pavilion and could do the most damage over a wide area, but the diagrams looked right and they would not only have been thoroughly checked at the start but would be continually checked by security hypnos.

Once in a while he would see Kalia, almost always with a different drol man, but she never even exchanged glances with him. He began to worry that she had fallen a bit too easily into the drol life, and that she might no longer really be on the job, but he knew better than to blow her cover to allay his worries.

Tobrush continued to get occasional indications of telepathic activity, not only in the pavilion area that Josef was working but also from a *Quarg* pavilion area down a bit on the other side, but nothing that could be pinned down. Robakuk had actually spent nights atop the pavilion roof, unseen but seeing, watching for any signs of nocturnal mischief. So far, he had seen nothing of consequence.

Time was ticking by. Clearly something was planned, something was up, but what? Why hadn't they been able to see anything at all, discover at least some evidence of tampering?

He was acutely aware of how fast the time was going. If they couldn't unearth the plot, if they couldn't figure it out and then prevent it, he'd be up at that castle again and under one of their nasty machines, where they'd burn out that part of his brain that gave him his hypno powers, along with, as an inevitable consequence, much of his long-term memory retrieval and a few other ugly side effects. Then they would send him back, not even as supervisor, to return to Vronsky as a drol worker and be worked to death.

The answer, he knew, was right in front of him somewhere. It stood there, in plain sight, almost shouting at him yet somehow still eluding him.

Damn Lord Qabar!

Fun And Games

With only two days to go, it was Tobruck who called in the heavy hitters; master telepaths, making no particular attempt to hide themselves or conceal their Talents, moving into and up and down the regions where activity was suspected.

There were no human telepaths of any power available, but since they were trying to flush out the malefactors or maybe get lucky with some of the non-telepathic members of Qabar's team, that didn't seem to matter.

Josef was not the only one wondering why no human telepaths had been brought in from the start. It would have made more sense to pair him with one of those rather than the empath girl, who might have gone native so much that he hadn't seen a trace of her in two days.

The telepaths went through the crowds, their races fearsome to the drols and causing a lot of superstitious nonsense as well as generalized fear among them. They came up pretty empty at the end of the day. That wasn't exactly a big surprise; if you had six hundred frightened drols all radiating fear and concern, how the hell could even the best telepath be expected to pick out those who were nervous or afraid for specific reasons? Well, at least when they demanded his report before executing Summary Judgment on him for failure, he'd be able to tell them to their faces that the next time they wanted results like this they should listen less to their damned

the drols for a diet for the rest of their elaborate the considerable creatures . . . importantly all these drols personnel computers and more to the chief field agent who would be responsible.

Tobrush agreed that their failure so far was due mostly to the limitations in personnel imposed on them and the heavy-handedness of Imperial Security rather than any laxity on their part. Not that it would help. Nobody ever executed a judge for sending an innocent person to his death. When you're on top, with no one above questioning *your* judgment, blame can always be shifted with a clear conscience.

At this point, they were resigned to their fate. "The only hope I have now," the Julki told him, "is that one or more of the Hidden Masters will be here, as is likely, and will call the Hive Master and perhaps the Lord to account."

That cheered him a bit. He was willing to accept responsibility; willing, even, to die for that failure—it was the price of being a freeman—but his death would have far more meaning if the ones above were also to join him in the Great Darkness.

"You think, then, that they're not going to have any more luck than we have."

The Julki gave a kind of spitting noise, then said, "They could not find an enemy who was in full uniform and had a sign painted on him! That is why they are mere soldiers and not free agents. Great power is meaningless if you have the brains of a stone. It means you become merely an instrument, a well-treated, well-paid drol of someone with even the brains of a cloud."

"I doubt if even our best free agent telepath could do anything now," he responded glumly. "By now, whatever they've set up is set up, and they've been hypnoed into being just ordinary drols until something triggers them and the action begins."

"They better have more than that planned. One of the ways for a Host Lord to cut costs is to eliminate the considerable expense of transporting all these drols from so many races back where they came from. After the tear-down, all but a few will be sent to the Great Dark. One suspects that, particularly if they get away with it, the only human drols left on this entire planet will be you and the girl. If they don't have a way out, their very success will kill them, too."

He hadn't thought of that. The logic of it depressed him even more. Not the fact that almost it these drols would be executed in another ten days or so—they were only drols and there was always a surplus of drols. It was the idea that his Summary Judgment for failure would be that he and the girl would most likely be lobotomized and set to roam here, the only two of their kind on the planet. Even worse, she might well be given the honorable way out, as the others surely also would, and allowed to commit suicide; he, on the other hand, would be required to report and accept full blame and judgment in the name of the team, condemning him not only to a life but an eternity all alone, and at a status *lower than a drol*.

The hell with it. There was still one day left. If these Qabar assholes really did get away with whatever it was without him figuring it out and stopping them, then he didn't *deserve* any better! Although the distant skies echoed with the booms of visitors arriving from all over the Empire, and the castle was taking on a festive air, there was still one day left before they were forced to clear the area and cell personnel took over.

His harem awaited him. They knew he was some kind of friend of the Julki by now, but being drols, they wouldn't go within a hundred meters of such a monster. They had been more distraction than cover, and he was losing patience with them. The damned sluts weren't much better than animals, anyway. Less valuable than animals, really. If they did the work that animals did, they would deserve more attention.

There was some commotion down the way that almost

drowned out their calls. Lots of technician teams were in now, clearing away the drols and doing the final wiring, lighting, and the like, checking all the pavilion hookups, seeing that everything was just so. It looked like they'd brought in some heavy equipment to dig behind the main pavilions on Tobrush's side of the valley. Sewage disposal was a real tricky problem in this large a crowd, especially when one race's sewage was the other's steak.

The girls were suddenly all around him and jabbering away and he had to shout, "Shuddup! Vronskygirls hush or bleed whipass!"

That, alas, wasn't much of a threat. They were used to the whip, to a degree. The degree he was thinking of, though, would take them out for the count and they seemed to sense it and quieted down.

He stalked deliberately up the hill, neither looking nor feeling very drolish right about then. To hell with cover. He'd played drol and it had gotten him nowhere. He strode up to the galley area, got a crude wooden cup, and pumped some water and drank it, then sat there, leaning on the pump, trying to think.

Suddenly, he froze, then slowly looked down at the cup, then moved away from the pump and turned and stared back at it.

And he felt at that point just as stupid and angry at himself as he'd predicted he would when he had the answer.

Why weren't *all* the races of the hive here? Certainly protocol demanded it. Answer: Some were water-breathers, while others breathed stuff noxious to anybody and anything. What did the vast majority here have in common? They were all carbon-based life forms—with a couple of exceptions that didn't really count.

And what was the heart of all carbon-based life? *Water!*

The water and sewage lines had been buried here

by expert technicians long before the drols had arrived, and would have been checked out again and again—but they terminated in exposed caps above ground to the rear of the structures now built. Pipe had to be fitted just to get the water to this pump—and probably all the others as well. More pipes to and from the pavilions themselves. Hell, some of his girls had done some of that work. It was easy, flexible, and simple, and there were piles of tubing all over—more than enough raw material that wouldn't be missed. It wouldn't be that tough to run a little private, off-the-diagram sequence, even after all the regular connections were made. Hell, those picture plans were all over—they'd even posted blueprints to pick out their interception points!

And it would take no more than a matter of minutes to cut a still-inactive line and run another junction point to wherever you wanted within the pavilion itself. There were so many parallel pipes running in the ceiling of the main kitchen area behind the pavilion that not even the technicians checking the work would notice one more. Not with this much to check. They'd turn on the system, see that it worked, check for leaks by running high pressure, then go on.

It was diabolically simple—and even more diabolically clever. One person could do it, maybe turn one valve, and foul the water of a whole side. Tobrush said there was another area—the Quarg, he recalled—where some other agents might have been working. On the other side. Both main lines.

But what could this junction hook into that would ensure that the entire water supply would be fouled? To all races, up and down each main water line. Adding something to the water line wouldn't be enough—the water pressure would send the stuff to the water taps, not back into the line. Unless . . .

He started walking toward the kitchen area, barely

aware of anyone else, still followed by his harem.

It wouldn't even have to be that hidden, just out of the way enough so no particularly officious plumbing tech would notice and ask what it was.

The altar? There'd be some large tank down there of some highly compressed flammable liquid or gas so that the altar flames could be lit and kept burning. No—too risky All that pressure would have to come against one little valve. If it had to last for a couple of days, it might blow prematurely and give the game away. Hell, the only way to be reasonably sure was if you had something of roughly equal pressure. . . .

He walked into the kitchen area but found that all the diagrams had already been taken down. He stalked back out, then started searching. One area, under the main seats and below the outer exposed part of the pavilion, wasn't in plain view from any point. It would not only be a natural place for the suspected valve, but maybe, just maybe, somebody had forgotten to take down the plumbing map there.

He stepped into the area, which, unlit and unreachable by the sun, was quite dark. He strained to see. By the Oaths of the Ten Martyrs—there were so many damned pipes and valves crisscrossing every which way in here, you could be piping *champagne*!

But it wouldn't be piping champagne. He just stared at the pipes in the semidarkness, impressed in spite of himself by the simplicity of the plan and its uniform effectiveness. The small pipes carried water; the larger ones carried the garbage and other wastes away under high pressure—higher pressure than the water had by far—so that all the sewage, from all the races, would be swiftly carried to a central dump and vaporized, the energy used to power much of the pavilions in the valley. How simple.

Just one diversionary valve, turned just so at just the right time, or at almost any time it was possible, and the high-pressure sewage pump, also under the pavilion, would send that sewage back through the entire water line. Human waste might even be toxic to some of the other races; certainly only a few of the weirder ones would want to drink it. Hell, maybe it was two-way. Then *all* the excrement from all the races further on would be flushed via this diversion into the water supply, pulled *up* by the wrong pump and pushed *back* by the right one.

It was sheer genius.

"Thanks for the compliment, smart boy," said a crisp, strong, but oddly familiar woman's voice from behind him. "*Hold it, hypno! Don't turn around!* I can kill you before you can fix your beady little eyes on me!"

"I might try anyway," he warned her. "You're going to kill me anyway, and probably right here." He fingered his whip and really considered it, but he knew the odds. Trained, she almost certainly could break his back before he even got turned around enough to take her on physically. *<And you're the telepath, too, aren't you? So there'd be no surprises.>*

"You are the smart boy. And right now you're thinking that your Julki friend is reading all this or maybe some of those mind-reading creeps will pick us up. Won't happen. You got smart too late and in the wrong place, hypno. A strong telepath can carry great distances but it's strictly line of sight. You ought to know that. Sorry, big man. I kind of liked you."

He braced himself for what had to come, and there was a sudden loud *crack* and he started, thinking at first it was him.

"Stop shaking and turn around, slaver," Kalia said in her usual sour tones. "She can't read anybody's mind, either, right now."

He turned and saw her standing there, and, between them, the limp body of the pushy Vronsky woman who'd put the make on him from the start.

"Is she dead?" he asked her.

"Probably not," the empath responded, sounding almost disappointed, "but she won't be any use for a while and she won't be doing any running."

He felt doubly stupid. "Her all along. . . . And the others?"

"Only one of 'em. The rest are just dumb pieces of meat added for cover—and diversion. One of us better step out and make a mental yell, though, before the others learn about this and crawl into their holes."

She backed out, and he stepped over the unconscious Qabar telepath and went out himself.

"All right, we're being sealed," he said with a sigh, still unable to believe how doubly dumb he'd been. "So how do we find the others?"

"Well, we got your other little lover spy over here and she's not in great shape but she's conscious. If you're any good with that Talent, she ought to be able to finger the others, although I got a couple of ideas already."

For someone who had gone from near certain death to a probable promotion in sixty seconds, he was amazingly depressed. "I suppose you also know just what they did and it's already being worked on."

"I haven't the slightest idea. Don't you? I figured that's why she was blowing cover." She paused as she saw his expression change. "You suddenly went from a black cloud to higher than a stratoliner. What's with you, anyway?"

He grinned. "Nothing, nothing at all." *But I know something you don't know!*

The other spy, one of the biggest mouths of the group, looked in pretty bad shape. In fact, she was still writhing in agony.

"I had no time to do anything to secure her, so I just smashed both her knees," Kalia explained matter-of-factly.

"Great," he grumbled, then sighed. "Let me see what

I can do." He bent down, and Kalia helped hold the girl firmly. She looked up at him, mouth open, screaming in pain, but suddenly the scream was cut short and she seemed to relax, and go limp.

A fairly large crowd of curious drols had assembled, but they started retreating quickly when they realized what he was and what he was doing.

"You feel no pain, no fear, no worry," he intoned softly. "I can keep it that way if you trust me, if you give your mind to me. Will you?"

"Yes," she responded dreamily.

"Other than you and the telepath, how many more of you are here?"

"Three more here. Five Quarg."

That fit. "How many of the others are Talents? And how many of those are humans?"

"Farita is the telepath. I am an empath. Ibrana is a hypno. Zoa and Maz are TK's. The same mix is on the Quarg team. I do not know their names. One Quarg looks much like another to me."

"Your entire team is female?"

"Yes. Drol women are virtually ignored and would be most likely to work on stringing pipes. I do not know about the Quarg."

That made sense, at least for the humans. Whoever had cooked this up and sold it to Qabar had thought it out very well. "How do we spot the rest of your team? How can we find them?"

"They are as average-looking as drols. Ibrana works as a food server. She is small and dark and her head is shaved. Zoa and Maz are twins, and lovers. They are short but large. Other than that, nothing to mark them."

"How did you plan to escape?"

"There is a pickup point in the mountains. Ibrana has programmed two master plumbers to do the work. Other freemen are under her power to help. She is very powerful. We are all very powerful."

Not anymore, he thought with some satisfaction.

He was starting to get up and turn around when something in the corner of his eye triggered an automatic response; he dropped, rolled, and, in doing so, received only a glancing blow. He jumped quickly to his feet and saw that his attacker was—Kalia!

"*Murderer! Slaver spy!*" she screamed, and came at him again.

She caught him in the chest with a nasty kick, but he managed to lash out and take her down with him, falling on top of her and knocking some of the wind out of her as well.

She was, however, too strong and in too good a condition to keep down. Avoiding her knee to his groin, he managed to look straight down at her glazed, maddened eyes. "Kalia! Look at me! *Look at me!*"

She stiffened and seemed almost frozen in place.

"Close your eyes," he ordered, "and don't move until I say that you can!"

He struggled up and then glared angrily at the group of drols who had formed a semicircle about fifteen feet away. The pain in his chest was bothering him, but he couldn't stop to think about that now. Finally he spotted her. Small and bald, Qabar's empath had said. And powerful.

He locked eyes with her, mad as hell. "You want to take me on?" he shouted to her. "Come on!"

The crowd shrank back even farther, but Ibrana did not. "You have no power over me!" she called back to him defiantly. "But do you know how many drols come through the food line? *All of them!* They are my army, if I but command! No hypno in the *universe*, not even I, could stop all of them before the rest tore out your heart!"

Damn! Why hadn't *he* thought of that?

"So? You can kill me, yes. But that won't save you or your companions or get your job done," he responded confidently. "Even now I can see and hear Security closing in."

"Whether we survive or not is of no consequence!" Ibrana told him. "Zoa! Maz! One of you throw the valves, the other open the gas ducts under the altar tank! The first fool that fires more than a spear or arrow will blow this pest hole to the Great Dark and then let us see your precious Lord unfoul this place by tomorrow midday!"

He saw the other two agents run from the crowd and thought, *they really* are *twins*! As telekinetics, if they knew just what to throw in that maze of pipes, ducts, and connectors, they could throw it all without even actually going in or touching anything.

One of them went to the dark area between the buildings where, as far as Josef knew, the telepath was still out cold. The other agent headed for the area under the altar. He'd been out-thought and fooled all along by these people, and now he was faced with a situation that was almost the ultimate terror to any hypno—a feeling of complete helplessness amidst a mob of raw material. For the first time in his life, outside of training, he got a sense of what it must be like to be on the other end of a hypno's power.

Security personnel were all around now, on the ground and even on gravity sleds above, but they were not yet in position to fire, or were awaiting orders to do so. The idiot in charge apparently hadn't grasped what was happening and was still thinking about avoiding damage to the pavilion.

As the one twin reached the altar area, she passed by a small, cube-shaped metallic cabinet that had been there since the beginning. Nobody had given it much thought, but now, as the spy came past it, it suddenly grew a set of tentacles that flowed and oozed from the cube, diminishing its size a bit. They wrapped themselves around the woman, and then they began to squeeze.

The whole altar area seemed to suddenly shake of its own accord; objects flew with abandon against the "cabinet" to no effect, just bouncing off, but the platform itself seemed to have something alive beneath it, shaking it like an earthquake.

Blood was now everywhere around the cube, and the woman's eyes bulged. Then she exploded in a gooey mess. The shaking stopped, but even from this distance, Josef could hear a slight hissing sound.

At that moment, the dark shape of a Thion emerged from the area between the buildings, where the first girl had gone in.

"She was most delicious," commented Robakuk.

Ibrana was suddenly conscious of the fact that she was entirely on her own. On her own, and now an easy target from above, but not helpless.

"Ilitika kabalah!" she screamed. "Light the altar flame with torches!"

Instantly a horde of drols within earshot of her command, were galvanized into action, taking or lighting torches from the cook fires and moving toward the altar.

"Kalia! You can move! Run like hell!" he shouted, and took off himself.

The escaping gas from below the altar was dense enough to catch before the mob got halfway there. Flame from the nearest torches seemed to leap up and ignite the air and, like a living thing, fly to the center of the altar.

As the whole complex erupted in a massive explosion, Josef felt heat on his back and he hit the dirt hard.

First the holding tank under the altar blew, then the backed-up connector lines caught but were prevented by automated safety valves from getting into the main line. The heat and pressure in the line that ran under the pavilion was enormous; even as the fireball over the remains of the altar was subsiding, the line under the other buildings blew, and, with it, the buildings themselves exploded in a shower of debris and sounds like thunder.

Dizzy, still reeling from the explosions and feeling the hurt in his chest even more, he managed by sheer willpower to get to his feet and look around for Ibrana's small form.

A loud, amplified male voice from above said, "She headed for the woods in back but can't have gone far. We've got the energy barrier there up now. She can't go anywhere."

He would have to leave that chase to others, because suddenly the whole world was spinning and he collapsed in a heap on the ground.

His first visitor, after he came out of the surgical system and regained consciousness, was the Hive Master himself.

"Just lie at ease," the Hive Master told him, waving off his attempt to show respect. "It will be a few days before you'll be able to get around. How do you feel?"

"I am a bit high on drugs, my master," he admitted. "It keeps me from knowing what the rest of my body is like."

"You might like to know that His Lordship is most pleased with you and with the performance of your team. *Most* pleased."

"But—they had the upper hand at the end! The altar, the pavilion, all of it blown . . ."

"Of no consequence to the main festivities. Unlike the water and sewer lines, the gas lines are well regulated, and damage was restricted to the immediate area. It's a bit of an eyesore, I admit, but that's all. Lord Qabar, it seems, has developed some sort of illness and has sent his last-minute regrets, so we have another human pavilion area to use. It must have been quite a sudden illness; his ship turned around when it was almost here."

Josef managed a smile. "I trust it will not be nearly as severe as the illness awaiting the planner of this enterprise upon his return home."

"Um . . . Yes. One hopes Lord Qabar is so enraged he does what you suggest. Whoever was behind all this is a plotter of considerable skill and a superb selector of personnel. It would be quite to our advantage if that individual were no longer around. It might well have worked, you know."

"It almost did," he admitted, still feeling less than victorious. "They successfully manipulated me almost to the end—diverting me, wearing me out, and then probably drugging me to take me completely in. When I am able, I shall go to a temple and pray for that team in its new journey through the Great Dark. They made no errors and suffer no dishonor. The plan itself was at fault, although no other plan that I could imagine would have any fewer complexities or problems. To actually have the nerve to attach themselves to me and then perform the sabotage under my very nose! If Kalia had not come by when she did, I too would be lying dead and they might still have gotten away with it."

"Kalia did not just happen by," the Hive Master told him. "It had been her intention to stick closer to you, in fact, but after you had taken on that drol entourage she knew that they had spotted you as one of our people, the telepath probably alerting them while on the voyage here. I know you wondered why we placed an empath rather than a telepath in with you. We assumed that they had a telepath along; we knew that we could not keep our telepath's existence secret from theirs if ours used its powers, and you were a public enough target. When Kalia approached you, she could read the emotions, the raw, primitive drol feelings, from all of those women—all but one. She knew that at least one empath was part of your company, and so backed off, keeping hidden but always with you in sight. She is quite good; my telepaths state that they never once could pick her out."

"But they still knew about her. They would have picked it from my mind and sent the information on. That scarred and twisted lip of hers is a dead giveaway."

"Indeed? In a crowd like that? If you had possessed a detailed description of the spies ahead of time, could you still have picked them out that easily? Particularly when they were trying hard not to be seen? She had already identified the twins and determined their less dangerous Talent; she assumed that the rest were around you."

"She identified the twins without them also recognizing her?"

"Yes. They couldn't resist showing off how very strong they were to the big men in the area, both to show superiority and to keep them respectfully distant. Of course, they couldn't really lift what they were lifting and carrying—not in the usual way, but the combined telekinetic powers of synchronized identical twins of your species seems to be considerable indeed. Word spread of them, reached Kalia, and *they*, of course, were not difficult to spot. She, in turn, made certain not to get too close to them just in case they had a description."

He nodded. "And she made no further contact with me, knowing that the odds were that they'd pick the information out of my mind and probably arrange a little accident for me."

"Precisely. Robakuk stationed himself atop the galley roof, unseen and out of the way but observant. Kalia was able to report to him, and he, in turn, could get messages non-telepathically to Tobrush so that there would be no interceptions. It worked out well. The wild card was the hypno. We could not spot her, could not telepathically scan for her—she was as good at that as Kalia, and it would simply have tipped them all off— and, until we could dig her out, no other action seemed meaningful as long as there was time left. Desreth was our wild card. With the Corithian ability to mimic certain inanimate objects, and their relative immunity to Talents, Desreth maneuvered to see if any of the known agents could lead us to the hypno. Since she was at food service, though, it never happened. Finally, Desreth staked out the position that you saw, where the entire area could be kept in sight."

"Is Desreth all right? It would have been right next to that first big explosion. . . . And what about the others?"

"Explosions of that sort aren't much bother to a Corithian. Robakuk has some burns but they are not serious. A Thion can really make speed when it has to. Kalia had some serious burns on her backside and sprained a wrist but is up and around. You got the worst, and, I fear, it was mostly from Kalia in her hypno trance. Two broken ribs, a punctured lung, internal bleeding, and a slight leg fracture—only the last was caused by the explosion."

"I consider myself blessed to have escaped with that," he admitted, not just for show, either.

"Do not denigrate yourself so," the Hive Master scolded him. "That breeds defeat and eventual failure. You did what you were sent in to do. Find the spies and then prevent them from doing harm. You were up against the best, and you broke the case by using your brain, not your powers. You were chosen because the computers said you had such a mind; your Talent, rather than being the crutch it is with most Talents, you used only to protect your mind so that you could use it properly."

"But *did* we prevent anything?" he asked the Hive Master. "They weren't the only ones."

"No, but if there was any fatal flaw in their plan it was in using humans at all. The fact that we were convinced that Lord Qabar's own ego and racial pride would make that inevitable made the rest possible. If he had chosen other races, unrelated to himself and unassociated with his highest nobles, as he *did* do with the Quarg, we would have never have found them until too late. As it was, feverish work through the night was able to undo most of their nasty work, and we were able to compensate for anything we did not catch. But for the burnt-out pavilion, no one at all would know. No, we are quite pleased all around. And this opinion is shared in even higher places. Have you given thought to what you would like to do once you are out of here?"

Although still not as impressed with himself as the others were, he knew better than to not accept accolades, or possible rewards. "I shall go wherever my Baron and our Lord commands me, and carry out my commission to the best of my abilities as always," he responded.

"A suggestion has been made for a higher calling. If you wish it, a full commission in Imperial Security is yours."

No empath was needed to read his excitement at that. *Imperial level!* "I—I would be most honored, master."

"Master no more, once you accept the commission. I began the same way. You would get some training, some additional schooling, then be assigned command of a patrol boat, probably out on the frontier. That's where they put the green ones usually, with mostly a green crew, on routine duty. It is an education, and a challenge. Much of it is quite boring, I assure you, but if you find the opportunity to accomplish a major task, it will be noted. As always, Destiny and you will decide where you go from there."

"I shall do my best, sir." *And someday I'll come back here and take your job, Hive Master. Or maybe even your boss's job.*

The training and schooling the Hive Master spoke of was definitely *not* boring; it was one of the hardest things

Josef had ever undergone. Even in his lowliest days as
a pupil in the hypno training colony, which, up until
now, he'd thought was the worst possible experience,
he'd never been through anything so low and degrading.
The physical demands were brutal; the punishment,
abuse, and degradation meted out by the security robots
who ran the program (and who were immune from any
Talent) was almost beyond belief. There were no letups
and no breaks. Thirty candidates began the training.
Like Josef, they were all there because they'd already
proven themselves very tough and very good in major
and often dirty field-assignments.

By the end of the training, seven of them had
committed suicide; five more had died at the hands
of the instructors, and three had died as a result of
training mistakes. Of the fifteen that remained, only
seven, including Josef, received full field commissions
as ensigns. The other eight were assigned to Hive
Security—a promotion, yes, and a good job, but not
Imperial level.

The training did not end with his commission. He
and the six other ensigns were now technical specialists
and introduced to an incredible variety of weapons,
espionage techniques, equipment—and then the survival
suits. The ultimate test would be to drop him, as if crash-
landed, on a horrible, screaming hell of a planet about
which he had received no briefing whatever, and with
only his rust-red survival suit and the equipment that
would normally be a part of it. With no maps, no nothing,
he would have to find a monitoring beacon that was
hundreds of kilometers away and call in a pickup from
there. The world, he was assured, was uninhabited, but
the atmosphere was poisonous and, the temperatures
ranged from freezing to near the boiling point.

The seven finalists would be dropped all at the same
time, although at different points. The first six to make
it, if there were six who made it, would graduate—finally.

The last one in, if they all made it, would be forced to go back and take everything over again, from the very beginning.

Before being dropped, he was given his one and only chance to resign, to accept an administrative post rather than a field commission. By then he'd gone through too much to call a halt; he would make it, or die. If he did not make it, he did not mind death at all in this honorable quest—nor, in fact, would he wish to live knowing that others like the old Hive Master had passed just this sort of test.

More than once, when it looked hopeless, he knew that the old Josef, even the one looking for spies at the celebration, would have given up, would have simply declared the situation hopeless. But one of the things indoctrination in this program did was to beat any sense of defeatism out of you. The training was harder than almost anything he might be likely to encounter later, yet you could get through it by using your brain and new-found knowledge.

About two thirds of the way there, his food synthesizes malfunctioned, and he doubted he had the strength to make it the rest of the way without at least some basic food. Besides, it endangered the far more vital water recirculation and purification system in the suit.

He decided that he could not be the last; if he were, it didn't matter if he died, anyway.

There was a range of high, barren, windswept mountains between all of them and the beacon, and the best and most logical place to cross was a small pass that at several points was only a few meters wide at the bottom. He staked it out, dug in, shut down all but essential power, and waited. On the second day, one of his comrades—he couldn't even tell who—came through. He shot the man down at full stun from ambush, right in the back, and as the cadet lay there he removed the packs he needed, replacing them with his own malfunctioning unit. Refreshed and repaired, he made the beacon. Only one of the seven did not. He lost no sleep, nor celebrated any less, for that lost man.

Walking down the corridor at Security Base Twenty-Nine, however, did make him a bit nervous. He was resplendent in his dark red uniform and black boots, and justly proud of the single star on his left breast pocket that marked him as a full field ensign, but now he was to meet his first crew, probably as green as he, and that made him nervous indeed. He would be firm, ruthless, a disciplinarian, he told himself, and drill them into a single machine.

He walked into the room, then stopped, totally amazed. Although it had been only a year, the memories suddenly jogged forward seemed a lifetime away and almost to belong to someone else.

"Kalia?"

She was, if anything, a bit uglier than he remembered although the hair, once fairly long, was now so short it barely covered her scalp, and revealed the missing right earlobe he hadn't known about—or, perhaps, she hadn't had it then. The cleaned and pressed uniform of a Sergeant, Junior Grade, only set off the fact that she hadn't, even now, done anything to repair those scars or enhance her appearance.

She snapped to attention, but he could see a trace of a smile, more of resignation than happiness, at the sight of him.

The others, who also looked familiar, he was less sure of. "Tobrush, I assume," he said to the Julki, whose own sort-of uniform bore the insignia of a Warrant, Junior Grade.

The tendrils rose in what he guessed was a salute. "Sir, the company is assembled," Tobrush responded. "I assume introductions are not necessary for the others."

"Robakuk, then," he said, nodding to the Thion. "And—Desreth? A *Corithian* in the Imperial Service?"

"Many of us are in the Imperial Service, sir," the emotionless, hollow-sounding voice of the strange being responded. "We are considered quite—useful. And if I survive, the experiences and knowledge I bring back will go into the Universal Fund of Knowledge for my people."

He sighed. "Well, be at ease, everyone." He took his seat, and only then did Kalia do likewise. The others had no use for chairs or their equivalent.

Josef looked over at Kalia. "Only Sergeant? I should have thought you would have been in *my* group." In point of fact, only Tobrush was also an officer warranting an officer's respect, although on a track below his. Robakuk and Desreth were basically just—crew—and the only reason Kalia had the Sergeant's grade would be because she finished first in her training.

"I did not choose to be an officer," she told him. "Just as I did not choose to serve with you, sir, or any of the rest of you, nor you with us. It appears that someone believed we worked well together and complemented each other."

"And so we do," he responded. "The fact that we all underwent the most rigorous training known and all of us came through speaks well for us. Now we are being given a ship and duties and we must carry them out, not as individuals, but as part of a team." He sighed. "I was going to say that we are no longer the same people as we were when we worked together for that brief week a year ago, but that isn't really true. We *are* the same. We were good then. We are better now. It was teamwork that got us here. We must be a perfect team to survive and prosper."

"Have we been assigned a ship, Captain?" the Julki asked him.

He nodded. "An older class of picket ship—*Blood*

Throne class. The quarters are close and not the best for creature comfort, but it's very fast and extremely well armed. I doubt if much could catch it, or that there is much we could not catch. Modifications are automatically made for racial needs, so all of us will have at least a minimal level of comfort. But before we go down to her, I want to know your specialties."

"I am officially the navigator, Captain," Tobrush responded. "What it means in practice is that I am a computer repair person and troubleshooter who can fix the basics if everything goes down. As a telepath, I double as Security Officer."

He nodded. "Robakuk?"

"Loadmaster and small weapons control, Captain."

"Kalia?"

"Boarding, inspections, and field expeditions," she told him. "Otherwise, I assist as needed. I can also operate minor weapons and can assist in interrogations, but my primary function aboard is maintenance."

In other words, a soldier on the ground and the ship's housekeeper aboard. He was surprised she would accept such a role when she clearly was capable of more. Another piece of the Kalia enigma.

"Desreth?"

"Communications, cryptography, and major weapons, Captain," the Corithian responded. "I am also capable of ship-to-ship fighter plots."

"Captain?"

"Yes, Kalia?"

"I feel it important that I give you a warning. The Security Officers gave me their highest marks, but were very concerned about my one major failure, which, as you know, was a particularly low resistance to hypnos. As a result, I was required to spend some time—I do not know how long—in conditioning chambers and under programming drugs and machinery. You may examine my personnel records for what they found; I do not understand much of it. However, as a consequence of the conditioning, any attempt by a hypno to take control of my will without my permission will result in an instant and totally automatic response requiring me to attack and render him unconscious or dead. I cannot control it."

That startled him, both bothering and reassuring him at the same time. she had given him *quite* a kick a year ago, and although he liked to think he was more than a match for her or almost anyone else now, the fact was that she had also gone through harsh training and might still have an edge. In the back of his mind, he'd been worrying about whether she'd be reliable in a situation with another hypno. Now he knew she was—but somebody who would attack any hypno wasn't exactly the kind of person he felt comfortable around, either. How could he trust her now in a social situation, or a tentative one, where some hypno might just put it on her to try and sell her some stupid junk or to have a good time? He'd have to think about this one.

"Well, thank you for the warning. All right, everyone—shall we see what our new home looks like?"

It felt good to be in command, to be in space, to have his own ship and the level of freedom and responsibility that went with it. Perhaps he would sour on it later, perhaps the predicted boredom would get to him, but, for now, it was just who and where he wanted to be.

The sealed orders could not be opened and fed into the ship's computer until they were well underway. Only then did he receive his first operational orders:

"You will proceed to the frontier post grid location now being fed into your computer. Upon reaching that point, you will patrol the assigned region from boundary to boundary, coordinating your picket with the other

ships like yours in the region, and subject to the orders of Zone Military Control. Under normal duty, you will respond to any calls for aid or assistance from any Imperial colony or vessel within your range, and you will also intercept and capture or destroy any enemy vessel encroaching on your zone. Our military forces are light in the region, where our border is pinched to a mere sixty-two light-years, with the Mizlaplan to one side and the Exchange to the other. Although much of the work will be tedious, you may expect the unexpected in the region, as we have operatives working the enemy frontier zones and they undoubtedly have some in ours. Applicable known star maps, tactics, and codes are included with these orders, not only for us but for the other two Empires as much as we know them. Any enemy movements or communications, even outside of our own space, will be monitored and reported at all times. . . ."

It was pretty clear, and pretty much what he expected. The primary problems aboard, after that lifetime year of training, would be fighting boredom and keeping in reasonable physical shape. After that, Destiny would have to take a hand.

It was a long journey, and he spent much of it drilling them over and over again and trying to get a feel for their strengths and weaknesses. Also, in his command chair above the rest, he got around to reading their full files, starting with Kalia. It explained many, although not all, of her enigmas.

She was far younger than he thought—a mere twenty-four, or so they estimated, with a face and mind and body of someone much older. She had been born a drol on Pusabi, as he already knew, in a fiefdom ruled by a knight named Mahaht, a sadomasochist with a fancy for very pretty, very young girls. She was picked out, brought to the manor house, and for many months thereafter she became his favorite plaything.

The psychological officer who did the report thought she had been no more than eight years old at the time.

After that, she was put to work as a housemaid and was no better than a drol with a higher standard of living—until she blossomed, early, at about age eleven or twelve. With puberty had come the emergence of her empathic talent. She was then sold or given to a freeman named Peshwar who ran some sort of traveling entertainment troupe on Pusabi. He then trained her as a woman of pleasure, a special kind of slave. Young and attractive empaths of both sexes were part of the Pleasure Corps, as Peshwar called it. She was fed hormones and drugs to make her extra pliant, then conditioned and trained by hypnos using a combination of their Talent and electric shock to remold the empath slaves into new creations capable of becoming whatever the freeman or noble customer might want.

Apparently she was not beyond servicing large numbers of people, like security troopers for fiefdoms and even quads. Using broadcast empathy to leave no customer unsatisfied, she and the others in her group were forced to suffer any level of abuse and degradation demanded by their hypno handlers.

Shit! No *wonder* she hated hypnos!

And no wonder she couldn't resist them.

After several years of this, when she was beginning to show a lot of wear and tear, an elderly Duke took a fancy to her for some reason and got her from Peshwar. With the scars and markings she already had from years of other people's idea of fun, he no longer considered her a long-term asset, since he had others and, particularly, since he'd have to pay for cosmetic repairs in a while.

The Duke was an odd sort who wanted her around only for the pleasure of looking at her with her slave chains. He apparently hadn't desired his concubines, in some time, either, and the chief one mistakenly saw

Kalia as the reason why she was no longer in favor. This concubine apparently played up to the Duke's guard, got into his bedroom when he wasn't there, caught Kalia chained and alone, took a ceremonial dagger, and proceeded to carve a few new notches in the girl. The most obvious was that disfiguring facial scar.

Security hadn't realized the concubine's intent, and now the guard knew that there'd be hell to pay when the Duke found out. He freed Kalia, got her immediate medical attention, then tried to figure out what to do. While he was still deciding, she got up, sneaked out, found the chief concubine, and slowly strangled her to death.

The psychologist said that the years of conditioning and that sort of life and treatment in one so bright had affected her mind, creating a kind of split personality, often called "possession" by the untrained. The second Kalia was all that the first was not; most importantly, where sex was everything to the original, the other substituted violence. The new Kalia was a violent, sadistic killer with a very short fuse, whose empathic ability was used to instill fear and terror and helplessness in others. She got a particular charge out of causing someone's death.

The Duke had been enraged when he saw her disfigured face, and had tossed her out. He was better able to accept the murder of the concubine, seeing it as justice.

Kalia I and Kalia II were always both present; remarkably, she could bring either one she wished to the surface with near total control. It was this that gave her an innate ability to totally confuse telepaths.

Using her empathic powers to induce guilt in the guard, she managed to become an adjunct to the local security staff, where her ability to befuddle even skilled telepaths drew quick notice. The staff undertook to train her and get her into condition. A particularly ambitious officer recognized her primary usefulness as an assassin, and she was put to work in that capacity. Her successes got her into the service itself and took her through the hierarchy right up to the Baron himself.

She could have availed herself of the best medical technology to totally remove her scars, even restore her face, but she would have none of it. When she was pretty she'd been an object, a helpless plaything of others. When disfigured, she had found freedom, independence, and respect—and she had risen. Her scars, her ugliness, were her security. The psychologist even theorized that if she ever did get full repairs, Kalia II would be submerged and Kalia I would become the sole, dominant, voluntary personality again.

And Kalia I was of no use whatever to anyone, while Kalia II was very useful indeed.

It was estimated that she had killed at least forty people—so far.

And now she was Imperial trained.

They *had* thought of the problem Josef had when she told him of her conditioned reaction to hypnos. Apparently unknown to her, any officer in her chain of command could countermand her conditioning, nor would it be triggered by a hypno of officer rank in the Security Services.

One other mystery was solved in the documentation, one that had never even occurred to him. She was a brilliant fighter, actress, assassin, whatever . . . but at no time had she had even the slightest formal or genteel education. Kalia I had neither the opportunity nor the need for it; Kalia II saw no purpose in learning anything that did not impact on her job. She had a phenomenal memory, and whatever was demonstrated to her she grasped quickly if she could see any use to it, but for anything else she was as ignorant as a drol.

She could never have become an officer, not even a warrant officer.

Kalia could operate a security suit, assemble and disassemble it blindfolded; she could kill in a hundred ways; she could cook, clean, do carpentry, and shoot the wings off flies at great distances.

But Kalia could neither read nor write.

Book Four:

The Quintara Marathon

The Demons At Rainbow Bridge

Alarms sounded all over the place, and Josef rolled out of his bunk and shook himself quickly awake, then headed for the forward communications and fire control station below the bridge.

"What have we got?" he asked Tobrush, who was manipulating about nine different sets of instruments with her back tendrils, while keeping eyestalks fixed on a long scan.

"Something very strange, Captain," the Julki responded. "Computers on the longest reach scan picked up a probable intruder from the Mizlaplan side, moving at a moderately fast pace through our territory. We've plotted the course and trajectory and it appears to be designed to avoid any major colonies or bases we have."

"Warship?"

"Impossible to say at this range, but from its characteristics I'd say not. The fact that it is only doing Force Six, yet is clearly making all deliberate speed on evasive course, indicates either that it is some test of our defenses or that it's a vessel of some mass. We've correlated Force Six with known Mizlaplan craft and determined that the speed and ballistic characteristics are consistent with a Mizlaplanian freighter going all out. Of course, if it's a test of our defenses and has only an automated crew, it might make some sense to use an old freighter, but I suspect that it is more likely some kind of smuggling operation."

Robakuk's black pulsating form gripped the top side of the hatchway and looked down from that perspective. "What have we got?"

Josef ignored him. "Plot a chase and intercept course and give our position and situation to Frontier Control," he ordered. "I'll take the con."

"Some action at last!" Kalia breathed excitedly as he squeezed past Robakuk and came through the hatchway.

Josef went immediately to the command chair. On the screens around him data, graphic plots, and estimates were popping up almost too numerous to follow. Fortunately, Desreth *could* follow them.

"Can you plot probable destination of quarry?" he asked.

"Not within the Empire unless major corrections are accomplished very quickly." The Corithian's voice came to him from the combat center amidships. "The best estimate of intent is that someone is trying to get from the Mizlaplanian frontier to the Exchange frontier, using the shortest possible route."

The patrol ship rumbled into life, and all aboard felt the sudden sinking sensation of rapid acceleration into the induced subspace vortex that allowed them, in progressive jumps, to quickly hurdle distances that would otherwise be impossible.

"Intercept point?"

"Too far away, Captain. We will not be able to get in range of them in less than six hours. By that time they will be at the boundary of Exchange space."

He frowned. Where the hell were the other pickets and border ships that were supposed to have intercepted this fellow by now? Were they all asleep at their posts?

"Any response yet from Frontier Control?"

"Initial only," Tobrush reported from below. "They order pursuit and overtake capture if possible, destroy if not. The standard instructions. There is nobody closer."

Easy for them to say, he thought sourly. *We are just*

far enough out not to be able to catch them, and they order us to do the impossible.

"When will we be within hailing distance of the vessel?" he asked.

"About two hours. But if this fellow is as competent as he appears to be, he'll simply ignore us and continue to outdistance us."

"Well, give me all you've got. Let's see if we can at least scare him."

As they got closer, instrumentation allowed a better picture of what they were chasing. It *was* a freighter, *Hochin* class—old but obviously in top condition.

"The course is parabolic, very wide," Desreth reported. "Quarry did not come from very far inside the Mizlaplan. A backtrack indicates probable origin to be disputed colony of Medara sixteen light-years from the border and on the edge."

That just didn't make sense. If the colony was disputed, but in enemy hands, the odds were good that Imperial Security was working something there. With this narrow neck of Mycohl that some incompetent had trapped them into, it wouldn't be any shock at all to discover that the Exchange was running some kind of operation there as well. If something nasty went down on Medara, it could mean that somebody else needed a quick getaway.

"If they do not deviate from their plot, where are they headed in the Exchange?" he asked.

"They must deviate, Captain," Tobrush responded. "If they do not, then they are heading right off the star maps to where stars have numbers, and lesser bodies are not fully charted."

What the hell?

"Well, somebody's got *something* out there," he commented. "A *Hochin* class freighter needs a light-year at that speed just to slow down to manageable sublight."

"Another message from Frontier Command, Captain," Tobrush reported. "They want to know if we can intercept. I have responded in the negative and fed them our figures as we have them."

"Very well." And it was; it passed all the responsibility from his lap to theirs.

Almost another hour passed during which they continued to close but not soon enough.

"Message in highest-class code, Captain," Desreth reported. "Frontier Command reports that there is no appreciable military strength on the Exchange side in that region. We are directed to maintain pursuit. If the course and trajectory of the quarry are not changed, we are to match speeds and follow them to their destination but *not* to intercept within the Exchange boundaries. If it changes course or trajectory to take it into the main region of the Exchange, we are to break off and return unobtrusively. Otherwise, they want to know where the quarry is going."

"They are directing me to cross the border?"

"Affirmative. But avoid engagement, particularly with any vessels of the Exchange."

Easier said than done, he thought irritably. Still, this was what they had trained for and it suited him just fine.

Four hours into the pursuit, Tobrush reported, "Quarry is at the Exchange boundary. We will be within their aft sensor range, assuming normal *Hochin* class instrumentation, in nine minutes."

He sighed. "Slow to matching speed and maintain that nine-minute gap," he ordered. "Any sign that they are slowing or changing course?"

"None beyond what would be termed minor course corrections. In a practical sense, if they were going to do so, it would logically be no later than two hours from now—at about the time we cross the frontier boundaries ourselves. If they do not slow and turn by that point,

Captain, all computer modeling suggests that they have no intention of doing so and are heading at that point off the map."

"Very well. *He* knows where he's going, anyway. Advise Frontier Command."

"I have already done so. They are sending a response now. Their experts believe they know where the ship is headed, although not what is there, or so they say. There have been repeated distress calls on Exchange frequency and in commercial code from a point very close to where the Mizlaplanian ship is heading. Frontier Command states that this distress call is quite peculiar, but that it gives full justification for our incursion should we face a challenge. Although this ship did not intercept the call, the Exchange won't know that, and, in any event, we are simply being ordered to assist according to interstellar treaties."

"Did they send a copy and triangulated estimate of origin?"

"Yes, sir. The estimate of origin is almost forty light-years off the maps and further out than we thought the Exchange had even gotten. That indicates that they are only in the most preliminary stages of claims."

"Is the message from a scout, then? *Nobody* goes after scouts. It's an occupational hazard."

"Not a scout. I'll put the translated intercept on the ship's intercom."

"*All ships . . . any ships . . . Exchange registry . . . This is Research Vessel* Wabaugh. *Coordinates based on special map frontier zone one one four eight two stroke five. Coordinates are Rainbow Bridge. Send assistance fast. They are all dead. They are all in there with the demons and they are all dead. Only one left. Can't leave. Approach with extreme caution! Power adequate for maintenance only. Any Exchange registry. Approach with caution. Demons at Rainbow Bridge! Coordinates . . .*"

"The man is mad," Josef muttered "if that's anything like an accurate translation."

"You don't believe in demons?" Kalia asked him in a tone that indicated that she herself didn't much believe in anything. "We have one in our little shrine right aboard ship."

There was no need for her to remind him of that. In the Mizlaplan they had angel figures who fought what they called demons. In the Mycohl, they had demons who battled the forces of stasis, represented as angels. Two sides of the same coin, he'd always thought. In a truly literal translation, the Mizlaplan and Mycohl terms, and their underlying positive or negative sides, were essentially reversed.

To the Mycohl, however, and to the others, the word "demons" did have a more basic meaning. It was one of the great mysteries, and probably explained more than anything else why such primitive superstitions hung on even among intelligent people.

Most races, clans, even families, had some kind of local spirits, both good and evil. It was always so on almost all worlds. The angel side was ambiguous, though, and in a great many cultures did not exist in clearly defined form.

But the demon did. The Thion both worshiped and feared a figure different from the human demon, yet in the essential details very similar indeed. The demonic figure—humanoid even on planets whose races were not, and filtered through different cultures and standards and concepts but still very much there—existed in the vast majority of all known cultures. Evil in most cultures, malicious or indifferent in others, they were the epitome of evil in the Mizlaplan and to some faiths in the Exchange, while in the Mycohl they were a supernatural warrior race that precisely matched the Mycohl vision of life and death and the values they represented.

Most people believed in them, or at least gave lip

service to them; many, however, rejected the superstition except as a social tool of the Empire or, like Josef, regarded it with total indifference.

"It is now relatively easy to deduce the situation," Tobrush commented. "The Mizlaplanians are fanatics. The demon figure to them represents the ultimate in evil, and they really believe that. Somehow, some fanatics of the ruling priesthood intercepted this message and in their somewhat psychotic social state took it literally. Literally enough to take a ship through the Mycohl and into the equally hostile Exchange, into a region off the maps, to chase demons. It is quite sad, really."

"Perhaps," Desreth put in. "However, one does not build and maintain a relatively powerful interstellar empire for so long on such irrationalities. It may be surmised that Frontier Control drew the same obvious conclusion at the start. The fact that we are still ordered to pursue, violating Exchange space, indicates that they have some knowledge that something in that new area of the frontier is going on of possible interest or threat to us. If that is the case, the distress call provides a way to find out. And, if indeed that is the case, wiser Mizlaplanian heads might see it exactly the same way. We must never forget that while we have two enemies in close proximity at this location, so do they."

"Point taken," Josef responded. "Maintain the two-hour nine-minute interval. Full shields up, scrambling sensors on, report any change in course of that ship ahead."

He looked at the main plotting screen. "Battle stations," he ordered calmly. "We have just invaded the Exchange."

Gun Roh Chin put his cigar down in the ashtray by his bridge chair and wondered idly if he would live long enough to finish the humidor. He flicked on the intercom and said, "Holies, I'm correcting course and going directly for the plot point. My sensors show no transponders or vessels, major or minor, in the region, although we are getting some odd interference along our track out of Mycohl. As soon as the correction is made and locked in, I am going to commence a very slow braking which may cause some noise and vibration. It is normal. I have to bring her down very gently after maintaining this kind of speed for this long. However, if you wish to meet me on the aft part of the bridge in—oh, two hours from now—I believe we will be close enough and slowed enough to get a scan of our destination.

"For the record, the active ship's channel on which the message was transmitted is still intermittently open, but only the emergency locator beam is still active. I would say that whoever or whatever is out there, if they are still alive, has powered down to minimum and is probably living in a suit. A thousand pardons for interrupting you, but I thought you would like to know."

He sat back and gave a kind of half smile to himself. It was fun to be a captain sometimes, and be able to outrank and even interrupt high clergy.

Only Morok, the titular superior of everyone outside of ship's operations, and Krisha, in charge of security, showed up, but, he noted, they showed up right on the button two hours later.

"Do you have anything for us yet, Captain?" the Stargin asked, a bit impatient after all this time.

"Any moment now . . . *There!* Solar system, G-type star, very promising in its composition. I make four inner solid planets and four gas giants, a nice mix. A bit small, but the fourth from the star is within the carbon-based life zone. See it on the diagram, there? And the red line, that's your signal. Bouncing around a bit, but—there! Yes, fourth planet. Since it's a rather fixed signal, I expect them to be in geostationary orbit, which probably means it was supporting a landing party."

"It was supposedly a research vessel," Krisha pointed out. "That would imply some sort of scientific or research base down there. No military monitors, though; not even automatic defense probes. They weren't expecting anything hostile."

"No, they weren't," Chin said approvingly. "No surprises for us, either. At least until we have to face whatever surprise got to *them*. On our current course and brake rate I can have us essentially alongside them in, oh, six hours. If they are in a high enough orbit, and from the data, I think they are, I might be able to close to where we could jetpack over."

"Begin automatic hailing of the vessel," Morok ordered. "Let me know at once if there is a reply."

Chin's eyebrows rose in surprise. "Are you sure? If there is anything hostile hiding in the immediate vicinity, or any Exchange patrol ships in this area, we're going to draw attention to ourselves by doing so."

"If there was anything closer than we, I think we'd have it and it us on our scopes," the Stargin responded. "In any event, it is the correct procedure to follow if we are to keep up the pretense that we are responding to a legitimate distress call. We may still have to answer to someone here, remember—and we must in any event have a way back."

"I agree," Krisha put in, nodding. "The only reason we don't have a whole fleet of Exchange ships in here by now with a signal that strong and that wide, is the geostationary orbit. It takes the ship around in an orbit that beams it almost directly across the Mycohl and into the Mizlaplan, but even though most of the time it beams towards the Exchange, it beams towards frontier areas and, if the maps are trustworthy, very sparsely settled territory. I am not surprised to find no Exchange ships in the area yet, although they will come, but I must admit to being mildly surprised not to find the Mycohl taking advantage of this opportunity to snoop."

Chin looked over at his instruments and pointed to the aft monitor. "That's what worries me about that interference to our stern. It *could* be natural, but it is also very much like a military scrambler would look if it were turned on and aimed at us. I, too, am very surprised not to see the Mycohl here ahead of us, but I very much fear that the odds are at least even that they are not that far behind us."

"It couldn't be an Exchange craft?" Morok asked him, although that was only slightly better.

"Unlikely on our same course. They wouldn't be coming from that way if they were the Exchange, and they wouldn't waste time and effort getting in behind us if they came from any sane Exchange point. If so, it's likely to be some sort of military craft, possibly a Mycohl picket ship. I need not remind you that Mizlaplanian freighters are not exactly bristling with armaments and battle computers."

"They are just as much invaders as *we* are," Morok pointed out. "They wouldn't *dare* do anything to us *here*. Not in Exchange territory."

Chin was unimpressed bit the comment. "Begging your pardon, Holiness, but I am very much afraid that this location and these conditions give them pretty much of a free shot at us. I doubt if the Exchange would bother lodging a diplomatic protest because one interloping enemy popped another interloping enemy, even if it *was* on their property."

Krisha decided to head off Morok's officiousness and faith-based optimism. "What do you recommend, Captain?"

"Well, they have been matching us—if that's what that is—and not closing. They're faster than we are, and can probably brake much faster as well—almost anything can—but if I were their captain, in enemy territory, knowing his quarry was unarmed, I'd hold off, let us get parked, get out, and have an initial look around—just in case there's a whole stranded Exchange Marines battle station down there. Come in slow, check it out, and have us where we are separated from the ship and most vulnerable. I'd say he'll give us two, maybe three or more hours, particularly if we show on his sensors as doing just what he expects."

"But we plan to do just that," Morok pointed out.

"Maybe, maybe not. I'm going to plot us a different sequence. I intend to get in fairly close but not achieve orbit or even come to a full stop. I will pilot the shuttle manually and we will come in first on that orbiting vessel. I'm going to leave the Klees aboard and have them gun this thing out of there and into the asteroid region between the first and second gas giants and park there until we call for help or they have to come out."

"Won't the Mycohl just pursue the ship, finish her, and then come back for us at their leisure?" Krisha asked him.

"They could, but I doubt it. I've been on one of their picket ships. It is loaded for planet killing and almost single-handed war, and its crews are chosen for their toughness and total and complete ruthlessness. The problem, for them, is that it's less a picket ship than a pursuit ship. It can go quite slow or it can go incredibly fast, but it isn't much good at a moderate speed. The odds are still against us, but I'm betting that the Mycohl captain's orders are to get in here, find out all he can about what is going on, and get out before he's boxed in by the Exchange. He can't afford to be 'at his leisure.' He's as much an invader as we are. If he chooses to come in rather than give chase, or even thinks hard about it, I have enough confidence in the Klees and my computers to pull if off. After all, it's not like we can come out of those asteroids and pick *them* off. With what?"

Gun Roh Chin sighed. "No, he'll come in, make orbit, and repeat our moves until he catches us. He won't chase this ship because he doesn't have to. It's got to come back in to him to pick us up sooner or later, or it's going to either have to make a run for it or be interned by the Exchange."

"You are talking as if this were a suicide mission and that we have no hope of escape," Morok said uneasily.

"There is always hope, Holiness, and prayer. I *did* warn of this possibility, remember. We are committed now. If I break off, he'll come in fast and finish us, then go in alone. I respectfully suggest that you eat and drink, even if you have been fasting, check out your survival suits and weapons and equipment, and then get what rest you can. I will meet you in the shuttle bay with whoever you designate to go with me, in . . . five hours and fifteen minutes. I am commencing automatic hailing of the ship in distress, using Treaty codes."

"They're not achieving orbit!" Tobrush reported. "They're detaching a shuttle on the fly and accelerating out-system!"

That pig of a Holy Captain has read my mind! Josef thought angrily to himself. Aloud, he said, "Then he knows, or at least guesses, that we are here."

"We could catch it and cut them off!" Kalia exclaimed excitedly. "I should like to be the one. I have never blown up a spaceship before."

"And you won't now, either! Not yet, anyway. I'm not worried about that massive hunk of metal and synthetics. It won't go far because it *does* have to come in and pick them up—or abandon them. Either is perfectly acceptable to us. We will get him afterwards—if time and circumstances permit We might waste several hours before we found and destroyed it, giving them time down there."

"So what?" the human woman responded. "Whatever they learn will die with them."

"Do you think they don't know that? That their gamble has failed? They are fanatics. They will die before they will be taken by us, and they know negotiations are useless. If they find nothing of hope, I would expect them to destroy or damage anything that might be of use to us. I have no intention of giving them that opportunity. I want everyone ready in full survival suit and battle gear. I'm going to put this thing close to that Exchange ship, and we are going to see just what is going on there."

"All of us are going?" Robakuk asked, more excited than nervous.

"This ship is fully capable of maintaining itself, flying itself, defending itself, or, if need be, destroying itself to keep from enemy hands. There is nothing that freighter could do to it except present it with an automatic target. Those Mizlaplan shuttles can hold up to nine people, depending on the races involved, and the races involved are unknown as of now. I do know that I am not going to underestimate that captain. Full gear—we all go. And don't get cocky or overconfident. As I said, these people are fanatics, who will gladly die if they could take one of us with them, and they are *not* stupid or ill-equipped. Many of them are probably priests, but don't let that fool you. Almost all the priests they let loose like this are Talents and they're trained and they're good. And, most of all, they are going to be there ahead of us. If it were *us* in *their* situation, with them coming in on top of us but we have the same kind of lead, what would *we* do?"

"Traps and ambushes," Kalia responded. "The only chance they've got is if they can wipe us out."

"Agreed, and while it's on unknown ground for both

of us, they will know it better than we, having been there first."

"I would recommend ordering the ship in stand-by, with partial shutdown of all but our monitoring codes," Tobrush put in. "It's tempting to have it close at hand, but if the Exchange shows up while we're down there, we're in no better shape than they are. If the Exchange shows up first weak and curious but unsuspecting, we can fight our way out. If it shows up in strength, we can then try and talk our way out."

"All right. Agreed. Desreth, you've been very quiet."

"I have been considering the odds that the Exchange is already here," the Corithian responded.

"Huh?"

"If they *did* show up first, they would have detected at least the Mizlaplanian ship before they themselves would be detected. They might well wonder what a Mizlaplanian ship was doing so far from home that it was willing to risk crossing Mycohl to answer a distress signal. In that case, they would lie back and monitor, just as we and the Mizlaplanians are doing, until they see what happens. It would be the practical thing, since both of us are now only rather lamely within the law. If we started shooting at one another or going where we have no right going—namely down to the planet— we would then be undertaking not a rescue mission but an overt illegal act within their territory."

Josef didn't like that. "What do the rest of you think? Is the Exchange that devious?"

"They are," Tobrush responded. "Yet I doubt the scenario. The Exchange in strength would have intercepted both of us by now and told us just where to go, or else, keeping us well away from that place. They would only lay off in weakness, where they feared that either of us might eliminate them just to save our honor. In that case, they are irrelevant."

"I would prefer they not be around, strong or weak,"

the captain responded. "Still, it would be interesting, would it not? A three-way battle to the death on a planet alien to all. It would be a magnificent challenge. I should like to think we would win such a battle."

"*Agh!* Priests and scientists and traders," Kalia scoffed. "It would not even be a contest."

Josef whirled around. "I told you not to underestimate these people!" he snapped angrily. "Do that and you die and take the rest of us with you! I don't care if those Mizlaplanians believe their souls will become gods by eating grass and rolling in the mud and howling at the stars! One on one, in a real fight, they are most certainly our counterparts. No common freighter captain I know of would have detected us, let alone pulled that maneuver, and he did it coolly, knowing the odds. No matter what the vessel, they wouldn't send amateurs on a mission like this, and they are no amateurs. Any more stupid bravado like that, and I will leave any of you who think that way here with the ship!"

They didn't really quite believe that anyone, particularly the Mizlaplanians, could be close to their equals, but they shut up because they wanted to go and to prove it.

This is where the greenness of the crew begins to show, Josef thought grimly. *And, damn it, I'm as green at this sort of thing as they are.*

Although, by treaty, the Mizlaplanian survival suit was officially categorized as "gold in color," that was simply to get around different racial perceptions of color. The suits were not shiny but rather dull, less gold than dark yellow with just a bit of orange. The form-fitted suits, customized for each individual, differed only in detail, and in color of course, from those used by the Mycohl and the Exchange. Gun Roh Chin had always wished that the diplomats had insisted on charcoal; he felt like a beacon in the damned thing, and a very good target.

Even though he timed his drop and his thrust perfectly, it took him close to thirty precious minutes to maneuver up to the Exchange ship, and, when he did, he found it with beacons and running lights off and no sign of power.

"It doesn't look damaged," Krisha noted, trying to see what detail she could. "I am telepathically scanning, though, and I get nothing at all."

"Nor I," added Savin, who was a powerful empath. Empaths often received signals at far greater distance than telepaths, although, in both cases, they weren't expecting to feel or monitor anything intelligible—just some sign that there was life aboard. "It feels like a dead ship."

Manya looked up from her instrument cluster. "It *is* a dead ship," she told them. "No power levels at all. Even the emergencies have been drained. Only the broadcast emergency transponder, which is opposite the planet's surface, shows any energy at all. It is inert. No life forms, no internal power. We will have to cut through an airlock just to board her."

"You're certain of that, Manya?" Morok pressed her. "No life, no internal power? It can't just be shielded?"

"No. If there were any attempts at shielding, then the shields themselves would register. There is nothing alive aboard. Even its computers are out."

"*Somebody* survived whatever it was," Krisha noted. "Somebody sent that message along with the distress beacon."

"Yes, but how long ago?" Gun Roh Chin put in. "Many days, certainly. Perhaps longer. With life-support down, they might not have been able to find a way to keep going. They might have lost hope after nobody came. They might have gone mad."

Savin's huge eyes scanned the surface of the research

vessel. "Holiness—the escape pods are still intact. Not a one has been fired. Not even the ones away from the surface that show some trickle charge—enough to use manually."

"Yes? So?" Morok was more spooked than irritated. They all were.

"Holiness—at least a few near the transponder are almost certainly usable, power drain or not. They weren't used. The first implication is that whatever happened here happened very quickly and to everyone. Everyone but one. He, she, it—whatever—survived, possibly by being in the only place, near the transponder that's still active, and was possibly only knocked out when everyone and everything else went. They would likely not have a huge crew on this sort of ship anyway. That person is not aboard now, or, if aboard, died there. Died there right next to a getaway system. Or got away without using the pods."

Gun Roh Chin nodded. "The pod would have taken him to the nearest survivable planet. We assume that they wouldn't assign races to this who couldn't survive down there, since the climate and atmosphere measure safe for us. It would have taken our survivor to the surface, with enough supplies and shelter for a month or more. That means . . ."

"It means," Krisha finished for him, "that he chose to die, either horribly or by his own hand, rather than go down to that world."

"There is a shuttle missing," Morok noted. "I saw its empty nesting bay on the underside."

"Within range of whatever it was, though," Savin pointed out. "I would assume that the shuttle was on the surface with the main scientific party. Since whatever killed this ship came from down there, I think it highly unlikely that anyone there risked flying up here to get that survivor off. Or was able to."

"Do you want to board her?" Chin asked them.

"Yes," responded Morok, "but not now. If there is no life aboard, we must first determine if there is still life below."

"Well, there is surely *something* below," Manya commented. "The energy pattern on the ship clearly indicates that it took a jolt of almost inconceivable power, pure energy, from a point below on the surface. It shorted out all the systems, shorted the computers, and most likely electrocuted almost everyone. Our survivor was probably the only one in some sort of insulated situation and so did not get the full jolt."

"If I am to be electrocuted, I should like to know who is doing it to me, and why," Morok said in a flat, hollow tone. "Take it down, Captain. Land at their camp below. Everyone check suits and weapons. Yes, again. *Now!*"

It wasn't difficult to find the camp below. It was a world covered with trees and seas, but the camp appeared to be the only sign of any animal life on it. There were a number of temporary, prefabricated structures down there as well as parabolic communications antennae, all of which were easy to spot.

"A standard scientific field station, not much different than the way we would do it," Manya told them. "The only thing I cannot understand is that large—house, or building, or whatever it is. It is of a totally different design than the others and looks quite permanent. In fact, it almost looks as if it were tooled from a single, unimaginably huge quartzlike crystal."

"More likely the object under study," Morok guessed. "Is it the odd light or my eyes, or does that—thing— seem slightly different, almost as if it moved?"

"I have been plotting it," Manya reported. "It does change, somehow. Not really in mass or even dimensions, but subtly, in detail."

"Could it be alive?"

"It might be—but if it is, it is like nothing we know

as life in any form. I simply do not know what it is, and I suspect that they didn't, either. That is why they are here."

"The base station has normal power," Chin noted. "Looks rather cozy, in fact. But we're not being scanned by anything I can detect. It's as if everybody down there is asleep. Ah—see! Their shuttle's there, in that clearing. I think I can put down close to it. No use in sneaking up. If anything's left alive down here, it certainly knows we're here by now and should come out and welcome us with open arms."

There was no welcoming committee. They put on their helmets, pressurized, and went out, even though all the instrumentation said that the air was perfectly safe and the temperature was quite pleasant. Until they knew more, none of them wanted to take anything for granted.

"Dead like the ship," Krisha said. "Nothing. I get nothing at all. Savin?"

"The same, although I do get some very odd intermittent sensations from the area of that object there. I can't really explain the sensation. It's not like anything I have ever experienced before. Whatever it is, I do not think it is directed at us."

"That will have to do for now," Morok told him. "Check out their shuttle first, then the prefabs, one at a time. Use caution, keep weapons drawn."

Gun Roh Chin took the shuttle. It wasn't difficult to enter, and, inside, he found it rather bizarrely arranged but nothing he could not have figured out. It was clearly not designed to be flown by humans, although there were two human-shaped seats in the rear. The rest he put down to different designs and a different shuttle design philosophy. Still, he could tell almost from the moment he entered that it was powered, fully charged, and could be operational with a few flicks of some switches.

"Shuttle is perfect and operational," he reported through his helmet radio.

"Then it could have picked up our survivor," Morok came back.

"Unlikely. Without power up there, they'd have had to cut away the outer airlock faceplate to get to the manual controls. They didn't. This thing was here before and it's been here all the time."

"The square prefab! Come quickly!" Krisha shouted.

They were all there on the run as soon as they got their bearings, piling into the door and then stopping dead just inside.

"May the gods embrace their innocent souls and reincarnate them to a life of peace," Morok intoned.

Gun Roh Chin was not prayerful. Even protected from the stench by his suit, he still wanted to throw up.

Savin bent down over a bloody form. "Krisha, exobiology is not my strong point, but isn't the human heart mounted roughly in the central chest cavity?"

Krisha swallowed hard. "Yes, roughly. What . . . ?"

The huge Mesok grabbed a shock of white hair atop the head of a human corpse, its face locked in a horrible and grotesque death mask. He yanked it up unceremoniously so that the chest was exposed.

The central area of the chest had been torn open, as if by some wild creature, possibly, even probably, while the man had been still alive. They all caught their breaths, but Manya scurried over and began using her portable instruments to examine the awful-looking wound. Even the tough, fanatical Gnoll seemed a bit shaky, though.

"It . . . has been torn from his chest," she managed. "Several of the others have equivalent mutilations. Something with great strength just pushed them down, like a child's plaything, and ripped key organs out of them, which depended on the race of the victim."

"How long have they been dead?" Morok asked her.

"Seven days at least. This happened at least seven days ago. The bodies are dried up and beginning to decompose."

Gun Roh Chin wanted to avoid the sight of the research party, its nice little lab smeared in red human blood, and *Zalerian* green, and gray, and purple, and other colors of other races who had been here. He walked over to the far side of the lab and began to examine a huge hole that had been smashed into the wall around what had once been a window. He pushed away the debris and looked out, to the strange, slightly changing opaque structure just beyond.

In the small administration hut there was much the same scene, only here the door had simply been kicked or blown in. Here, too, were several armed security officers; apparently these and a couple found outside had been the only armed members of the party. Some had clearly gotten off a lot of shots, and even in their present condition they looked like the kind who didn't miss.

Whatever had come out of that thing and killed them was hardly subtle; it had just come, on and on, oblivious to anything that they could do.

He had been around, seen hundreds of worlds and races, seen violence and cruelty as well as gentleness and good, but he had never seen anything like this.

"*Something big,*" Kelly Morgan had told him. Something perhaps *too* big, even for them.

Krisha called to him. "Captain, I hate to ask, but I need you. We've found the depository recordings and none of us can read the writing to tell which is which."

He returned to the ultimate horror scene, noting how peaceful and gentle this world itself was, how *quiet*, and reentered the lab.

He scanned the cabinet full of small labeled cubes she'd found, then picked one out. "This is a good place to start," he told her. "It says 'Preliminary Report on Remote Autopsy of Unknown Forms.' "

"There's a player in the office over there," she told him "And no bodies. The recording system is different than ours. I'm not certain I know how to work it."

He took it, went into the office, which looked as if it had just been left for a moment by its occupant, then found the small previewer machine. "It's not difficult," he told her. "It's just that instead of the full-blown presentation we get a small representation on the viewer plate, there. Switch your suit to translate standard Exchange"

The power was on; he simply turned on the machine, inserted the cube, label side out, and pressed the large actuator switch.

Much of it was simply a dictated interim report to some superiors back home, probably a record copy, but the small, three-dimensional images it projected of the research materials told them something.

"Subject A is a male of the species, 2.4381 meters tall, weight estimated at two hundred forty to two hundred and sixty-eight kilograms. It won't be possible to totally eliminate the material in which they are embedded without extraction from the estimations. Sorry. The main body surface area is very tough, very dense. The skin is at least one point two centimeters thick, more aptly described as a 'hide' than mere skin, and various vital areas seem further protected by bony plates at or very near the exterior. Both hands and feet are overly large in proportion to the body and are hairless, with that mottled texture consistent and the palms probably rock-hard to the touch, although they certainly bend and flex in the expected manner. The talons at the ends of the fingers are suited to ripping and tearing flesh, consistent with the teeth, which contain no herbivorous molars at all. They are true flesh-eating carnivores, no question."

"By the gods," Krisha intoned under her breath as the long-dead voice went on. "I am looking at the scans but they mean little to me."

"Or me," Chin agreed. "Manya?"

The Gnoll was trembling visibly, her eyes fixed on the small viewing plate, intoning prayer after prayer.

Krisha seemed somewhat stricken herself and looked up at Chin. "Her mind keeps saying 'Demons! Demons! They have awakened Hell personified.'"

"*Manya!*" Morok shouted at her.

The science officer seemed not to notice, then pointed a gnarled finger at the projection. "There! The full scan! Now they will pull back and restore it!"

The tiny figure, still a computerized diagram, now showed a full figure. Humanoid, big—bigger than Savin by a head—and, slowly, more and more detail was laid in as the voice continued to drone on with its observations.

"Oh, gods of eternity, protect us!" Savin prayed. "Manya is right. Look! Look!"

Gun Roh Chin had to admit that even the hair on the back of his own neck was tingling as he saw what they had found.

The creature didn't look quite the way his own religious teachers had pictured them, but it was still clearly recognizable, from the small horns on its head to the dull red eyes, fanged mouth, even the cloven hooves.

There was no question in his mind that he was looking at, not a representation, not an abstract estimation, and not someone's imagination, but a real, three-dimensional photograph of an actual, in the flesh, classical demon.

"There must have been bodies in that thing," he commented dryly, his feelings at the moment impossible to describe. "They thought they were dead. They put a lid on this because they knew the effect this sort of discovery would have not just on our religion or even the Mycohl's but on their myriad faiths as well."

He could see the scene now; these cold, pragmatic, utterly materialistic scientists with their faith firmly rooted in what could be seen, felt, touched, and demonstrated, excited by the discovery of what must have been a burial place, intact, for what might have been the galaxy's earliest spacefaring civilization. They had poked, probed, and scanned for weeks, probably months, to learn what they could before physically attempting to disturb or remove the remains, just in case exposure to air or light might cause damage or deterioration.

Finally, though, they had all they could get from their instruments, their data filling those recording cubes and probably being beamed back to the highest levels of the Exchange. Finally, there came the time when they could do no more without physically extracting the bodies from the sarcophagi they lay in.

And the sleepers had awakened and wreaked horrible vengeance on those who had defiled their tomb and disturbed their sleep.

"I almost hesitate to ask this," he said, his throat curiously and almost painfully dry, "because I'm not sure I want to know the answer, but it must be asked."

"Yes?" Morok responded, watching in added horror as a *second* scan was being dispassionately discussed on the tape.

"They were in suspended animation, not dead. They were freed, awakened, whatever. They came out and they killed all these people and somehow also fried the ship up there. Then what?"

"Uh? What do you mean?"

"Where did they go next?"

At that moment there came a roaring noise from outside, and in their current mental shape all weapons snapped to the ready and they ran out, leaving the recording playing.

Near both the research shuttle and their own, they could see another, differently designed shuttle coming in for a landing.

"The Mycohl!" Chin swore. "I'd forgotten about them! Just what we really needed right now!"

The Jugglers' Race

The star-shaped Durquist draped himself over his instruments, then said, "There is nothing alive on that ship. Nothing."

"Scan the colony," Modra Stryke instructed him. "I want to know if anything's alive anywhere here." She paused and shook her head. "What in God's name could have happened here?"

<*Gives you the creeps, doesn't it?*> Grysta commented to Jimmy McCray.

"It's the dunes world all over again," the telepath swore under his breath, not really replying to the parasitic creature on his back. "This smells really bad."

"It is even worse than it looks," the Durquist reported. "I do not scan any living forms below, but I scan not one but *three* parked shuttles."

Tris Lankur rushed to the command screens. "Put them up, Durquist. Full enlargement."

McCray, Lankur, and Stryke all gathered around the screen.

"What the hell?" Tris Lankur exclaimed, frowning. "The brown rectangular one there is from the orbital vessel. It's similar to ours. That dull gray oval one, though—that's Mizlaplan! And the black one that's kind of beetle-shaped—that's Mycohlian!"

"They had a bloody interstellar *convention* down there," McCray commented.

"I read no higher form anomalies below, either," the

Durquist reported. "And if those are foreign shuttles, where are their base ships? And what the hell were they doing here in the first place?"

"That's easy enough," Lankur replied. "They're here, someplace. Either automated or with a standby skeleton crew, watching us from out there someplace. Or chasing each other. I can't see those two groups in particular having any sort of friendly arrangement."

"You think the winner's getting ready to jump us?" McCray asked. "I mean, what if them bastard heathen Mycohl jumped the research ship and camp down there 'cause they were on to something real important and stuck out here in the middle of nowhere? The Holy Joes get wind of it and figure on an ambush—or vice versa. You said yourself they're all pretty close by here, all crunched together."

"Yes, but this is *our* territory, damn them!" Modra Stryke responded, feeling oddly angry at the sight. "And if they're here to get something, they have to pick it up and run. More of our people will be here in just a few days."

"Aye, and the winner of their free-for-all will be all set to prove that they came here in response to a legitimate distress signal, found everybody already dead—whether they did or not—and the colony abandoned. Then they'll stake their own claim on it and there'll be hell to pay," McCray theorized. "I'm no patriot, and I'm not keen for a fight, but how many of our people would be represented on a thing like this? Forty, fifty in the ship, maybe half as many down? It sticks in my craw that if we just sit here, they might just get away with it."

<Another way to try and commit suicide, Jimmy?>

Modra looked around at them. "McCray's right. This is *our* space, *our* territory. And if anybody's going to put in a claim on a planet so important it would tempt both of our enemies, it's going to be us."

"As an officer of the Exchange I've *got* to investigate," Tris Lankur reminded them. "As a member of this team, my presence is as good as all of us for our own claims. I *have* to go down. The rest of you could lay off and give me what cover you can."

Modra Stryke shook her head firmly in the negative. "Oh, no, Tris. No offense intended, but, God help me, you're a dead man. You look like Tris and talk like Tris and mostly act like Tris, but we have no idea what you have in your head or whose marching orders you follow in a pinch. The Exchange thought this was so important they didn't even put it up for bids. They kept it, and kept it quiet, too. As far as I'm concerned, that doesn't put you squarely on the Team's side in this. Uh-uh. We go down as a *team*. Same as always."

"I hate to keep bringing up nasty and inconvenient things," the Durquist put in, "but all evidence seems to indicate that whatever hit that ship did so from the planet's surface, not from space. And no matter if the Mizlaplan and Mycohl both have shuttles down there—*I am registering no known lifeforms on the surface, either!* I think that suggests several prudent courses of action."

Tris Lankur nodded. "All right, then, if it's a full team job, then we have to approach it that way. For one thing, we don't land where they did. I'd much rather come in from the other side if there's any sort of clearing, even if it means a little walk. Tran will drop the I.P. inside the camp but will then withdraw. I'd like to keep this ship in orbit for a lot of reasons, and I'm not really nervous about attack from enemy vessels—even if one of them *did* do all this, hitting us as well in our own territory would make it impossible to explain. I am concerned that nothing from down there does to this ship what it did to the research vessel. We'll drop a relay beacon here so we can be in touch, then Tran will lay off and out, but within range, so he can come in quick and dirty if need be. Understood?"

"Agreed," Modra responded. "Full packs and equipment, too. Durquist, any last bad news?"

"I am just trying to figure out what that structure or outcrop down there is," the Durquist responded. "It has rather—bizarre—properties, and is certainly what these people were studying."

"Well, I don't care what it is right now," Tris told him. "I think we'd better get suited up and ready and drop that beacon and get down there as fast as we can. It's going to be almost dark by the time we get into that camp, and I don't want any nasty surprises just in case that thing's masking our instruments or has a Mycohl military team inside it just waiting for us."

Back in the ready area, Jimmy McCray was surprised to see Molly come in and start rummaging around. "What are you doing here? You can't come with us on this."

"Where you go, I go," she told him. "Besides, Molly did what bigbrains couldn't. Molly got funny suit. Molly go with Jimmy."

The fact was, she did have an environment suit, although she couldn't do much with it other than exist on the automatic systems. She had to have a suit; you couldn't go into space on anything less than a capital ship without one.

<Order her to shut up and stay here!> Grysta snapped. *<She's just gonna get us both killed.>*

For once, Jimmy agreed with his unwanted mate. "No, Molly! It's too dangerous! This isn't like being off the Hot Plant."

Molly stared at him. "Jimmy say Molly free girl?"

"Yes, but—"

"Didn't Jimmy say back there that Molly part of team?"

"All right, damn it, but I didn't—"

"Then Molly go," she responded with a note of finality.

"Molly," Modra put in sweetly, trying to be kind. "There might be a lot of bad people down there.

Shooting and killing. We're afraid you might do something because of that, something that might get some of us killed."

"Molly had lotsa bad men in life. Molly not as dumb as folks think!"

Modra looked around. "Tris? Durquist?"

"I don't like it, but we can lose what little light we have arguing with her," Tris Lankur pointed out. "Either somebody's got to club her into unconsciousness or she's going to go."

"I agree," said the Durquist with a sigh. "Molly, if you come, you must be a full member of the team. You must be very quiet and do exactly as we say, no matter whether you agree with it or not. You must obey us instantly, because we have done this before and you have not."

"Molly understand. Molly also know rest of you had first time sometime, right?"

Modra Stryke sighed. "Give it up, Jimmy, and help her into her suit."

Molly *had* been very good and very cautious, and she was strong as an ox, which allowed Lankur and the Durquist to bring some extra equipment and supplies along.

They had landed about four kilometers northwest of the camp and trekked in. It wasn't an easy walk, but compared to some of the worlds they had been on, it was almost absurdly simple. They arrived at the camp just at sunset, then fanned out to find out as much as they could.

"Don't enter or even touch the foreign shuttles," Lankur warned. "We want to know if anybody's aboard, dead or alive, but nothing more. They're almost certainly boobytrapped."

The grisly scene of carnage that had shocked and baffled the Mizlaplanians had no less effect on them.

More, in some ways, because all of them were *their* people, Exchange citizens.

"There's been a fight here, too," Modra noted. "See some of the searing on the exterior walls there? Whichever of them was here first fought at least a brief battle with whoever came second."

"No signs of foreign dead, though," the Durquist noted, a bit shaken to discover that some of the original victims of the carnage had been Durquists as well. He felt as if he were looking at his own end. "None of the victims we found were shot, and all the clothing and equipment here appears to be ours. I did an entire surface scan."

Tris Lankur stood in front of a huge cabinet in the administration hut, which had clearly been filled with the accumulated scientific recordings made there. "Maybe nobody shot these folks, but somebody shot the data," he noted. "I bet there isn't a single intelligible or salvageable data cartridge here. Somebody wanted to make sure that we had as little to go on as possible."

"Or, more likely, whoever was here first didn't want the newcomers to know what they were in for," the Durquist said from behind him. "And they did a very nice job of that, too."

"I wouldn't worry so much about the data," Modra replied. "There are surely tons of materials on the ship in safely insulated interior regions, or maybe already sent back to the Exchange. This vandalism is just senseless."

Jimmy McCray, still in the research prefab, turned and surveyed the lab, with its twisted, wrecked bodies and dried blood of a half-dozen races all over everything. "And this makes sense?"

Molly had been more shaken by the gruesome sights than she wanted to let on, still fearing they'd send her back up. She wandered over to where a huge hole had been made in the side of the building.

"Whoever do this thing don't like doors," she noted.

McCray went over to her and examined the hole. "My dear, you're absolutely right. Whatever monstrosity came through, came right through here—everything's bent inwards. And if they came on a straight line, then . . ." She followed his eyes as they looked at the bizarre structure not too far up on the bluff.

Molly frowned thoughtfully, something she rarely did. "Jimmy, you think that be somebody's house? They maybe not like be broken into?"

He stared at her in surprise. "You might just have something there, darlin'." He suddenly paused. "Huh. Gettin' pretty dark in here. I think either I better find the lights or I'm gonna be spooked right to Jesus."

"Somebody already got lights on," she said, pointing.

In the near darkness, the huge alien structure was definitely glowing, although only slightly.

"There's no two ways about it," Tris Lankur told them, shining his light on various signs of a fight leading from the camp, up toward the thing embedded in the bluff. "We either camp here and wait for something to happen, or we go up and see just what the hell that thing is, with the likelihood that either it will kill us or it contains both whatever did all this and two very mean and fully armed foreign crews."

<*I vote to stay here!*>

"Shush, Grysta. You don't get a vote in this."

"Alas," the Durquist sighed, "I fear he's right."

Modra looked around in the near total darkness. "I think I'd rather take my chances up there than spend the night in this morgue," she said. "And I don't see how waiting until morning will help us. I think we call into Tran, make our report, then go on in. Funny. I'm feeling remarkably wide awake for somebody who's walking right into death."

<*Shit!*> Grysta swore.

"You can always hop off now," Jimmy McCray suggested hopefully.

"Team to *Widowmaker*, team to *Widowmaker*," Tris called. "Do you read me, Tran?"

"Coming in fine," Trannon Kose responded. "I wish I were down there with you."

"I wish I was up there and *you* were down here," the Durquist commented.

Quickly but thoroughly, Lankur made his report on their findings, which would supplement and detail the recordings of their intercom communications automatically registered on the ship.

"People go in there and they don't come out, or so it seems," Lankur concluded. "As a result, I recommend that nobody, repeat, nobody, follow us in. At least not until experts have recovered the data on those cartridges and know exactly what they are facing. Instead, I recommend active quarantine of the planet until they are a lot more confident, and I also recommend a military sweep of this system. If the foreign ships are hiding out in there, they could probably learn a lot from them."

"Affirmative, Tris. You sound like you don't think you're coming out, either."

"I don't know. None of us do. But—come in briefly and blow up the foreign and base camp shuttles as soon as we go in. Understand? Blow them up. Make them unable to fly. If anybody *except* us comes out of there, I don't want them getting off this hell hole. But you blow them and then back right off. you understand? Come in, blow, and withdraw. Then you wait, either for us or for reinforcements."

"Understood. Take care, all of you. I should very much hate having to break in another team."

"You can bloody well afford the best, Trannon Kose," Jimmy shot back. "If we don't come out of there, you get the whole bloody payment!"

Kose was silent for a moment, then responded, "I hadn't thought of that, McCray. Now I *know* I'll see you again. The way you've been, you'd come back from the grave to claim that money before you'd let me have it all."

"All right," Lankur sighed. "We'll keep our monitors on, but since we're not getting even carrier signals from the Mycohl or Mizlaplanians, the odds are pretty good that ours won't carry, either." He drew a deep breath. "All right, everybody—let's see what the hell this is all about."

They walked up the well-worn path in the eerie darkness.

"Place feel real strange," Molly commented as they neared it.

Modra nodded. "I feel it, too. Something on the empathic band, but not like anything I've ever felt before. It's almost as if that were some kind of new life form rather than a structure. Something somehow *alive*, yet so different, so alien, it's like nothing we know."

<*I knew it! It's some kind of gigantic stone beast and we're walking right into its stomach!*> Grysta cried to Jimmy McCray.

Jimmy tried to ignore that comment as he did most others, but damned if it didn't echo his own dark thoughts. He could sense second-hand what they were feeling by scanning their thoughts, but scanning the object produced nothing except the creeps. "Nothing on my wavelengths," he told them.

"The glow is very low-level energy," the Durquist reported. "Essentially a trickle charge almost too low to measure at all. The stuff, whatever it is, must be built to glow. It might even be simply radiating back absorbed sunlight."

Standing at the end of the structure, they could see where someone, presumably the scientific team, had laid down a plastic carpet up to what had to be the entrance. It looked dirty and well-trod.

"Well, if anybody thinks it's going to eat us, I think that should disprove at least that much," Lankur noted. "From the looks of this and the data modules and equipment, I'd say our people have been going in and out of here for a long time."

"Strange how it seems to change, somehow, every time you look at it," Modra commented. "And yet, you can't ever catch it in the act."

"Weapons on full lethal except Molly," Lankur stated flatly. "Don't give anything or anybody a chance to pick you off first. Check equipment, then report."

Molly didn't even draw her pistol. She doubted if she could harm anything, even something trying to kill her. The fear of death, or the unknown, didn't enter her mind. To the Syn, it was always "now."

"Okay, everyone. Let's go in," Tris Lankur said in a flat, yet determined voice.

The eerie, opaque, cream-colored walls seemed almost to be dissolving about them, although intellectually they all knew it was really just an effect designed by some mind alien to each and every one of them.

"Keep your suit lights on," Lankur warned them. "We get to depending on this place and suddenly something cuts the power. On your guard."

"We may be nuts but we aren't dumb," Jimmy McCray muttered in reply.

"I'm going through that entrance there," the cymol said, pointing. "Durquist—left. McCray, right. I'll go through the middle, you two follow on my signal or if I open fire."

He crouched down and let the other two get into position, then checked and double-checked his rifle, took a deep breath, and charged into the nearly heart-shaped opening.

For a moment there was silence, then Tris Lankur's voice said, "It's all right. Come on in. There's nothing alive here . . . now. Modra, come on up with us if your stomach will take it. It's worse than the base camp. Molly, you were bothered by that scene. I'm not real sure you should see this."

That brought them all in in a hurry, with Molly, somewhat indignant at the patronizing, charging right through. She and the others stopped dead just behind Tris Lankur, who was standing stock-still, seemingly transfixed by the scene.

Everywhere there was blood. Red blood, green blood, blue blood, all the colors of the rainbow, smeared all over in such abandon it seemed like the work of some mad artist.

The chamber was huge, far larger than could be accounted for by the apparent size of the "house" or whatever it was, with the slightly rounded floor characteristic of the rest of the place, and in the center were the remains of what had once obviously been two pillars rising from floor to ceiling, although it appeared to need no support—which was good, since a substantial portion of the pillars was now gone, shattered fragments mixed in with the blood.

It was Lankur who moved first, walking over to the closest remains of what might have once been a living creature. The heaps of bone, flesh, and muscle were so mangled and distorted that it wasn't even possible to determine its racial origin.

He approached the bloody, twisted lump cautiously, almost as if he expected it to come alive in some hideous form and leap upon him, even though cymols were supposedly immune to fear and imagination's tricks, and that thing was through ever leaping anywhere.

"It's been gnawed," he said hoarsely. "Who—whatever did this, it indiscriminately tore up and gnawed on every one of them. It was a blood feast, without any sense or reason at all. The ones back at the camp were just sadistically murdered—not these. What in *hell* did they set loose in here?"

The Durquist moved next, over to Lankur's right and near the ruined pillar. "It was our doing, whatever it was," he noted. "This is—*was*—a Durquist. Mangled, but ungnawed. Whatever it was knew not to eat a Durquist."

Of all the known creatures, the Durquist was the only one whose flesh had proven toxic to any living thing that consumed even a small part of it.

Modra Stryke walked carefully through the carnage and up to the base of the shattered pillar nearest the Durquist. She was shaken, certainly, by the sight, but she was also a pro. She could be sick later.

"There appears to have been some kind of hollow center in the pillars," she noted. "The rubble isn't quite enough for solid posts of that thickness and height." She stooped down and picked up two shards, not randomly chosen but selected for their obvious difference.

"Look at this," she said, holding one shard in each hand. "The one here is better than ten centimeters thick. This one, though, is very thin, very fragile—a few millimeters, no more."

The Durquist's stalked eyes turned away from the sight of his dead relation to the contents of her hand. "Interesting. Two enclosures, then, one inside the other. The outer thick, perhaps for protection and support, the inner—a capsule? You suppose that whatever it was was in some sort of capsule, suspended, and then the pillar was poured from the top down, over it, to seal it in?"

"Yeah, but what was inside the thing?" McCray asked, looking nervously around. "And where is it now?"

"Not here," the Durquist responded. "Not now. Whatever it was was *big*. Look at the teeth marks here.

And those really nasty marks there—What could make them? Fangs?"

"Their weapons seem to be still here," Tris Lankur noted. "I found a few. Small stuff but it should still have been adequate to have stopped just about anything I know."

"If they had a chance to use 'em," Jimmy put in.

"They did. you can see the marks on the walls all around you, and at least the one pistol I just checked is totally discharged. It's a near certainty that whatever it was wasn't invisible, or faster than lightning, and there were a fair number of people here. Whatever it was got hit all right. Got hit—and kept on coming. And it was *fast*. There wasn't even the obvious element of surprise implicit in the base camp attack. I—Uh-oh."

"What's the matter?" Modra asked, tensing. Lankur kneeled down before another mass of mangled flesh, then reached out and began peeling parts of it away. Modra, even McCray, found themselves averting their eyes. "What the hell you doing cymol?" Jimmy asked.

"You said it right," Lankur responded. "I am a cymol and this is all that's left of another. *Jesus*! The skull's been crushed!" There was a sickening popping sound. "Ah! Got it!"

"What the hell are you doing, Tris?" Modra almost screamed. It was like a dead man loose in a slaughterhouse.

"Sorry to be so ghoulish," he responded, "but I got what I was looking for. Maybe damaged, maybe not. Hard to tell until I connect up."

They all turned in spite of themselves and saw that he was now standing, holding something that resembled a crudely shaped lump of some dull, lead-colored material to which small bits of organic matter still clung.

"I have one of these in my head," he told them. "Different size and shape, probably different capacity, but something like this just the same. Odd—never actually *saw* one before."

"That—that's the cymol part?" Modra asked weakly, wondering if in fact she *could* wait until later to be sick.

He nodded. "It's inert—now. No thought, no life left in it. But if its recording function is intact, I might well be able to learn just what happened here."

"You want to take it back to the ship?" she asked hopefully.

"I think I want to try it here. But—uh, sorry. Let's move back into one of the outer chambers."

They got no argument, even from the Durquist, and when they entered the antechamber they found Molly already there, looking as if she'd just puked.

Lankur unlatched the small case he wore on his belt, did something, and the case opened to reveal a dull metallic checkerboard surface. He removed a cable, stuck one end on the box, where it seemed to stick like glue, then reached up and removed a small section of his hair. Modra watched in horrified fascination, unsure whether this sight was worse or not as bad as the one in the other room.

"This won't take long. Not at the speed I can operate in that direct mode," he told them, sticking the other end of the cable into the plate in his skull.

Somehow they all expected him to assume some trancelike state, but he seemed much the same, eyes darting to each of them, face nearly expressionless. After a minute, perhaps less, he sighed and said, "It is badly damaged. I can't believe the kind of strength this would take. I don't have it all, but I think I have enough. I can tell you just what was inside there, and a little of what happened right at the end."

"The demon message was correct, no matter how mad the fellow was," Tris Lankur told them. "About three months ago, a scout discovered this world and this place, the only artificial structure on it. The scout didn't enter but *did* send in a probe, and got back pictures of that central chamber in its original state. You were right, Modra—two bodies, one in each pillar, sort of like giant stalagmite sarcophagi, each containing the body of a demon"

"Demon? What do you mean, 'demon'?" Jimmy McCray asked him.

"Just what I said. It was always theorized that we'd find at least the remains of them sooner or later. Hundreds of worlds, hundreds of races, and two out of three of them have demons. Even some water-breathing and silicon-based races have demons. Changed, altered, filtered through countless generations of legend, superstition, and racial viewpoints, but demons all the same. Tall, bipedal creatures—the one looked to be two and a half meters easy, the other maybe two—with horns, blazing, fiery eyes, ugly expressions, fangs, cloven hooves, pointed tails—the whole business. Ugly as sin and twice as fearsome-looking. My old Islamic grandfather would have recognized them in an instant, as would your Catholic priest, McCray, or your high priestess, Modra. Even you, Durquist, would have known them instantly, although they look considerably more humanoid than your people's version."

"Demons," the Durquist mused. "*Xotha*, in my mother tongue, which is, by the way, the exact same word as ours for 'evil' but for the inflection that makes it refer to a living thing rather than a concept. The universal personification of evil—except to the Mycohl, who have them in place of demigods or angels or whatever."

Tris Lankur nodded. "It was long theorized that such memories couldn't have arisen independently, even on early worlds like Mother Earth, where cultures and religions were so different, let alone on worlds that had no creature in any way resembling them on their planets. An early, brutal, interstellar race that made such an impression that ancient cultures preserved their memory in legend and myth."

"Some impression," Jimmy McCray muttered. "The personification of evil."

Lankur shrugged. "Well, you saw the other room," he noted. "I'd say that they more than lived up to their reputation."

"*They* did *that*?" Modra asked, incredulously. "Just *two* of them did all *that*?"

Lankur nodded. "Just two. And two who'd probably been in some kind of suspended animation for thousands upon thousands of years."

"The two—a set?" the Durquist asked him.

He nodded. "Yes, a male and a female. Conventionally bisexual, racially, although his organ looked big and half bone."

"The story now appears obvious," the Durquist said. "As far as it goes, anyway. Such a discovery caused the Exchange to rush their best scientific team here, along with a military guard ship to keep everybody else out, both entrepreneur and Mycohlian. Then they tested, poked, probed, and eventually got to extracting the pair from their tombs. When they broke the seals, the two awoke and—well, fulfilled expectations. But how did they also cream the naval frigate?"

"That's not in here," Tris told them. "It must have happened either after they did this or simultaneously. I played back the end scene frame by frame and it's still not really clear. Too much disorientation and shock, too much damage. But it appears they only cut through the base of the female—that was the one on the left— and suddenly this whole place lit up. I get a picture of the light being much brighter all of a sudden, and of a kind of pulsing, almost like this building was a living organism. It's like—well, maybe examining a bacterium under high magnification. Fluids moved, tiny things pulsed and flexed—I'd say this place as alive, somehow."

Jimmy McCray looked nervously around. "Jonah all over. And we walked right into the whale's *stomach*!"

"Artificial life," the cymol responded. "No offense, Molly, but you're an example of the earlier stages that this represents. They grew and designed artificial life as their housing, as their machines, everything. It probably thinks, even anticipates. Don't worry—I *think* I know what happened. I think they cut a little too high. I think they were going to cut just a little of the female's right leg, at least if my figures are correct. It triggered the defensive mode of this place. It revived the pair and shattered the external casings, which kept her from being sliced, and at the same time it automatically reacted against everything that could be perceived as a threat. That means it has the power to shoot and take out even a warship in high orbit."

"You mean—this—*place*—did that to them in there?" Modra asked, growing more and more nervous by the second.

"No," replied the cymol. "Not this place."

The cutting laser was having trouble with the substance, even though it could cut through the toughest known alloys. It did slice, but not cleanly, nor easily, nor particularly straight. It began to get jagged, and the robot-saw stopped a moment and said, "Warning! I cannot guarantee that I can get through without raising the angle. This has the potential of cutting into specimen."

Professor Makokah, a Brudak, flared its umbra in frustration. "What do you think?"

The Durquist, a female of high rank, snorted. "Too bad, but we have to get them out of there. She won't feel a thing. My instruments show she's been dead a mere three-quarters of a million standard years more or less."

"Any chance of better luck with the male?" asked Juria,

a matronly looking human cymol who was the theoretical official in charge.

"Negative," the robot responded. "The problem is the thickness of the base and the nature of the material. I am the finest precision cutting tool we have. Something catches and twists the beam but does not weaken it, and their interior chambers give almost no latitude at all, being, as you noted, form-fitted. The tolerances built into me should be adequate, but they are not. My own abilities do not foresee a way to prevent loss of at least most of the foot."

Juria sighed. "My computations do not see any way out. The drill knows what it talks about. We shall have to accept the damage or leave them there."

"Very well," the Professor responded. "Proceed, then. The anticipated damage is rather minor compared to the value of an actual autopsy."

The drill turned itself back on, and in that moment the walls, floor, and ceiling of the chamber suddenly burst into illumination, but they no longer had the hard, quartzlike appearance and texture. It seemed instead as if there were a tremendous network of transparent veins and arteries, cells and other objects, suddenly alive, suddenly moving, like some great beast.

The drill, programmed to stop at any unusual occurrence, shut down, and the people in the room were still gaping, in shock and wonder, when the two pillars burst at the center with a loud double explosion that both deafened them and nearly knocked them down.

Great demon figures stepped out, and from their backs spread large barbed, leathery wings. They did not step out as if suddenly revived, nor were they groggy, fearful, or even, apparently curious.

The only two words Tris Lankur could come up with were imperious, and, somehow, arrogant.

The guards' weapons came up and even as Juria shouted, "No! Don't shoot them!" the pair made *incredible leaps on the nearest living things and began to use razor-sharp claws and fangs and great strength to tear head from body and limb from limb. The soldiers hesitated for fear of killing others, but when they saw the ferocity of the demons they opened up, pouring every bit of their charges dead into the two attacking monsters.*

The demons appeared to find the shots, sufficient to vaporize part of the inert drill, mildly irritating, and immediately went after the soldiers, falling upon them and making of them very quick work.

Several of the team members, including the cymol, started to make for the exit, but to their horror, the wide, ovoid opening through which they had entered suddenly shut, as if it were more valve than door, trapping them inside!

It did not take the demons long to finish them off at that point, going next for the cymol, whose memory and sensors became disoriented, then failed, but not, as first suspected, of immediate damage.

As the first demon, the male, touched her, there was a sudden shock, a sudden opening of receptors, and some kind of contact, somehow, was made between the cymol computer in her head and whatever that thing was. There was a sudden, tremendous surge in her head, like contact with the Guardians themselves but with a difference; with a strange, terrible alienness about it, and crude, terribly crude, without regard for what it might do to her. She felt the contents of her cymol capsule being written out, copied somehow, but the two-way contact fed her such a totally alien stream of incomprehensible thoughts and images that she could not grab hold of them, nor make any sense of them, even as her cymol half tried to do so.

Then, suddenly that cymol brain assembled something—a thought, a concept, a distorted and meaningless misinterpretation based on overload—who could tell? It said:

"The Quintara—they still run!"
Then all was blackness.

"I wish I could show them to you," Tris Lankur told them. "Alive, animated, they are like nothing I've ever seen before, even though they are in every sense the classical demon. It's not just the size and strength and form, it's something else, something *inside* them, that radiates out from them with every look, every gesture, every move. Almost the way . . . well, that an entomologist might look at a collection of insects. Only, no, even *that* doesn't convey it. Maybe . . . the way he'd look at a collection of *common* insects, of no particular interest. The kind even an entomologist wouldn't hesitate to step on without another thought. It's not even viciousness— they're too damned smugly superior for that. But it *is* power. Incredible power."

For a moment, there was silence, and he asked, "Any questions?"

"Yeah," Molly said, voice trembling slightly. "What the hell we still *doin'* in here?"

"She's got a point," the Durquist noted. "On a strictly pragmatic level, our current weapons aren't even a match for the soldiers', not really, and we have no idea how far back this structure goes. The demons certainly didn't go out onto the surface—we'd have detected them as life forms, at least—and they didn't just spread their wings and fly off into space. Whatever they are, I refuse to renounce the laws of physics. That happened days ago in there. They were certain to be hungry—pardon— with three-quarters of a million years between supper and breakfast, but one would suspect that by now they would have at least a passing interest in lunch."

"I'm afraid it makes no difference," Tris Lankur commented. "If this place is alive, it's monitoring us right now. If it's got armaments capable of what we know it has, then we're no safer up there than we are down here right inside it. In other words, if it wants us, there's not a damned thing in creation that can stop it."

Jimmy McCray let out a long breath. "Well, that sort of says it all, doesn't it? Kept around like mice in a snake house until the snake gets hungry. And if we try and leave, it can bloody well just blow our ship to kingdom come."

"Wait a minute! Wait a minute! This thing's got us all spooked!" Modra snapped at them "There's no evidence that we're anything of the sort. It did nothing to the scout's probe, nor to the people here until they made a decision that would have harmed one of the owners. It didn't just shoot us out of the sky when we arrived, so it isn't in defensive mode all the time even now, and maybe it can't use all that stuff on its own initiative. Maybe, just maybe, it has to be directed to shoot."

"A telepathic link to machinery?" Jimmy McCray scratched his chin thoughtfully. "Well, it's been attempted for centuries, but I don't know that it's ever been done or can be."

"I think she is right," the Durquist put in. "Consider that all prior attempts have been to link people to machines. This isn't a machine—not in the sense we think of it. It's no more a machine than Molly there is a machine, and they found a way to induce broadcast empathy in Molly. If the Exchange knows how to do *that*, who knows what sorts of creatures with what sorts of powers they're producing or at least working on right now? And, if the Exchange can do that, how much of a stretch is it to imagine that a technology that could create a place like this couldn't build in telepathic abilities as well?"

"You make me feel like some kind'a space suit or somethin'," Molly responded sorrowfully.

"No offense meant, I assure you," the Durquist responded.

"Well, Grysta just pointed out to me that it's no skin off us," Jimmy commented. "We've done the job, right? We answered the call, inspected the deed, didn't disturb the evidence much, and it's now up to us to make our report for other, wiser heads to follow up, and then head home to collect on our successful mission. Personally, I don't give a damn *where* those demons are so long as they're not near me."

Tris Lankur thought about it, then nodded and put away his equipment. "All right. Your little companion is a hundred per cent right as far as my own obligations are concerned. Still, I hate like hell to turn this over to anybody else after we beam the report. After all, a claim's a claim and salvage law is still the law."

"You mean—claim this place as salvage?" Modra was appalled by the idea. "But—that would mean some of us would have to stay here until the salvage claim was registered."

"We'll have to stay in the area, anyway, until somebody else gets here," Lankur pointed out. "You can bet that the Mycohl are headed this way as well. They *had* to pick up that call. If we're here, they won't get the claim— they'll be blamed for it if they try anything straightaway. Only if we aren't here and can't file a report, can they get in under the same salvage law."

"Well," the Durquist said with a sigh, "if we are stuck, and we are, and if we are targets anywhere, which we are, I suggest that we are much more comfortable targets aboard *Widowmaker*."

"Agreed," responded McCray, and the others nodded. "Let's get out of this accursed place."

They picked up their gear and started back the way they came, with Molly, this time, taking the enthusiastic lead.

They walked for some time, from chamber to chamber, but there was no sign of the entrance.

"Wait a minute! We've gone much further than we

did coming in," McCray commented. "We must have taken a wrong turn."

"Impossible!" Lankur snapped. "It was a straight line and we retraced our steps exactly. Trust me."

Hearing this, Molly suddenly stopped. "Uh-oh! I got bad feelin' 'bout this. *Real* bad."

"The instruments aren't working right in here," Modra said, "so I can't say for sure, but I think you're right, McCray."

"Press on for a little," the cymol urged them. "It's this place. It's got us all spooked."

But after a half hour or more and chamber after chamber, even Tris Lankur had to admit that something was wrong.

"Who'd have thought this thing was this *huge*?" Modra said in a puzzled tone.

"A tesseract," the Durquist mumbled. "We're in a real, live tesseract!"

"A what?" Molly asked, looking totally confused.

<*A what?*> Grysta echoed to Jimmy.

"A what?" asked McCray.

"A tesseract. Purely theoretical, of course. Or was. A structure of some sort built in a shape or form that intersects more than the usual dimensions. The plaything of mathematicians for centuries. Any structure, even us, exists in the three obvious dimensions plus time. A tesseract is folded so that it goes through more dimensions than just those. That's how this place seems larger on the inside than on the outside and why it appears to change its dimensions now and again. It seems larger because it *is* larger. The rest of it is folded through other dimensions we can't perceive. But, since we're inside, we're carrying our own dimensional perceptions with us, so nothing appears to change—it's just a lot roomier. One wonders what a pair of *anything* needs a place this big *for*."

"Maybe they don't," Lankur responded. "If you're right, if this *is* a true tesseract, and everything indicates that you are, it might just be that all these rooms are necessary only because they're needed to create just the right folds. Who on our side knows how to build one of these things? What needs to be included to maintain structural integrity? A tesseract must be potentially incredibly unstable."

"I think I get what you mean, sort of," Modra said, sounding like she really didn't. "But if I follow you at all, then the front door might still be wide open. We might just have taken a wrong turn into some other dimension or something."

"Possible, but unlikely," Lankur replied. "The scout probe got in and out in a straight line, and that team was here for months and never had a problem. Unless . . . Hmmm . . . Perhaps it was triggered to switch when the place activated. Become a one-way door."

"In which case it's probable that the owners are indeed still inside," the Durquist noted uneasily.

"No, they can talk with the place, remember? They can open the door any time they want and have an illuminated road map and complete directions. No, you have to ask why they'd *want* to go out the front door."

"To get outside, I assume," the Durquist replied.

"To what? A world of trees and oceans, totally deserted, and all creation inevitably bearing down on them? Uh-uh. But maybe you only have one exit at a time. If this thing folds through space and time, they might not even *need* spaceships. I'm sure they had plenty of time to read the chronograph in this thing and all the other data and they know how long it's been. And if *I* woke up under those conditions, the first thing I'd try and find out is what happened to the rest of my people. What's home like? And that . . . Uh-oh. Now *there's* a wrinkle I hadn't considered."

"What's one more in a furrowed brow?" McCray asked tartly.

"They got a complete readout of the cymol data from

that dead cymol back there. Not enough for military secrets or stuff like that, but it's a good bet that they know pretty much what we know. They know about the three empires, about the various races, the systems, that sort of thing."

"Three-quarters of a million years ago my ancestors were slithering through the jungle marshes in a constant search for food and worshiping our sun," the Durquist noted, "and probably communicating in grunts and whistles. I suspect that your ancestors were not that much more advanced. Even the Guardians themselves were an interstellar civilization within the last hundred thousand years. A civilization this high and this pervasive a quarter of a million years ago would either be gods of the universe by now or they are extinct, at least until that pair breeds. Hmmm . . . I wonder how many children they have, and how quickly?"

"I wonder about that last enigmatic thought that the cymol got," Tris Lankur responded. *"The Quintara— they still run.* Suppose, somehow, it was a last analytical gasp. A warning, in hopes that another cymol would pick it up, as I did? If these demons are the Quintara . . . Well, you see what I mean."

"They can't *still* be around!" Modra asserted. "It's got to be just some garbage. After all, she *was* being torn to pieces at the time. Even a cymol is bound to be a teensy bit less than clear under those conditions. Like the Durquist said—if they were around, and were at this level that long ago, as is probable from the demon legends, then we'd know."

"That pair of demons was around a quarter of a million years," Tris Lankur pointed out. "And we didn't know about *them* until recently."

"What do you—oh! I see! How many more are there out there? Sleepers? Sleepers who now can be awakened. Oh, my God!"

"The front door was open," Tris Lankur noted. "I

assume that the back door is now open. All we have to do is find it."

"And go where?" McCray asked.

The cymol shrugged. "Anywhere. Anywhere but here."

"And then what?"

"I don't know. We'll find out when we get there. We can't stay here. We'll run out of food and water eventually, and power too. As for me—they've got at least a four-day head start."

All the others suddenly started and stared at him. "You intend to pursue?" the Durquist asked.

"If I can. Things will have changed in all this time. They, too, have to eat—that's obvious. And drink, presumably. The preliminary reports said they were carbon-based life forms, fairly standard for all the extraordinary abilities and immunities they showed. I think they can be tracked. And, of course, I doubt if it would even *occur* to them that any one of the likes of *us* would give chase. After all this time, I don't think they'll be in a hurry, and subtlety isn't their strong suit."

"And then what?" McCray pressed. "Suppose you catch them? Your pistol's useless. Your strength's no match for them, and they know at least a little more of the stashes along the route than you do. You're going to wind up in a loincloth with a homemade spear, stalking them in their own element. The odds of you catching up to them, let alone catching them, are remote. And, if you do, the best you can do is be dessert."

Tris Lankur looked at the telepath squarely. "McCray, did you see any Mizlaplan bodies around? Any Mycohl? No. And neither did I. There was nothing in here that recently dead." He stopped, stooped down, and picked up something off the floor. He examined it, then showed it to them.

"A cigar butt?" Modra responded, looking at the curiosity.

"Yes. A cigar butt. Not dried out, either. The tobacco

is still moist in the unsmoked part. That small yellow band there near the end tells me that it was a Mizlaplanian who smoked it."

"I didn't know any of them had *any* bad habits," McCray commented dryly.

"One of the foreign teams landed, found what we found, and probably also still had use of the recordings back in the office. They know what was here and what was done. The second team surprised them and they had to fight, eventually taking refuge inside this thing, whatever it is. The newcomers, maybe fearing a trap, maybe just out of good sense, didn't pursue right away. They went back, probably found the recordings that the first group watched and saw them, too. Then they destroyed them, in the hopes that nobody could or would follow them soon. Then they, too, came up here and came in. I don't think the second group found the first one. In this sort of place, it would be nearly impossible for *everybody* to miss, and I can't believe they're all lousy shots."

"One can imagine what being faced with live, real demons would do to the Mizlaplanians," the Durquist noted. "It would be like their angels were suddenly face to face with the physical forces of Hell itself. No, force other than death itself would prevent them giving chase, no matter how hopeless it seemed."

"And the Mycohl venerate the demon figure as a kind of demigod," Tris Lankur pointed out. "Although, to be fair, they are about as deep-down religious as the average Exchange citizen, which is to say, not much. But if they followed the Mizlaplanians in, and found them gone, what were they going to do? Go on a hunt, or camp out by the front door until the Exchange came in and, at best, arrested them? They had no choice— and they at least have some reason to believe that, of all three systems, these demons will be more favorably disposed to them than to the other two."

"They're probably all dead," McCray pointed out.

"Probably. But what if they're not? What if this back door opens right into some ancient base world of the demons' civilization? What if these two are all that's left? Think of the knowledge, and power, represented here. No, go camp out front for a few weeks or come with me."

Modra shook her head in wonder. "I don't think we have a choice. If there *is* a back door to someplace else, perhaps another world, perhaps another dimension, as the evidence, over logic, seems to suggest, I'd rather go there than camp out here and hope against hope that somebody will come in and rescue us. If there is only one exit, you take it."

"Consider the possibility, though, that it does *not* lead directly to them, but rather to intermediate stops," the Durquist chipped in. "Perhaps a great number of intermediate stops. A tesseract is a rather odd thing. That would mean that we would be in both a chase, and a race, with two teams of mortal enemies, to catch up with representatives of an ancient race we might be powerless to do anything to. All the time, the three teams would be going not only after the same unholy end, but fighting each other every step of the way. And we are already behind, perhaps half a day, perhaps more. One feels the firm bounds of reality slipping madly away in this, particularly when such an insane race is in fact the more desirable course!"

Jimmy McCray gave a wan smile and looked at each of the others in turn, then said, "Hurry! Hurry! Hurry! Step right up, ladies, gentlemen, others, those of all races and creeds and nationalities! Three highly trained teams are about to set out on a racecourse blindfolded, where they will attempt to murder one another in their quest to catch creatures that will certainly eat the winners! Yes, indeed, beings of all races! Don't dare miss—*The Quintara Marathon!*"

<*Shut up, Jimmy!*> snapped Grysta.

DAVID WEBER

The Honor Harrington series: *(cont.)*

Field of Dishonor
Honor goes home to Manticore—and fights for her life on a battlefield she never trained for, in a private war that offers just two choices: death—or a "victory" that can end only in dishonor and the loss of all she loves....

Flag in Exile
Hounded into retirement and disgrace by political enemies, Honor Harrington has retreated to planet Grayson, where powerful men plot to reverse the changes she has brought to their world. And for their plans to suceed, Honor Harrington must die!

Honor Among Enemies
Offered a chance to end her exile and again command a ship, Honor Harrington must use a crew drawn from the dregs of the service to stop pirates who are plundering commerce. Her enemies have chosen the mission carefully, thinking that either she will stop the raiders or they will kill her ... and either way, her enemies will win....

In Enemy Hands
After being ambushed, Honor finds herself aboard an enemy cruiser, bound for her scheduled execution. But one lesson Honor has never learned is how to give up! One way or another, she and her crew are going home—even if they have to conquer Hell to get there!

continued ☞